CO-ACO-793

Dear Romance Reader:

This year Avon Books is celebrating the sixth anniversary of "The Avon Romance"—six years of historical romances of the highest quality by both new and established writers. Thanks to our terrific authors, our "ribbon books" are stronger and more exciting than ever before. And thanks to you, our loyal readers, our books continue to be a spectacular success!

"The Avon Romances" are just some of the fabulous novels in Avon Books' dazzling *Year of Romance*, bringing you month after month of top-notch romantic entertainment. How wonderful it is to escape for a few hours with romances by your favorite "leading ladies"—Shirlee Busbee, Karen Robards, and Johanna Lindsey. And how satisfying it is to discover in a new writer the talent that will make her a rising star.

Every month in 1988, Avon Books' *Year of Romance*, will be special because Avon Books believes that romance—the readers, the writers, and the books—deserves it!

Sweet Reading,

Susanne Jaffe
Editor-in-Chief

Ellen Edwards
Senior Editor

Other Books in
THE AVON ROMANCE Series

FORBIDDEN FIRES

ELIZABETH TURNER

AVON BOOKS ◆ NEW YORK

FORBIDDEN FIRES is an original publication of Avon Books. This work had never before appeared in book form. This work is a novel. Any similarity to actual persons or events is purely coincidental.

AVON BOOKS
A division of
The Hearst Corporation
105 Madison Avenue
New York, New York 10016

First Avon Books Printing: July 1988

AVON TRADEMARK REG. U.S. PAT. OFF. AND IN OTHER COUNTRIES, MARCA REGISTRADA, HECHO EN U.S.A.

Printed in the U.S.A.

K-R 10 9 8 7 6 5 4 3 2 1

To Rosalie:

critic,
cheerleader,
friend

Prologue

London, 1757

Exquisite. The word sprang to his mind. She was by far the most exquisite creature he had ever seen.

Behind him, the solicitor's monotone droned unheeded. All Justin Tremayne's attention was arrested by the lovely young woman in the street below. He drank in the sight of her, unable to slake his thirst.

Dark curls peeked from beneath a frivolously beribboned bonnet to frame a delicate oval face. A blush of rose tinted finely sculpted cheekbones, accentuating the fairness of her skin. In Justin's bemused state, each feature seemed perfection—the small, straight nose, the sweet mouth that hinted of an innocent sensuality. Feathery black lashes surrounded eyes that were large and widely spaced. Brown? Hazel? Green? From this distance he couldn't discern their color. His gaze left her face and traveled downward. The pink watered-silk gown revealed a figure that, though small and slender, was flawlessly proportioned, with rounded breasts and a tiny waist his hands could easily span.

She stood outside a milliner's shop with a companion, a girl near her own age, which Justin guessed to be eighteen. Something the friend said caused the girl to smile. As warm and sweet as a day in early summer, it stole his breath away. Is this how it feels to be struck by lightning? he wondered.

1

He was too absorbed to notice a pair of urchins begging for coins on the nearby street corner until the younger, a girl of about three, reached out a grubby hand and clutched a fistful of pink silk. Obviously as captivated by the beautiful woman as Justin was, the child simply stared. Incensed by the urchin's audacity, the companion issued a sharp rebuke and slapped the small hand away. The frightened child burst into tears. A boy stepped forward to wrap a protective arm around her quaking shoulders.

Taking out a lacy handkerchief, the beauty wiped away the little one's tears. She smiled once more—that radiant smile that had such a profound effect on Justin's breathing—and succeeded in drawing forth a tentative response from the child. She beckoned to the lad. When he came closer, she loosened her purse strings and emptied her coins into the boy's cupped hands. At first the children were dumbstruck by their good fortune. Then, recovering, they mumbled their thanks and scampered off. Justin's initial surprise kindled into admiration. The woman's beauty had stirred his desire, but her impulsive, generous act now captured his heart.

A black lacquered carriage emblazoned with a coat of arms rolled to a stop before the women, and a footman alighted to assist them inside. Justin swallowed. In another minute she would disappear down the street and out of his life forever.

"Hightower, come here. Quickly!"

The solicitor let the sheets of parchment flutter to the desk's polished surface and joined Justin to peer out the multipaned window.

Justin motioned to the carriage. "The lady in pink. Do you know who she is?"

Henry Hightower, his balding head not quite level with Justin's shoulder, adjusted his monocle with great care before replying. "That, my dear fellow, is Miss Eden St. James."

"Eden," Justin repeated. Never had a name seemed so

appropriate. "Miss? You did say miss? Then she's not married." Justin felt an absurd sense of relief.

"This is her first season. Although, I daresay, judging from her appearance, I shouldn't be the least surprised if an offer weren't soon forthcoming."

"Can you arrange an introduction?"

The solicitor's myopic eyes widened at the blunt request. These colonials were a strange breed, he thought to himself, carefully schooling his features so as not to reveal his dislike. "I did hear mention of a soiree being given tonight by Lady Butterick. Since your late uncle, Hubert Wyndom, was a friend of hers, I'm certain her ladyship could be persuaded to extend an invitation."

"Wonderful!" Justin slapped the smaller man on the back with such vigor that his monocle went flying along the length of its silk cord. "I'm in your debt, Hightower."

"Boorish colonial," Henry Hightower muttered under his breath as his client's footsteps clattered down the stairs. He clasped his hands behind his back and watched Justin emerge below, then walk away with a jaunty step. "Presumptuous fool," he said with a sneer. Fat chance if he fancied himself the lady's suitor. Eden St. James's stepfather was a member of the House of Lords. No matter how wealthy Hubert Wyndom's will had left him, Justin Tremayne didn't stand a chance. No one less than an earl would be an acceptable match. There were even rumors of a match with an Italian count.

Buffeted by a gale of indecision, Justin prowled the rooms of his uncle's luxurious town house. He should be celebrating his good fortune. Hours earlier he had learned that, as the sole beneficiary of his late uncle, he had inherited an amount that increased his already-substantial assets more than two-fold. He paused to examine an onyx paperweight on the ornately carved desk, then set it down abruptly and resumed his restless pacing. What had come over him this morning in the solicitor's office? He was far too sensible, too practical, to be diverted by a pretty face.

It was totally unlike him. Yet, if Henry Hightower hadn't known the girl, he would have chased the carriage down the street until he discovered her identity. A fitting exercise for a man obsessed, he thought with wry amusement.

The invitation to Lady Butterick's soiree arrived in due course. The remainder of the afternoon crawled at a snail's speed, but at last the appointed hour was at hand. In the elegantly appointed salon, the men's attire rivaled the ladies for grandeur. They all came clothed in velvets and lace, glittering with silver and gold. All wore wigs, many large and elaborate, in contrast with Justin's simple hairstyle. Not possessing a wig and disdaining the use of powder, he had brushed his unruly locks into submission and restrained them with a ribbon at the nape of his neck. Although he was dressed in his finest, Justin felt decidedly ill at ease, a grouse amidst peacocks.

Why was he so uncomfortable? Justin wondered as he stood to one side of the crowded drawing room observing the guests. After all, he had attended similar gatherings in the past. What made this one different? The answer was simple. In the Tidewater, he had always been an integral part of the group, not an outsider, a foreigner. More than just an ocean separated England from the Colonies. The English exuded a condescending attitude that grated on his nerves and put him on the defensive. If one more person asked about red skinned savages and wild beasts . . .

Silence fell and heads turned. Abruptly conversation resumed in a rush. Justin let out his pent-up breath. The wait was over.

If anything, Eden St. James's beauty was all the more devastating at close range. In spite of an intricate pile of whitened curls that looked too heavy to be supported by her slender neck, he would have recognized her from her smile alone. While he looked on, Lady Butterick rushed up to greet her newly arrived guest. Justin stepped forward lest his courage desert him.

Lady Butterick dimpled. "This young man has been most eager to meet you. He's the nephew of an acquaintance of mine, the late Hubert Wyndom. Miss Eden St. James, may I present Mr. Tremayne.'' Before she could say more, she was diverted by another guest and left them to become better acquainted.

Eden extended her hand. Justin silently wished he could surreptitiously wipe his damp palms on his breeches. What did one say to this breathtaking creature clothed in white satin? Struggling for a modicum of composure, he bent low over a soft, dainty hand that had undoubtedly never suffered a day's toil. When he looked up, her head was tilted to one side, her lips curved in a slight smile.

''Violet.'' He spoke his thought out loud. Her eyes were the same shade as the delicate flowers found in April in the deep woods of his native Virginia.

''I beg your pardon?'' She carefully withdrew her hand, her smile deepening.

''Your eyes. They're violet. When I saw you this afternoon, I tried to guess what color they were.''

''You must forgive me. I'm afraid I don't recall our meeting.''

''We didn't. You were shopping with a friend. I saw you from a distance and resolved we'd meet.''

''I see,'' Eden murmured. Her gaze swept over him, taking in the conservative cut of his coat and its lack of adornment. He was taller than most and well muscled, as though accustomed to physical activity. She found him attractive in an unassuming way.

Justin shifted his weight. Eden St. James had the ability to make him feel like a callow youth. He began to doubt the wisdom of this meeting.

''From your speech and manner of dress, Mr. Tremayne, am I correct in assuming you're from the Colonies?''

He smiled. ''My home is in Virginia, not far from the capital of Williamsburg.''

Recalling tales her stepbrother had told her, Eden asked, ''Is it true that red skinned savages and wild beasts roam the forests?''

Justin's smile vanished. Did she seek to ridicule him, like others he had met? "Much of my country is still a vast wilderness," he answered soberly. "While it's true there are Indians and wild animals, there are also areas which are quite civilized. Should you ever decide to visit the Colonies, I would be only to happy to prove to you that Virginians lack neither culture nor hospitality."

"I didn't mean to imply they were uncivilized." Her expression was equally somber. "I was merely curious to learn if the stories I had heard were true. If I've offended you, I apologize."

Justin wished he could begin the conversation anew. "I should be the one asking forgiveness. It seems of late I've grown overly sensitive. Many of your countrymen tend to view me as an oddity."

Eden found herself responding to the stranger's quiet charm. At the same time, she was disconcerted by the man's unwavering stare and direct speech. His clear gray eyes seemed to plumb her soul. That frightened her. While adroit at parrying compliments and deflecting amorous advances, she wasn't accustomed to sharing her innermost thoughts.

Justin sensed her withdrawal, but wasn't sure of its cause and attributed it to his stumbling demeanor. He was behaving like a dolt. Not only must he seem incapable of carrying on a simple conversation, he was ignoring the social graces as well. "I've been remiss." His tone had become stiff and unnatural. "Please, allow me to get you some punch."

At her nod of assent, he hastened in search of the refreshment table. While waiting to be served, he was unable to avoid overhearing the conversation of two men standing near the punch bowl.

"Did you notice that brash colonial monopolizing Miss St. James?"

"How could one not notice when the gentleman is in such dire need of a tailor?"

"And a wigmaker," the second added, chortling.

"Miss St. James is too much a lady to put him in his place."

A glass in either hand, Justin turned on his heel and went in search of Eden. She was no longer where he had left her. He glimpsed white satin on the balcony just beyond the French doors and was about to join her when he realized she wasn't alone. A dandy clad in plum velvet stood at her side, speaking in a snide voice.

"I daresay these colonials are a vulgar breed. Boorish savages, all of them. Aren't you pleased I came to your rescue?" The man's high-pitched laughter drowned Eden's quiet response. Justin noted the slight movement of her white head.

He had seen and heard enough. Eden St. James was no different from the rest of the English nobility. It had been folly to hope otherwise. Emotion had clouded his reason. Shoving the two untouched punch glasses into the hands of a liveried servant, he bid a terse farewell to his hostess and left. Common sense had deserted him this day. He usually knew where he didn't belong. He had been chasing rainbows, but the storm had passed. In its aftermath was the bitter calm of self-recrimination.

"Fool," he snorted in disgust.

It was time to return home.

Chapter 1

Virginia, 1758

"Stop yer bellowin'. You wanta wake the mistress?" Cook's gravelly voice jolted Eden awake.

"No, no, of course not. I'm sorry." Eden mumbled, still disoriented by the dream that had made her cry out loud.

"Good. See that you don't. Some of us puts in a full day's work around here and needs our rest." Cook's heavy footsteps crossed the wooden floor to her own bed under the eaves.

Eden shivered. The coarse muslin nightgown clung to her; wisps of hair were plastered to her forehead and brow. The dank scent of fear oozed from her pores. Terror kept her eyes wide lest she fall asleep again and see Rodney's bloody face. His threat still rang in her ears. Even with an ocean separating them, Eden didn't feel entirely safe from him.

Pulling the thin blanket closer around her shoulders, Eden snuggled deeper into the cornhusk mattress. Don't think of Rodney, she told herself. Think of more pleasant times. Remember the lovely bedroom at Sommerset with its pale lemon walls, billowing silk curtains, and lace-trimmed satin sheets. It was as large as this attic room she now shared with three other indentured servants. Only a year ago, she had lived in such luxurious surroundings, yet it felt like a century ago.

Leaden weights seemed to settle on Eden's eyelids, and she fell into a deep void of sleep, one finally untroubled by spectres from the past. The sweet oblivion was all too brief.

"Wake up!"

Eden tried to ignore the command. There was nothing she wanted more at that moment than to burrow into the lumpy mattress and escape for a while longer into a dark, dreamless tunnel of sleep.

"Wake up, you lazy chit." Someone shook her roughly, forcing her to consciousness.

Eden pried her eyes open. Cook stood, her hands on her ample hips, scowling down at her. "This is no time to lie abed. There's much to do before company comes."

"The party," Eden mumbled, remembering. For weeks, servants at the Wainwright plantation had labored from sunup until long after sundown preparing for a lavish affair to celebrate Charles Wainwright's twenty-first birthday.

"Yes, the party," Cook snapped. "Now get your arse outa bed before I tell mistress." Tucking gray strands of hair under her starched cap, she lumbered off.

Eden raised herself on one elbow. A single tallow candle sputtered in the predawn gloom. Bess and Polly, the others who shared the attic space, were already nearly dressed.

"Well, well, her ladyship's awake," Polly mocked. "I thought she was waitin' for us to fetch her breakfast in bed."

If being reduced to bond servant wasn't penance enough for Eden, Polly's spiteful tongue was. The girl had the face of an angel, but the temperament of a shrew. From first glance, Polly had taken an instant dislike to Eden. Time and again, Eden found herself the object of Polly's sarcasm and pettiness. With a weary sigh, Eden tossed aside the covers and swung her legs to the floor.

"Leave her be, Polly," Bess said, timorously coming to Eden's defense. "If we don't hurry, Cook will eat the raisin cakes you were savin'."

Polly peered into the small piece of silvered glass hanging from a hook and carefully settled the cap on her fair curls. "Good thing mistress keeps the sugar under lock and key, else Cook would eat that, too."

"If Miss Caroline didn't beat her to it." Bess shook her head in wonder. "I've never seen anyone more fond of sweets."

"Not even Cook." Polly twisted golden tendrils to frame her face. "She'll soon be bigger than her Ma, mark my words."

Rough-sawn boards scraped Eden's bare feet as she crossed the room to the washstand. The cold water shocked her into wakefulness. She glanced over her shoulder to see Polly leave the attic room.

"Cook's in a foul mood. Best you hurry," Bess advised. Tying her apron strings as she went, she clattered down the stairs after Polly.

It was good advice. Eden knew she mustn't dawdle, for if Cook was in a foul mood, it would be folly to test the temper of Mrs. Wainwright. Her sour disposition had been one of Eden's first discoveries upon entering this household. Tugging off her nightdress, she slipped into a blue-gray dress of coarse homespun that was badly faded after repeated launderings in lye soap.

The house party had been planned months in advance. Guests would begin arriving this afternoon, and most would stay the better part of a week. Mrs. Wainwright was apt to be in a vile humor if the least thing went awry. Quickly combing and rebraiding her hair, Eden shoved her feet into sturdy black shoes and blew out the candle before leaving the attic.

She was still fastening the thick coil of hair around her head as she stepped through an outer side door and sped across the narrow tract of land that separated the manor house from the row of dependencies, or outbuildings. Dawn spread a pink stain in the dun-colored sky, silhouetting the small wooden buildings which housed the kitchen, smokehouse, dairy, and laundry. Donning her servant's cap, Eden entered the nearest building.

A variety of wrought-iron cooking utensils filled the whitewashed interior. Logs blazed in a great smoke-blackened fireplace that occupied most of an entire kitchen wall. In an oven built into a wall of the chimney, heated by coals from the fireplace, Cook was baking pies and cakes. The odor of well-prepared food lingered pleasantly in the air.

The three other bond servants were seated at a work-worn table in the center of the room, consuming a hearty breakfast of cold, sliced venison and cornbread. Eden perched on a bench and spread honey across a thick slice of crusty bread.

Polly ignored her arrival. "Caroline has been in a twitter for days," she said as she reached for a raisin cake. "It seems she hopes a certain young man will ask for her hand."

Bess nodded knowingly. "I've seen her smile and stare off into space when she thinks her mother isn't watching."

"She's got half a dozen new dresses." Polly made no attempt to hide her envy. "You'd think Caroline was the one havin' a birthday, not her brother."

"It ain't every day a young man comes of age." Cook wiped crumbs from her mouth with the back of her hand. "The Wainwrights can well afford to go all out for their only son."

"What about you, Eden?" Polly's smile was cunning. "Do you agree Charles deserves nothin' but the best?"

Eden chose to ignore the insinuation. She had long suspected Polly was aware of Charles's flirtation with her. In fact, she had begged him to be less obvious with his attentions. She shrugged. "As cook said, Charles is their only son."

Bess poured another cup of tea. "What's that fancy name for the law where the daughter gets a dowry, and the son gets everything?"

"The eldest son," Eden corrected. "It's called primo-geniture."

Polly folded her arms on the trestle table and leaned forward. "Tell us, Eden, is that what happened to you? Poor little rich girl, reduced to bond servant? That would explain all your fancy airs."

Her peel of laughter was cut short by cook's gruff reminder of chores to be done, but the jibe had come painfully close to the truth and Eden kept her face averted. Polly would surely puzzle over her sudden loss of color. God only knew what conclusions she might draw.

The ensuing hours passed in a blur of activity. Eden's fingers were soon nicked and bleeding from slicing and chopping under Cook's critical eye. Knowing that she frayed the woman's patience to the breaking point only increased Eden's clumsiness. She received a summons from Mrs. Wainwright with relief. Wiping her hands on her apron, Eden flew up the stairs to the sewing room.

"It took you long enough." Millicent Wainwright, a woman of generous proportions who abided nothing short of perfection from her household staff, glared at Eden. "Caroline wishes to wear her blue sprigged muslin this evening. That idiot seamstress made the gown so tight it strains at the waist. As you can see, it'll tear the first time she raises her arm. Fix it!" She sailed out of the small room.

Resentment stirred within Eden. She, too, had once been in a position of authority with a staff of servants at her beck and call. Never once had she spoken to them in the insolent tone Millicent Wainwright used with her. It made her feel like an object, not a person.

"Don't mind Mother." Caroline pirouetted in front of the cheval glass. "She has a lot on her mind. It's important that everything be absolutely perfect for Charles's birthday."

Eden studied the way Caroline's full skirt met the snug-fitting bodice and silently agreed with Bess. If Caroline wasn't careful, her penchant for sweets would gain her the full-figured shape of her mother. Aloud she said, "I think I know how to remedy the problem."

As Eden reached for the sewing basket, she caught sight of her reflection in the mirror and scarcely recognized the image. Memories continued to taunt her. The lady of renowned grace and beauty had vanished, replaced by a ghost of her former self dressed in shabby servant's garb. Long ago, she had possessed more gowns than she had space to put them. Now she owned two of homespun, a shift, nightdress, cap, apron, and a pair of sturdy black shoes.

Her hand rose instinctively to her throat. Oh yes, she had nearly forgotten the locket. She touched the smooth metal concealed beneath the bodice of her gown. Sometimes it was hard for her to comprehend the changes of the past year without feeling bitter.

"Eden?" Caroline called, breaking through her reverie. "You look a bit strange. Are you all right?"

"Yes." With a shake of her head, Eden forced herself back to the present. "If you'll just slip out of the dress . . ."

Caroline was happy to comply, but she made no move to leave the sewing room. Instead, clad in her petticoats, she curled up on a cushion on the floor. "I can hardly wait to see Justin again. Last time he was here I was only a child, but now he'll see that I've grown into a woman."

Eden busied herself with pins and pincushion. Only three years separated the girl's ages, but Eden felt infinitely older and wiser. Though Caroline stood on the brink of womanhood, she often acted with the emotional maturity of a child. "Tell me about this Justin of yours," Eden encouraged. "Is he attractive?"

"Oh, Eden, wait until you see him. He's tall and handsome, with hair the color of nutmeg, and his eyes . . ." She rolled hers heavenward. "Sometimes I think they're the palest blue. Other times they look clear gray. He's got perfect white teeth and looks a bit like a pirate when he smiles. Not that I've ever seen a pirate," she added, giggling.

Eden had cause to regret she had ever asked about this marvelous creature who, according to Caroline, resembled a fairy tale prince more than a mortal being. The needle flashed in and out of the cloth in tiny, even stitches as Eden quietly listened to Caroline's rambling. It was restful here in the cluttered sewing room. Eden, an accomplished seamstress, would have been content to serve out her indenture as such. But it wasn't to be. Millicent Wainwright had been quick to observe her only son's infatuation with the comely bond servant. In the blink of an eye, Eden had been banished from sewing room to kitchen.

"What about you, Eden? Did you have a beau in London? Have you ever been in love?"

"Love?" Eden paused, the needle poised in midair. "Love? I'm not even certain there is such a thing."

"Eden!" Caroline squealed in dismay. "Surely you can't mean that."

Eden resumed sewing. "But I do."

Caroline leaned forward, her strawberry curls falling over her shoulders. "But what about your parents? Didn't they love each other?"

"I can't say. My father died shortly before I was born. My mother remarried a man much older than herself. She died in childbirth when I was quite small. I scarcely remember her."

"Oh," Caroline murmured, at a loss to deal with distressing facts unwittingly uncovered.

Eden shrugged. "It's the way of things." She tied off a knot, snipped the thread, and rethreaded the needle. "I was taught that love has little to do with why people marry. Marriages are arranged for monetary reasons and according to social station. If fortune smiles, an affection will develop between the couple."

"Well"—Caroline's pale brows drew together in a frown—"I suppose that's partly true in Virginia, too. It would never do for me to marry just anyone. Why, father would have apoplexy if I decided to marry say"—she groped for an example—"a boot maker."

"Or a bond servant?"

Caroline had the grace to flush and look away.

* * *

Guests began arriving by late afternoon, some from as far away as Richmond and Norfolk. Most traveled the tidal rivers and creeks in small boats, which they tied at the Wainwright's dock; others came by carriage. Eden was kept busy running errands, pressing gowns, and helping in the cook house. She was about to hurry from the kitchen with a tray of sweetmeats when Charles Wainwright waylaid her.

"Eden!" He snatched the tray from her hands and set it on a nearby bench. "I've been looking for you." Grasping her upper arm, he pulled her around the far side of the building, away from curious eyes.

"I have work to do, Charles," she protested, half scolding, half laughing. He was pleasant to look at, tall and sturdily built, with reddish brown hair and eyes much the same hue as his sister's.

"My fair Eden, what a drudge you're becoming." He smiled down at her. "Hasn't anyone told you that all work and no play makes Eden a dull girl?"

"You're incorrigible. Whether I've heard that or not, your mother hasn't. What would she say if she knew we were together?"

"Forget Mother. I'm of age now, or I will be tomorrow," he amended. "I no longer have to answer to my mother." He dismissed her objection with a wave of his hand. "I've only a minute. Promise you'll meet me tonight at the rose arbor."

Eden looked down at the scuffed toe of her shoe. Like his mother, Charles expected his requests to be met without question. "I'm not certain that's a good idea."

"Not a good idea! Please, Eden," he coaxed. "What can it hurt?"

Eden's fingers wandered to the neckline of her dress and felt for the slender gold chain beneath the cloth, a mannerism she sometimes resorted to in times of stress or uncertainty. Indeed, what could it hurt? she asked herself, meeting his gaze. Charles's attention was flattering, his persistence a balm to her wounded self-esteem. Since her arrival in the Colonies, he was the only one who had treated her with kindness and consideration. Now, more than at any time in her life, she needed a friend.

Often she caught herself daydreaming about what it would be like if their friendship deepened into a permanent commitment. Marriage to Charles would solve all her problems. How astounded everyone would be, she mused, at how easily she adapted to any social situation. Being mistress of the house was a role she had once assumed was her birthright. And Charles was interested; a woman could sense these things. "All right," she agreed at last. "Tonight."

Eden hurried off before she was missed. In her haste, she failed to note the calculating gleam which brightened Charles Wainwright's blue eyes. Patience, he counseled. The prize would be worth its price.

Although dinner was customarily served between two and three in the afternoon, in deference to the guests who had spent the day traveling, tonight the large meal would be served at six. Dining was considered a fine art in Virginia. Planters took pride in setting their tables with greater quantities of food than the guests could consume. Millicent Wainwright was no exception. She personally supervised the huge quantities of food that graced her table. No general marshalling his forces could have been more attentive to detail, or more critical.

"Get a move on, girl," Cook snapped, adding a tureen of peanut soup to the already-overburdened pewter tray Eden carried.

"Yes, ma'am." Eden tightened her grip. Painstakingly, so as not to spill the precious contents, she made her way from kitchen to house.

"Remember, now," Cook called after her, "Polly and Bess will do the serving. Your task is to hold the tray steady."

Millicent and Jasper Wainwright presided over a long

damask-draped table. Fine china and crystal sparkled in the light of beeswax tapers set in twin candelabrum that flanked either end. Animated conversation flowed as freely as the delicate wines imported for the occasion. No one paid the least attention to the servants, who unobtrusively performed their duties. By the time the first course had been served, Eden's arms ached from the strain of holding the heavy tray.

"Bess," Millicent Wainwright said in an undertone, "leave the tureen on the sideboard in case someone should request more. Eden, go back to Cook and return with the next course."

Eden ducked her head obediently. Without glancing up, she felt Polly smirk. The other girl was inordinately pleased to see her relegated to the chore of fetching and carrying. Eden, her face impassive, retraced her steps from dining room to kitchen and back again. Platters of deviled crab cakes, scalloped oysters, and soft-shelled crabs were placed on the sideboard, then once again the girls circled the dinner table, this time removing soup dishes. The muscles in Eden's arms quivered with fatigue, and she gritted her teeth in determination.

Turning from the sideboard, Polly set the partially full tureen on one end of the pewter tray, unbalancing the heavy load and causing it to tilt precariously. Before Eden could right her burden, several china dishes slid off and crashed to the floor.

"You clumsy chit!" The sharp rebuke silenced the talk as effectively as a hot knife slicing butter. "See what you've done! My best china!"

Eden's cheeks flamed. "I'm terribly sorry, Mistress Wainwright." Setting the tray on the floor, she knelt to pick up the broken china. What was wrong with her? Was she truly as inept as others seemed to think? She couldn't seem to do anything right, not even the most menial task. Tears of mortification blurred her gaze, forcing her to keep her eyes downcast.

"Little harm done, Millicent." The lazy male voice

that came to her defense was rich in timbre and pleasing to the ear. "Only one dish broken. The other two escaped without so much as a chip."

The scraping of a chair alerted Eden that her rescuer was about to offer further assistance. Her vision cleared, then focused. A ruffle of fine white lawn trailed over a pair of beautiful masculine hands—a pianist's hands. But unlike those of a pianist, the skin was bronzed by the sun. She studied his fingers. Though lean and tapered, they hinted at a strength acquired from more strenuous pursuits than striking ivory keys. Fascinated, Eden watched them pluck the final fragment of glass from behind a table leg. It fell to the tray with a gentle clatter.

She looked up to thank her gallant benefactor. Her lips parted in surprise. Her words of gratitude died unspoken.

It couldn't be.

But it was.

Chapter 2

Horrified, Eden stared into the clear gray eyes of a man she had once been introduced to in a London drawing room. She had been a fine lady, he a rustic foreigner. Now the tables were turned. She was the stranger, a lowly bond servant, and he, judging from his presence in this elite group, was one of Virginia's landed gentry! Fate had, indeed, played a cruel prank on her.

Justin glanced up from where he knelt with one bent knee on the dining room floor. Instead of the mumbled thanks or shy smile he had expected, he saw stunned disbelief etched on the servant's features. Beneath a starched cap which concealed most of her hair, the girl's face was incredibly beautiful. It could even be called exquisite. His brows drew together in a puzzled frown. Exquisite . . . ?

Recognition dawned slowly. It was impossible, he thought, yet no two women could claim eyes that exact shade of violet. What stroke of fortune had brought her back into his life? Her name formed on his lips, but an almost imperceptible shake of her head kept him silent.

"The girl is useless." Millicent Wainwright broke the spell that had held Justin and Eden motionless. "For the life of me, I don't know what Jasper was thinking the day he bought her articles of indenture. Why, she doesn't even know how to spin. Imagine!"

Eden picked up the heavily laden tray and struggled to her feet. Justin rose quickly, too, reaching out a hand to

19

steady her. He stared unabashedly. It was difficult to reconcile the elegant satin-clad creature who still haunted his dreams with this serving girl wearing faded homespun. Her beauty, however, was undiminished, luring him as before into its seductive, silken web.

"You should be relieved, my dear Millicent." A male guest, his bagwig slightly askew, addressed his hostess. "Jasper's acute eyesight is to be commended. The girl did not come without certain assets to recommend her." Ribald laughter followed the remark.

Hectic color stained Eden's cheeks. The sting of humiliation was great. Too embarrassed to meet Justin's gaze, she stepped back so that his hand fell to his side. With her back stiff, her head high, she turned and left the dining room. "Boorish colonials," she muttered under her breath. The pricking of tears behind her eyelids belied her proud carriage.

"Now, now, Millicent," Jasper Wainwright placated, "you know how Willard likes to jest. Certainly you're aware indentured servants become more scarce each year. Soon we'll have to rely entirely on black slaves for household help."

Millicent shuddered. "I can't abide the idea of their dark faces everywhere I look—even in my own home!"

Eden returned a short while later. Concentrating on completing her tasks without further mishap, she moved slowly and awkwardly. Each time she approached the table, she was conscious of a pair of silver eyes following her everywhere. Desperately, she wished he'd stop watching so intently. It put her nerves on edge.

Justin added little to the conversation flowing around him. His thoughts centered on Eden. The year had enhanced her breathtaking loveliness. Her face was thinner than he remembered, with subtle hollows that emphasized her fine bone structure. The delicate bloom of color had faded from her cheeks, leaving her skin as smooth as alabaster. Her eyes shone like highly polished amethysts in her pale face. He leaned back in his chair, absently twirling the stem of his wineglass. Before this night ended, he vowed, he would find out what had brought her to the lowly station of indentured servant.

For Eden, the meal was an ordeal, and she was grateful when it ended. After the last dish had been rinsed and wiped dry, she wrapped a woolen shawl around her shoulders. Complaining to Bess of a headache and the need for fresh air, she strolled down the path toward the rose arbor.

The evening's events had contrived to make her temples pound and her spirits plummet. For the second time that day, she doubted the wisdom of meeting Charles. If Millicent Wainwright ever suspected their association, she would make the remainder of Eden's indenture a living hell. But Eden had promised Charles, and his wit and flattery always made her forget her troubles, at least for a little while. It wasn't his face though, but another's, who stole into her thoughts now.

It had been a great shock to see someone from the past, someone who had known her when she was a lady of quality. Eden pulled the shawl tighter to ward off the damp chill of late March. Frowning, she tried to recall the meeting at Lady Butterick's. Memory stirred, bringing forth a hazy picture of a man who appeared at odds with his elegant surroundings. Too big, too plainly clothed, he had looked decidedly ill at ease. How strange, she reflected, since tonight he had seemed in his element. She shook her head in wonder. His charm had even defused Millicent Wainwright's wrath.

Try as she might, she couldn't remember his name. She walked slowly, her head bent in thought. Another memory surfaced. In London, his manner had troubled her. That hadn't changed. It was still much too direct for her peace of mind.

Upon reaching the arbor, Eden sank down on a wrought-iron bench. New worries assailed her. Would the man reveal that he had once known her? How amused everyone would be to learn that the former Eden St. James, stepdaughter of the Earl of Rutherford, was now a servant.

Could he be so heartless? No, she didn't think so. She sensed an innate goodness in him that was evident in the quick way he had come to her defense. What kind of man lowered himself to help a servant?

The pounding in her head intensified. Closing her eyes, Eden massaged her temples with her fingertips and inhaled a deep breath of air that was fresh with the promise of new beginnings. Except for the gentle rush of wind through the tangled vines overhead and the distant hoot of an owl, all was quiet. The garden was peaceful, lulling, and gradually she began to relax. So seldom did she have a chance to be alone, she valued such rare moments of privacy. At the sound of bootheels striking a bricked pathway, Eden reluctantly opened her eyes and rose to her feet.

"Charles?" she called softly.

"Miss St. James?"

She froze at the already-familiar drawl.

Justin's breath caught. She stood trapped like a startled doe in a shaft of moonlight that speared through the lattice of snarled vines. Never had any woman seemed so beautiful, or so vulnerable. For an instant, he was overwhelmed by a desire to protect, comfort, and cherish her.

Eden waited without saying a word while he drew nearer. He stopped in front of her, seeming to tower over her, taller and bigger than she recollected. The top of her head barely met his chin.

"Miss St. James, I've been searching for you. I feared the other serving girl, the timid one, had been mistaken when she said you intended to stroll in the garden." His mellow tone had the power to both soothe and unsettle her.

"Forgive me, sir." His size was intimidating, and Eden sought refuge behind a shield of indifference. "I'm afraid I've forgotten your name."

Her admission was like a sharp slap in the face. Justin's expression hardened. Obviously their previous meeting had made no impact on her, he acknowledged bitterly. Yet without the slightest effort, Eden St. James had made a profound impression on him. More the fool he for wishing otherwise. Perhaps he should be flattered she remembered him at all. He tried not to let his irritation show. "Since you don't remember, permit me to introduce—or rather, reintroduce—myself. I'm Justin Tremayne." He made a knee.

Was the gesture a deliberate mockery? she wondered. Or was she being overly sensitive? "I recognized you instantly, Mr. Tremayne, but I have a poor memory for names. It's a fault for which I've often been chastised."

Justin accepted her explanation. Time enough later to judge its truthfulness. "Our faults are what distinguish us mortals from the gods."

She inclined her head graciously, the action reminiscent of their first encounter. For a moment he was transported back to London and Lady Butterick's soiree. At the time, he had believed this woman was destined to be a princess, a duchess, or a queen. Never a bond servant!

Eden sensed the direction of his thoughts and tried to divert them. "Justin?" she mused. "Ah, so you're Caroline's Justin." He was handsome in a rugged sort of way, she admitted grudgingly. She could see why the younger girl was enamored.

"Begging your pardon, Miss St. James, but you're mistaken. I am neither Caroline Wainwright's Justin, nor anyone else's." A trace of a smile softened his denial.

His bald statement confirmed her earlier impression. Here was a man who was direct and honest, unlike the males of her limited experience. It increased her uncertainty. Crossing her arms over her chest, she brought the edges of the shawl more tightly over her shoulders.

"I didn't seek you out to discuss Caroline's misguided notions." Justin hesitated, then cleared his throat. "I don't mean to pry, but all evening I've wondered what circumstances forced you to sell yourself into bondage."

Eden held herself stiffly erect. She didn't want this man's pity. "My affairs are no concern of yours."

She was proud. Justin saw it in the defiant thrust of her

chin, in her erect bearing. If pride was a fault, it was one of which he, too, was guilty. He silently cursed his tendency to be blunt. "I've offended you. I apologize. My intentions, if not my method, were honorable." Her expression might have daunted a lesser man, but Justin forged ahead. "I had hoped there might be something I could do to ease your burden. I thought perhaps you were in need of a friend."

His sincerity nearly shattered her composure. *A friend.* Had he really said *friend?* Or had it been merely an echo from her soul? How could he know? Was it so apparent that she longed for someone to confide in, to ask for guidance? The offer was tempting, but caution prevailed.

"That's very kind of you, Mr. Tremayne—"

"Eden!" Charles's voice carried in the still night air. "Eden, is that you?"

"Yes, Charles. Over here."

Charles emerged from the shadows, resplendent in a powdered wig and braid-trimmed finery. "Justin!" he blurted upon seeing the other man. "I didn't expect to find you here."

"Evidently not."

The men faced each other. Eden watched uneasily. The two were nearly identical in height and breadth of shoulder, but there the similarity ceased. While Justin's form was sleek and well muscled, Charles's girth was already substantial. The initial surprise on Charles's face was replaced by a look of smug proprietorship. Justin appeared as though he was holding his anger on a tight rein. The air was heavy with tension.

"I realize my concerns were untimely." Justin's words sounded stilted. "My apologies for interrupting a lovers' tryst." He turned and stalked away, his broad-shouldered figure disappearing into the darkness.

Eden reached out as if to hold him back. She wanted to explain. But explain what? she asked herself. That Charles wasn't her lover? Why should she defend herself? Justin Tremayne meant nothing to her. She let her arm drop.

Charles took a step forward. "What happened between you? Did Justin make advances? I daresay, he's not accustomed to being rebuffed by the ladies."

"No." Eden shook her head, strangely subdued by this information. "He was a perfect gentleman."

"Hasn't my sister bored you to tears about the marvelous Mr. Tremayne? Justin has earned quite a reputation as a ladies' man."

"Is that right?" Eden angled her head to stare up at him. Did she detect a note of envy in his voice?

"Stay away from him, Eden," Charles warned. "Justin likes to toy with a woman's affections, but he never gets seriously involved. He's too busy with his own pursuits to settle down. Undoubtedly, he believes variety adds spice."

"Hmm." Eden quietly cataloged this bit of information, not finding it to her liking. "I suppose an attractive man grows accustomed to having women fawn over him."

Charles's mouth turned down at the corners. "Let's not waste precious time discussing Justin Tremayne." He stroked her arm from shoulder to elbow. "Have I told you yet today what a pretty wench you are? You'll make some lucky man a fine wife."

Eden smiled with pleasure. This was what she wanted to hear. Needed to hear. She had been brought up to be the wife of an influential man, not to scour kettles and scrub floors. An alliance with Charles would solve all her problems. "Thank you, Charles." She rested a hand on his coat front.

Emboldened by the simple act and the spirits he had consumed that evening, Charles jerked her against his chest.

"Charles!" Eden protested, trying to pull back.

"Come, Eden, don't be coy."

"I'm not fit company tonight," she demurred, alarmed by his impatience.

"Don't tease." His hold tightened painfully. "This is the moment we've waited for all day. Your beauty drives me to the brink of madness.'' His lips swooped down, seeking hers.

The smell of his wine-sour breath, the feel of his wet lips grazing her cheek, made her stomach churn. ''I never should have come.'' She closed her eyes briefly.

''The time for games is past, my dear Eden.'' Charles stilled further protest by holding her head in a fierce grip and grinding his lips against hers in a demanding kiss.

Through the fabric of her gown, Eden felt his hand explore, then fondle, the fullness of her breast. If this was a game, the rules had suddenly changed without her knowledge.

With a rush, she recalled another time, another place, another man. He too had praised her beauty while pawing at her bodice with clumsy, grasping fingers. The episode had filled her with revulsion, as had her stepbrother Rodney's plan to marry her to the drunken, lecherous count. Eden placed both palms against Charles's chest and shoved. She was rigid with indignation by the time she succeeded in freeing herself from his rough embrace. ''How dare you treat me like some doxy!''

Anger colored his ruddy complexion more vividly than usual. ''I thought you welcomed my attentions. What's wrong with a kiss or two?''

The situation had gotten out of control. The last thing Eden wanted was to antagonize him. She drew in a deep, steadying breath. ''Please, let's not argue. I have a splitting headache, and you've had too much to drink. Let's forget this incident ever happened.''

Clutching the edges of her shawl with one hand and holding her skirts with the other, she fled down the garden path. The scene with Charles distressed her, but equally unsettling was the accusation, the disillusionment she had seen in a pair of crystal gray eyes.

One day fair, three days foul. March teased the Virginia countryside with the promise of spring. This particular Thursday was especially dreary. Heavy rain-soaked clouds hung low, concealing any traces of blue. A biting wind whipped down from the north, causing tender buds to furl more tightly against its sting.

The boisterous spirits of the guests weren't dampened by the elements. Their numbers swelled hourly as more arrived from Williamsburg, a half day's journey from the Wainwright plantation. At the grand ball that evening, Charles's twenty-first birthday would be toasted on the stroke of midnight. Since inclement weather prohibited outdoor activities, tables had been set up so everyone could amuse themselves with games of chance. Later, in preparation for the gala festivities, all of the ladies and many of the gentleman would retire for an afternoon nap. Then the elaborate ritual of dressing and primping would commence.

Eden's dismal mood reflected the weather. She went about her tasks mechanically, replenishing trays of food and refilling goblets of drink. The sooty smudges beneath her eyes hinted at her lack of sleep the previous night. With disturbing regularity, her gaze strayed to the corner of the room where Justin Tremayne, with Caroline as his partner, was playing a game of whist. Caroline was flirting outrageously and basking in his attention. Justin was an exceptionally attractive man, Eden concurred.

His nut-brown hair was clubbed with a black ribbon at the nape of his neck, while a tumble of curls spilled over his broad forehead. His repartee came easily, his smile frequently. The brilliant slash of white, even teeth conveyed a wicked devilish appeal. A pirate's grin, Caroline had said, and Eden decided the description was apt.

She watched his long, tapered fingers curve around a glass and raise it to his lips. Of their own accord, her feet moved toward him. As she bent to refill his cup with cider, her breast lightly brushed his arm, causing a pleasant tingling sensation to chase along her nerve endings.

Justin flicked Eden a dismissive glance, then returned his attention to Caroline. "I don't recall seeing her on my previous visit. Has she been here long?"

"Not very." Caroline frowned at the cards fanned in one carefully manicured hand. "Father brought her back from Yorktown last fall. Shame on you for not visiting more often."

"Does she have a name?"

"Of course, silly." Caroline giggled.

Eden simmered. She was being treated like a stick of furniture. How demeaning! How rude! Anger tinted her pale cheeks a becoming shade of pink and added a bewitching glitter to her violet gaze.

Caroline played a trump card. "Her name's Eden."

"Eden, hmm." Justin lounged back and studied Eden boldly. "I was introduced to a woman of that name while in London last year. I remember thinking it an unusual name for an unusual lady."

Eden gripped the handle of the pitcher so tightly that her knuckles blanched. What kind of sport was this man seeking? Was he going to expose her identity? Were her fears of the night before about to become reality? Moving to fill Caroline's glass, she darted a worried look at Justin over the girl's red-gold curls. His bland expression gave her no clues as to his intention.

"Does the wench have a surname?" Justin's tone was redolent of idle curiosity.

"Doesn't everyone?" Caroline countered their opponent's move with an ace, winning the trick. "Pray tell, Eden, what is your surname?"

"St. James," she bit out. "My name is Eden St. James." A guest at the adjoining table raised his empty glass, and Eden moved away.

Though her back was turned, she was still within range of their voices. "Seems Miss St. James has a temper," Justin drawled. "That can be quite unflattering in a servant. For your sake, I hope she doesn't have a long period of indenture."

Caroline shrugged a plump shoulder. "I have no idea. Father takes care of those matters. Why such interest, Justin? She's only a bond servant."

"You're absolutely right, Caroline, my sweet. She's only a servant."

Eden whirled, clutching the pitcher as if it contained the last dram of self control, sorely tempted to empty the cider over Justin Tremayne's arrogant head—and damn the consequences!

Justin glanced over at the next table and met her glare. His steady look seemed to read her chaotic thoughts. His mouth curved up in a parody of a smile, as though he was perversely pleased to have ruffled her feathers. Still wearing that infuriating grin, he turned his attention back to the cards.

Furious, and struggling for control, Eden rushed from the room, down the wide center hallway, and outdoors. She leaned against the rough bricks of the house and drew in great drafts of air while she fought to compose herself. What was Justin Tremayne up to? Perhaps it was only her imagination, but she had the distinct impression he delighted in goading her to her limits.

She pressed a flushed cheek to the cool metal pitcher. She was angrier than she ever remembered being. With a start, she realized it felt wonderful. After masking her feelings for years, she had nearly forgotten how marvelous it felt to let them show.

Her mood lighter than it had been in months, Eden entered the cook house, where a blast of heat from the great hearth greeted her. Cook, Bess, and four black women put into service for the occasion, were busy preparing vast quantities of food to be served at a midnight buffet. A Negro lad of seven or eight turned a spit, which held haunches of beef and venison. The mouth-watering aromas mingled with that of wood smoke. Pastries of every description vied for space on tables and shelves.

Cook spotted Eden. "You, girl, over here. And be quick about it."

Eden threaded her way across the cluttered kitchen.

"As if all this ain't enough, Mistress Wainwright ordered me to bake silver cake." Cook wiped her perspiring face with the corner of a stained apron. "Here." She thrust a hard, cone-shaped mold of sugar imported from the West Indies into Eden's hands. "Scrape this. And make sure it's free of lumps. It's the one thing you're good at, girl. Find a spot where you won't be underfoot."

"Yes, ma'am," Eden agreed readily. The tedious chore provided a welcome respite from the day's bustle and confusion, as well as an excuse to avoid a certain guest. She hurried from the kitchen, past the laundry where the laundress was using a handbox iron heated on glowing coals to erase stubborn wrinkles from frilly ball gowns, to a wooden bench near the well.

Eden sat quietly, enjoying the solitude. Occasionally the clouds parted, allowing a ray of weak sunlight to filter down to earth before the clouds regrouped to choke off its feeble warmth. Winter was nearly over, she knew, and soon spring would breathe new life across the land. If she was fortunate, perhaps spring would also mark a brighter time for her. She slowly began to scrape the cone with a dull blade. How she hated her loss of freedom. It bruised her soul and battered her spirit. Her every waking moment, every single breath, every stitch of clothing was owned by another. But had it ever been different? Had she ever really been free?

Even in England, her every action had been accountable, to her stepfather, then later to Rodney. Sometimes she wondered if fate would have been kinder had she acceded to Rodney's outrageous demands. No! she answered without hesitation. At least in this strange country—provided she survived the next four years, five months, and thirteen days—there was hope.

Eden was too preoccupied to hear approaching footsteps.

"Well, well, what have we here?"

Justin! Her startled gaze flew upward, and a flood of awareness swept through her. There was something about him that drew her yet frightened her as well. She dropped her gaze and scraped the sugar cone with renewed vigor.

Justin placed a well-shod foot on the bench next to her and casually draped an arm across his raised knee, a thin cigar clamped between his fingers. "Since Charles is being monopolized by Rosemarie Hughes, I hope you won't object to my humble company."

Eden shrugged. "Should I?"

"Does it annoy you that Charles is busy elsewhere?"

"Charles is expected to be attentive to a girl he's known since childhood." Justin was forgetting her background. Who understood better than she the importance of social obligations? They had been drilled into her since childhood.

"A woman who isn't jealous . . . ?" He studied her. She either hid her concern well or was truly naive. "You are, indeed, a most unusual woman, Eden St. James."

Flustered by his presence, Eden continued her task. The earthenware bowl in her lap was half-full of fine white crystals. Without thinking, she raised her right hand and one by one licked her sticky fingers.

Justin could almost taste their sweetness. Fascinated, he stared as Eden's pink tongue meticulously cleaned each fingertip. Sparkling granules clung to her moist lower lip. When the tip of her tongue slid over the tempting, ripe curve, he contained a groan. The action was both innocent and provocative. He yearned to capture her mouth with his and savor its honeyed essence.

Suddenly he scowled. She had the face of an angel and a form that made a man ache with longing. Could she really be untouched? Or was she a temptress well versed in the art of pleasing a man? Maybe that was why she wasn't concerned that Charles's affection might waver. He was probably only one of many conquests. Justin swallowed a spurt of irrational jealousy. He had no call to sit in judgment, but the notion of other men in her life was most unsettling. "What kind of woman are you, Eden St. James?" he asked softly.

"And what kind of question is that, Mr. Tremayne?" Eden pushed a strand of hair away from her face with the back of her hand. "You speak in riddles. I only know you seem to derive unusual pleasure from baiting me."

"I should feel honored. At least today you remember my name." He drew on the cheroot and exhaled a swift stream of smoke.

A hint of a smile softened the sober line of her mouth. "Did it irk you that after a brief meeting months ago I failed to recall your name?"

His scowl returned. Not only had this slip of a girl stumbled on the truth, she also found it amusing. "In some circles such forgetfulness would be construed as a sign of poor manners."

"There are many things that can be interpreted as such," Eden returned calmly.

"Such as?"

"Such as discussing a woman who is present as though she were not."

"Some people would term it rude," he agreed.

"Not to mention unkind and insensitive."

"Typical behavior from a boorish, vulgar colonial, wouldn't you agree?" He flicked his cigar into the shrubbery and stalked off.

Boorish, vulgar colonial.

The familiar phrase sang in Eden's mind. She stared after him, her task forgotten. Where had she heard those words before? Slowly it came to her. At Lady Butterick's soiree! A silly fop in purple velvet, whose name and face she no longer remembered, had used those same words to describe Justin Tremayne. Could Justin have overheard them and assumed she shared the sentiment? If so, it would explain his abrupt departure that evening.

For the second time in less than a day, Eden had been tried and found guilty by this man. Why should she care what he thought? Pride prevented her from arguing in her own defense. Besides, what was the use? Too much time had elapsed, too many events had occurred, her world had tilted on its axis. She rose wearily to her feet and started toward the kitchen.

* * *

In one corner of the ballroom, a trio of musicians played a sprightly tune while dancers advanced and retreated in the precise, measured steps of a minuet. As he stood on the sidelines, Justin was oblivious to both music and dance. Not even Caroline's incessant chatter could command his attention. He wasn't proud of himself. Amidst the gaiety of the ball, he berated himself for his abominable behavior that afternoon. It wasn't fair to make Eden the target for his anger and frustration. And, he admitted, his jealousy. Why should it matter if Charles Wainwright had captured her fancy?

Punch sloshed out of Justin's glass as he was jostled by a young man overeager to reach his partner. He cut short the man's apology and dabbed at the moisture staining his sleeve. Stuffing his handkerchief back into his breast pocket, he scowled into his drink.

While Eden's beauty held him in awe, her singular disinterest had dealt a crippling blow to his male pride. Her cool detachment intrigued and irritated him. Her assessment of him was probably more accurate than he cared to admit. Whenever he was near Eden St. James, he did act boorish. He sipped at the drink. To make matters worse, he was no closer to finding out what dire circumstances had driven the proud beauty to relinquish a life of luxury for one of drudgery.

"Justin," Caroline whined, tugging at his sleeve, "you aren't listening."

"Sorry, pet. I've been remiss." He smiled into her upturned face. In truth, he had been so preoccupied he had nearly forgotten Caroline's presence.

"I was asking about the horse you brought for the race. What did you say his name was? Thunderfoot?"

"Thunderbolt."

"Close enough." She giggled. "Thunderfoot. Thunderbolt. They sound alike to me."

Justin caught sight of Eden through shifting sets of dancers. A starched white apron and neckerchief covered most of her dress. The ruffled cap he was growing to detest concealed her glorious ebony tresses. Even attired like the other servants, she was conspicuous. Her rare beauty had the power to transcend the shabbiest costume. He admired her quiet dignity as she moved among the guests with glasses of rum punch and mulled cider. Never once did she smile.

"Justin!" Caroline scolded. "You're doing it again."

He shook his head in self-disgust. "My dear Caroline, I promise you my undivided attention. If it so much as wavers, please feel free to trounce on my foot."

She coyly batted pale eyelashes. "But if I do, you won't be able to dance."

"Should that occur, you'll discover a long line of young men, each eager to be your partner."

"I don't want another partner." Caroline stuck out her lower lip. "Do you really think your horse can beat Charles's? I'm betting five pounds on Thunderbolt. Father allowed me to chose the prize and is letting me present it to the winner. I do hope you'll share it with me."

The minuet gave way to a reel, and a young man claimed Caroline for the dance. Justin set his glass aside and joined the others. Rosemarie Hughes was the next woman who tried, but failed, to capture his wayward musings. After her came faceless others, like so many hothouse blooms in brilliantly colored gowns. As he circled the ballroom, aglow with candlelight, Justin came to a realization. He didn't covet a hothouse flower. He wished for one special woman to fill his arms, one with the incomparable beauty of an elusive, delicate wildflower.

The hands of the tall case clock moved toward twelve. Jasper Wainwright, his family at his side, signaled the musicians for silence. Servants circulated bearing trays of long-stemmed glasses brimming with sparkling wine.

"My dear friends," Jasper said in a voice that boomed with pride and authority, "this is truly a momentous occasion. As you are aware, my wife, Millicent, and I invited you here to help celebrate the twenty-first birthday of our son, Charles. My pleasure tonight is two-fold. I ask you to join in a toast, not only to salute Charles's coming of age, but also in honor of his engagement. Miss Rose-marie Hughes, daughter of our longtime friends and neighbors, has graciously consented to become his wife.''

The burst of loud applause that followed was inter-spersed with murmurs of congratulations and approval. The guests' raised glasses clinked together.

Over the rim of his glass, Justin spied Eden standing somewhat apart from the others, her back pressed against the wall. He watched thoughtfully. Her face, devoid of expression, could have been a beautiful porcelain mask; even the dull sheen of her eyes added to the illusion. Her lack of expression puzzled him. Had he been mistaken about her involvement with Charles? As he watched, she raised a slender hand to stroke an object hidden by her neckerchief, just below the hollow of her throat.

Once again Jasper raised his hands for silence. ''Allow my servants to refill your glasses, then follow Charles and his lovely bride-to-be into the dining room for a midnight repast.''

Like a statue coming to life, Eden slowly and method-ically poured champagne into outstretched glasses. Her stepfather's training stood her in good stead. Under his strict tutelage, she had become adept at hiding her feel-ings. Although she wanted to scream and cry, to stamp her feet and pound her fists, she poured glass after glass of sparkling wine. Hurt, betrayed, humiliated, Eden con-trolled her inner turmoil with a skill honed by years of practice.

The effort cost her dearly. By the time the last guest was ready to retire, her tenuous control was ready to snap. Not bothering with a shawl, Eden ran from the house and once again sought the sanctuary of the rose arbor. She sank onto the hard iron bench. Her arms clasped around her body, her eyes tightly closed, she began to rock back and forth.

Tears swelled inside her like a tidal wave. She rocked

faster, trying to hold them at bay. A low, keening sound escaped. Hot salty drops squeezed beneath her lids and rolled down her cheeks. Her shoulders shook and her chest ached from the effort to contain her emotions. With a convulsive sob, she abandoned the attempt. The storm of weeping she had avoided for the past year overtook her.

Chapter 3

Tortured, raspy, agonized gasps.

Listening, Justin paused, his head to one side. They seemed to be coming from directly ahead of him at the end of the pathway. He wanted to hurry forward, but was hampered by an inky darkness that spilled across the night, blotting out everything but the vaguest shadows. There wasn't even a glimmer of moonlight to guide his steps. The sound inexorably drew him near.

Squinting into the gloom, he glimpsed a patch of light against dark just inside the rose arbor. He could barely distinguish a slight form huddled on a bench partially hidden from view by the trellis. It was a woman, weeping as though her heart were breaking. Justin's feet dragged to a halt. He felt more confident confronting a bear protecting her cubs than he did a sobbing woman. Tears rendered him helpless. He hesitated, torn between the impulse to beat a cowardly retreat and the desire to offer comfort. The latter won.

He advanced cautiously. It was undoubtedly some young girl with an empty dance card. Or perhaps a wife who had found another woman in her husband's arms. But it was neither.

Although the woman's head was averted, her face buried in her arms, Justin could tell by her drab clothing that she was not a guest. The starched white cap, neckerchief, and apron proclaimed her station. When she turned her face, his gut twisted into knots.

"Eden!" Her name slipped easily from his tongue. Following instinct, he sat down next to her. The tears were unrelenting. Tentatively, he reached out and touched her shoulder. "Eden," he repeated, wanting desperately to console her but not knowing how. Consumed by misery, she remained unaware of his presence.

Justin watched with growing concern. Her sobs were so violent they seemed to be tearing apart her slender frame. His initial reserve melted and compassion filled him. He gathered Eden in his arms and held her. "Hush darlin', please don't cry," he murmured over and over, but to no avail.

Gently cradling her, he swayed to and fro. Ragged, convulsive shudders rippled through her slight body. He could feel her pain, her anguish. Angry at whatever circumstances had reduced her to servitude, he snatched the cap from her head and tossed it to the ground. A heavy, braided coil tumbled out. He wove his fingers into the thick, silken plait, loosening the strands until her hair spilled free, shrouding her in an ebony mantle. "There, there, it's all right." With great tenderness, he stroked the glossy mass, all the while rocking slowly.

The motion was soothing, almost as comforting as the softly spoken words. Eden clutched his coat front and wept bitterly. Though her tears dampened his cravat, Justin could not have cared less. After what seemed like eons, the torrent of weeping subsided, except for an occasional hiccoughing sob. Emotionally spent, Eden rested against Justin, absorbing his warmth and his strength. For the moment, she accepted the solace without questioning its source.

"Does Charles mean so much to you?" Justin's usually smooth voice was gruff. He needed to know the truth, yet feared the answer. *He* wanted to be the only man who mattered to Eden St. James. The sudden realization shocked him.

With a sinking sensation, Eden recognized the familiar voice. Somehow it seemed inevitable that Justin Tremayne should be the one to find her. "I . . . it . . . it's . . ." she half stammered, half sobbed, her head moving from side to side in denial. "I—it's not Charles." A shiver raced through her, causing her to instinctively press closer to share his body's warmth.

"Damn," Justin swore under his breath. Belatedly it occurred to him that the girl must be chilled to the bone by the damp night air. He was a lout not to have thought of it sooner. Holding Eden against him, he shifted her from one arm to the other while he shrugged out of his woolen coat and spread it over her shoulders. *It's not Charles.* The phrase echoed in his mind, filling him with giddy relief. "If not Charles, what is it that makes you so unhappy?" he persisted.

"Everything." Eden squeezed her eyes against renewed tears. "E-everything has gone wrong since that night in London."

Justin fumbled in the pocket of his vest and brought out a handkerchief. Drawing back slightly, he tilted her face to his and wiped away the tears that still glistened on her cheeks. He handed her the cloth and instructed, "Blow."

Black spiky lashes raised slowly to reveal eyes that reminded him of rain-drenched violets. Something akin to horror filled their dark purple depths.

"Go ahead. Blow your nose."

Bowing her head, Eden did as she was told. She was mortified. There was no ladylike way in which to blow one's nose. Added to this was the heinous offense of having a stranger witness her total loss of restraint, an unforgivable crime. Both her stepfather and Rodney would have gloated in meting out punishment for such an infraction.

Thrusting the handkerchief at Justin, she pushed away from him and hastily scrambled to her feet. "Please, forgive my outburst. My behavior was inexcusable. I hope you won't think the worse of me." The episode had unleashed in her memories of nearly forgotten scenes from her childhood, incidents in which she was a defenseless child at the mercy of an overly strict, often-cruel stepparent. Again she felt like that small, frightened little girl.

"My display of emotion was deplorable, but I thought I was alone. Please don't think it's a reflection on my upbringing. I don't know what possessed me just now. F-f-forgive me." The words burbled out unchecked. Eden shivered again and hugged the coat more securely around her shoulders.

Justin rose slowly, his brows meeting in a frown. Involuntarily, Eden took a step backward, her eyes enormous in her pale, distraught face.

Puzzled by the effusive apology, Justin chose his words with care. "No explanation is necessary. There's nothing wrong with tears. All of us feel the need of them at times." He reached out, intending to draw her closer, but at his touch, Eden whirled and bolted down the garden path.

Justin was left holding his coat and grasping at air. A ghost of her warmth, and the delicate scent of wildflowers, clung to the wool, an elusive reminder of the woman who had slipped from his arms.

The following day Eden avoided both Charles and Justin, a feat which required little effort. Charles was occupied with his bride-to-be; Justin simply kept his distance. It was best this way, she told herself repeatedly. Justin must be thoroughly disgusted with her after the uninhibited bout of weeping he had witnessed the night before.

Eden stacked the soiled dishes from the midday meal. How her stepfather had detested tears. Each time her eyes filled or her lower lip quivered, he would fly into a cold rage. His rapier tongue would flay her sensitive nature until she cringed with shame and despaired of ever pleasing him. Knowing this, kindhearted Nanny Wadkins would admonish, "Never let the sun catch yer cryin', sweetkins." By the time she was ten, Eden had learned to restrict her tears to the privacy of her room late at night, their sound muffled by goose down pillows.

Still, Eden reflected as she stole a glance at Justin stand-

ing in the broad central hallway just outside the dining
room, he hadn't seemed repulsed. Quite the contrary. His
actions had been gentle, even tender. For a brief interlude,
it had been heaven to be held in those strong arms. Never
could she remember a time when she had felt so protected,
so safe.

"I have ta hand it to you, girl."

Eden glanced up, dismayed to find Polly watching her.

"You sure don't let any moss grow under your feet.
With Charles out of the picture, you've already got your
sights set on another."

"I don't know what you're talking about." Eden picked
up an empty platter from the table, and balancing the tray-
load of dishes, left the room by a side door.

Polly followed close on her heels down the hallway and
out a back entrance. "I seen the way you've been watchin'
Justin Tremayne when you think no one's lookin'."

Eden quickened her pace. "You're imagining things."

"Am I?" Polly clutched Eden's sleeve, halting her midway along the path. "Way it looks to me, if you can't get
the master of the household, you're willin' to settle for
Caroline's beau."

"That's absurd." Eden twisted loose.

"Is it?"

"Look, Polly, all I want is to serve out my indenture
with as few problems as possible."

"Then, girl, you better get rid of those high and mighty
airs." Polly stepped closer, her china blue eyes bright with
menace. "You've always fancied yourself a cut above me
and Bess. Well, we're gettin' fed up. You better come
down a peg or two, or you'll find out what real problems
are." She left Eden staring after her.

The rest of the day seemed interminable. When it finally
drew to a close, Eden lay on her narrow attic cot, staring
up at cobwebby eaves. An uncertain future stretched before her. It had been folly to pin her hopes on Charles.
She didn't love him, and he had toyed with her. She meant
nothing to him—nothing whatsoever. Oh yes, he had called

her beautiful. He had told her she would make a fine wife. What he hadn't said was that she would make a fine wife for him. She had heard only what she wanted to hear. She was a dreamer without a whit of common sense.

Eden drew the meager blanket closer around her shoulders and rolled onto her side. Cook's loud snores broke the silence. Four years, five months, twelve days. It might as well be a lifetime. Polly's animosity earlier that day had been upsetting. The girl meant to cause trouble, Eden was sure of it. Polly had taken an instant dislike to her since she had first set foot in this household. Bess, the more timid of the two, would surely side with Polly.

Eden's delicate jaw firmed with resolve. The tears of the previous night had washed away emotional baggage she had been carrying since she had fled England, leaving her free to confront the future. Somehow, she vowed, she would not be bested by this hostile land. She would survive. Somehow . . .

The much-talked-about horse race was set to take place shortly. Most of the guests were already milling about the fallow field where a crude race track had been improvised. On her way to join the spectators, Eden was hurrying past the dependencies when a hand reached out and pulled her into the deserted dairy.

"Charles," she gasped when her eyes adjusted to the gloom. It was cool and dark inside the small outbuilding, the air smelling faintly of soured milk.

"Who else?" he said with a laugh. He took her by the shoulders and pressed her back to the rough siding, blocking her exit. "We haven't had a minute alone in days. Have you missed me?"

Eden shook her head in disbelief. "How can you act as if nothing has happened? What if someone should see us?" She moved to skirt around him, but he braced both arms against the wall on either side of her.

"There isn't a soul in sight. No one will miss me as long as I'm there in time to win the race."

"Charles, please, just leave me alone."

"You're not mad because I had a little too much to drink the other night and tried to steal a kiss?"

"I was thinking of your betrothal." Eden made no effort to hide her contempt. "What about your fiancée?"

His grin was cocky. "What about her? Rosemarie has nothing to do with us."

"Wrong," Eden corrected. "Since you are engaged to be married, there is no more *us.*" Wounded pride prevented her from looking at the boyish face so close to hers. Instead she fixed her gaze on a point above his shoulder.

"Eden, look at me," Charles ordered, taking her chin and forcing her head around. "All I'm asking is one little kiss. Wish me luck. Surely that's not too much, is it?"

Eden's eyes widened at the brazen request. "Charles, you led me to believe you were interested in me."

"I am interested, sweet." He flashed a grin. "Very interested."

"If that's true, how do you explain your engagement?"

The amusement on Charles's face was replaced by amazement. He stared at her as though she had gone daft. "Certainly you didn't think for a minute there could be anything serious between us. Why, you're a servant! And an indentured one at that!" He drew himself up, tall and straight, and peered down at her. In the blink of an eye, he became a haughty aristocrat, she a lowly peasant. "Don't forget my family owns you. From the cap on your head to the soles of your shoes, you're our possession. You belong to us just as surely as one of the black field slaves, the only difference being you have years of service to contend with, they a lifetime."

Eden couldn't believe what she was hearing. Never had she suspected Charles capable of such cruelty. His saber-sharp words lacerated her pride, shredded her self-esteem. "Thank you for the reminder," she said through numb lips, and started to turn away. She could barely breathe. The walls were beginning to close in on her.

"Eden." He grabbed her arm. "I didn't want to hurt

you, but you needed to be reminded of your place. You were getting above your station.''

She glared at him, her hands curled into tight fists at her sides. You cloddish colonial, she wanted to hurl at him. In England, you would never even be considered a possible suitor. Why, I could have married an earl, or a count.

But you are no longer in England, an inner voice taunted. Her anger ebbed, leaving empty despair.

His grip tightened. ''Mark my words, sweet Eden. Servant or no, you're a comely wench and I mean to have you.'' He released her abruptly and straightened his coat with a tug. ''And I always get what I want.'' He flung the door wide on its hinges and stormed out.

Eden stood in the open doorway, staring at Charles's retreating back. Hugging her arms for warmth, she absently massaged the place where his hand had touched her. Charles's threat chilled her to the bone. Thoughts of Rodney resurfaced. Again she had the feeling of being trapped, cornered. Only this time, there was nowhere to run.

With a heavy sigh, Eden left the dairy and started across the sunlit meadow, moving toward the sound of voices. The sun's rays failed to penetrate the icy shell that seemed to encase her as she approached the noisy crowd.

Both servants and guests were already assembled for the contest. Virginians, she observed, shared an inordinate fondness for a good horse race. Even the weather cooperated. The sky was a cloudless blue, the air crisp but not uncomfortably so. A carnival atmosphere prevailed with much gaiety and laughter. People chattered, excitedly making last minute wagers. The women appeared to be enjoying the occasion every bit as much as their male counterparts. Eden was shocked to hear Millicent Wainwright loudly wager ten pounds on her son's horse.

Eden shielded her eyes with one hand to better view the impromptu racecourse. It comprised roughly one-half mile in circumference, staked out with posts tied with bright red and yellow flags. Two men selected as judges positioned themselves at the end posts. Another man was chosen to act as starter, and yet another to hold the money that had been wagered.

Six horses with hand-tooled saddles pranced impatiently. One steed in particular commanded Eden's attention. As black as coal, as sleek as an otter, its barely restrained muscles rippled under a satiny coat. Justin Tremayne himself clad in a black coat, tight-fitting black breeches, and highly polished black boots, stood beside the magnificent animal, allowing it short rein. A starched white linen shirt and scarlet vest added a dash of color to Justin's attire, making man and beast a striking pair. Eden tore her gaze away from Justin and surveyed his challengers. In comparison, Charles's mount looked like a docile brood mare. The other horses rated little better in her estimation.

For the moment, Eden set aside her problems. The excitement of the race was contagious. Were it possible, she knew she would wager fifty shillings, the entire amount of her indenture agreement, on Justin's magnificent horseflesh. She shouldered her way forward, wanting an unrestricted view of the race.

Bess sidled up and stood next to her at the far edge of the racecourse. "Do you have a favorite, Eden?"

She shook her head, knowing it was a lie. She *did* have a favorite—Justin and his splendid black stallion.

"I heard people talking." Bess dug her hands into her apron pockets. "They say Mr. Tremayne's horse is called Thunderbolt."

"Thunderbolt," Eden repeated, thinking the name well suited for such a powerful animal.

"Isn't he wonderful?" Bess sighed wistfully. "I'd bet on Mr. Tremayne, but I don't have any money. He's the most beautiful man I've ever seen."

Eden almost smiled. "Mr. Tremayne isn't the one doing the racing, Bess," she chided gently. "His horse is."

Blond curls peeked beneath Polly's white ruffled cap, bouncing with each step as she approached. "Bess, you ninny." Bess seemed to shrivel under Polly's assault. "Are you still talking about Justin Tremayne? Don't you know your homely face doesn't have a chance against the fair Eden's?"

Mottled color stained Bess's sallow cheeks. She dropped her eyes and scuffed at the loose turf with the toe of her shoe.

"That remark was uncalled for," Eden said in Bess's defense. "Furthermore, I have no interest in Mr. Tremayne, and he has none in me."

"Is that right?" Polly smirked. "Then why was he so anxious to find you the night after the ball? I offered him my company, but it was yours he wanted. He even gave me five shillings if I could tell 'im where you had run off to. I didn't care a fig if he found you or not, but I told 'im to look in the garden." She reached inside the bodice of her dress and withdrew the coin, holding it before Eden's startled gaze. "Properly grateful he was, too."

So Justin's finding her hadn't been a coincidence! Why had he sought her out? Eden wondered.

"Tell you what." Polly eyed her slyly. "What about you and me makin' a little wager? Say my five shillings against your locket?"

Eden's hand flew to the smooth metal disk suspended from a gold chain around her neck.

"But, Polly, it's real gold," Bess protested. "It's worth more than five shillings."

"Ha! That's what her highness would like us to think. It's probably nothin' but polished brass."

"No, I couldn't."

"C'mon, Eden. I've watched Charles's horse win more than one race. I'd pick his any day over that flashy black stallion."

Eden was tempted. But the temptation wasn't prompted by the desire to win five shillings, or to wipe the smugness from Polly's face. Justin Tremayne had given her comfort at a time when she had desperately needed it. For that, she would be eternally grateful. Her fingers fondled the locket resting against the swell of her breasts, its gold warmed by the heat of her body. She felt torn. The locket, a gift from Rodney on her sixteenth birthday, was her only connection with the past. It linked the person she had once been with the one she had become. To lose it would be like losing part of herself. She couldn't take the risk.

"Well, what're you waitin' for?" Polly interrupted with growing impatience. "Make up yer mind. The race is about to start."

Eden's glance strayed toward the course and found Justin watching her. Their eyes met and held. Win, Justin, win. You can do it. I know you can, she wanted to tell him. Instead she addressed Polly. "I can't bet the locket. I have nothing else of value."

"Coward!" Polly sneered. With a swish of her skirts, she marched off to join a small cluster of servants standing nearby, most of whom had accompanied guests to the Wainwright plantation.

Bess rested her hand on Eden's sleeve. "Don't let her bother you."

"Bess!" Polly shouted. The girl quickly let go of Eden's arm. Giving Eden an apologetic look, she scurried to hover in the blond girl's shadow. Eden remained somewhat apart, observing the activities around her. All the while, her index finger stroked the golden locket.

At a given signal, the riders valuted into their saddles, quirts in hand. The horses sidestepped and tossed their manes while their owners struggled to align them at the starting line.

"Ready gentlemen?" the starter asked.

"Ready!" came the reply.

"Good fortune ride with you. Go!"

As though shot from an invisible cannon, the horses catapulted down the track. Hooves thundered over hard-packed earth, causing the ground to vibrate beneath their feet. Excited shouts rose from the crowd. A thick cloud of brown dust nearly obscured the riders. Eden leaned forward. Already four horses had fallen behind. In moments it became a two-horse race, Justin's black stallion against Charles's gelding.

The gelding started to take the lead. Eden's heart pumped furiously, her mouth dry as cotton. Charles glanced over his shoulder and flashed a triumphant grin. It proved premature. His horse broke stride as Justin's Thunderbolt surged ahead in a blur, black on black. Flexing and stretching its powerful legs, the stallion flew across the finish line.

Eden wasn't aware that her own cheers had joined the others. Neither was she conscious that for the first time in months she was happy. Her smile lingered as she watched Caroline Wainwright present a painted tin of imported chocolates to the winner. Justin accepted the prize. Then, seated on his mount like a conquering hero, he surveyed the crowd before spying the one he was seeking. Ignoring the onlookers who surged forward to congratulate him, he nudged the stallion forward and reined to a halt in front of Eden.

Oblivious of the gawking crowd, he presented the tin with a flourish, his mellow words intended for her ears alone. ''To the fairest of the fair, the sweetest of the sweet. For you, Eden.''

Chapter 4

Eden's hand trembled as she reached to accept the tin Justin offered. Grasping the gift firmly in both hands, she hugged it to her breast. She was unable to force words past the stricture in her throat, but her smile was eloquent. It mirrored her pleasure and reflected her relief. Justin hadn't been repulsed by her tears of the previous night. He wasn't angry.

Justin couldn't tear his gaze from Eden's face. Her radiant expression held the warmth of a summer day, the promise of a Christmas morn, the brilliance of a shooting star. As it had nearly a year ago on a London street corner, her beauty stole his breath away.

The stallion snorted and tossed its head, sending flecks of foam flying from its mouth.

"Whoa boy, steady," Justin commanded. The huge beast quieted at his soothing drawl.

"He's a magnificent animal." Tentatively, Eden stroked the velvety muzzle. "The minute I saw him, I knew he'd win the race."

With an exaggerated swing of well-rounded hips, Polly walked over to join them. "Since when is a serving wench an expert on horseflesh?"

Eden's expression sobered. Polly was deliberately trying to embarrass her. The moment of happiness turned sour. Withdrawing her hand from the horse's muzzle, Eden clutched the painted canister tighter.

"Poor Caroline," Polly cooed. "Looks like she got

herself a terrible bellyache. She don't look none too happy.''

Eden glanced over her shoulder. Caroline was standing not more than ten feet away, staring at Justin, a stricken expression on her round face. Immediately, Eden felt guilty. The girl cared for Justin. Eden had never meant to interfere. Caroline's gaze shifted to her. Anger warred with hurt in the girl's pale blue eyes. Then, stomping her foot in frustration, she whirled and flounced off toward the house.

"Caroline is plenty miffed, if you ask me," Polly observed, chortling.

Justin locked his gaze on Eden. "Don't worry. She'll recover."

Polly shot Justin a brazen grin. "Seems your Thunderbolt put Mister Charles to shame. To my mind, it's the first time he's ever been beat."

Leaning forward in the saddle, Justin patted the stallion's lathered neck. "Charles's horse ran a good race."

"But yours ran better." Polly eyed the animal dubiously. At close range, the steed seemed gigantic. Having been raised in the streets of Liverpool, Polly had scant experience with horses, and no desire to learn, but not wanting to appear a coward, she tried to imitate Eden's familiarity. Inching forward, she gave the stallion three sharp raps on its snout before she lost her nerve.

Thunderbolt whinnied, protesting the abrupt treatment by raising his lips in a display of great yellow teeth. With a frightened squeal, Polly leaped backward.

"Steady, boy." Justin controlled the restive horse with a firm hand.

"How can you just sit there?" Polly demanded, emboldened by her scare. "Give him a taste of your crop! Your precious beast nearly bit my hand off."

"You're quite safe." Justin flashed a grin. "He's well fed on hay and oats and has yet to be carnivorous."

"Humph!" Polly eyed the horse skeptically and forgot for a moment she was addressing one of the guests. "Don't waste no fancy words on me. Even an idiot can tell from the look in his eyes that horse would like nothin' better than to chomp on my fingers.''

"He's a Thoroughbred, Polly," Eden intervened. "And Thoroughbred's are high-strung animals. You just startled him, that's all.''

Polly turned on her. "Since you're so smart, too bad you didn't have sense to place a small wager. You'd be jinglin' my five shillings in your pocket right now.''

Justin frowned. "What's this about a wager?''

"N-nothing.''

"Ha!" Polly snorted. "Miss High and Mighty here didn't see fit to wager her precious locket. You against Charles. So much for her knowin' horses. Maybe she thought Charles would win.''

Justin sat straighter in the saddle. Coolness seeped into his tone. "You disappoint me, Miss St. James. Your actions show a distinct lack of faith.''

"It wasn't like that," Eden protested, her voice faint.

"Then how was it?''

A satisfied smirk on her face, Polly rolled back on her heels and watched the two.

"Well?" Justin prodded. "Tell me, why did you hesitate to make the wager?''

And why do you always have to twist things? Eden wanted to ask. It was as though he deliberately misunderstood her, each incident cutting more deeply than the one before. Whatever the reason, it was a puzzle that would keep till later. She squared her shoulders, her expression remote. "Think what you will, Mr. Tremayne. My actions aren't accountable to you. You don't own me.''

"You're absolutely right, Miss St. James, I don't.'' Nudging the stallion's flanks with his knees, Justin tugged on the reins and, wheeling the horse about, rode off to join a group of gentry. True, he didn't own her. But he'd like to. Lord, how he'd like to own Eden St. James.

His eyes narrowed thoughtfully. The wench was entirely too arrogant. If she didn't exercise caution, her pride could bring about her downfall. What she needed was a firm but gentle hand. Like his.

"Well, girl, you gonna hog it all? Ain't you gonna share?" Polly demanded.

"Of course, I'll share." Eden pried the lid from the box of chocolates and offered a piece to the blonde. While Polly stuffed the sweet into her mouth, Eden walked over to where the other servants were congregated and passed the tin to each in turn. "Go ahead," she whispered when she came to Cook. "Take another. I don't really crave sweets."

Cook's plump fingers whisked the candy from the box in the blink of an eye. "That's real generous," she mumbled, flashing Eden a chocolate-coated smile.

When the others finished helping themselves to the confections, Eden glimpsed her reflection on the bottom of the tin. Only one piece of candy remained, but Eden didn't mind. The thought of Justin's gift would stay with her.

"Miss Caroline wants a word with you," Polly informed Eden shortly before the evening meal. "She said she'd be waitin' in the sewin' room."

"But I'm to help serve. Are you certain she wants me now?"

"I'm sure."

"Very well." Eden set the platter of sliced ham on a side table and swept an errant lock of hair inside her cap. "If Cook asks, tell her where I've gone."

"Don't worry. I'll tell 'er."

Eden shot Polly a troubled look. Given an opportunity, the girl would relish stirring up trouble.

"Caroline's waitin'," Polly urged with a bland smile.

Eden nodded, then hurried up the back stairs and pushed open the door to the small room at the end of the hall. Two narrow cots had been brought in to accommodate the overflow of guests. Both were strewn with ribbons, undergarments, and discarded dresses. Silk stockings dangled off one bed to trail on a braided rug. A clutter of hair ornaments, brushes, and cut-glass containers of powder and scent competed for space on a mahogany dressing table. The cloying smell of roses perfumed the air. The room's other occupants had already finished dressing and departed, leaving Caroline alone. She stood staring out the window, her back to Eden.

"Polly said you wanted to see me."

Caroline swung around. "How could you?" she wailed, her hands balled into fists at her sides. "I thought you were my friend."

Eden observed that the girl's eyes were red-rimmed and puffy from recent tears. "Caroline, I never meant—"

"You sat in this very room and listened to how much Justin means to me, yet you deliberately tried to steal him. Well, you're not going to get away with it. He's mine! I saw him first!"

Eden walked to the nearest cot and smoothed the wrinkles from a carelessly discarded gown of yellow dimity. "As far as I'm concerned, Mr. Tremayne is yours and always has been."

"Justin ignored me. And in front of all my friends. It was so embarrassing, I could have died." Tears welled in her eyes and threatened to spill over. "Why, Eden? Why did he give you the candy instead of me?"

It was a question Eden had asked herself many times over. She kept her attention on the gown, taking great care to ease its full skirt into neat folds. "Perhaps your Mr. Tremayne is a bit like Sir Galahad."

"Never heard of him," Caroline said with a sniffle. "Is he a friend of King George?"

"No," Eden murmured with a trace of a smile. "He was a knight of King Arthur's Round Table."

"You're not making sense." Caroline's lower lip protruded in vexation. "What has this to do with why Justin gave you his prize?"

"Sir Galahad was reputed for his gallantry." Eden proceeded to pick up the stockings, fold them, and place them on the bed next to the dress. "Mr. Tremayne probably felt sorry for me. Remember, I'm only a servant and not likely to have many opportunities to sample sweets." It was a feeble explanation, Eden realized, but one that seemed to pacify the girl.

"Well . . ." Caroline considered Eden's logic, then brightened. "I suppose that does make sense. Justin is the most thoughtful man." She pushed past Eden to peer critically into the small mirror of the dressing table. "What do you think, Eden? Will everyone know I've been crying?"

Eden stared at the girl, amazed by her abrupt change in mood. "A splash of cool water should remedy the problem."

"What a good idea! That's exactly what I'll do." Caroline twisted a golden curl to fall in a spiral over a plump shoulder. "Mother promised to seat Justin next to me at dinner." She took the stopper from a glass decanter and dabbed perfume at the base of her throat, between her breasts, and behind each ear. "I'm glad we had this little chat. I feel ever so much better." With a rustle of starched petticoats and smelling like an overblown bouquet, Caroline sallied forth.

Eden's glance shifted to the untidy room. In England, had she ever been guilty of leaving such disarray for Jennie, her lady's maid, to set right? Yes, she had, Eden recalled with shame. On many occasions she had chosen then discarded gowns, experimented with hairstyles, and debated her choice of jewels. But anxiety rather than vanity had prompted her indecision. She hadn't wanted to give her stepfather, or Rodney, reason to fault her appearance. Frequently, she had endured their meals together under an unrelenting barrage of criticism.

Still, that was no excuse for such slovenliness. Eden replaced the stopper of the perfume bottle and quickly rearranged the toiletries. Until now she had never considered the thankless task confronting Jennie. She had been self-centered, inconsiderate. It was ironic how the tables had been turned. How Jennie would chuckle if she knew.

"There you are, you lazy chit!"

The hairbrush in Eden's hand clattered to the floor as Millicent Wainwright launched her considerable bulk into the small room. "Shirking your duty! I might have known. Fortunately, Polly knew your whereabouts."

"Caroline wanted to speak with me." Eden forced herself not to back away. Mrs. Wainwright was livid.

"As well she might after her humiliation this afternoon." Millicent crossed her arms over her ample bosom. "What have you to say for yourself, girl?"

"There is nothing to say. Mr. Tremayne was only being kind."

"A likely story! Caroline may be gulled by your mealy-mouthed excuses, but not me." She advanced on Eden, a huntress moving in for the kill.

Eden tensed. Instinct honed by years of experience screamed danger.

"I've watched you in action, missy. I've seen you work your wiles—first on Charles, and when that failed, on Justin Tremayne!"

"You're mistaken, Mrs. Wainwright—"

A vicious slap cracked across Eden's cheek, causing her head to snap back. Pain scalded her cheek, bringing a sting of tears behind her eyelids.

"Don't talk back to me, missy, or next time I'll give you the strap."

Eden could barely hear Millicent Wainwright's next words over the buzzing in her ears.

"Listen to me and listen well." Millicent spit each word. "You're nothing but a cheap little trollop. A wanton. A woman of loose morals, luring family and guest alike while thumbing your nose at respectability." She jabbed her forefinger into Eden's breastbone, driving her backward with each poke. "Well, I won't stand for it! Do you hear me?" Her finger skewered Eden's spine to the wall.

"Yes, ma'am," Eden croaked.

"Luckily for you, I'm a generous, God-fearing woman.

I'm giving you another chance. But should your disgraceful behavior ever again come to my attention, your articles of indenture will be sold to a tavernkeeper in Williamsburg within the day. A suitable place—one where you'll have ample opportunity to ply your trade. Do I make myself clear?''

The hurtful hand left Eden's chest and fastened on her jaw, forcing her chin upward. "Well, girl, I'm waiting for an answer."

Eden gathered her composure. "Yes, Mrs. Wainwright, I understand. Perfectly." The calm in her voice was testament to her skill in hiding her feelings.

Millicent Wainwright's pale eyes bored into her, but Eden met them without flinching. At long last, the woman released her tight grip and stepped back. "You're to stay away from the guests. Polly and Bess will serve the meals. In return, you'll take over extra cleaning chores. If Cook can't find you enough tasks in the kitchen, you're to help Mathilda with the laundry. Now, out of my sight before I reconsider."

Eden didn't need to be told twice. She dodged around the portly figure, which didn't budge a fraction to accommodate her passage, and quickly left the room. The scene had been unnerving. She desperately needed time to collect herself. Her knees were like pudding; at any moment they might collapse and send her sprawling.

Thank goodness the rear stairway was deserted. Eden darted down the narrow flight, her ears attuned for the sound of voices. From the muted rumble of conversation behind the closed drawing-room doors, she surmised some guests were sipping aperitifs before being summoned to dine. Careful to make no sound, she made her way down the central hallway and was nearly out of the house before she noticed that the door to the dining room was slightly ajar. Her attempt to slip by unnoticed failed.

"Eden!" Polly called out sharply. The door opened wider. "My, my, whatever happened to you? Looks like you've been in a fight." The blonde surveyed Eden's pale face. "You poor thing," she crooned solictiously. "Your lip is cut and bleedin'."

Eden became aware of the salty taste of her own blood as she touched the small wound with the tip of her tongue. She probed it gingerly with a fingertip, which came away warm and sticky with a bright smudge of red.

Polly cocked her head to one side, a broad smile on her face. "You're gonna have a nasty bruise across your cheek. Pity."

"It's kind of you to be concerned," Eden replied with icy dignity.

"Think nothin' of it, ducks," Polly replied, chortling. "By the by, Mistress Wainwright asked me to keep an eye on you." Turning, Polly swaggered off with a saucy grin.

Justin noted Eden's absence at supper. He was also quick to observe Caroline's forced gaiety and Millicent Wainwright's efforts to throw them together. During the musicale that followed, his thoughts wandered. It wasn't that he didn't like Caroline. After all, he had known her since she was a child and was fond of her. Maybe that was where the problem lay. Caroline was still a child, and he wanted a woman.

There was an unmistakable void in his life. As hard as Justin tried to ignore the feeling, it returned to plague him in quiet moments. Not once had he regretted his decision to leave Baltimore and return to his mother's beloved Virginia. After his parents untimely deaths, he had sold his father's share of the shipyard and the fleet of merchant ships, and used the proceeds to pursue his dream of becoming one of the most prosperous landowners in the Tidewater. For nearly ten years, with single-minded determination, he had gone about his plan. He was thirty now, and he was succeeding.

He was familiar with every aspect of tobacco growing. He had mastered every task. By laboring long hours beneath a blistering summer sun, he had coaxed secrets from the Virginia soil. He knew which fields were fertile and which to leave fallow. Because of his perseverance, the land had yielded its precious bounty.

Vaguely aware that Caroline's quavering soprano had ceased, Justin let his perfunctory applause join the others. Rosemarie Hughes was next on the program. Charles stood alongside the pianoforte, ready to turn the pages of music. After taking several minutes to arrange her skirts prettily on the rosewood bench, the bride-to-be smiled at her audience and began to play. Justin winced at the abuse she gave one of his favorite pieces. It was best not to listen, to think of other things instead, such as the home he was building.

Greenbriar. It's beauty was unrivaled. Barring unforeseen difficulties, the house would be completed by harvesttime. His brows drew together as his vague unease persisted; his dream was incomplete. He needed an adoring wife and children to bring his plans to full fruition.

Restlessly, he crossed and then recrossed his long legs. Recognition of this need had prompted him to leave Greenbriar to attend the Wainwright's party. Every eligible girl in the Tidewater would be present. The time had come to reacquaint himself with them, yet he'd found that none of the guests appealed to him. Indeed, no woman had since he had chanced to look out a solicitor's window almost a year ago. He had lost his heart the moment he set eyes on Eden St. James. The question was, what was he to do about it?

Ignoring Millicent Wainwright's tight-lipped disapproval, Justin quietly left the room. He shrugged into his greatcoat and, after lighting a cigar from a flickering candle, stepped outdoors. Fog from the James River cloaked the land in a moist shroud. As dampness crept through the folds of his coat and seeped into the woolen fibers, Justin tugged the collar closer about his neck. Cigar clamped between his teeth, hands buried deep in his coat pockets, he strolled slowly down the mist-slicked pathway.

He took great pride in being a sensible, practical man, not one given to impulsive acts—except where Eden St.

James was concerned. In the space of a heartbeat, she could make him jealous, angry, frustrated, remorseful, protective . . . and as besotted as an adoring schoolboy.

The rose arbor appeared out of the eerie white vapor like a ghostly apparition. For a long moment, Justin stood motionless, staring at the latticed structure. Narrowing his eyes, he peered through the darkness. There was no sign of movement. Disappointment spread through him. He was alone.

He walked the brick pathways, his steps a hollow echo in the deserted garden. Heedless of the light drizzle that had begun to fall, he sank onto the partially sheltered wrought-iron bench and blew out a thin stream of smoke. What was it that drew him to the woman? Her beauty? Yes, he couldn't deny he'd passed many a sleepless night wondering what her skin would feel like, how her mouth would taste. But the attraction went beyond the physical. She had a rare quality others seemed to lack, a vulnerability he found undeniably appealing. And on several occasions he had witnessed a spirit in her that was both unselfish and generous.

Yet she was so guarded, so cautious. It was as though she held the world, and him included, at arm's length.

Memory of Eden had served as his inspiration for the past eleven months. He had envisioned her descending Greenbriar's intricately carved staircase, pictured her opposite him at the gracious dining room table, felt her presence in the magnificent music room. Now that he had found her again, he refused to let her go.

Justin drew again on the thin cigar, watching its smoke mingle with the enveloping mist. Perhaps he'd have a rose arbor built at Greenbriar. If so, he'd never be able to set foot inside without being reminded of Eden. Eden and Greenbriar. Greenbriar and Eden. The two were as inseparable in his mind as smoke and fog.

Tossing the cigar to the ground, he crushed it beneath the heel of his boot and rose to his feet. Thoughtfully, he retraced his steps. If only the timing were different.

Greenbriar was still months from completion. Until then, he had nothing to offer Eden St. James except a crude shelter in the woods. Leaving her behind would be difficult, but only temporary. He would return for her in the fall, when she could grace his home not as his servant but as his wife.

Chapter 5

Eden put down the scrub brush and stretched to ease the cramp between her shoulder blades. She had already been working for hours, sweeping and scrubbing the hearths in each room on the lower floor of the great house, then meticulously piling logs on the grate so that they would ignite when spark met tinder.

The crack of gray visible through a gap in the draperies seemed a shade lighter than the last time she had looked. It would soon be dawn. Eden dipped the brush in soapy water and scoured harder. Mrs. Wainwright's instructions had been specific—the task was to be completed and Eden out of the house before the first guest began to stir.

"Good morning," a familiar voice drawled.

Eden jumped, bumping the bucket and sending suds sloshing over its rim. Looking toward the doorway, she found Justin lounging against the frame, a broad shoulder propped against the jamb, arms folded over his chest, one ankle crossed over the other.

"I . . . a . . ." Eden told herself it was the unexpectedness of his presence that caused her heart to hammer in her ears. "You startled me."

"I would never have guessed." His somber agreement brought a puzzled expression to her face. "I'm being facetious," he explained with a grin. "Haven't you ever been teased before?"

Eden sat back on her heels and considered the question. The sophisticated repartee of London drawing rooms could hardly be called teasing. In England, at Sommerset, laughter had been rare, smiles infrequent, good-natured teasing nonexistent. To her way of thinking, there was a subtle yet distinct difference between repartee and teasing. "Not that I can recall," she answered at last.

Humor fled his gray gaze. What kind of upbringing had she had, this beautiful girl on the brink of womanhood? He knew so little about her and wanted to know so much more.

Eden felt self-conscious under his solemn perusal. She wished he'd go away and leave her alone. Turning her back, she wiped up the spill and resumed scrubbing.

Justin pushed away from the door, closed it softly behind him, and sauntered into the shadowy music room. "Were the chocolates to your liking?"

"They were delicious, thank you. Everyone enjoyed them immensely."

"I noticed the others were quick to get their share. I hope that in their greed they left you a sample."

The candy was unimportant. Eden had cherished Justin's thoughtful act more than the gift itself. "It was kind of you to think of me, Mr. Tremayne. However . . ."

"However . . . ?"

He was close enough to touch. Panic welled inside her. What if Mrs. Wainwright found them together? Or Polly? Eden dipped the stiff-bristled brush into the soapy water and applied it to the stone hearth with renewed vigor. "I appreciate the gift more than I can express. I only regret that Caroline's feelings suffered."

He leaned against the mantelpiece and studied her. "Caroline behaved like an overindulged child having a tantrum."

"Nevertheless, she cares for you, and I don't want to cause any problems." Eden glanced nervously at the door, fearful that Millicent Wainwright would burst through at any moment, brandishing the indenture agreement, ready to haul her off to a tavernkeeper.

"Is something amiss?"

"No, nothing," she replied a trifle too quickly. "Why do you ask?"

"You're acting as skittish as Thunderbolt before the race yesterday."

Eden attacked the soot-stained bricks with a vengeance. "I have no time for idle talk. There's much to do before the other guests waken."

While this was undoubtedly true, Justin wasn't convinced it was the sole cause of her nervousness. He decided to test his theory. Wandering over to the pianoforte, he plunked the notes of a half-remembered tune.

"What are you doing?" Horrified, Eden scrambled to her feet, raced across the room, and snatched his hand from the keyboard. "Shh! Someone will hear."

Justin complied with a grin. "Is my playing that bad?"

"No, no, of course not." She shook her head in exasperation. "That isn't what I meant. Actually you play quite well." She shot another worried look at the closed door.

"I assumed you received music lessons as a young girl. Did you detest them as much as I did? Or perhaps you were more talented?"

"I loved my lessons. More than anything, I miss being able to play." In a rare, unguarded moment, wistfulness flickered across her features.

The last vestiges of humor disappeared as he stared into her distressed face. "Why weren't you helping at supper last evening?"

Suddenly Eden became aware that she was clutching the sleeve of his jacket. Releasing it, she clasped her hands together to still their agitation, keeping her eyes downcast. How humiliating. She wished she could disappear through the cracks in the floorboards, but there was no avoiding the issue. The man showed no sign of budging until he learned the truth. "Mistress Wainwright threatened to sell my indenture papers to a tavernkeeper in Williamsburg if I so much as talked to you." Her voice was scarcely a whisper.

A long silence followed.

"So that's the way it is," Justin said at last.

She swallowed the cold lump of pride lodged in her throat and, raising her chin, met his clear gray gaze. "Please, Mr. Tremayne, I don't want any more trouble. Just go away. Forget we've met."

"You ask the impossible." His long fingers reached out to gently cup her chin. "Trust me, Eden. I won't let any harm come to you."

She would almost believe he spoke the truth. Almost. His mellow voice flowed over her like a balm, soothing her fears, assuaging the hurt. When his thumb began to stroke her cheek, it was like a caress. She felt a strong urge to turn her face and press a kiss into the palm of his hand.

Abruptly his hand stilled its gentle movement. "Come closer to the light." The tone of his voice had changed. This wasn't a request but a command.

Eden allowed Justin to propel her to the window. He jerked on the cord, opening the wooden slats and allowing watery light to spill into the room. Keeping a firm grip on her upper arm, he reached into the pocket of his waistcoat and brought out a linen square. "You have soot on your cheek." He dabbed at the spot with a corner of his handkerchief.

Eden winced and pulled back.

"So! A bruise! I suspected as much." Anger roughened his touch. Again he gripped her chin and turned her face first one way and then the other. In the paltry light, he could make out a dusky imprint marring the ivory perfection of one cheek. "Who struck you?" Rage deepened the color of Justin's eyes to dull pewter. A muscle ticked along his jaw. "Tell me, Eden. Who did this?"

Her gallant knight was transformed into a fierce warrior. Eden found it difficult to reconcile the change. His hands dropped to her shoulders, their grip viselike and painful. "Tell me!" he demanded. "Was it Charles? God help him, he'll pay dearly."

"N-no," Eden stammered. "Charles had nothing to do with it."

"I want the truth, Eden, and I want it now." Justin shook her. "Who hit you?"

Eden was frightened, not so much for her own safety but for the target of Justin's fury. "Mr. Tremayne, please, let it be. Mistress Wainwright only meant to protect her children."

"Millicent did this?" Justin's already firm grip tightened even more. "I can't believe the woman would be so vicious. The bitch!"

Eden moistened her dry lips with the tip of her tongue. "Most mothers, I suppose, would react similarly if they feared their children's future was in jeopardy."

"How in God's name do you pose a threat to Charles and Caroline?" Justin's hands left her shoulders and angrily sliced the air. "They live in the lap of luxury, while you're clothed in rags and reduced to drudgery."

"Mistress Wainwright thinks Charles's flirtation with me may threaten his engagement. She was also afraid I might spoil Caroline's chances of having you as her suitor."

He ran a hand through his hair. "Eden, I swear I don't understand you. How can you try to justify what she did? Her conduct was inexcusable. You're either a fool or a saint."

His bafflement was so genuine, it brought a ghost of a smile to her lips. "I'm neither, Justin," Eden answered, unaware she had called him by his Christian name. "I'm simply trying to survive."

"There is nothing simple about you, Eden St. James." His voice took on the slow, smoky sound she found so compelling. "You are the most complicated creature it's ever been my fortune to meet."

He rested his hands on her shoulders. This time his touch was no longer angry, but gentle. Responding to Justin's velvety tone and eyes of liquid silver, Eden stood pliant. Every sense, every nerve vibrated with awareness of this man. Part of her brain warned her that danger was imminent, to flee while she could. Yet she was incapable of pulling her gaze from his. Emotion flickered in those clear gray depths, causing anticipation to trickle through her veins, spreading a pleasurable warmth. With a flash of certainty, she knew he was going to kiss her.

"Eden!" Bess burst into the room. "There you are! I've been sent to . . ." The girl skidded to a halt. It was apparent from her expression that she had realized for the first time Eden wasn't alone.

"M-Mister Tremayne," Bess gaped, one hand poised over her heart as though to still its fluttering.

Justin gave Eden a rueful smile and released her. He crossed the room in long strides and gazed down at the red-faced, obviously flustered servant. "I was just having a word with Miss St. James." He picked up Bess's clammy hand. "As a special favor to me, don't mention you found us together."

The girl gulped noisily and nodded. "On my mother's grave, sir, I won't tell a soul."

"You have a kind heart, Bess."

When Justin brushed a kiss against the back of her hand, Bess looked as though she might dissolve in a puddle at his feet. He was gone before she could collect her wits. Dazed, she closed the door and leaned against the panel. "Oh, Eden," she sighed. "I'd give anythin' to change places with you. You're so lucky!"

"You don't know what you're talking about." Eden crossed to the fireplace, feeling strangely disappointed. If only Bess could have delayed her untimely appearance for just a few moments longer. Now she would never know whether or not Justin's kiss fulfilled its promise.

"If Mr. Tremayne looked at me, even once, the way he looks at you . . ." Bess sighed as she stooped to help gather the scrub brush and mop. "He loves you, you know."

Eden froze, broom in one hand, bucket in the other, and stared at the girl. "Have you gone daft?"

Bess wasn't deterred. "You're the one who's addled if

you haven't noticed. He cares for you a great deal. When he gave you the box of candy yesterday he reminded me of a prince in one of those fairy tales my ma used to read.'' A dreamy smile transformed her plainness until she looked almost pretty. ''Wish I coulda heard what he whispered to you when he handed over them chocolates.''

Eden hurried from the room without comment, a telltale flush tinting her fair skin.

That afternoon the young negress, Reba, injured herself with scalding water, and Eden was singled out to escort her home. Reba would be fine, Hennie, the girl's grandmother, assured her. A thick paste made from slippery elm applied over the burned arm relieved the pain, and the patient was resting comfortably by the time Eden left the slave quarters and started back to the great house. Cook considered Eden a jinx in the kitchen and had told her not to hurry back. In fact, the woman had seemed happy to have her out from underfoot.

The sky was overcast, the clouds heavy with the threat of rain, but the temperature mild. Eden picked her way slowly along the wooded path. In spite of the weather, she enjoyed the chance to stroll through the woods. Brave green sprouts poked their way through the underbrush, and the swollen buds on the branches appeared ready to burst. The landscape reminded Eden of England. A swift pang of homesickness wrenched her heart. She missed Sommerset, her stepfather's country estate. While her stepfather and Rodney had spent most of their time abroad or in their London town house, Eden had led a cloistered existence in the English countryside. She hadn't minded. It wasn't until a little more than a year ago that she had been summoned to London to make her debut. Only a year ago? Who could have foreseen the chain of events that had brought her to this strange land?

She reached a hilly elevation where the woods thinned to reveal a panorama of cleared fields and a broad river. Telling herself she wouldn't be missed, she spread her skirts on a flat rock jutting from the base of a tree and sat down to enjoy the view. Virginia wasn't unlike the countryside of her girlhood, she decided. Given other circumstances, she might even grow to like the Colonies. The area's temperate climate had much to recommend it.

A rumble in the distance drew her up straighter. She glanced skyward, half expecting a deluge of rain or a streak of lightning. The rumbling grew more insistent, followed by excited shouts and barking hounds. From her vantage point, Eden saw a red blur streak across the field and disappear into the brush. Men and women on horseback followed in close pursuit. A fox hunt was in progress. Eden had participated in several, and she, too, had been caught up in the excitement of the chase. Today, however, she found herself sympathizing with the fox. One little animal against so many. The odds didn't seem fair.

Hoofbeats thundered along the path behind her. She stood up quickly, pressing her back against the bark of the tree in the hope her presence would go unnoticed. A horse and rider passed within yards of her hiding place. She let out a sigh of relief, only to realize with sinking dismay that the rider had slowed his mount, wheeled it about, and was approaching the spot where she stood. Not wanting to appear a coward, she stepped out from her poorly concealed refuge.

"Are you a witch or a wood sprite?" Justin's laughter laced the question.

"Neither, sir," Eden replied, tilting her head to study his expression. "Am I correct in assuming you speak in jest, Mr. Tremayne? That once again you are indulging your fondness to tease? Or do you require proof that I am truly flesh and blood?"

"My dear lady, of that I have little doubt."

Eden immediately wished she could call back her impulsive words. Would Justin think her bold and brazen? Now that there was no Mistress Wainwright lurking about, did he think she would invite his advances? She gestured in the direction the other riders had taken. "The fox is leading the pack. If you tarry, you'll miss the kill."

"Perhaps I prefer a chase of a different kind. I find you much more elusive."

There it was again, the directness she found so disconcerting. She should scurry back to Cook, yet for some unknown reason she didn't want to leave this man's company. Besides, astride his magnificent beast, he blocked her path. Thunderbolt snorted and moved restively, looking like a mighty destrier from an illustration in her stepfather's library, power and beauty personified in the animal's sleek, muscled form.

Eden reached out to stroke the horse's muzzle. "You are a beauty," she murmured.

"I couldn't agree more," Justin concurred, his gaze trained on Eden's slender form. Dismounting, he patted Thunderbolt's neck. Eyes twinkling with humor, he peered around a tree trunk.

"What's the matter?" Eden whispered. "Is something wrong?"

"Shh," he cautioned. "I'm checking to make sure Millicent isn't spying behind a tree, ready to send you fleeing like a scared rabbit."

Eden's bewilderment faded, and as the absurdity of the notion struck her, she laughed, the sound low and musical.

Justin felt inordinately pleased that his actions had had the desired effect. "You don't do that often, do you?"

"Do what?"

"Laugh."

"No, I suppose not." Eden smoothed the horse's mane and wished she had a lump of sugar in her apron pocket.

"And why is that?"

She shrugged. "There's been little reason."

"If I had my way, I'd make sure you laughed at least once a day."

"Sounds like doctor's orders." She hazarded a small smile, then cocked her head to one side. "What about you, Mr. Tremayne? Do you follow your own advice and laugh once a day?''

"Indeed, my lady." Though his expression was grave, his eyes danced with deviltry. "Some days even twice."

He was doing it again, teasing her. Or was he serious? At Sommerset any laughter had often been at another's expense. Imagine, she mused silently, a place where it was heard daily!

Justin crooked a finger and tilted her chin up so that their eyes could meet. "A shilling for your thoughts."

Eden wasn't ready to reveal them. Regardless of his charm, this man was still a virtual stranger. Her lashes lowered, and she took a half step back from his touch. "My thoughts are all I can truly claim as my own, Mr. Tremayne."

His expression darkened. Damn! It seemed he couldn't be near the girl more than five minutes without reminding her of her station. "I'm sorry if I've offended you, Eden. I ask no more than you're willing to give."

"I'm often overly conscious of my . . . altered circumstances. Perhaps I'm the one who should apologize."

"Let's forget it. For now, all I want is to spend part of a spring afternoon with a beautiful woman. I know you have a generous heart. Can you spare a boorish colonial a few precious minutes?"

"I mustn't tarry overly long or Cook will be angry," Eden explained hesitantly. Then she confessed, "I never thought you boorish, Mr. Tremayne."

"Not even at our first meeting?" he asked with a wry smile. "Never have I felt as out of place as I did that evening."

"Though you may have felt a foreigner, you had the manners of a gentleman. It was the others who were rude."

"Allow me to walk you at least partway home." At Eden's look of consternation, Justin added, "You needn't fear. No will will see us."

"All right," she consented. Side by side, they walked

along the narrow path. Justin loosely held the horse's reins, the stallion picking his way behind them.

Justin cleared his throat. "About Charles's betrothal," he said, broaching the subject cautiously. "Are you still disappointed?"

"No." Eden shoved her hands into her apron pockets and answered honestly. "I was a fool to believe Charles would see me as a suitable mate. Though I would have made him a good wife," she added defensively, "regardless of what anyone may think."

"Then you don't love him?" Justin tried to keep his tone casual. It was vital he pose this question and once more hear Eden's denial.

"Love?" Eden scoffed with a shake of her head. "First Caroline and now you. I daresay you colonials are full of romantic notions."

"And I gather you English are not?"

"We're far more practical when it comes to marriage."

Justin studied her. "I'm well aware it's the custom among the upper classes to marry for wealth and social position."

A bloated face with bleary eyes and sour breath flooded Eden's memory, then quickly receded, leaving behind a residue of revulsion. "I could never wed for money and position alone."

Justin ducked a low-hanging branch. "Go on."

"I view marriage as a business partnership, an arrangement between two people willing to work toward a common goal."

"Interesting." Justin glanced down at her, but the ruffle of the starched muslin cap that confined her glorious black hair also concealed her expression. "However, just for the sake of argument, keep in mind that women are the weaker gender, often in need of a man's protection. What can they contribute to this partnership you describe?"

"Like other men, you underestimate a woman's role," she replied spiritedly. "It's a woman's place to make the home a haven, to create an atmosphere of comfort and beauty. In addition, a wife supervises all entertainment, and"—delicate color suffused her face—"provides her husband with heirs."

"You speak in generalities, Eden. What is it you expect from a husband? A man who will shower you with jewels and dress you in satin? Must he be handsome, witty, and charming?"

"Those traits are unimportant." Eden paused to watch a chattering squirrel poised on a swaying branch high above their heads. "There has to be more," she said as she resumed walking. "There has to be a certain feeling of compatibility, some foundation upon which affection can develop, and, of course, mutual respect."

"That's what you want from marriage? Affection? Respect?"

"And kindness."

"Kindness?" She uttered the word so softly that Justin wondered at first if he had misunderstood. "Kindness," he repeated under his breath. The wistfulness in her tone tugged at his heart. Had she known so little kindness as to make her value it so highly?

Noting Justin's surprise, Eden regretted the admission, the first time she had voiced her unspoken thoughts. It was folly to think he might understand. The row of dependencies became visible through the thinning woods. Eden paused at the fringe. "It's best I go the rest of the way alone so as not to run the risk of being seen. Goodbye, Mr. Tremayne." She gave him a brief smile. "If I don't see you before you depart, Godspeed."

Eden's heart felt encased in lead as she walked toward the cook house. Already she felt the pain of Justin's departure. How easy it had become to think of him as "Justin." Though she had known him only a brief time, he had made a lasting impression on her. He had dried her tears, coaxed a laugh, and for a suspended moment in time, made her feel like a woman.

Enough! she admonished herself. You're growing fanciful. Remember, Justin Tremayne is one of the landed gentry. Like Charles, there can be no future with him.

Justin watched until Eden disappeared from view. His foot in the stirrup, he was about to spring into the saddle when he chanced to look down. His booted foot had nearly crushed a delicate plant with heart-shaped leaves. A violet. As yet there was no evidence of the fragile blue-purple flowers, but given sunlight and warm days, the plant would soon bloom. Could it be the same with Eden? he wondered. With patience and kindness, would she blossom into an affectionate, caring woman? He felt certain of it.

Humming under his breath, he mounted the stallion and rejoined the others.

"Psst, Eden." Bess beckoned. "I have somethin' for you."

Eden wiped her wet hands on her apron. Giving the mountain of unwashed pots and kettles a parting glance, she went to the narrow doorway separating the main room of the kitchen from the smaller one used as a combination storage and scullery area. "What is it, Bess?"

"Shh." Digging into a pocket, Bess produced a folded sheet of vellum. "He said to give this to you." She cast a nervous look over her shoulder. "But not to let the others see."

"Who did?" Eden asked, taking the note.

"Shh!" Bess shook her head in warning. "He did! Mr. Tremayne. You know how to read, don't you?" she added worriedly.

Eden nodded, her hand shaking as she unfolded the paper. She had said farewell to Justin that afternoon. What could he want now? Quickly she scanned the bold script. The missive was brief. He asked to meet her later that evening at the rose arbor but offered no explanations.

"He wants to see you again, doesn't he?" Bess whispered, her green eyes bright with excitement.

Eden gnawed her lower lip in indecision. "I'm not sure . . ."

"Go, Eden, go." Bess pressed a thin hand on Eden's arm. "What harm can it do? Don't worry about Polly. She won't find out. I'll tell her Cook gave you extra chores, and you won't be done for hours."

"You won't be telling a lie." Eden stuffed the note into her pocket. "With Reba hurt, Cook has me doing her chores besides the extra ones Mistress Wainwright assigned. By the time I finish, Mr. Tremayne will have long since given up waiting for me."

"Bess! Get yer scrawny arse over here! Supper's awaitin'." Cook shouted, waving a dripping spoon for emphasis. "If Miss High and Mighty has time on her hands, I'll have ta find more fer her to do."

"Comin'." Giving Eden a commiserating look, Bess rushed off to help Polly carry trays of roast meats.

It was near midnight when Eden looked about a final time to make sure she hadn't forgotten anything. Every pot was scrubbed and shiny. Each gleaming utensil hung from its customary hook. The giant hearth was swept clean of cinders, and logs laid on the grate. The kitchen was ready for another day. At last she was finished. Her bones aching with weariness, Eden blew out the sputtering tallow candle.

"Well, well, Polly was right. She said I'd find you here."

Eden spun toward the voice. "Charles!" He lounged just inside the doorway, his shoulder braced against the frame, a tankard of ale in one hand. "What are you doing here?"

"I craved a sweet." His words slurred together. "And, to my good fortune, I find the sweetest morsel of all." His movements slow and clumsy, he entered the darkened kitchen.

"I'm not available." Eden nervously fingered the gold locket. "What would your fiancée think if she got word of this?"

He tipped his head and took a large gulp of ale. "My dear fiancée has a distinct talent for stoking embers into a raging inferno." Eden sensed rather than saw the humorless smile that stretched his mouth. "However, she refuses to quench the fire."

Eden's fingers tightened around the disk at her throat. "And while you'll accept her refusal, you won't accept mine."

The truth of her statement went undisputed. His laugh sent a chill down her spine. "She's a lady. You're a bond servant." He advanced further into the room. "You should be honored I'm so persistent. I've managed to restrain myself—until now. But I need a woman tonight, and you'll suit."

Eden retreated a step. "Your mother," she said. "She'll be furious when she finds out. Polly will tell her."

"Mother may not approve, but like it or not, there's little she can do. Men have always had mistresses—and always will. Some wives, I'm told, are content with such an arrangement."

The hard edge of the table pressed into the small of Eden's back, preventing her further retreat. Eden fought a rush of panic. Memory of the fox hunt flashed before her. She could imagine the hounds closing in for the kill. Only in this instance it was she, not the fox, who would be the victim.

Charles drained the tankard, then wiped his mouth with the back of his hand. "Never fear, I'll make it worth your while." He jingled the coins in his pocket.

Her stomach lurched. "I'm not for sale," she spat.

"Now, now, Eden, don't be hasty," he said with a lopsided grin. "A clever woman knows how to improve her lot in life." He weaved across the space separating them. "Enough talk." The tankard sailed from his hand, crashed against the wall, and clattered to the floor.

Eden groped behind her, searching for something with which to defend herself. Her fingers curled around the pewter candlestick at the precise instant that Charles lunged. He caught her shoulder, and the sleeve of her homespun gown ripped from the bodice. Eden raised the candlestick and struck out blindly. Charles ducked, then cursed as a glancing blow struck his temple. Her memory flashed to another scene: *A river of blood pouring down a man's face. Warm. Red. Sticky. Streaming from a gaping wound.* The candlestick dropped from Eden's nerveless fingers.

Charles viciously kicked the object aside. "Like to play rough, do you?" he snarled. "Good! You've got spunk." Snatching off her cap, he grabbed a fistful of hair to still the movement of her head, in a grip so fierce that it brought tears to her eyes. He took advantage of her gasp of pain to grind his lips against hers, ravishing her mouth with his tongue. The ale he had consumed affected his balance. He bent over her, causing Eden's back to arch. She clung to his shoulders to keep from falling.

"Excuse me," Justin's smooth voice intruded. "Sorry I interrupted."

Wrenching her mouth free, Eden flattened both hands against Charles's chest and shoved. "Justin . . ." she gasped. "Help."

Justin whirled Charles around and grabbed the lapels of his coat. "Touch her again and you're a dead man." Steel laced his words.

"I'll touch her whenever I damn well please," Charles answered belligerently.

Horrified, Eden watched as Justin's arm crashed against Charles's jaw with a sickening thud. Charles flew backward. His leg hooked a chair and sent it scraping across the floorboards. He was brought up short against the fireplace and slumped slowly to the floor.

Eden leaned against the table, holding on to the scarred wood, her legs as wobbly as a newborn colt's. Charles lay at her feet. Justin, his hands bunched into fists, towered over the prone form. "Keep your hands to yourself," he warned with a cold finality.

Charles staggered to his feet. Dabbing at his bleeding

mouth with a handkerchief, he glared at Justin, then lurched out of the kitchen.

"Are you all right?" In the diminished light, Eden's eyes appeared like dark, fathomless pools in a face as pale as alabaster. Justin wanted to cradle her in his arms and comfort her as one would a small child, to hold her tightly, absorb her pain, and share his warmth. But he did nothing. He was afraid to. She seemed so fragile that he feared she would shatter into a million shards.

"I'm quite all right, thank you." Her voice sounded faint and faraway.

"Yes, I can see that," Justin said with a trace of asperity. Damn her pride! She was shaking like an aspen in a gale.

Drawing on her reserves of strength, Eden released her grip on the table and pulled herself upright. "Your intervention was timely. I'm indebted to you. How did you find me?"

"Bess told me she had delivered my message. When you didn't come to me, I decided to go to you instead. I'm glad I did."

"I'm very grateful." An aftershock rippled through her as she thought of her narrow escape.

Justin swore softly. Reservations be damned! He loved her. He couldn't stand idly by and watch her suffer. Guided by instinct, he enfolded Eden in a tender embrace. She resisted initially, but when he spoke in calm, soothing tones, she quieted. He made no demands, simply held her.

For the second time in their brief acquaintance, Eden experienced the unique refuge of his arms. She rested her cheek against his broad chest, held fast to the lapels of his jacket, and was lulled by the steady beat of his heart. Is this what it's like to feel safe and cherished? she wondered. If so, she would be content to remain here for a lifetime.

"Feel better?"

"Mmm," she murmured against his chest.

"I need to talk with you." He drew back slightly so he

could peer into her face. He was reassured to find the unhealthy pallor had vanished. "Fresh air will do you good. Walk with me."

Eden murmured her consent. Away from his warmth, cool air whispered through her torn gown, causing her to shiver. Seeing her discomfort, Justin shrugged out of his coat and slipped it over her shoulders. Swift and painful, an awareness of her reduced station coursed through her. Shame bit into her, its fangs sharp, the venom lethal. Her clothing in tatters and without means to cover herself, Eden's spirit cringed in mortification. She slanted a quick glance at Justin and saw pity on his handsome face. Pity was the last thing she wanted . . . especially from him. Pride stiffened her spine. With quiet dignity, she swept past him, leaving him to follow.

Neither spoke as they walked down the garden path leading to the arbor.

"I'm leaving tomorrow," he said, catching her arm and looking into her eyes. Suddenly all his clever phrases deserted him. There wasn't time for pretty speeches and gentle wooing. "I want to take you with me."

The breath squeezed from her lungs. Her heart slowed, then began to race. Eden stared at him wide-eyed, scarcely believing what she had heard.

Chapter 6

Eden bristled. Charles had wanted her to be his mistress. Apparently Justin Tremayne did, too. Disillusionment swelled inside her. She had envisioned Justin as a gallant knight. In reality, his motives weren't any nobler than Charles's. "No," she replied sharply.

"No?" Surprised, Justin released her arm. It hadn't occurred to him that she might refuse. "Surely, madam, you don't mean that?"

"You heard me."

Justin stared down at her, but she refused to return his look. Etched in moonlight, her profile was as pure and delicate as a cameo, and just as emotionless. He felt her slipping away. He was losing her. "Why?" He pulled her around so that they stood facing each other. "Tell me why."

"If it's a servant you want, certainly you can find one more skilled than me."

"And if it's more than a servant I desire?"

Any remnant of doubt about his offer fled. Anger lit a violet flame in her eyes. "If it's a whore you seek, Mr. Tremayne, I advise you to look elsewhere. It shouldn't be difficult to find someone more knowledgeable than I in the ways of pleasing a man."

Shocked disbelief spread across his features. He cupped her face in his hands. "It's neither servant nor whore I seek—but a wife." He watched the fury flicker and die, her eyes fill with unspoken questions. "I'm asking you to

79

marry me, Eden St. James. In good times and poor, I want you at my side all the days of my life.''

His words were honeyed, ripe, and sweet with promise . . . and they filled her with nameless terror. ''Why?'' she whispered, stepping away from his touch. ''You hardly know me.''

''A man can't live without his heart,'' he said simply. ''I lost mine the first time I saw you.''

She shivered in spite of the warm coat. Was Bess right? Did Justin love her? ''I don't know what to say.'' She felt confused. Everything was happening so fast. ''I need time to think.''

''Time is something I don't have, Eden. I've been away from my home long enough. I must return tomorrow—with or without you.'' Making no further move to touch her, he stood tall and straight, regarding her soberly.

''I need to think,'' she repeated. She turned and walked briskly away. His proposal had caught her by surprise. She supposed she should leap at the chance to marry a man like Justin Tremayne, but all she felt was steadily mounting panic. Being indentured had taught her an invaluable lesson. Never again would she take freedom for granted. It was bad enough to lose five years in the service of others, but marriage might mean a lifetime of servitude. Dear God! How she hated having so little control over her life.

''I realize my proposal is sudden.'' Justin matched his pace to hers. ''I wish I had time to properly court you and win your love, but''—he shrugged—''I must get back. Certain matters require my attention.''

Upon reaching the arbor, Eden sank down on the bench with a sigh. ''I can appreciate your situation. But this is all so . . . unexpected.''

''Is that why you hesitate? Or do you love another?''

''No,'' she said quietly. ''There is no one else.'' She looked at him for a long moment. ''I can't marry you.''

''Can't—or won't?''

''I can't. Please, try to understand.'' She spread her hands in supplication.

His head bent in thought, Justin paced back and forth in front of her. Didn't she realize that the choice wasn't hers? That once he purchased her articles of indenture—and for her own safety that was what he intended to do—she would be legally bound to him? He was doing the honorable thing. Didn't she realize the scandal that would result from an unmarried woman being indentured to a bachelor? He was offering matrimony to protect her reputation.

He cursed under his breath. Who was he trying to fool? What part did honor play in all this? He was offering marriage because he loved her. He had lost her once; he wasn't about to lose her again.

"I know life is far from ideal with the Wainwrights," she began, "but . . ."

"Far from ideal?" Justin snorted in disgust. "You have a unique way of phrasing your predicament." He stopped pacing to glare at her. "Millicent Wainwright is a cruel, domineering woman bent on turning you into a drudge. Caroline is jealous and spiteful. Charles is determined to have you—with or without your consent. Far from ideal?" he exclaimed. "You may not think me a gentleman for being blunt, but, woman, you must be daft."

"How dare you!" Eden sprang to her feet and glared back.

"Then kindly explain your reasoning, or rather, the lack of it. If you can," he challenged.

Eden took a deep breath. "I happen to have two very good reasons for rejecting your proposal. In another four years, five months, and ten days, my term of indenture will be over. I'll be free to live life as I choose. Should we marry, it would be a lifetime commitment."

Did she find the idea of marriage to him so repulsive? he wondered. "And your second objection?" he asked after a long pause.

Eden had hoped he wouldn't ask. She didn't want to hurt his feelings, but he had been honest with her. She could be no less with him. "You love me, but I don't love you. I'm sorry.'' She stared down at her laced fingers. ''You're a fine man, Justin Tremayne. You deserve better.''

At his silence, she stole a quick upward glance. She had hurt him. His pain was clear on his face, glowing in his eyes.

''I see,'' he said quietly, and immediately his pain became hers. Already she regretted her decision. He was by far the most decent man she had ever met, yet she was sending him away. But because she admired him so, she wanted his happiness. Maybe his assessment was right. Perhaps that made her daft. ''Good-bye, Justin.'' She forced the words past a stricture in her throat.

''Wait!'' He caught her as she started to flee. ''What if I convince you that your objections aren't valid? Will you marry me then?''

The intensity of his gaze held her captive. Speech impossible, she nodded.

Hands locked behind his back, his tone matter-of-fact, he stared down at her. ''As for the first objection, you have my word that at the end of four years, five months, and ten days, if you still want your freedom, I will give it to you. I will pay for your return to England and see that you have the means to live comfortably. Do you find that agreeable?''

''Quite, but—''

''As to the second,'' he continued as though she had never spoken, ''while I appreciate your candor, I realize it was premature to reveal my feelings. Someday I hope you will reciprocate my love, but it's much too soon. I can be patient, Eden. I want no other for my wife.'' He saw her resolve weaken and pressed his advantage. ''This afternoon you spoke of marriage as a business arrangement. Why can't it be that way with us? I'll be all the things you want in a husband. You will have the protection of my name.'' His voice took on the low timbre she found so compelling. ''I promise you a wealth of love, laughter—and kindness.''

Eden didn't think the lump in her throat could get bigger, but it did. He had stated his case so eloquently. His plea was so earnest, so sincere, she thought she would strangle on emotion. He was once again her knight in shining armor. Still, some tiny part of her insisted she give a full accounting of her shortcomings.

"I know little in the way of managing a household in the Colonies." She paced as she talked. "Cook says whenever I'm near, cakes fall and bread burns. I was never taught to spin. We purchased candles and soap instead of making them. Life is much different here than in England." She whirled to confront him. "How can you be certain I would be a suitable wife?"

A smile tugged the corners of his mouth. "Trust me, Eden."

Oh, how she wanted to. But experience had taught her to trust no man. *Don't be afraid,* an inner voice prompted. *Take a chance. Trust.* Caution aside, Eden succumbed to the temptation. Drawing a shaky breath, she held out her hand to seal their bargain. "If your offer still holds, I accept."

Justin took her hand in his larger one. Absently his thumb stroked the back from knuckle to wrist, finding the skin rough and chapped. His brows drew together. Holding her hand securely, he trailed a fingertip along the short, ragged edges of her nails. Turning her palm over, he raised it for his inspection, seeing the ridge of calluses. This was no longer the soft, dainty hand he had held ever so briefly in a London drawing room.

It took every ounce of Eden's willpower to endure Justin's scrutiny. She could read his thoughts as clearly as printed words on a page. Her work-worn hands loudly proclaimed her station. *Servant!* Her cheeks crimson, Eden fought the urge to snatch her hand free and hide it behind her back.

Just when she thought she could bear it no longer, he pressed his lips against her callused palm. For a split second, she felt the soothing rasp of his tongue against her flesh.

"Allow me to escort you back to the house. Try to get a good night's rest before the morrow." Justin spoke as though nothing out of the ordinary had transpired. Taking her elbow, he guided her along the brick path.

"There is one request I'd like to make," Eden said as they reached the back entrance. "Please promise me you'll tell no one of my background."

"But why don't you want anyone to know? It would ease your acceptance into the gentry."

And it would also make it simpler for Rodney to trace her whereabouts, Eden thought, feeling a flutter of nervousness at the thought. "Such a revelation would only prove embarrassing. It would raise questions I'd prefer to leave unanswered." She saw his lingering doubt. "Please, Justin. I left the past behind when I sailed for the Colonies. What's important is that we have our whole lives ahead of us."

Justin studied her thoughtfully. She was right. Why quibble about the past when the future stretched ahead so brightly? "Whatever you wish, my sweet." He placed a light kiss on her lips. "Sleep well. I'll speak with Jasper first thing in the morning."

Eden stepped inside and trudged up the stairs to the attic room, pausing on the landing. Bemusedly, she became aware that her right hand was curled into a loose fist. She had imprisoned Justin's fleeting kiss as securely as an elusive butterfly. Pressing it to her breast, she held her hand against the heavy beating of her heart.

Trust me, he had said. But could she?

Voices rose behind the closed door of Jasper Wainwright's study. Eden glanced around nervously. She knew it wasn't wise to be inside the great house. There would be hell to pay if she were caught. Still, she lingered in the deserted hallway just outside the study. Her fate, her very life, was being sealed at this moment.

The morning had brought a bedlam of activity, with most of the guests trying to get an early start home. Noontime was now fast approaching, yet so far she had not seen Justin. Word had just arrived in the kitchen that dinner would be delayed. Cook fretted that the meal would be ruined.

The study door burst open, then banged shut. Caroline stormed out, her face blotchy and her round cheeks glistening with tears. Upon seeing Eden in the hallway, she brought herself up short.

"I hate you," she exclaimed, and fled up the stairs.

Her hand on the banister, Eden stood at the bottom of the staircase. The younger girl was heartbroken, and it was all her fault. Should she go after her and apologize, or would that only make matters worse? Eden gnawed her lower lip in indecision. Caroline loved Justin and she didn't. Caroline should be the one Justin wanted for a wife, not her. It wasn't fair, but then life was rarely fair. Sighing, she returned to her vigil outside the closed door.

She jumped when the door crashed open a second time. If looks could kill, Eden would have died on the spot.

"You sly, conniving slut." Millicent Wainwright marched over to her. "We gave you food, clothing, shelter, and you repay us by stealing Justin away from Caroline the minute my back's turned."

"Mistress Wainwright, I'm truly sorry—"

"Save your lies," Millicent snapped. "Men are such fools when it comes to a pretty face." She shook her head. "Mark my words, you'll always be a misfit here in the Tidewater. Your sort can never mingle with the gently bred. After Justin's infatuation wears off, you'll be a constant embarrassment."

"You're wrong, Madam." Eden refused to cower under the woman's attack. Squaring her shoulders, she met the venomous look calmly. "Justin will have no cause to regret his decision."

"Time will be the judge of that. We're a close-knit group in the Tidewater. Our paths will cross again. A Tidewater wife is many things to her husband. I'll be eager to see how well you measure up.''

''And hoping I don't?''

''In spite of your fancy airs, you're ignorant,'' Millicent said with a sneer. ''Why, you can't function unless someone is standing over your shoulder telling you what to do. Gather your things and get out of my house!''

''Your hospitality is sorely lacking, Millicent.'' Justin stood framed in the study doorway.

''Justin! You startled me!'' The woman clapped a plump hand to her heaving bosom. ''I prayed Jasper could talk sense into you. To set this girl up as your mistress is one thing, but why marry the chit?''

''As my wife, Eden will be your equal, Millicent. I trust you to remember that. I would hate to see a feud divide our families.''

''That won't happen, will it, my dear?'' Jasper asked, coming to stand beside Justin and appearing dwarfed by the younger man.

Despite his diminutive size, Jasper's quelling stare silenced Millicent's tongue, at least for a second. ''No, of course not.'' She couldn't let the matter rest. ''I only hope, Justin, that you will not come to rue this day.''

''I sincerely doubt it, Millicent. But if so, you'll have the pleasure of reminding me of my folly, won't you?''

''Humph!'' Millicent turned on her heel. ''If you'll excuse me, I must find Caroline, the poor lamb.'' She brushed past Eden and bustled off.

Justin turned his attention to Eden. ''How soon can you be ready to leave?''

''Whenever you say.''

''Good. We depart in ten minutes.''

Jasper slapped Justin on the back. ''I'll have the horses saddled and brought to the front. Come with me and you can select a proper mount for, ah . . . your . . .'' He floundered searching for a way to describe Eden's new role.

"Future wife," Justin supplied easily. He shot Eden a reassuring look, then followed his host.

Five minutes later, Eden clutched her pathetic bundle of possessions and hovered uncertainly outside the front entrance, filled with anxiety. Once, she had been eager to flee England, but her high expectations of a new land had been cruelly dashed. Perhaps her plan to leave the Wainwright's and wed Justin Tremayne would also bring disillusionment. But Justin had asked for her trust. She had to give him a chance.

The large house seemed conspicuously vacant. No servants were about, no family members. It was as though everyone was collectively holding their breath, waiting and watching. Eden turned as light footsteps padded across the porch.

Bess threw a nervous glance over her shoulder before reaching into her apron pocket. "Here, Eden, this is for luck." She pressed a pale blue satin ribbon into Eden's hand. "Every bride should have somethin' blue."

Moisture sprang to Eden's eyes.

"It's not much, but I wanted you to have it."

"Thank you, Bess. I'll keep it to remember you by."

"I'm so excited. Mr. Tremayne will make a fine husband. I told you he was in love with you. Be happy!" She gave Eden a quick hug and darted off.

Eden looked at the ribbon, then after Bess. Without Polly's interference, she and Bess might have become friends. But Polly demanded complete loyalty, and Bess was easily intimidated. It was too late for regrets. In all probability they would never meet again. Eden bent and added the ribbon to her meager belongings.

When she straightened, she saw Justin mounted on Thunderbolt. He was leading two horses, one bearing heavy saddlebags, the other a sidesaddle. He dismounted and came toward her, a frown forming as his gaze swept from her cotton cap to her sturdy, scuffed shoes; his frown deepened when his eyes rested on the threadbare shawl draped around her shoulders.

"Enough of Millicent's rags!" Before she guessed his intent, he tore off the offending garment and tossed it in a heap. Slipping off his cloak of fine gray wool, he spread it over her shoulders, making sure the clasp was secured below her chin. "This should keep you warm."

The warmth she felt had little to do with the richness of the fabric. Heat seemed to radiate outward from deep within. She told herself it had nothing to do with Justin, but even as she did, she knew it had everything to do with him. . . . She stared into eyes of clear gray and swallowed hard. "Thank you." Her voice was a throaty whisper.

"You're quite welcome," he returned, then stepped back. "I assume you know how to ride. If not, Jasper will loan us a carriage. It's a half day's journey to Williamsburg. Horseback will be quicker."

"I can ride."

"Good girl."

Justin led the mare toward the mounting block and assisted Eden. She swung into the saddle with natural grace, carefully arranging the folds of the cloak around her. She sat with her back straight, the reins held with the easy assurance of a born horsewoman. With a nod of approval, Justin placed a booted foot in the stirrups and vaulted into the saddle. His expression darkened as he glanced once more at Eden.

"One more thing." He nudged the stallion closer and reached out to snatch the servant's cap from her head, sending a thick ebony braid tumbling down her back. Hurling the despised cap to the ground, he watched in satisfaction as the white muslin was trampled in the mud under the stallion's hooves.

Giddy exhilaration surged through Eden. The gesture proclaimed her free, no longer any man's slave. Along with this feeling came one of resolution. Justin, she vowed silently, would never have cause to regret granting her her freedom. *Never.*

"Shall we go?"

Eden glanced toward the plantation. Except for Bess,

not a soul had emerged to bid them Godspeed. The windows of the great house gleamed like sightless eyes, but Eden wasn't deceived. She knew that behind each drape and blind, every detail of their departure was being observed with keen interest and would be discussed for days.

It didn't matter to her. Putting the past behind her, she set aside her fears. The future beckoned. She turned to Justin with a brilliant smile. "I'm ready."

Side by side, their horses cantered down the winding drive.

It was late afternoon when they arrived at Williamsburg. Slowing their horses to a walk, they turned down Francis Street, lined by neat rows of ruddy brick and white weatherboard homes. Eden noted the carefully pruned boxwood hedges and glimpsed gardens tucked behind white picket fences. She imagined how it would look in summer with benches hidden in shady nooks, orderly beds of flowers, and fruit trees heavy with plums, peaches, apples, and figs.

Justin watched covertly, pleased by her interest. "What do you think of our capital?"

"It's lovely," she answered honestly. "I like the way fences separate one home from another, yet link them all together. Each is distinctly individual, but part of a greater whole."

"Your description of Williamsburg could apply to the inhabitants of the Colonies as well," Justin replied. "Strong, determined individuals working to mold a new land. Alas, sweet"—he smiled—"the fences aren't just for decoration, but serve a practical function as well. A town ordinance decrees that lots be enclosed to keep stray horses and cattle from wandering into neighboring yards."

They rode the next block in silence.

"Will we be staying at an inn?" Eden asked.

Justin shook his head. "Ladies never stay in taverns. I know a better place."

He reined to halt before a stately two-story home in the

middle of the block, where he dismounted, looped the reins over a hitching post, then lifted Eden down from her mare. She looked askance, but Justin ignored her expression and, holding her elbow, escorted her to the front door and boldly banged a brass knocker. The door was opened by a young negress with a voluminous, starched apron over a dress of bright yellow muslin.

"Who is it, Prudence?" A tall, stately woman with gray hair and eyes the same shade as Justin's came forward.

"It's Mister Justin," Prudence announced.

"Well, Nephew, it's about time," the woman scolded. "Prudence and I have missed you these long winter months." She raised her face for a kiss.

"Sorry, Aunt Nora." Justin brushed his lips across the wrinkled cheek. "I brought someone for you to meet." He moved aside and, putting his hand on the small of Eden's back, gently propelled her forward. "Aunt Nora, I'd like you to meet Miss Eden St. James. Eden, this is my aunt, Mistress Nora Cunningham."

Eden inclined her head. "It's a pleasure to make your acquaintance, Mistress Cunningham."

"And it's a pleasure to meet you." Nora Cunningham studied the girl at her nephew's side with undisguised interest. Wisps of hair had escaped the single plait to frame a delicate face. The violet eyes were strikingly beautiful, but guarded. Nora's gaze settled on the scuffed shoes peeking from beneath a masculine-looking wool cloak. How odd, she mused, sensing something amiss.

Realizing she had kept them on the doorstep, she motioned them inside. "Forgive my lack of manners. You're just in time for tea."

"Here, ma'am," Prudence offered. "Let me take your wrap."

Eden slowly unfastened the cloak, loathe to reveal the faded homespun dress it concealed. The masquerade of gentility had come to an end. Like her work-roughened hands, the gown proclaimed her lowly status. Her face a careful blank, she handed the cloak to the servant and saw amazement spread across the black countenance. "Thank you, Prudence," she said with quiet dignity.

Her head held proudly, she faced Justin's aunt. "Tea would be lovely after our long ride."

With a polite smile, Nora bid Eden and Justin follow her into the drawing room. The walls were Dresden blue with white wainscoting, and a cheery fire blazed in the hearth. A book lay open on a Chippendale tea table next to a wing-backed chair. Nora indicated for her guests to be seated on a damask settee and waited until they were enjoying tea and cakes before seeking to satisfy her curiosity. "Tell me, Nephew, what takes you away from home when planting time draws near?"

"I've been visiting the Wainwrights to help celebrate Charles's coming of age."

Nora fixed her puzzled gaze on Eden. "Were you a guest also, Miss St. James?"

"No." Eden's fingers tightened on the handle of the fragile china cup.

Justin crossed one leg over the other. "Eden has agreed to marry me, Aunt Nora. We'd like your blessing."

Nora carefully lowered her raised teacup. "Isn't this rather sudden, Nephew?"

"As sudden as a bolt of lightning." He chuckled, resting his arm along the back of the settee.

Nora sighed in exasperation, then directed her questions at Eden. "How long have you known each other? Did you meet at the Wainwrights? Forgive my curiosity, but your attire is hardly that of a lady. It's more like that of a . . ."

"Servant?" Eden's brow arched.

"Precisely." The woman's wintery gaze assessed her nephew's choice of brides. Miss Eden St. James posed a mystery. Despite her lowly attire, her voice was soft and cultured, and there was nothing servile in her demeanor; if anything, her manner was proud, almost regal. Nora's lips pursed. The girl was an enigma.

"Eden's background shouldn't concern you, Aunt." Justin's words cracked with authority.

"It's quite all right, Justin." Eden set her cup down. "It's better your aunt hear the truth from us than have gossip distort the facts. I was a servant for the Wainwrights. A bond servant."

Before Nora had time to assimilate Eden's shocking disclosure, Justin added another. "We wish to be married this afternoon."

"This afternoon?" The pitch of Nora Cunningham's voice rose. "Justin, you haven't . . . ?"

"No, I haven't." He leaned forward and spoke earnestly. "I must return home tomorrow. I had hoped you could use your influence to help expedite matters."

"Forgive me, both of you, if I've been presumptuous. Of course, Justin, you know I will do whatever I can." Nora turned to Eden. "My dear, I'm sure you'd like to freshen up. Prudence." She waved at the young slave dallying near the doorway. "Show Miss St. James to the guest room and see that she has everything she needs." She speared Justin a look that fixed him to his seat. "Meanwhile, you and I will have a nice chat."

The moment Eden was out of hearing, Nora came straight to the point. "How well do you know this woman?"

"As well as I need to, Aunt."

"But she's a servant." Nora gestured impatiently with one hand. "What kind of wife will she be for a man in your position? What will people say?"

Justin's first impulse was to tell his aunt everything he knew about Eden, but he remembered his promise of the previous night. "Rest assured, Eden's behavior will never bring disgrace."

Nora fidgeted with the handle of her tea cup. "Justin, I hope you realize I'm not trying to be rude or difficult, but you're like a son to me. I'm concerned for your happiness."

"I know that, Aunt Nora." His stony expression softened. He replaced his cup on the tea table and leaned forward intently. "All we want is your blessing."

The gray eyes so like his own regarded him steadily. "Do you love her?"

"Deeply." Nora heaved a sigh of resignation, thought for a moment, and then plunged into wedding plans with the zeal of a field marshal organizing a major campaign.

Chapter 7

Not only did Eden look like a bride, she was also beginning to feel like one. As a flower responds to sunlight, she basked under the tender ministrations of Nora Cunningham.

"Let's see," Nora murmured, stepping back and studying Eden critically. "Something old . . ." Her finger rested on the gold locket at the hollow of Eden's slender throat. "Something new . . ." She cast an approving glance at Eden's ice-blue brocade gown. How fortunate. The dress, with its square-cut bodice and long, fitted sleeves, suited the girl as though it had been made especially for her. "Something borrowed . . ." She handed Eden an embroidered lace-edged handkerchief.

"Something blue," Eden added, reaching up to touch the ribbon Bess had given her. The strand was artfully entwined with her ebony curls, which were arranged on the crown of her head and embellished with tiny silk flowers.

"And a lucky sixpence for your shoe." Nora completed the verse and handed Eden a shiny coin. She nodded with satisfaction while the girl slid it inside her slipper. "There, dear, I think that takes care of everything."

"You've been very kind, Mistress Cunningham."

"Call me Aunt."

"Aunt?" Never having had a female relative, Eden found the notion held an intriguing appeal.

"Or Aunt Nora, if you prefer." Fussing with the folds

of Eden's skirt, she asked hesitantly, "Dear . . . has any-one ever explained a woman's wifely duties to you?"

Eden's face pinkened. Surely the woman wasn't referring to the intimate aspects of married life? She chose to disbe-lieve that possibility. "My needlework is of the finest quality," Eden enumerated matter-of-factly. "I play the pianoforte with some degree of competence. And I do have experience supervising a household, though I must confess the ways of the Colonies are still foreign to me."

"Those you will learn in time, child. What I meant was"—Nora cleared her throat—"has anyone ever ex-plained what transpires between a man and a woman?"

In truth, Eden knew next to nothing about the marriage act. However, in her innocence, she didn't realize the depths of her ignorance. The sum of her knowledge had been gleaned from a conversation she had overheard be-tween two acquaintances in London. One girl had stated with conviction that all that was required was for the wife to be submissive. Men, she had elaborated, soon spent themselves and fell asleep after doing the necessary work. The act was not painful after the first time and had only to be endured. All one had to do was lie there.

"I know what is expected of a wife," Eden confessed, nervously patting her curls.

"Good!" Aunt Nora said, relieved not to have to dis-cuss such matters further. "You look like an angel." She embraced Eden and brushed a kiss across her cheek. "Jus-tin is a very special man. I trust you will make him happy."

"I'll try my best, Aunt Nora."

Moisture shone in the older woman's eyes when she drew back. "Fortunately, even with short notice, a few of my closest friends will be able to join us. As you've prob-ably already discovered, Virginians are a sociable lot. They would never forgive me if I didn't invite them to my only nephew's wedding." With a swish of silk skirts, she hur-ried off to attend to last minute details.

As the hands on the mantel clock neared the appointed

hour of the wedding ceremony, Eden became increasingly confident, a growing sense of optimism blossoming deep within her. She was doing the right thing in marrying Justin Tremayne. Justin was gifting her with the opportunity to start life anew, and although she had little to give in return, whatever he asked she would grant unstintingly.

A short while later, Eden heard piano keys tinkle with more enthusiasm than expertise. Knowing this was her cue to venture downstairs, she drew in a steadying breath and, turning her back on the past, faced the future.

Flames danced atop a dozen tapers, casting intricate patterns of light and shadow along walls and ceiling, scenting the room with bayberry. Arrangements of dried flowers decorated tables and flanked either end of the fireplace, where the minister stood waiting. The music swelled dramatically. Silk and satin rustled as Nora's friends and neighbors turned for their first glimpse of the bride.

From the first moment Eden set foot on the stair tread, Justin's gaze never wavered. His chest swelled with pride, and his heart overflowed with emotion. Eden was a vision, a dream come true, his passion . . . his bride.

He drank in the sight of her descending the stairs, her movements graceful, her face, though pale, shining with a madonnalike serenity. Behind a screen of feathery black lashes, her eyes were luminous violet pools that mirrored an inner calm. As she took her place beside him, the candlelight gave her an ethereal loveliness. Justin felt as though he had been presented with a priceless treasure. Promising himself he would always be patient and gentle with her, he took her small hand in his.

In a deep sonorous voice, the minister began to read from the Book of Common Prayer. "Wilt thou, Justin Wescott Tremayne, forsaking all others . . ."

Justin repeated his vows.

It was her turn.

"Wilt thou, Eden Elizabeth St. James . . ."

As Eden repeated the vows, a strange contentment settled over her. Filled with a sense of rightness, she accepted the union without reservation. For better for worse, for richer for poorer, in sickness and in health, she pledged to love and cherish a man she scarcely knew.

"Those whom God hath joined together, let no man put asunder." The minister gave Justin an indulgent smile. "You may kiss the bride."

Eden lifted her face for Justin's kiss. His lips were warm and firm, their touch tender—and . . . all too brief. In the pit of her stomach a fluttery sensation stirred.

Nora Cunningham planted a resounding kiss on her nephew's cheek, then another on Eden's. "You make a splendid couple," she gushed. "May your years together be long and fruitful."

In the flurry of introductions and good wishes, not a single name registered with Eden. Somehow she managed to make appropriate responses, acutely aware of Justin's hand resting protectively on the small of her back.

His easy charm smoothed over the rough spots when blatant curiosity about his bride bested courtesy's dictates. "Eden and I were first introduced in London a year ago," he explained repeatedly. "When we chanced to meet again in Virginia, I exerted all my powers of persuasion to convince the lady to wed and return with me to Greenbriar."

"Your home, Justin," began a scholarly looking man in his sixties, "I'm anxious to hear more about it."

Justin clapped the man on his back. "Later, Randolph. Aunt Nora is signalling us that it's time for refreshments." He grinned. "We wouldn't want to incur her wrath."

"Heaven forbid, sir," the man said, chuckling.

Eden was amazed at how much Justin's aunt had accomplished in such a short time. Nora Cunningham graciously presided over a table spread with fine linen, pouring tea from a silver tea service into delicate porcelain cups. Prudence, puffed with self-importance, circulated among the guests with a tray of cakes and cherry tarts.

In her imagination, Eden had always pictured herself wed amidst pomp and splendor befitting her stepfather's position, in a lavish ceremony witnessed by a horde of

strangers in a chill granite cathedral. Instead, this ceremony had been simple, intimate, and infinitely more to
her liking. She made her way across the crowded room to
Nora Cunningham, placed her hand lightly on the older
woman's arm, and bestowed a radiant smile. "Thank
you," she said simply.

Looking into Eden's glowing violet eyes, Nora knew
why her nephew was so enamored. Such breathtaking
beauty would turn the head of a monk. Yet her doubts
nagged. Nora hoped she was wrong, but she had watched
the young couple closely. While Justin was openly affectionate, Eden seemed reserved and remote, her emotions
carefully controlled. Justin was obviously in love with the
girl, but did she reciprocate his feelings? Nora feared not.
With an effort, she thrust her worries aside. "You don't
have to thank me, dear. After all, isn't that what families
are for?"

Eden's smile faded. *Families*. The very word conjured
up a host of bitter memories. Family meant criticism and
fear, manipulation and control, being a pretty object that
was put on display then ignored. She glanced across the
room and caught Justin watching. She knew he loved her,
but was he only in love with her beauty? What did he
know of the person inside? In London, men had lusted
after her, some had even claimed to love her, but none
had ever delved beneath her surface and sought to know
and understand her in a deep and intimate way.

Justin's gray eyes bored into her as though trying to
decipher her most private thoughts. Eden hid them beneath
a smooth, unsmiling mask, as she had disciplined herself
to do since childhood. Disappointment flickered across his
face before he turned back to the discussion in which he
was engaged.

An hour later, the small gathering began to disperse.
With her usual directness, Nora declared that the newlyweds needed privacy. With Justin's hand riding on Eden's
waist, he escorted her up the staircase, down the hallway,

and pushed open the door of the guest room she had occupied earlier.

He surveyed the room with pleasure. "Aunt Nora outdid herself."

"Yes." Eden's voice was a whisper. A crackling fire dispelled the evening chill; the counterpane had been turned down in silent invitation; a small table had been readied for an intimate dinner for two. Clearly, the bedroom had been deliberately transformed into a lover's bower. Her nerves coiled tighter.

Justin gently urged Eden into the room. The latch clicked shut behind them, the sound seeming uncommonly loud. Eden walked to the fireplace and spread her hands toward its warmth. She didn't turn when Justin answered a rap on the door.

"Sorry to burst in," Prudence said with a giggle, "but Mistress Nora said to bring ya'll a bite of supper." The young negress set a tray of thinly sliced beef, cornbread, fruit, and cheese on the table along with a bottle of wine. "Mistress said to be sure to tell you this wine here is a weddin' gift from her neighbor, Mr. Jessup." Black eyes dancing, she looked from Justin to Eden. "Don't guess you need me no more." Overcome by a fit of giggles, she put her hand to her mouth and quickly left them alone.

"Allow me, my lady." Justin pulled out a chair. With a sweep of his arm, he indicated Eden was to be seated.

Eden complied. Remembering how severly her stepfather—or Rodney, for that matter—would have dealt with a disrespectful servant, she was perplexed by Justin's good-natured grin. "Prudence meant no harm. I hope you bear her no ill will."

"Whatever for?" Justin seemed genuinely puzzled as he took the opposite chair.

Eden shrugged. "Some might deem her impertinent."

"I would not want a household in which laughter is considered disrespectful." Justin poured wine into the stemmed glasses. "A toast is in order." He raised his glass and smiled at Eden. "To my wife, whose beautiful eyes are surpassed only by the radiance of her smile."

A band formed around Eden's chest at Justin's extravagant praise. A comely face. A pretty smile. He kept alluding to superficial attributes. Was she destined to be an ornament her entire life? Was she to be a newly obtained and costly acquisition for a prized collection? The stricture around her lungs tightened painfully. She wanted more, so much more. She longed to be loved for herself, for the way she was inside and out. Only then would she be truly satisfied.

Summoning a smile that threatened to falter, she raised her glass. "To my husband."

Justin's eyes deepened to the color of smoke. *Husband.* Hearing the word from her lips pleased him greatly. Yet, had he imagined that for the briefest instant disappointment had flickered in her violet gaze? Nonsense! What woman would fault compliments to her beauty?

"Shall we eat?"

Eden looked on while Justin filled a plate from the generous repast and placed it in front of her. He doubled the portions on a second plate, then waited for her to begin.

Her appetite waned. Resorting to a diversion she had learned in childhood, she began cutting her meat into tiny pieces. "Your aunt is a remarkable woman. I was amazed at how much she accomplished despite such short notice."

"Aunt Nora is a bit of a rogue. She's not above pirating a cake here, a pie there, with a servant or two thrown into the bargain. Tidewater people are generous. They're always willing to help a friend."

"You, too, have been most generous. My gown is beautiful. Thank you."

"It's you who lends beauty to the gown, love. Though, I confess, it's yours more by accident than design. Luckily, a trousseau had been ordered for the youngest daughter of a planter, but she eloped with an army sergeant. Her irate father refused to take delivery of the gown you are wearing, as well as several others." Justin helped himself to another slice of meat. "I regret we can't remain in Williamsburg long enough to acquire a suitable wardrobe for you. However, the mantua-maker has your measurements and should have gowns ready for a fitting on our next visit to Williamsburg. I was told you are skilled with a needle. Aunt Nora has purchased bolts of fabric in the hope you can fashion some clothes for yourself in the meantime."

"Your aunt seems quite fond of you."

"The affection is mutual."

Eden picked at her food. "Tell me about her."

"She's my maternal aunt. She lost two children in infancy, which may explain why she's practically adopted me. Uncle Robert, her husband, taught philosophy at the College of William and Mary until he passed away from lung fever the winter before last. Aunt Nora still has many friends among the faculty and was able to use her influence to have Reverend Hughes officiate at our wedding." Justin finished his meal and leaned back in the chair.

"I like your aunt very much." Eden spread the bite-size pieces about her plate and hoped Justin wouldn't notice she had eaten little. "Do you have other family as well?"

"My sister, Emma, lives in Philadelphia. She and her husband expect their first child in late summer."

"And your parents?"

"Dead." Sorrow was evident in his voice, in his expression. Justin raised his wineglass and drained its contents.

Impulsively, Eden placed her hand over his. She regretted asking a question that had elicited painful memories. It was obvious he still mourned their loss. "Forgive my asking, Justin."

For a long moment, he stared at their joined hands. Candlelight reflected off the wide gold band on her third finger. Raising his eyes to Eden's face, he saw her gentle compassion, and his spirit lightened. "What about you? Do you have relatives?"

He watched all the color leave her face just as surely as

chalk was erased from a slate. "None." She withdrew her hand.

Silence dropped between them, stiff and uncomfortable. A log fell in the grate with a shower of sparks. Eden toyed with her food while Justin poured more wine. Still neither spoke.

Captivated by the play of firelight across the sculpted planes of his face, Eden stole frequent glances at the man she now called her husband. Justin Tremayne could eschew the silk or velvet trappings other men relied upon. He came by his good looks honestly. No stiffly powdered wig held greater appeal than his curling brown locks. His firm, sensual mouth needed no artifice of a gummed patch to attract a woman's attention. How could anyone ever consider him boorish? she wondered in amazement.

In another part of the house, a clock chimed the hour. It was already late. Behind her, the feather bed promised an answer to unspeakable mysteries. The longer they talked, the longer she could postpone the inevitable. "Is your home far?" she asked.

"A day's journey."

"Will we travel by horseback?"

"At this time of year the roads are almost impassable. A boat will be quicker. I'll send someone for the horses later."

Her store of small talk swiftly depleted, Eden drank the remainder of her wine, praying its effects would quickly blunt her senses.

"Don't you think you've shoved those little pieces of meat around on your plate long enough?" Justin asked. "The hour is late, Eden." His look was meaningful. "It's time we retire for the night."

Embarrassment colored her cheekbones. Justin hadn't been deceived by her tactics. Except for the flush in her cheeks, no other sign betrayed her anxiety. Her face void of expression, she rose with a rustle of brocade skirts and crossed to the mirrored dressing table. Reaching up, she began to pull first the silk flowers, then the blue ribbon, from her elaborate coiffure.

Soundlessly, Justin came to stand behind her. Desire spread through him in a heated rush, bringing an ache to his loins. How many times had he dreamed of such a moment, only to despair of ever realizing it? For, in fact, fantasy was a sorry substitute for reality. God, how he wanted her! The need to possess her struck him like a physical blow.

"You're far lovelier than my wildest imaginings," he murmured.

Her arms were raised. The lush fullness of her breasts strained the heavy fabric and threatened to spill over the deep, square-cut neckline. Passion darkened his gaze, and he watched hungrily as Eden took out the bone hairpins. One by one thick curls spiraled down her back in glossy corkscrews.

To look and not touch was sheer torment. Yielding to impulse, Justin picked up a silken strand and slowly ran its length through his fingers before bringing it to his lips. Closing his eyes, he drew a ragged breath and inhaled the faint, sweet essence of wildflowers.

The tenderness of his gesture beguiled her; the action was as intimate as a caress. Eden's eyes flew to Justin's reflection. With the firelight behind him, his face was shadowed, his expression unreadable. She wondered what it would be like to feel his arms around her waist.

She gasped in surprise. As though able to read her thoughts, he pulled her firmly against his chest and held her there, pressing her against his solid length. Bending his head, he nuzzled aside her dark curls and touched his lips to a sensitive spot on her jaw, savoring the taste of her skin.

"Justin . . ."

"Shh, darlin'. Let me love you."

Warm breath tickled her neck. A delectable shiver shimmied down her spine. With tantalizing slowness, his lips skimmed the slender column of her throat, stopping at the juncture of her shoulder.

Her head lolled helplessly against his chest. "Justin . . ."

"Hush, love! Don't talk." His voice was low and husky, flowing over her senses like golden honey. "Don't think." He began to unfasten the hooks of her gown. "Let yourself feel."

Her willpower, indeed her very ability to reason, was sapped. Eden felt the dress slide from her shoulders, then heard it fall in a soft *whoosh* about her feet.

"Corset and stays. Hoops!" Impatiently, he eyed the contrivance formed of slats banded with strips of fabric. "What fiend from the Inquisition decreed these fashionable?"

A nervous bubble of laughter escaped before Eden could prevent it.

The offending hoop was unfastened and tossed aside. With an impatient tug, the strings of her corset were loosened and removed. He stared, devouring her with his gaze. "Your body doesn't need these contraptions. It's perfect."

Naked and vulnerable, Eden squeezed her eyes shut and fought the instinct to shield her body from his searing gaze.

"Open your eyes, Eden," he ordered softly.

"No." She mouthed the denial, shaking her head from side to side.

"Yes, love. Go ahead. Open your eyes," he coaxed.

Responding to his gentle command, her lids slid open, and she looked at herself in the pier glass, scarcely recognizing the girl staring back with heavy-lidded eyes of brilliant amethyst. The pale face was surrounded by raven tresses in glorious disarray, her lips parted as though eager to be kissed. She was the same, yet different. It was the face of a familiar stranger.

Justin turned Eden to face him. "Never be ashamed, sweet. Your body is beautiful. It could rival that of Venus."

She met his look. "I want to please you, Justin, but I don't know how."

"You already please me, Eden. Your very existence brings me joy." His hands resting on either side of her jaw, he tilted her face to his. "But right now it would make me happy if you would kiss me."

Eden balanced on tiptoe, her hands resting lightly on his shoulders, and gravely touched her mouth to his.

The world was his. The most beautiful woman he had ever seen was in his arms, his wife. One hand tangled in her hair, the other traced her spine to mold her slender hips against him. The pressure of his mouth increased. When her lips parted in answer to the unspoken request, his tongue dipped inside to plunder the sweet nectar, teasing, tantalizing, until it kindled the desired response.

The first stirrings of passion awakened within Eden, forbidden fires. Her arms crept around his neck, and she melted against his hard length. The kiss deepened as ardor flamed. She moved sinuously against him, feeling as though the two were about to meld into one. Her full breasts, the nipples taut and sensitive, brushed his chest and encountered the rough wool of his clothing. A soft moan echoed her frustration at finding a barrier. *Feel.* Justin had told her to feel. Eden wanted his flesh against hers. Impatient to learn the texture of his skin, she peeled his coat from his shoulders, pushing it roughly down his arms.

"Ah, Eden." Justin laughed deep in his throat. "What a delight you are, all fire and ice."

Scooping her off her feet, he turned and placed her on the bed. Not taking his eyes from hers, he shrugged out of his coat and began to untie his cravat.

Eden gnawed on her lower lip. The crucial time was at hand. The last thing she wanted was to disappoint Justin. He had been kind, loving, and generous to a fault. She owed him so much. Recalling the advice of her London acquaintances, she tried to imitate what a proper wife should do—lie quietly while the husband performed the so-called marriage act. But it was hard to be passive when everything inside her clamored for motion. Yet she wanted to put Justin's pleasure above her own. Drawing in a slow, calming breath, she forced her body to relax, her mind to empty, her emotions to still.

Justin saw the fire extinguish from Eden's gaze, and his brows drew together. Limbs stiff, her body lay sprawled just where he had placed it, like a lifeless rag doll. Bending down, he moved his lips over her mouth, hoping to fan a spark of feeling. Though swollen from their kisses of minutes ago, her mouth was now cool and unresponsive. "What's wrong?" he asked, peering into her face. "Did I do something to offend you?"

Eden stared at the ceiling. "Of course not. Nothing's wrong."

Her slender figure glowed opalescent in the firelight. Desire heated Justin's blood. His hand roved up and down her body, trailing feather-light caresses. Eden wanted to squirm in pleasure; instead she grabbed the counterpane. Justin stopped to cup the weight of her breast in the palm of his hand, his finger flicking the hard nub of her nipple. Eden bit down on her lip to keep from crying out. His frown deepened.

"Don't be afraid, Eden. You know I'd never harm you."

That wandering hand of his, the source of delight and consternation, strayed downward across Eden's flat abdomen. She choked back a moan. She didn't think she could hold still for another second under his erotic assault.

"Please, Justin. Be done with it."

The unexpected words abruptly doused his desire. He drew back, his expression hard. "It appears I was wrong in my assessment. The lady is, indeed, more ice than fire."

"That's not fair." Eden blinked up at him, hurt and confusion warring for dominance. "I am willing to be a wife to you—in more than name only."

"Why?" he asked, his voice harsh.

Eden nervously ran her tongue over her lips. "Because you're my husband. Because I owe it to you."

"Owe it to me!" His incredulity exploded in the quiet room. "You're willing to let me bed you because of a misguided sense of gratitude? Is that all you feel for me?" Even before he asked, he knew the answer. Eden had been honest with him from the start. She had never professed to have deep feelings for him. Why did he keep hoping for more than she was able to give? Must his pride be assuaged? Or did he love her so much that he was unable to accept reality?

Eden pulled herself up on one elbow. "If it wasn't for you, I'd still have years as a bond servant to the Wainwrights, or worse, as a common tavern wench. By choosing me for your wife, you have restored my honor, my self-respect. Naturally, I'm grateful."

"Naturally," he echoed. Disappointment knifed through him. Getting up from the bed, he stooped to pick up his jacket from the floor and slung it over his shoulder.

Eden's eyes rounded in disbelief. "Where are you going?" She could barely speak.

"To find myself a common tavern wench who won't be a block of ice."

He flung open the door and slammed it behind his retreating back.

Chapter 8

Hurt and bewildered, Eden stared at the closed door. What had she done wrong? Why would Justin seek the company of a tavern wench—and on their wedding night? She sniffed back tears. All she had wanted to do was show her appreciation.

Swinging her legs over the edge of the bed, she climbed down and walked to the dresser, opened a drawer, pulled out her nightgown, and slipped it over her head. *Gratitude*. Justin had spat out the word as if it left a foul taste in his mouth. He didn't want her gratitude. In fact, he seemed angered by it. What was so wrong with feeling grateful?

She left the candle burning for Justin's return and returned to the four-poster bed. What did Justin want? she wondered, snuggling under the covers. What did he expect? Eden sniffed more loudly. To be honest, gratitude wasn't all she felt for Justin Tremayne. A myriad of emotions had sprung up inside her at his touch, feelings that caught her by surprise, aspects of her personality she hadn't known existed. Justin had called her fire and ice, and ladies, she had been led to believe, were expected to be the latter. Eden brushed away a tear with the back of her hand.

"It isn't fair!" she muttered to the empty room. How could Justin fault her behavior when she had only done what she had been told was proper? It had been no easy task to lie perfectly still while her body was bombarded with strange sensations. Every ounce of self control was needed to master the urge to cling and caress. She had felt as though she were teetering on the brink of discovery. Instead she had fallen to earth with a thud.

Eden punched the goose down pillow, then rolled onto her side, dissatisfied without knowing why. Weariness washed over her, crushing her into the feather bed. Finally she slept.

Justin was the last to leave Raleigh Tavern. Upon his return to Francis Street, he found Eden asleep. Her raven tresses flowed over the white linen pillowcase, framing a countenance that had the innocence of a child, the purity of an angel, the allure of a temptress. Three tankards of ale had failed to erase that face from his thoughts. Though the barmaid had hinted her favors were for hire, Justin hadn't been interested. For him, there was only one woman.

"Damn!" he swore under his breath. Eden had come to the marriage bed willingly. Indeed, she had spread herself before him like a sacrificial offering. That, he decided, tugging at his cravat, was the entire problem. When he made love to Eden, he didn't want her sprawled beneath him as limp as a rag doll. He wanted her warm, willing—and loving.

Justin paused in the midst of undressing, the shoe in his hand forgotten. He had unearthed a passion beneath her cool facade that had surprised him, but something had happened to spoil the moment. The instant he had placed her on the bed, the flame had been extinguished. Perhaps it wasn't so strange, he thought, frowning. No doubt, Eden was still a virgin—and fearful. Why had he reacted like a disgruntled suitor?

"Humph!" He shook his head in self-derision. "So much for being patient!" Once again this slip of a girl had shown him for a bumbling lout. His shoe thumped on the floor. It had been a mistake to storm out. But anger, not to mention injured pride, had overridden his better judgment.

He slipped out of his coat and tossed it over the back of a chair. He glanced at the small form under the mound of bedclothes. She looked young and defenseless. His expression as dark as the March night, he finished undressing and blew out the candle Eden had left burning. He had meted out cruelty to one who craved kindness. His actions were despicable.

A new worry assailed him as he slid into bed. He didn't own a nightshirt. He fervently hoped Eden wouldn't be affronted by his nudity. As though to soothe his doubt, Eden unconsciously sought his body's heat and curved around him.

Dawn brings another day, he reminded himself. Tomorrow we start afresh. Putting his arm around her, he drew her close.

Eden wakened slowly, averse to leaving the peaceful realm of slumber. Her eyes still closed, she nuzzled the solid warmth at her side. Inhaling deeply, she detected an unfamiliar though not unpleasant musky scent. Her eyelids opened a slit to reveal a broad chest furred with chestnut curls. Small and pale in comparison, her hand rested on the muscled expanse. Gold winked from the wide band on her third finger. Her eyes flew open. It wasn't just any gold band, but a wedding ring!

"Already there are advantages to married life." The corners of Justin's mouth curved upward.

Eden snatched her hand away.

"Had I but known," Justin continued in his rich-as-molasses drawl, "I would have embraced the institution sooner."

"Why didn't you?" she blurted. Her face burned at her boldness.

"Truth is, I was never tempted until I spotted you."

She regarded him skeptically. Even with a day's growth of beard shadowing his cheeks, he was truly pleasing to look upon. Eden wondered what it would feel like to graze her knuckles over the stubbled chin. "Surely there were many women who would have been happy to end your bachelor days?"

Justin rolled over abruptly, pinning her beneath him. The pirate grin she found so engaging flashed in his face. "Jealous, sweet?"

"Of course not." She tried to sound indignant. At close range, she could see tiny flecks of white in his soft gray irises, rimmed in charcoal.

His warm breath fanned her cheek. "My parents enjoyed a long and happy marriage. When I asked my father how this came to be, he told me their secret."

It was difficult to concentrate on his words when his nearness was so distracting. Eden couldn't help but admire his clean, evenly chiseled features, with a jaw that bespoke strength but hinted at obstinacy.

"Well . . ." he prompted. "Aren't you at least a bit curious?"

"Very," Eden breathed. However, it was Justin, not his parents, who piqued her curiosity.

He smoothed a lock of hair from her brow. "Actually, there were two suggestions. The first was never go to bed angry."

Saying nothing, Eden stared transfixed at the face so near her own.

"I'm ashamed of my actions last evening, Eden. I promised to be patient, yet I behaved worse than a child denied a treat. I didn't seek out another. You're my wife. I want only you."

Until now, she had refused to acknowledge how much she wanted to hear those words. She felt absurdly happy at his admission. "I'm the one who should apologize," she risked saying. "Somehow I disappointed you. I'm sorry."

"You have a most generous and giving nature, Mistress Tremayne. I think that was why I fell in love with you." He traced an index finger along her downy cheek.

For the second time in as many minutes, Eden was speechless.

Justin gazed at her tenderly. "Don't you want to know the second piece of advice my father gave me?"

"Yes." Her voice was husky. "I'd like very much to know."

"He advised me to start and end each day with a kiss. I think the time is ripe to carry on a family tradition."

Mesmerized, Eden watched Justin's mouth descend to claim hers. Her lips parted in response. The sweetness of the kiss teased her senses. One taste failed to satisfy her craving, instead making her hungry for more. Tentatively, she touched her tongue to his, then quickly withdrew at Justin's sharp intake of breath. Had she done something wrong again?

She needn't have worried. He deepened the kiss, carrying her with him to a state of mindless ecstasy while his tongue plundered, explored, teased the hollows of her mouth. He took. She gave. Both wanted more.

"Mister Justin!" Prudence banged on the bedroom door. "Your aunt done tol' me to fetch ya'll hot water. Said you was leavin' bright and early."

Justin tore his mouth free and gave Eden a rueful smile. "As usual, father's advice was excellent." He swung his legs out of bed.

Eden smothered a shocked gasp. Justin wasn't wearing a stitch of clothing! She knew she shouldn't stare, but she couldn't help it. She simply couldn't pull her gaze away. Never having seen a man unclothed, she found the sight intrigued and fascinated her. Sleeping nude was a barbaric custom, of course, but . . .

With his back turned, Justin was unaware of Eden's perusal. He reached for his breeches, stepped into them, and opened the door.

"Here you is. Plenty nice hot water," said Prudence, beaming. The servant entered the room with a pitcher. "Mornin', Miss Eden." She gave her a broad wink, and

Eden was sure Prudence had noticed her flushed cheeks, tousled curls, and rosy just-kissed lips.

"Good morning, Prudence," Eden managed, feeling at a disadvantage.

Justin took the pitcher and placed it alongside a matching bowl on the rosewood dresser. "Tell my aunt we'll join her for breakfast."

"Yessir, Mister Justin. Sure hope I didn't come at a bad time. I tol' Mistress Nora, them newly hitched folks likes their rest."

"Don't worry, Prudence. My aunt knows I wanted to get an early start this morning."

"See ya'll downstairs." Prudence backed out the door, grinning from ear to ear.

As Justin turned to Eden, he couldn't help thinking what a fetching sight she made with the bedclothes clutched to her chin. "If you don't object, I'll shave and dress, then leave you to your toilette. I have some details to discuss with Aunt Nora. I'll send Prudence up to help with your gown."

"No . . . I-I mean yes," Eden stammered, suddenly overwhelmed by the intimate aspects of married life. "Thank you. That's quite agreeable."

Facing the dresser, Justin poured water into the basin. Eden turned on her side and watched as he set out soap, brush, and a razor. After working the soap into a lather, he spread a thick layer on his face. He stropped the razor against a leather strap, then placed the blade near his right earlobe and scraped. He repeated the process until there were flesh-colored swaths striping his cheek.

Eden shifted position, conscious of the play of muscle and sinew as he stretched and reached, bent and straightened. Justin Tremayne looked fit, like a man accustomed to regular exercise and not the type to go soft with excess flesh. Her gaze dropped. Tight-fitting breeches showed off the lower part of his body to good advantage, the well-turned calves, firm thighs and buttocks.

Justin noted her interest in the mirror. "Is everything to your liking, madam?" he teased.

Eden lowered her eyes and plucked at the flower design on the counterpane. "Do you always sleep . . . uh . . . unclothed?"

"I haven't worn a nightshirt since I was a lad. Much to my mother's dismay," he added with a chuckle.

"Oh."

"Why? Does it distress you?"

"Not in the least." She shrugged. "Sleep as you wish."

A warm glow of approval lit his gray gaze before Justin resumed shaving, Eden watching surreptitiously. When he pressed the blade to his throat, she held her breath. He was so vulnerable. A single slip could end his life. She drew up higher against the pillows. The razor followed the curve of his neck until the bronzed column was free of whiskers. Eden slowly let out a long sigh, marveling that he had accomplished the task without spilling a drop of blood.

She found Justin grinning at her and felt silly. He whistled a jaunty tune as he quickly finished dressing. Before he left the room, he went to the bed and caught Eden's chin, brushing a light kiss across her mouth. "Hurry, love. We've a long journey ahead of us." Then he disappeared through the doorway.

Before the sound of his footsteps faded, Eden sprang out of bed, eager to begin the new day. Besides the gown she had worn at the wedding, she now owned two others which had been part of the uncompleted trousseau. Deciding that the simply-cut midnight blue challis was more suitable for travel, Eden hurriedly completed her toilette. She had already finished dressing when Prudence arrived to braid her heavy tresses and twist them atop her head in a silken coronet.

Nora Cunningham greeted Eden with a smile as she entered the dining room. "It takes a special talent to look fresh and lovely at this hour."

"Thank you, Mistress Cunningham," Eden replied, glancing about for Justin.

"I thought we settled that matter yesterday," Nora rebuked with mock sternness. "You're to call me Aunt."

Accepting the proferred cup of tea, Eden nodded. "I won't forget again, Aunt Nora."

"Good." Nora waved her hand at the covered platters of food. "Eat hearty, Eden. You'll find eggs, ham, stewed prunes, and for a special treat, I had Prudence fetch scones from the baker."

Not wanting to offend her hostess, Eden filled her plate. Much to her embarrassment, she heard her stomach give an unladylike rumble of anticipation.

Nora laughed. "And Justin feared you had the appetite of a sparrow."

Eden buttered a scone. "Where is Justin?" She tried to keep her tone casual. "I thought we would be breakfasting together."

"He bolted down a plateful twice the size of yours in record time." Nora poured herself more tea. "He claimed he had business to attend to."

"Business which, I am pleased to say, is successfully concluded." Both women turned toward the sound of Justin's voice. He strolled toward them, wearing a satisfied expression. "I was able to locate a sloop for the trip up the James. Even Mother Nature is cooperating by sending a brisk breeze. With luck, we should be at Greenbriar well before nightfall." He broke off a piece of scone and popped it into his mouth.

"What about the horses?" Eden ventured.

"A friend of mine will be coming to Williamsburg next month during Publick Times. By then the roads should be better. He can return the sloop and bring the horses back."

"How soon can I expect another visit?" Nora asked hopefully.

"You can plan to see us this summer, though our visit will have to be brief."

Nora looked disappointed, then brightened. "Perhaps

Governor Fauquier will be hosting a ball at the Governor's Palace. I can't think of a better way to launch Eden into Williamsburg society.''

''Eden's beauty will outshine even the Governor's magnificent residence.'' Justin shot her a proprietory glance.

She wasn't pleased. Justin's remark troubled her. Again she felt like an ornament. Then she recalled a comment he had made earlier about falling in love with her generous spirit and felt somewhat better. Maybe he did see below the surface after all. ''What are Publick Times?'' she asked.

''Publick Times are held every April and October when the courts convene. The House of Burgesses and the Governor's Council meet at the capitol to form the General Assembly,'' Justin explained.

''And Williamsburg wakes from a sleepy college town into a city befitting the capital of the king's largest colony,'' Nora finished proudly. ''The streets teem with people—statesmen and riffraff alike.''

''And she thrives on the excitement.'' Justin gave his aunt a knowing smile. ''It's a time of attending balls, fairs, theater, and getting the chance to catch up on the latest gossip.''

''Justin! For shame,'' Nora admonished good-naturedly. She added, ''Not that I don't enjoy your company, but if you intend to make it to Greenbriar by dark, isn't it time you leave?''

''Right as always, Aunt.''

''Hiram will take you to the landing.''

''Hiram is Prudence's husband,'' Justin clarified for Eden's benefit.

Just then, Prudence came in to announce that Hiram had the horses harnessed and would bring the carriage around front.

Nora gave Eden an affectionate hug. ''Come back soon, dear. You're always welcome.'' To Justin she said, ''Ask Hiram to drive down Duke of Gloucester Street so Eden can see Williamsburg before you whisk her away.''

"Yes, Aunt." Justin's meek reply was accompanied by a broad wink at Eden. Nora Cunningham's attention was occupied giving instructions to Prudence, and she was spared the necessity of issuing a stern rebuke to her nephew for his impudence.

Nora linked one arm through Justin's, the other through Eden's, and walked with them to the front hall where their bags waited at the foot of the stairs.

Prudence handed Justin his cloak. As on the previous day, he draped it over Eden's shoulders, then escorted her to the open carriage and assisted her inside, climbing in after her.

Hiram, garbed in mustard gold livery, slapped the reins smartly and the carriage, pulled by a matched pair of dappled grays, rolled down Francis Street. They left amid a flurry of farewells and promises to return.

"This is Duke of Gloucester Street," Justin announced as Hiram turned the carriage down the wide avenue that bisected the city. Eden's head bobbed from left to right as she tried to take in the sight of the many shops and taverns that lined the thoroughfare. Milliner, apothecary, silversmith, bookbinder, wigmaker, grocer, music teacher—each proclaimed their importance in a self-sufficient community.

The carriage veered to the right, narrowly missing a wagonload of squawking chickens. Justin reached out to steady Eden. "We're approaching Market Square." He motioned toward open-air stalls of produce and choice meats, where servants and housewives haggled loudly with red-cheeked farmers.

An adjacent building captured Eden's attention. "That strange-looking building"—she pointed to a sturdy red-brick octagon—"I've never seen another quite like it. What is it?"

"That strange-looking building, as you call it, is the magazine. It's used to store the king's arms and ammunitions."

"Judging from the height of the wall, the king keeps his treasure well guarded," she observed with interest.

"Actually it was the good citizens of Williamsburg who decided it needed protection."

"Really?" Eden arched a brow.

"With the French and Indian War being waged in the Ohio Valley, the residents wanted the arsenal well fortified in the event of attack. Rumor has it that the magazine contains upwards of three thousand Brown Bess muskets and enough shot, powder, and flints to outfit a formidable army."

Eden's face blanched. "Indians? Is the Ohio Valley nearby?"

"It's hundreds of miles away, sweet. The only Indians we're likely to see are quite friendly."

Somewhat reassured, Eden leaned back against the cushion. Her attention was drawn to the opposite side of the road. At the end of a wide, tree-lined green stood an imposing brick edifice. "Is that the Governor's Palace?" she asked, craning her neck for a better view.

Justin nodded. "It serves as the residence and official headquarters of His Majesty's chief deputy to the Colonies. And there"—he pointed to a church with a tall wooden steeple—"is Bruton Parish Church, and directly ahead of us is the College of William and Mary. The massive structure with the cupola is the Wren Building."

"Is that where you went to school?"

"No." A wry smile twisted his mouth. "I attended Harvard, which is in the colony of Massachusetts, near the city of Boston."

Eden glanced at him curiously. Had she detected a certain wistfulness in his voice? "But you would have preferred going to school here instead?"

"It was father's wish that I attend Harvard. I didn't want to disappoint him." Justin gave the college a final glance as Hiram rounded a corner and headed south.

Eden remained silent. She knew what it was like to surrender part of yourself in an effort to win another's approval. She only hoped Justin's attempt to please his father had been more successful than her futile efforts to gain her stepfather's affection.

The carriage followed a dirt road out of town which led to the riverbank. "Wait here," Justin ordered, climbing down. After looking over the moored craft, he selected the nearest sloop.

To Eden's unpracticed eye, the sloop looked frail and none too sturdy, while the river seemed treacherous. She had taken only one sea voyage. On that voyage she had met Amy. The ship had encountered a fierce storm. Eden had been terrified, certain she would drown in the stinking hold. Remembering, she absently stroked the gold locket. For two days, the winds had raged. The girls had huddled together, confiding their hopes and dreams—their secrets. By the dawn of the third day the sea had calmed. Amy and Eden had become fast friends. She would always remember her.

"I forgot to ask," Justin called from the sloop, "are you a good sailor?"

"I'm afraid not," Eden replied. Her gaze darted from sloop to river, then settled on the sloop. "Is it seaworthy?"

"It's fit." Justin finished rigging the sail, then came to the side of the carriage and helped her alight. In a voice too low for Hiram to hear, he asked, "Do you think I would put your life in jeopardy?"

Eden's eyes met his, and her breath caught in her throat. Trust me, his look seemed to say. She summoned a small smile and, placing her hand lightly on his arm, allowed him to lead her toward the boat.

She gingerly stepped abroad, sitting where Justin indicated. Hiram helped Justin push from shore, then stayed at the landing while Justin raised the sail. Looking back over her shoulder, she saw the servant's figure grow smaller and smaller. A breeze grabbed hold of the canvas sail, and the sloop began to skim gracefully across the water.

The James River was broad and curving, its surface a rippled blue-gray. Wind snapped the canvas sail and held it taut. Justin sat, one hand on the tiller, looking thoroughly relaxed. "Do you still doubt the craft's seaworthiness, sweet?"

"I haven't made up my mind about the sloop, but you seem skilled."

"Frequently those of us who live in and around the Chesapeake travel by water. Best you get used to it."

The trusty little boat tacked the width and breadth of the James, carrying them farther from Williamsburg and deeper into the unknown. Sitting stiffly, Eden peered into the dense woodland. The riverbank was flanked by primordial forests of towering pines. Animals and waterfowl were abundant. Justin directed her attention to a white-tailed deer poised in a copse of trees. There was a vastness to the land that was both peaceful and terrifying.

Tales of savage Indians surfaced in Eden's memory to plague her. Her fingers tightened on the edge of the seat. She tried to penetrate the thick forest with her stare, half expecting to spy a fierce warrior, his face garishly smeared with war paint, tomahawk in one hand, bow and arrow in the other. She moistened her lips. "I've heard stories of Indian brutality. Are they true?"

Justin adjusted the sail. "I won't lie. Some stories are undoubtedly true, others grossly exaggerated."

"Oh."

"The French and Indians are waging war against the British," he explained, "but I'm quite confident we're safe. The confrontations are taking place well to the north and west of our home. The only Indians you're apt to see are harmless."

Reassured, Eden tried to relax and enjoy the sensation of effortlessly gliding over the water. When the sun was high overhead, Justin reached for a sack of food, and they lunched on bread and cheese washed down with cider. Occasionally the forest gave way to a wide sweep of lawn leading to a palatial home, a reminder that the country through which they were passing was, indeed, civilized.

The sea air and hypnotic slap of waves against the side of the small boat lulled Eden to sleep. Justin absorbed her weight, positioning himself so he could rest her head on his shoulder while adjusting their course. Watching her, so content and trustful in slumber, he wondered if he was doing the right thing. He knew she expected a fine mansion such as those dotting the riverbank. How would she react when she learned a crude cabin would be their home?

"Eden." He shook her gently. "Eden, wake up. We're almost there."

Still groggy, she drew herself upright and looked about her. The purple shadows of dusk were beginning to gather as they rounded a bend in the river. On her right, a splendid brick house crowned the crest of a wooded knoll. The three-story house was designed in the Georgian style of architecture favored by Virginians. A series of shallow steps led to a porch that extended the width of the building, with six greek pillars supporting an upper balcony. Tall brick chimneys protruded on either end of a gabled roof, and a wide lawn sloped down to the river.

"What a beautiful house!" Eden exclaimed.

Justin smiled, but said nothing.

"If we're near your home, then will the owners of this house be our neighbors?"

"In a manner of speaking, yes." Justin narrowed his eyes and scanned the riverbank as though expecting someone—or something—to burst from the heavy foliage. A short time later, they arrived at a landing. Justin tossed a line over a post and secured the sloop, though he made no move to leave the boat.

Eden regarded him expectantly. He gazed back, his expression troubled. "I've asked you to trust me, but I haven't been entirely honest with you."

Eden felt a shudder of apprehension. "I don't understand."

Justin frowned at a path barely visible in the waning light. It would be dark soon, much too late to show her Greenbriar. Tomorrow, he decided. He would take her there tomorrow. After all, hadn't she already admired it from afar? Once she saw it up close, surely she could bear to live in a one-room log cabin until the big house was completed. Greenbriar was only months from being finished. September perhaps. October at the latest. Could she accept the fact that he hadn't been able to abandon her to the Wainwright's petty jealousies and acts of calculated cruelty? He'd wanted her safe. He'd wanted her with him.

"I've misled you, and I beg your tolerance."

"What are you keeping from me?" Eden asked. Justin wanted her trust, but trust was something she couldn't give heedlessly. It had to be earned.

"You'll see." He climbed from the boat, then assisted her to the landing, his hand firmly on her elbow, and guided her along the footpath.

A thick web of branches blocked out the remaining light. Any moment Eden expected the woods to thin, revealing a large house with dependencies. The path was narrow, scarcely wide enough for one person. Briars snatched at the hem of her cape. Twigs snapped underfoot. Justin uttered not a single word.

Eden glanced over her shoulder, but at the sight of Justin's set face, she bit back further questions. Her apprehension increased. At last they reached a clearing. In its midst sat a small cabin made of logs chinked together.

"This is where we'll live."

With a concentrated effort, Eden kept the shock from her face. This was Greenbriar? Surely this must be another example of Justin's teasing. She had assumed him to be a man of wealth and influence, not a backwoodsman! Her heart tripped at an alarming rate. At any minute he would flash his devilish grin and tell her this was some sort of jest. But no hint of merriment softened his somber gaze.

His grip on her elbow tightened as he led her forward. Running his hand along the ledge above the door, he produced a brass key and fit in into the lock. The cabin door swung open. Justin scooped Eden into his arms and carried her across the threshold.

"Welcome to your new home."

Chapter 9

Justin set Eden on her feet in the center of the cabin. "Wait here. I'll light a candle."

Flint scratched and feeble light vanquished the murky shadows.

"I know it's not what you expected."

Eden realized Justin was waiting for her reaction, but she couldn't meet his gaze. She schooled her features to impassivity and slowly pivoted to inspect her new surroundings. A bed covered with a colorful patchwork quilt stood against the far wall. To her right was a massive stone fireplace with a dutch oven. A neat pile of logs was stacked on the grate. Wrought-iron utensils hung from hooks nearby. A trestle table with two pine benches stood in front of the fireplace. A pine chest, corner cupboard, and a leather wing-backed chair that seemed much too grand for this humble setting provided the only other furniture. Exposed beams ran overhead, planked floor-boards underfoot.

She cleared her throat, her mind scrambling for a neutral phrase. "It's . . . cozy."

"Cozy?" he repeated. A muscle ticked in his jaw. "A polite way to describe a crude one-room cabin." This wasn't how it should be, he thought bitterly. He should be carrying her up the winding staircase at Greenbriar. She should be introduced to his home as chatelaine, not treated as a peasant in a rough-hewn shelter. The knowledge galled him.

Eden took a cautious step toward him. "I didn't mean to offend you—"

"Eden." Justin narrowed the gap between them and caught her hands. "There's something—"

The door flew open on its hinges and crashed against the wall. A grizzled giant of a man burst through; the small cabin seemed to shrink even smaller.

"Justin, ya laggard, it's about time. Too much of the fine life will make ya fat and lazy."

"Bear!" Justin greeted the intruder.

The men embraced with the enthusiasm of schoolboys, laughing and thumping each other on the back. Justin seemed to have forgotten Eden's presence, affording her the luxury of studying her new home unobserved. The room was spartan, plain, even primitive. She had been trained to supervise a large household, not a cabin in the wilderness. Nothing had prepared her for this!

Harsh reality overwhelmed her. This couldn't be Greenbriar. It just couldn't be! She had expected a home on a similar scale as that of the Wainwrights. How would she ever cope? She had no skills, no experience to draw upon. At that moment all she wanted was to fling herself across the bed and bawl like a baby. Dangerously close to tears, she sank her teeth into her lower lip to keep it from trembling.

Their exuberant greeting finished, the men held each other at arm's length, grinning from ear to ear. "There's someone I want you to meet," Justin told his friend, and beckoned to Eden.

She approached the pair cautiously, the stranger's dark stare making her uneasy. Already she sensed his animosity. *Hold your head high, girl,* her stepfather's reprimand rang in her memory. *Never show an opponent your fear.* Instinctively, she raised her chin.

Justin wrapped his arm possessively around her shoulders. "Eden, I'd like to introduce my best friend. Bear, this is my wife, Eden."

If Justin was large, this man was enormous, his girth

easily double that of Justin's. The visitor's face didn't resemble a profile as much as it did a craggy mountainside with generous features weathered by the elements and heavy brows jutting out like low-hanging cliffs. His coarse brown hair was combed straight back from a broad forehead, then fell about his shoulders to tangle with a full beard and shaggy mustache that sported red highlights. A battered felt hat with a wide brim dangled from one oversized hand.

"Wife!" Bear growled, his eyes narrowing to slits. He inspected Eden as though she were a serpent with two heads.

Feeling braver with Justin's arm around her, Eden extended her hand. "I'm very pleased to make your acquaintance, Mr. Bear."

Bear threw back his head and roared. Justin joined in the laughter. Eden glanced from one to the other, feeling excluded from their hilarity. Had she committed a blunder? She hid her confusion behind arrogance.

Bear grasped her hand as she started to lower it, wiping tears of merriment with his shirtsleeve. "Well, well, if that don't beat all. I've been called plenty of names in my day"—his laughter threatened to erupt again—"but never *Mister* Bear."

Justin's eyes twinkled with humor as he explained, "Bear is his nickname, sweet, the only name my friend answers to. His last name is Smith, but he refuses to tell another living soul his Christian name." He playfully punched Bear's shoulder. "I suspect it's been so long since he used it, he's forgotten what it is."

Privately, Eden concurred that Bear was more suitable than any other name she could imagine. "Excuse my blunder," she murmured, gently trying to extract her hand but finding it caught fast in Bear's huge fingers.

Bear directed his next remark to Justin. "Guess we weren't as close as I thought we were . . . friend. Didn't know ya were plannin' to wed."

"Getting married was furthest from my mind when I

left,'' Justin agreed, giving Eden a brief hug. "If circumstances had been different, you would have been the first one I told. You ought to know that."

Bear's attention shifted to Eden, and hostility glittered in his tea-colored eyes. Unable to find a flaw in her exquisite face, he let his gaze drop to the hand he still held. His thick brows drew together, forming a furry bridge over his hawklike nose.

Convinced that her work-roughened skin and calluses were the cause of his scrutiny, Eden defiantly returned his stare.

He dropped her hand. "Thought fer a minute Justin married hisself a lady, but yer hand says otherwise. Which is it, Mistress Tremayne? Are ya quality or servin' wench?"

Eden felt Justin's arm around her tense. Her eyes flashed. "I'm the wife of your friend. Nothing more . . . and nothing less." She drew out each word for emphasis.

"Guess yer lady gave me my comeuppance."

"One that shouldn't have been necessary," Justin added pointedly. "Come. You can help me unload the sloop." He squeezed Eden's shoulder. "Don't worry. We won't be long."

When the men left, Eden went to the bed and sank into the surprisingly comfortable mattress. Gazing around the log cabin, she tried to reconcile her lot. Primitive though it might be, at least the place was clean. The urge for tears had vanished, leaving only grim resignation.

"What's wrong with you tonight?" Justin asked Bear as they headed down the path toward the landing. "I expected you to wish us happiness."

"I seen 'er kind before. Worked fer one when I was hardly more than a lad in London. Treated me like dirt, she did. Looked down 'er nose at me same way yer lady wife just did." Bear tromped in front of Justin. "All I see ahead of ya is misery."

"Misery!" Justin laughed in disbelief. "Are you daft?

How can I possibly be miserable when I'm married to the most beautiful woman in the world?''

"Oh, she's a beauty, all right," Bear agreed easily. "But she's cold as they come. Mark my words, she won't be warmin' yer sheets when the winter winds blow.''

"You take too much upon yourself to fault my wife." Justin's tone hardened. "If you weren't a valued friend . . .''

"It's because I am that I'm trying' to talk sense into that stubborn head of yers. Yer wife has airs like a lady, but 'er hand's nearly as chapped and callused as mine. And,'' Bear raged, "isn't that yer cloak she's wearin'? How come?" he asked suspiciously. "Doesn't she have one of her own?''

Justin lengthened his stride to match Bear's. "Eden is a lady. It just happens that she's fallen on hard times.''

"How well do ya know 'er?''

"Well enough.''

"Where'd ya meet 'er? The common room of Raleigh Tavern?''

Justin grabbed Bear's arm and stopped the larger man in his tracks. "We met in London a year ago, then at the Wainwright's.''

"Where at the Wainwright's? The kitchen?'' Bear sneered.

"Yes, dammit! Eden was a bond servant." Justin's hands balled into fists. "Don't forget you came to Virginia as one yourself.''

"I didn't ferget. But I served my time. No doubt yer fine lady heard ya had more money than brains, friend, and marked ya as an easy way out. With her looks, there's no way of tellin' how many men she tried to trap into marriage.''

An angry haze clouded Justin's vision. Seizing Bear's shoulders, he slammed the burly man against a tree. "Listen, and listen well. Eden is my wife. I won't tolerate slurs on her character.''

"Ya lovesick pup!" Bear had seen the disgusted look

on the woman's face when she thought Justin wasn't watching. He effortlessly knocked Justin's hands away. "Yer lady wife doesn't give a tinker's damn about ya. She'll empty your purse, then break yer heart."

Justin's fist crashed against Bear's chin.

Staggering under the blow, but not going down, Bear stared back at Justin in amazement. "Don't make me hurt ya," he warned.

The two men crouched and circled each other warily. Justin jabbed with his right arm, but Bear dodged. The blow glanced harmlessly off his shoulder.

"So that's how ya want it." Bear swung his ham-sized fist and landed a punch, splitting Justin's lower lip.

Angered, Justin ignored the sting and lunged forward. Both men went down, rolling in the brush amid the crackle of dry leaves and snapping twigs, and were brought up against the base of a tree. Justin's hands went for Bear's throat.

"Sonofabitch!" Bear's outstretched fingers wrapped around a stout log. Grasping it tightly, he was about to bring it crashing against Justin's skull when a shred of sanity returned. He heaved Justin aside and lumbered to his feet. "See what that durn woman has done already!" He bent to retrieve his hat.

Justin slowly came to his feet, gingerly touching a knuckle to the trickle of blood at the corner of his mouth. "Don't lay the blame on Eden."

"I'm only tryin' to make ya see reason. She's usin' ya. Are ya too blind to see?"

"You're mistaken," Justin said tersely, then turned and continued down the moonlit path leading to the sloop. "Time will prove me right."

Bear trudged behind him. "Fool! She doesn't love ya. It's yer money, yer grand house she's in love with."

They reached the boat. Justin bent to lift out parcels and hand them to Bear. "Eden knows nothing about the house."

A package slid from Bear's grasp and narrowly escaped

falling into the water. Was it possible the twit didn't know the extent of Justin's wealth? That would explain why she had looked as though she had been hit with a poleax back at the cabin. He straightened. "Nothin'?"

"That's right. I won't be able to show her Greenbriar until tomorrow."

"Don't!"

Justin squinted at his friend-turned-foe, trying to read his expression in the darkness. "Why not?"

"If she cares for ya, really cares, it won't matter if she lives in a one-room cabin or a fancy house. Put her to the test." Bear retrieved the fallen package, pleased he had stumbled upon the perfect means to prove his point. "Unless, of course, ya don't think she'd pass muster. C'mon, Justin. I dare ya!"

Justin stared at his friend for long, thoughtful moments. He felt a twinge of conscience. He disliked deliberately misleading Eden, yet Bear was so sure of himself, so positive that Eden was only interested in his wealth, it would be worth a small deception to prove him wrong. "Very well." He thrust his hand forward. "You've got yourself a deal. I'll see you eat your words."

"Good." Bear pumped Justin's hand. "I'll make sure none of the workmen show up at the cabin and make 'er suspicious. I'll tell 'em to come to me with any problems."

"All right," Justin agreed grimly. "And I'll warn Eden not to venture south where she might accidently come upon Greenbriar."

It was a contest from which each man knew with absolute certainty he would emerge victorious. They gathered the parcels and baggage, and silently retraced the path to the cabin. Bear set the items he carried just inside the door and, giving Justin a curt nod, left without so much as a glance in Eden's direction.

Eden had spent Justin's absence exploring her new home, peeking inside drawers, poking through the cupboard. Everything was neat and orderly. Perhaps she had been overly pessimistic. Perhaps . . .

His face averted, Justin knelt at the hearth and lit a fire. Soon tongues of orange flame licked the dry timber, spreading a welcome warmth.

Eden started across the planked floor, wanting to tell him he musn't be ashamed of his simple holdings, yet afraid she might offend him further. "Justin?"

He looked up.

"Justin!" she exclaimed in horror. "You're hurt!"

He had nearly forgotten his bloodied lip and bruised jaw. "I must be a mess," he said, getting to his feet.

She ran toward him, rummaging through the pocket of her skirt for a handkerchief. "What happened? Did that brute strike you?"

She looked so outraged that Justin smiled, then winced at the sting. "Let's say we had a difference of opinion." When Eden's search failed to locate the required linen square, Justin produced one from his own pocket.

Rising on tiptoe, she stood between his slightly braced feet and dabbed at his mouth. "The bully! Hold still," she ordered when he would have jerked away.

She must think him a spineless coward, Justin thought. Should he try to explain it wasn't pain that had caused the sharp intake of breath, but rather the innocent brush of her soft, full breasts against his chest? Her slender body teased his manhood with it nearness. Close, but not touching. It was enough to tempt a monk. To steady her, he rested his hands on her hips. The faint, familiar smell of wildflowers drifted to his nostrils.

"How well do you know this Bear person?" Eden asked, pursing her lips as she studied the small cut.

The hold on her hips tightened; Justin pulled her fractionally closer, but Eden was intent on repairing the damage to his face. Lightly, she ran her fingertips over the purple bruise on his jaw and felt a lump forming beneath the skin. "What kind of animal would do this? And he dares call himself a friend!"

Justin's mouth curved in amusement. "You're angry."

"Of course, I am!" Eden was surprised at her own vehemence. "He's bigger than you. Meaner. He could have killed you."

"It sounds as though you care." Justin's voice had lowered, soothing her indignation.

Realizing she was still on tiptoe, Eden lowered her heels to the floor, conscious of their unintentional embrace. "Of course, I care. You've been very good to me."

"That's the only reason?"

She stepped back, not ready to explore the depths of her feelings. "Isn't that enough?" She shrugged. "What other reason could there be?"

Only one that really matters, Justin thought. Aloud he said, "I'm starving. I'll store the packages if you'll set out supper. Aunt Nora packed food in one of those baskets. Dishes are in the corner cupboard. Ask if you can't find something you need."

Eden lifted the checkered cloth covering the largest basket. The bountiful meal was typical of Justin's aunt. Nora Cunningham had thoughtfully provided cold fried chicken as well as other items from her larder. By the time supper ended, Eden was hiding a yawn behind her hand.

"You're exhausted," Justin observed from his place opposite her. "It's time you got some sleep."

This was the moment Eden had dreaded. Would it be a repetition of the previous night? She hoped not. She wasn't up to dealing with the frustration and strain of trying to please Justin, only to be rejected. When he remained at the table, she walked to the bed. Her nightgown was spread across the patchwork quilt. Justin had handled the garment. The knowledge was exciting . . . and unnerving. Swallowing, she glanced over her shoulder. He was still sitting on the bench at the table, his back turned to afford her some privacy. Quickly she unfastened the woolen dress and slipped the nightgown over her head, her fingers trembling slightly in her haste to fasten the buttons.

Modestly covered from chin to toe, Eden unbraided her

hair. Leaning forward, she drew a brush through the long tresses until they cracked and swirled about her shoulders and down her back like a lustrous satin cape. Setting the brush aside, she pulled her hair over one shoulder and began separating it into thirds.

"Leave it," Justin commanded gruffly when he realized her intention. "Please."

"It will be full of snarls." But her protest lacked conviction.

"You left it loose last night."

Eden hesitated.

"You have lovely hair. Some night I'm going to brush it for you." Justin's voice softened to the consistency of warm butter.

The cabin seemed to be alive with intimacy. The simple shelter provoked primitive feelings in her, as basic and elemental as wind and fire, heaven and earth, flesh and blood. Eden's heart seemed to beat in response to the strange spell.

"You could sit on a bench in front of the fire. I'll brush out the tangles with long, slow strokes, then gently massage your scalp until you're ready to purr. Your hair will sift through my fingers like strands of silk. And when you move a certain way, it'll become shimmering black satin."

His words painted vivid images in Eden's mind. A fluttery sensation, like moths batting their wings against a screen, started in her midsection, then spread downward. Her eyelids slid closed; her breathing quickened. How could this be? she wondered. Without a single touch, how could this man provoke in her such a disturbing response?

Justin came up behind her and wrapped his arms around her waist. "But for now, for tonight, it's enough just to hold you," he whispered. His lips grazed her temple. He wanted her, more than ever, but not when she was ready to collapse from fatigue. Patience, like other virtues, he reminded himself, required self-discipline and sacrifice.

Eden rested against his solid strength, thoroughly content. In a log cabin, in the midst of a wilderness, she felt as if she were truly home for the first time in her life.

Birds were chirping. The sky beyond the window glowed golden pink. Eden stretched with a sigh.

"Morning, sleepyhead." The bed sagged under Justin's weight as he tugged on his boots.

"Good morning," Eden returned, stifling a yawn.

"Stay in bed as long as you like. I'll be gone most of the day. I have planting to tend to."

"Gone? All day?" she murmured, still half-awake.

"Yes, but don't worry, you'll be safe here. Just don't stray far from the cabin. And whatever you do, don't venture south." Justin placed a soft, lingering kiss on her mouth, then he was gone.

The cabin was quiet, too quiet. Eden rolled onto her side and tried to go back to sleep, but she was no longer in the habit of sleeping until noon.

Climbing out of bed, she washed quickly, donned her blue traveling dress, and fixed a breakfast of bread and honey. Licking a sticky drop from her finger, she looked around. In broad daylight, the cabin seemed even more spartan than it had the night before. "It needs a woman's touch," she said out loud.

Her gaze chanced to rest on the bearskin tacked to a far wall. It must have once been a ferocious beast with its huge yellowed fangs. "Bears," she muttered in distaste, thinking of Justin's burly friend. Her husband seemed to have a peculiar affinity for that particular creature. "God only knows why."

For the first time she noticed the long-barreled musket hanging from a peg above the door. Her brow puckered in a frown. The gun wasn't there for decoration, she reasoned. Did wild animals prowl these woods? "Little good it's going to do unless I use it to club a beast over the head."

After breakfast, Eden decided to venture outdoors. Kissed by spring, the day was beautiful, the sky an unblemished blue. A light breeze whispered through branches and tall grass. The air was fresh and delicately scented. Eden leaned against the doorsill, her face tilted to the sun. She closed her eyes and smiled. It was so peaceful here—so safe. At last she felt truly free from Rodney's vengeance. Thanks to Justin, she had a new name, a new identity, and a home far from civilization. A glorious sense of freedom bubbled inside her.

Still smiling, she returned to the cabin. So this was Greenbriar, she mused. What an elaborate name for such a simple dwelling. Her happiness faded somewhat when she thought of the night before. Why hadn't Justin told her he owned nothing but a humble cabin? He must also own a plot of land somewhere, she decided. Or perhaps he merely worked property belonging to a plantation owner some distance away. Why had he let her think he was one of the gentry?

Recalling his proud carriage and the stubborn set of his jaw, she felt the answer was clear. Justin's pride wouldn't allow her to think otherwise. He had been ashamed he had so little to offer. *And she had let him down.* She had been so stunned to find this rustic dwelling instead of a home on the grand scale of the Wainwright's that she had let her disappointment show. Her violet eyes sparkled with determination. She would make it up to him.

The sun was slipping toward the horizon when Eden sat back to review her progress. She had spent most of the day rearranging furniture. The bed now faced the window where they could watch the sun come up each morning. The table was set at a right angle to the fireplace. The dresser and corner cupboard had proved too heavy so she had left them where they were. Her biggest accomplishment had been taking the dusty bearskin off the wall and laying it on the floor between the bed and hearth. In its place, she had hung the beautifully worked quilt. A search through the chest had produced a linsey-woolsey coverlet for the bed. Tomorrow she would start to make yellow calico curtains.

Eden glanced anxiously at the cold hearth. Justin should be home soon. It was time to start dinner. There was enough chicken for another meal, and she should be able to manage a simple spoon bread. To her delight, she had discovered a covered well behind the cabin. Inside the attached bucket was a jug of milk and half a dozen eggs. Bear had probably brought them for his friend, she decided.

"First, though, I have to start a fire and heat the oven," she said to herself. Imitating what she had watched Polly and Bess do, she carefully laid twigs and small sticks on the grate, then piled on firewood. Satisfied with the result, she brought out flint and steel. After ten frustrating minutes, she succeeded in directing a few feeble sparks into the small pile of tinder and gently blew on them until they began to glow and take hold.

"I did it!" Giddy with her accomplishment, Eden watched the flames curl upward. To her consternation, instead of going up the chimney, smoke began to fill the cabin. She fanned the dense cloud toward the hearth with her skirt. Smoke billowed into the room faster than she could shoo it away. Panicky, she threw open the door and windows. Eyes burning, chest tight, she coughed and sputtered. The smoke was so dense she could barely see across the cabin. With a surge of hope, she remembered the well. She would pump some water and put out the blaze. Picking up her skirts, she dashed out of the house.

Frantic with haste, Eden lowered the bucket until it splashed at the bottom, then using both hands, she cranked the handle with all her might and brought the pail to the top. Water sloshed over the rim and onto her dress as she dashed back toward the cabin.

Justin and Bear were three steps ahead of her and didn't see Eden round the side of the house. Smoke poured from the open door and streamed out the windows. The men raced into the cabin.

"What did I tell ya?" Eden heard Bear roar. "Durned woman's no good. Not only did she run off, but she's gone and set the place on fire!"

Chapter 10

Eden skidded to a halt, the bucket clutched to her chest. Justin, with Bear at his heels, nearly collided with her as they charged out of the cabin.

"Eden!" So great was his relief, Justin hugged her, pail and all.

"The cabin! Here," Eden instructed breathlessly, shoving the bucket into his hands. "Put out the fire. Quick, before everything's ruined!"

Justin smiled into her worried face. "It's all right. Everything's under control."

"Humph!" Bear grunted. "Durn fool woman!" He turned and stalked down a path leading away from the cabin.

Eden watched him disappear. "He hates me."

"Don't let Bear upset you," Justin said, setting the pail on the ground.

Eden cast an anxious look at the cabin. "Is the fire out? Did you mean it? Everything's really all right?"

"I'll never lie to you, sweet." He ran a finger down her cheek. "Everything's fine, or will be once the place airs out. You forgot one important step when you started the fire."

Eden mentally reviewed everything she had done. The missing piece of the puzzle eluded her.

"You forgot to open the damper."

"The damper!" She was deeply embarrassed; her head

slumped on her chest. "Oh, Justin, I'm so sorry. How stupid of me!"

"It's hardly the end of the world." He exerted gentle pressure on her braid, forcing her to meet his gaze. "I should have mentioned about supper. You didn't have to bother."

"But wives are supposed to fix their husbands' meals."

Justin's hands rested lightly on her shoulders. "Well, I'm not an ordinary husband."

"No, you aren't." Eden tipped her head to one side and stared up at him. "You're like no one I've ever met. I don't know quite what to make of you."

Justin felt himself drowning in the violet pools of her eyes. "I understand your sentiments exactly." Unable to resist, he drew her closer. His lips grazed hers. When her mouth parted and she melted against him, he deepened the kiss, leisurely sampling and savoring its ripe sweetness.

He stepped back reluctantly. If he weren't vigilant, his vow of patience would be short-lived. When he made love to Eden, he wanted to possess more than her delightful body.

"What is the dinner menu, Mistress Tremayne?" he asked, attempting to lighten the mood.

"Chicken." Eden tried to match his tone. If Justin could appear so unaffected by a kiss, so could she. "There was chicken left from yesterday, and I was planning to bake spoon bread. At least I was until . . .''

"Don't look so unhappy," he chided. "Virginians are fond of smoked ham. Perhaps you'll start a new custom—smoked chicken."

The corners of her mouth curved upward. "We'll be able to boast the largest smokehouse in the entire colony."

Justin threw back his head and laughed, a rich, happy sound. "Not only is the lady beautiful, but she has a sense of humor as well. What more could a man ask?" He offered his arm. "Shall we brave the smokehouse together?"

Arms linked, they entered the cabin. Most of the smoke had cleared. Justin paused inside the threshold and viewed the changes Eden had made in his absence.

She tensed. Maybe she should have left things as they were. Not all men liked change, she knew, thinking of her stepfather.

But Justin nodded his approval. "Very nice."

Eden released a breath she didn't realize she'd been holding. "Then you don't mind?"

"Not at all. I like it." Justin walked around, observing the details. "It must have been a struggle to take that heavy bearskin off the wall." His gaze traveled to the space it now occupied on the floor, and a vision formed. He imagined Eden lying on the thick pelt, her raven tresses streaming across the coarse fur, firelight playing over her creamy flesh, her eyes aglow with lambent passion, her lips smiling as she held out her arms. Justin shook his head to clear it. It was only a dream . . . but someday . . . Meanwhile, he would bide his time and win her trust. Patience. He must learn patience.

"You must be hungry," Eden murmured, recalling that Justin had a hearty appetite. He would be ravenous each night after working the fields. She busied herself setting out plates and the rest of the chicken. "About cooking—I'm sure I'll soon acquire the knack."

"Don't worry. The wife of one of my friends is an excellent cook. I've arranged for her to fix extra portions each day so you needn't concern yourself with preparing meals."

Apparently Justin remembered what she had told him about her limited culinary ability and had taken precautions to forestall starvation. It was thoughtful of him, of course, to relieve her of the task. She should be grateful.

But she wasn't. She set a tankard of ale down so forcefully that foam slopped over the rim. It was important that she prove her usefulness. Besides, she reasoned, taking her place at the table, Justin probably couldn't spare the extra coin to pay the woman for her trouble. "That's very considerate, Justin. All my life I've depended on others but now it's time I learned to depend on myself. I'll learn to cook."

A chicken wing in hand, he regarded her thoughtfully. "Your attitude is commendable, Eden, but mastering the art of cooking, I've been told, is a formidable task."

Her jaw set stubbornly. "You don't think I'm capable?"

"I never said that." He sighed in exasperation. "Have you had actual experience cooking, either in England or at the Wainwrights?"

"Well, no, not exactly."

"Not exactly?" One eyebrow rose.

Eden moved bits of chicken about with her fork. "In England, the chef and his staff did all the cooking. I wasn't allowed near the kitchen."

"And at the Wainwrights?"

"The Wainwrights bought my articles of indenture because I was skilled with a needle."

"And are you?" Justin prodded softly.

"Yes." Eden's chin came up, and she gave him a defiant stare. "You'll see. I won't ruin the cloth you purchased."

"I didn't think you would."

Eden's gaze fell to her plate. She felt somewhat foolish for snapping at him. "Mrs. Wainwright resented me from the very first. Nothing I did ever seemed to please her. Eventually she sent me to the kitchen."

"If memory serves, you weren't happy there."

"People expected me to know things no one had ever taken the time to teach me. I could never do anything right. The more they criticized, the worse I became." She put down her fork and stared at her food. "I was clumsy and inept at everything I tried, except for chores a simpleton could do. I became a scullery maid."

Her dejection tore at Justin's heart. But when Eden raised her eyes to his, it wasn't dejection he saw in her expression but resolve.

Looking at him, Eden remembered his earlier remark.

"I would never lie to you either," she said. "I meant it when I said I wanted to be a good wife, and I'm going to be. That includes cooking your meals."

"At least listen to my idea." Justin covered her hand with his. "Start with simple items. In the meantime, Sookie will prepare the main dish until you feel confident enough to take on the entire meal. Is that agreeable?"

"What about the cost?" Eden was uneasy about raising the subject of money. "Can you spare the coin?"

His expression hardened, and Eden grew fearful that she had angered him. He withdrew his hand. "In spite of what you may think, I am not a pauper."

"I didn't mean to imply that you were," she said quietly. "I merely thought your resources might be somewhat limited."

"Not so limited that I can't afford a woman to help my wife with the cooking."

They both fell silent for the remainder of the meal. Afterward, Justin excused himself on the pretext of having to do chores.

At the dock he paced up and down, the tip of his cigar glowing in the dark. He had Bear to thank for this predicament. Eden must believe she had traded one life of drudgery for another. Yet, at every turn, she surprised and delighted him. She was no spoiled, pampered beauty. No matter what hand life had dealt her, she played it squarely. There was no doubt in his mind that she would learn to cook. And do it well.

He stopped to gaze across the river flowing silver in the light of a full moon. Puffing on his cigar, he rocked back on his heels. The final satisfaction would be his. In due course, Bear would realize he was wrong about Eden and the truth would bring the ornery cuss to his knees. Yet a nagging guilt persisted within Justin for keeping Greenbriar a secret from Eden.

Moonlight filtered dimly into the cabin when Justin returned. Eden was already in bed, curled on her side. Thinking her asleep, he tried to be quiet. He pulled off his boots, nearly tripping on the bearskin rug as he groped his way to bed. He cursed under his breath, then undressed and slipped between the sheets.

"Justin?" Eden ventured timidly.

"Yes, sweet."

Eden hoped he wouldn't think her brazen. "Remember your father's advice about never going to bed angry?"

"Mmm-hmm." There was a smile in his voice.

"I was wondering . . ."

Justin gathered her in his arms. "I confess I was angry before, but not with you." Warm breath fanned her cheek. "Have I ever mentioned how well your name suits you?"

The cotton pillow slip rustled crisply as she shook her head.

"Your name implies a garden of never-ending delight." He ran a finger lightly along her jaw. "Just when I think I know all about you, I discover something beautifully new. Not only are you a joy to look upon, but you're sweet . . . generous . . . spirited. . . ."

He punctuated each attribute with a kiss that left her yearning for more. She wanted him to touch her, to caress her as he had on their wedding night. She wanted him to claim her as his wife, the indelible seal that would brand her as his alone.

His tongue traced the outline of her full bottom lip, then slipped into her mouth. She touched it, tentatively at first, then at his answering moan, with increasing ardor. Emboldened by her success, she threaded her fingers through the thick brown curls at the nape of his neck. The thick, soft, springy texture intrigued her. Her hold tightened when he began to trail moist kisses down her throat. She shivered as his hand cupped her breast, its heat seeming to scorch through the worn muslin of her nightgown.

Happiness soared within her like a rocket. At last, Justin was going to make love to her. With utmost care, she relinquished her hold on him. Drawing long, slow drafts of air into her lungs, she squeezed her eyes shut and forced herself to lie perfectly still. It was torture, not quite knowing what to expect, but she knew she mustn't wriggle and spoil things.

She waited. Nothing happened. Justin's hand no longer caressed her. The kisses had ceased; there were no more compliments. Eden's eyes flew open. He was braced on one elbow, staring down at her, somber and unsmiling.

"Good night, Eden." Without a word of explanation, he turned his back to her.

Eden faced the far wall, her spine rigid, waiting for Justin's breathing to become slow and steady. It seemed to take hours. Then, and only then, did she let the tears silently dampen her pillow.

In the days that followed, a pattern seemed to emerge. Justin was usually gone before Eden awoke. He returned at sundown, bringing food Sookie had prepared. Sometimes it was stew, or fish chowder, and once, a haunch of venison.

Eden would tidy the cabin, and when that was done, fashion gowns from the bolts of cloth Justin had purchased. If the day was mild, she would drag a bench outside and do her sewing there. If the weather was inclement, she would work inside. Her first project, however, was yellow calico curtains. Occasionally Justin joined her for a light noontime meal, but more often did not; he claimed there was too much to do with planting the tobacco crop.

Late each afternoon she would attempt to cook. Lighting the fire was the most difficult hurdle. The flame would often sputter and die before the water boiled for tea. Another time the heat was so intense, bread would have sizzled rather than baked.

Each evening, Justin kissed her a tender good night, then rolled onto his side and went to sleep. During slumber their bodies sought what their minds denied. Their limbs would entangle like two kittens, Eden's head nestled on Justin's shoulder, his hand twisted in her hair.

This behavior went on for nearly two weeks. Tension mounted. What was Justin waiting for? Eden wondered.

When was he going to claim her as his bride? The unanswered questions pricked her contentment.

As daylight waned one afternoon in mid-april, Eden heard voices and peeked out the window. Justin and Bear were coming up the path. Glancing in the mirror, she pinched her cheeks and smoothed her hair, then greeted them at the door with a smile of welcome.

"You look pleased with yourself," Justin observed jauntily.

Bear stood scowling. He hadn't been at the cabin since the disastrous affair with the closed fireplace damper, which was fine with Eden. His obvious dislike made her uncomfortable. Still, he was Justin's friend and, as such, deserved her hospitality.

"Hello, Bear." Her welcome sounded stiff. "I hope you'll join us for supper."

"Sorry, but—"

"He'd love to," Justin interrupted, overruling the objection. "Mmmm. Something smells good."

"I made corn bread."

"That'll go perfect with Sookie's stew."

Eden self-consciously wiped her hands on her apron. Bear pulled out the nearest bench and lowered his bulk, watching her so intently that his bushy brows beetled over his nose; his dislike was palpable. Well, she didn't care for him either.

Pewter plates banged as she set them on the table. The man was a bully! She remembered Justin's bloodied lip with renewed anger and shot Bear a hostile glare. What sort of man would assault his best friend?

The stew was hot, bubbly, and smelled delicious. Eden opened the oven door and bit her lip in vexation. The corn bread had baked unevenly in the pan, the lower end resembling overdone toast, the other end a pale, sickly yellow.

Justin brought out ale and poured it into tankards. Glancing over his shoulder, he noted Eden's dismay. "Your corn bread looks so good I could eat it all myself. Bear will be lucky to get a taste."

Eden could have hugged him. Her violet eyes mirrored her gratitude. She sliced the bread with a sharp knife and set the pieces on a plate. "I'm afraid I still haven't quite got the knack," she apologized, doubting the bread was fit to serve. She would have preferred to leave it for the raccoons.

Justin ladled a generous portion of stew onto Bear's plate and passed him the corn bread. Bear eyed it dubiously, then took the smallest slice.

"How did the planting fare?" she asked Justin, noticing he took the largest piece.

"Most of the tobacco is in."

"Then will you soon be working shorter hours?"

Bear snorted. "Shorter hours come after harvest." He shoveled in a forkful of stew.

Eden felt the rebuke. She knew so little of how Justin spent his time, whether he owned a small garden plot or large fields. But whenever she questioned him about his holdings, he was evasive. She assumed he was sensitive about his modest circumstances, so she didn't persist. "Since I'm still a stranger to your ways, perhaps you will be kind enough to enlighten me. When is harvest?"

"When the leaves are ripe," Bear retorted, his voice surly.

"Ahh." Eden daintily cut a small morsel of meat. "Does that occur in a predictable manner? Or must you consult a gypsy fortune-teller?"

Bear looked startled at her pert response. Justin chuckled and said, "Gypsy fortune-tellers are in short supply in the Tidewater. I'm afraid we must rely on more mundane methods."

"Such as?" Eden prompted.

"Around the beginning of September, tobacco leaves have a yellowish cast. They soon become leathery and thick enough to retain a crease. That's when we begin the first cuttings."

"And then the tobacco is shipped to England?"

"After it's cured and packed in hogsheads."

Bear took a bite of corn bread and chewed. His face contorted in a grimace. Tipping his tankard of ale, he drained the contents. "Speakin' of England, wouldn't ya like to go back?"

Justin slammed his tankard on the table.

"Don't go gettin' all riled," Bear countered. "I was only thinkin' yer wife might be gettin' homesick."

Eden stared at the burly man across the table, and her spine stiffened. His rudeness was intentional. "Naturally, I miss my homeland."

Bear helped himself to more ale. "Justin told me ya met at a fancy party in London."

Eden nibbled a piece of corn bread. For a moment she forgot Bear was waiting for her reply. She chewed thoughtfully. Something was dreadfully wrong. This corn bread didn't even vaguely resemble others she had tasted. A strange sensation occurred once it was inside her mouth. It became a gluey, flavorless wad with a predilection to stick to the roof of her palate. She, too, swallowed a drought of ale before speaking. "Yes," she answered absently. "Justin and I were introduced at a soiree."

Bear folded his arms on the table. "A soiree?" he smirked. "Sounds like ya were quite the lady back then."

To what extent had Justin confided in this man? Eden's cheeks burned at the possibilities. The notion brought a sense of betrayal, but she hid her hurt. "What else did my husband tell you?"

Bear's smirk widened. "Said ya fell on hard times."

"Hard times? How civilized." Eden's eyes glittered with the cold brilliance of amethysts. "I was an indentured servant." Pride kept her chin high. Her voice was clipped, cultured, her manner defying Bear to challenge her.

"Why?" Bear leveled his gaze at her, begrudging a faint stirring of respect. "What are ya runnin' from? What'd ya do, kill someone?"

All the color leached from Eden's face; her fork clattered to the table.

"Enough!" Justin banged his fist on the table, rattling

the plates and cutlery. "Calling yourself a friend doesn't entitle you to insult my wife."

Garbed in a simple woolen dress, her hair weaved in a French braid that fell nearly to her waist, Eden possessed the dignity befitting a duchess. She rose slowly and met Bear's blatant hostility with chilling formality. "How I came to be here is none of your concern."

Justin looked from one to the other, unhappy with their verbal sparring. He had hoped Bear had set aside his animosity. But once again, Eden had surprised him. Not the delicate flower she appeared, she was of a hardier strain. She could hold her own.

Justin gestured Bear toward the door. "Since you're done with dinner, I'll walk you partway."

The instant they stepped outside, Justin spoke his mind. "Eden's right. Whatever brought her to the Colonies as an indentured servant is not your concern. I won't have you harassing her. Do I make myself clear?"

Bear jammed his hat on his head. "We've known each other fer years. Are ya gonna let a woman get in the way of our friendship?"

"Eden's not just a woman. She's my wife!"

"And yer more than a man I work for. If I speak out, it's because I'm worried about ya."

"I know that." Justin's voice was curt. "And I appreciate your concern. You've taught me everything I know about planting and growing tobacco. I'm indebted to you. But don't push."

"If ya don't want me at Greenbriar, don't pussyfoot around. Just come out with it."

"If the time comes, I'll do just that. You're more than my overseer, Bear, you're my friend, my teacher. But Eden is my wife. Don't forget it. I don't want to have to choose between you, but if I must . . . the choice has already been made."

"Do yerself a favor. Hear me out."

"Say what you want and be done with it." Justin shoved

a hand through his hair. "Never have I met anyone so mule headed."

"Yer the one who's mule headed. That woman's usin' ya, man, and yer too blind to see beyond a pretty face. Tell me . . ." Bear jabbed a finger in Justin's chest. "Haven't ya ever wondered how she ended up indentured?"

"Of course, I've wondered," Justin retorted.

"Well? What did she say?"

"The same thing she told you," Justin said with a sigh. "Her affairs were none of my concern."

"And ya let the matter drop? Then yer the one who's daft!" Bear wagged his shaggy head in disbelief. "Don't expect me to believe the lady had a sudden urge to take a sea voyage but couldn't afford the passage. She's up to her ears in trouble."

Bear's conclusion was a grim echo of Justin's own. "Are you finished?" he asked quietly.

"Not quite. Yer precious Eden quickly found out it was much nicer havin' servants than bein' one." Bear's wide-footed stance blocked the narrow trail. "Ya offered a perfect escape. Ya know damn well servants love gossip. She got wind ya were a wealthy bachelor buildin' a great plantation. She only wants yer money! Can't you get that through yer thick skull? I watched her face that first night. She hates livin' in a log cabin. Give 'er half a chance and she'll hightail it to London so fast it'll make yer head spin."

"Are you finished?"

"Yeah, I'm finished."

"Then good night."

Justin stared after Bear until shadows engulfed his large form and distance muffled his footfalls, then he slowly made his way home. His thoughts centered on Eden. Bear was mistaken. Eden hadn't married him for money, though in all honesty, she had probably believed initially, after seeing him mingle with other Tidewater gentry, that she possessed considerable wealth.

Nevertheless, she seemed to have accepted a humbler station, determined to make the best of the situation. The cabin reflected her personal touch. Her thrift was evident in her effort to learn to cook rather than spend hard-earned coin. Justin shook his head, a half smile lightening his mood. He wished Eden would abandon her valiant but misguided attempts to prepare his meals herself. Never had he sampled such a sorry excuse for corn bread.

But as he neared the cabin, his doubts returned. In spite of his efforts, he was unable to dismiss Bear's warning. Why had Eden come to this country a bond servant? What secrets did his beautiful wife harbor?

Chapter 11

Wispy clouds decorated an azure sky. Tender green sprouted beneath winter's withered carpet. Birds chirped as they busily built their nests; small furry animals foraged through the thicket. Springtime. Eden sighed, the sewing in her lap forgotten. Spring usually filled her with a sense of purpose, but not this year.

A peculiar restlessness invaded her spirit. She wanted something—was waiting for something—but didn't know what. Her gaze fell to the nightshirt she was making for Justin. Absently she traced the monogram on the pocket. Justin, she thought, frowning. A kiss in the morning, a kiss each night . . .

Her movements stilled. Could it be that Justin was afflicted with the same malady as the elderly Lord Ashcroft, the man to whom Rodney had betrothed her? Perhaps kisses were all Justin was capable of. The old lord, Rodney had pointed out with glee, was unable to claim his husbandly rights. To Rodney's twisted reasoning, Lord Ashcroft would never be the wiser if Rodney's friend, Geoffrey, first claimed Eden's virginity. Only it hadn't worked out that way. Rodney hadn't anticipated Eden's resistance.

"No!" she cried as a vision of Rodney's bloody face intruded. She squeezed her eyes shut and pressed her fingers to her temples. "Don't think about it."

Drawing a calming breath, she opened her eyes. Resolutely, she folded the nightshirt, stuffed it into the sewing basket, and rose to her feet. Perhaps some exercise would help rid her of this strange mood. A walk might be just what she needed. She looked about with indecision.

Don't venture south, Justin had cautioned.

A strange bit of advice, Eden decided with a shrug, eyeing the tall trees surrounding her. Everyone knows the sun rises in the east and sets in the west, but, she wondered, how does one judge direction when the sun is directly overhead? She started down the path she had seen Bear take. A short way farther a lesser-used track bisected the first. Feeling adventurous, Eden followed it until it came to a gurgling creek, then she wandered along its bank.

She paused to admire a cardinal perched on a pine bough. As strange as it seemed, she had grown to like Virginia. Moving on, she let her thoughts return to Justin. Quite often she watched him when she thought he wasn't looking. He seemed so masculine, so virile. Somehow she knew he didn't suffer Lord Ashcroft's affliction. She snapped a twig from an overhanging branch. Yet why didn't he claim his marital rights?

She had once overheard servants gossip that some men didn't like women. "Surely not Justin," she said aloud. He most certainly liked women—and they him. Then why didn't he make love to her?

Eden plucked the shiny leaf of a plant that grew waist high and shredded it into tiny pieces, letting them drift through her fingers. She was tired of being a virgin! Perhaps it was time to take matters into her own hands.

While she hadn't the foggiest notion how to seduce a man, the situation seemed to call for drastic measures. The more she thought about it, the more the idea appealed to her. She'd wear the rose-colored gown and take extra care arranging her hair. She would do it tonight—before she lost her courage.

Turning a full revolution, her arms outspread, Eden laughed happily. Why hadn't she thought of this plan weeks ago?

Even nature seemed to cooperate. Wildflowers grew in abundance and would adorn the table that evening. Eden filled her skirt with pink saucer-shaped laurel and delicate arbutus. As she picked a final flower, she noticed a bush bearing small orange fruit that resembled persimmons. Curious, she picked one and took a bite.

"Ugh!" She grimaced, spitting out the bitter fruit after a single taste.

Eden started home. The first cramp caught her unawares. The wildflowers tumbled from her skirt as she doubled over. A second spasm, more severe than the first, scissored through her midsection. Nausea followed. Eden dropped to her knees and lost the contents of her stomach in the tall grass beside the creek.

Gasping for breath, her arms hugging her abdomen, she waited for the churning in her stomach to pass. Half staggering, half crawling, she made her way to the creek and, cupping her hands, splashed cool water on her face and rinsed out her mouth. She had to get back to the cabin, back to Justin. Unsteadily, she rose to her feet and retraced her steps.

The queasiness returned. Her skin felt hot and cold at the same time, and her stomach pitched like a ship in a gale. She stumbled over a fallen branch and lacked the strength to get up. Another cramp made her cry out. She retched violently, repeatedly, until only empty, racking spasms remained.

Spent, she fell asleep.

At last she stirred and saw the hem of a black cotton skirt swishing before her half-closed eyes. The motion antagonized her unsettled stomach. With a moan, she raised her head. An old woman with a wizened face peered down at her. So unexpected was the sight that Eden screamed.

The woman scampered into the woods.

"Come back," Eden called weakly. "I didn't mean to frighten you." She pushed herself into a sitting position. The abrupt motion started her stomach roiling. Another cramp knotted her midsection, and she was besieged by dry heaves that left her depleted. Telling herself she would rest for five minutes then continue home, Eden closed her eyes and once again dozed off.

"Here, missy," an unfamiliar voice rasped. "I brought you something."

Eden opened her eyes. The old woman had returned and was squatting next to her on the ground. Her gnarled hands circled a mug filled with a steaming liquid that smelled vaguely of mint. Eden felt too sick to be frightened. She raised herself cautiously and balanced on one elbow.

"Not going to scream again, are you?"

"No, I'm not going to scream again," Eden said wanly. The woman seemed more wary than she was. Given different circumstances, the situation might have been humorous. "Why did you run off?"

"Only sensible thing to do. For all I know, you might be a crazy lady given to screaming fits. Here, drink." She shoved the mug at Eden.

Eden leaned against the trunk of a tree, hesitantly accepted the mug, and sniffed its contents. "I don't—"

"Go ahead. Drink," the woman urged. "It'll help your stomach."

Too weak to argue, Eden took a small sip.

"Spearmint tea. Best thing for the digestion."

Eden took a larger swallow. "How did you know about my stomach?"

"After you quit hollering, I watched you from the bushes."

While she sipped the tea, Eden studied her benefactress with curiosity. The woman resembled a witch in a fairy story, but no witch would have worn a canary yellow shawl draped over her black gown. Wisps of scraggly gray hair had slipped from the haphazard knot that listed toward the woman's left ear. The tiny birdlike creature with her seamed face and sparrow-bright eyes, was of indeterminate age. Eden had no way of guessing if she was sixty, seventy, or even eighty.

As Eden handed back the mug and her hand brushed

the woman's misshapen knuckles, she felt a surge of compassion. "Thank you," she said.

"You're pretty."

"Thank you again."

"Pretty is as pretty does." The crone's voice was as dry as an autumn leaf.

"My name is Eden Tremayne. What's yours?"

"Mary." The old lady grinned. "Some folks call me Crazy Mary." She sat back on her heels and waited for Eden's reaction.

"Which do you prefer?" Eden inquired soberly. "Crazy Mary or will plain Mary do?"

"Want to hear a secret?"

Eden wondered fleetingly if she should pinch herself to see if she were awake or dreaming. The bizarre episode recalled childhood tales of fairies and leprechauns. Fascinated in spite of her reserve, she nodded.

"Promise not to tell?"

"I promise."

"I'm crazy all right." Mary's cackle sounded as if it hadn't been used for a decade. "Crazy like a fox."

Another wave of nausea washed over Eden, then subsided.

Mary observed her distress. "You in a family way, girl?" At Eden's startled look, Mary repeated impatiently, "Family way? You expecting a baby? Is that why you took sick?"

Only the persistent throbbing in her head kept Eden from laughing out loud. "No, I'm not pregnant. I tasted what I thought was a persimmon. It made me violently ill."

Mary squinted at her. "This persimmon of yours by any chance have big shiny leaves?"

Eden nodded. "It looked harmless," she said, finishing the tea and handing back the cup.

"Consider yourself lucky. You could have the flux."

Eden winced at the thought. "I'd better find my way home." When she climbed to her feet, she felt weak and light-headed. Mary scrambled up and reached out a hand to steady her.

"Good idea, missy. Your husband will be combing the countryside for you."

It was already getting dark, twilight descending like a veil shrouding the woods in purple shadows.

Eden remembered she had followed the winding creek. But which direction would lead her home? She glanced right and left, trying to decide which way to go.

Mary clucked her tongue. "I'll see you home."

"No, that's quite all right. I've been enough bother."

"It'll be a worse bother if I have to worry about you roaming about like a stray lamb. Come."

Eden followed the slight, round-backed figure. "This isn't the way I came," she protested when the woman veered from the creek.

"Don't trust people much, do you?"

"No, I suppose not," Eden acknowledged, picking her way behind Mary.

Though her nausea had declared an uneasy truce, Eden's headache escalated. She was relieved when the trees thinned, and she could distinguish the dark shape of the cabin. She started to thank the old woman for her help, but she was already disappearing into the woods.

With a weary sigh, Eden placed her hand against the cabin door. She was stopped by angry voices that penetrated the barrier.

"Told ya she'd hightail it out of here first chance she got!" Bear bellowed.

"And I'm telling you something must have happened to her! Are you going to help me find her or not?" Justin demanded, his tone equally fierce.

"Find 'er? The woman's probably halfway to Williamsburg."

"Dammit, man! I thought I could count on you."

The door was yanked from Eden's hand. Justin stood framed in the rectangle of light. The gentle, temperate man she called husband had been transformed into a formidable stranger.

"Eden!" He stared at her for a moment, as though unable to believe it was really her. "Eden," he rasped. He crushed her against him so tightly that her ribs creaked in protest, then held her at arm's length. "Where the devil have you been?"

"I'm sorry you were worried."

"Sorry!" His anxiety flared into anger. "Is that all you have to say for yourself?"

She flinched. She had been the subject of men's wrath often enough in the past. Now she dealt with it the only way that had proved effective. "Do you mind if I come inside?" she asked with cool detachment.

Her composure fueled his fury. How dare she act as if nothing had happened? Didn't she realize he had been nearly frantic? "By all means, my lady." Justin stepped aside with a mocking sweep of his arm.

Eden entered and shot a considering glance at Bear, who seemed to resemble his namesake more than ever. He stood near the fireplace, his feet planted apart, his arms folded across his barrel chest, and glared back.

"You, madam, deserve a thrashing!" Justin shoved his hands in his pockets to keep from shaking her senseless. "A sound thrashing!"

Dear lord! Eden shrank from the violence she had provoked. Justin meant to beat her! Not even her stepfather or Rodney had ever resorted to such primitive methods. Though her knees felt like rubber, she kept her head high. "I realize I disobeyed your order not to stray far from the cabin."

There, she had admitted her guilt. Let Justin beat her and be done with it. All she wanted was to curl into a ball and sleep till morning.

Eden's apparent calm heated his anger. He had entertained visions of her being kidnapped by renegade Indians or mauled by wild animals. "Pray tell"—Justin's voice was ripe with sarcasm—"where were you?"

"Yeah," Bear added belligerently. "Where was ya?"

"I-I . . ." Bile rose in her throat. Eden wasn't sure whether it was a recurrence of her earlier condition or the result of fear. She prayed she wouldn't disgrace herself by being sick again. She swallowed nervously. "I went for a walk."

"Humph!" Bear snorted. "A likely story."

Hands still in his pockets, Justin paced the width of the cabin with quick, angry strides before stopping to scowl at Eden. "Are you telling me you were strolling through the forest until dark?"

Eden feared her legs wouldn't support her much longer. Ignoring the possible consequences, she walked unsteadily to the table and sat down. "I had followed the creek some distance when I found what I thought were persimmons. Apparently I was mistaken, for one taste made me deathly ill."

For the first time since he had flung open the cabin door, Justin calmed sufficiently to notice her unhealthy pallor. He groaned at his stupidity.

"And that's it?" Bear remained skeptical. "Ya mean that's the whole story?"

"Not quite," Eden admitted tiredly. "I must have fallen asleep. When I woke up, Mary was bending over me. She fixed mint tea to settle my stomach, then brought me home."

"Who the devil is Mary?" Justin came to sit on the bench beside her, one arm resting along the trestle table. "I don't recall any neighbor by that name."

Eden sensed that his anger was much like a summer storm—full of lightning and thunder but soon dissipated. "Mary's a dear old lady who was kind enough to help me," she explained.

The two men exchanged puzzled glances. Bear scratched his head. "Surely she can't mean Crazy Mary? The old woman's daft. Crazy as a loon."

"Mary may be eccentric," Eden said in the woman's defense, "but she's as sane as I am."

"I'm not sure a woman who eats persimmons where none dare grow can think herself sane." Justin took Eden's chin and turned her face toward him. "You little fool. Don't you know you just poisoned yourself?"

Bear muttered unintelligible oaths under his breath. Neither Justin nor Eden noticed when he left. The concern mirrored in Justin's face was genuine. Tenderness, too, was evident in his soft gaze. Eden moistened her lips before voicing the worry uppermost in her mind. "Then you're not going to beat me?"

His grip on her chin tightened. "You really believed I could lay a hand on you? Do you have so little faith in me?" he asked. "I would sooner cut off my right arm than raise it against you in anger. More than life itself, I love you, Eden."

"I believe you," she admitted, her voice a husky whisper. "I won't doubt you again."

Justin folded her in an embrace. Eden snuggled closer, absorbing all the comfort, the caring, the love he offered.

He smoothed tendrils of hair away from her brow with gentle fingers, then drew back slowly to study her. Her face was milky pale with dark smudges beneath her eyes. "A good night's rest is what you need most, sweet."

She gasped in surprise when he picked her up as easily as he might a babe. In three long strides, he reached the bed and lay her gently on the mattress. With her trusting gaze upon him, he undressed her as dispassionately as a parent does a sleepy child and tucked her beneath the covers.

"Sleep well, my love." He brushed a light kiss across her lips, then retreated.

Hours later, Justin lay awake, his mind rife with confusion. Why had he been ready to believe that Eden had fled? Was it because of her caution, her wariness, her refusal to admit she felt anything toward him but gratitude? Once he penetrated the invisible armor with which she girded her emotions, he found her warm and yielding. But each time, a battle of words and wits preceded such a victory. He turned on his side and studied the smooth perfection of her features. Another thought chased his sleep away. What cruelty had Eden endured that made her so readily believe he would resort to physical brutality? Was it the same cruelty that made her place a high value on kindness?

With a fingertip, he traced the sculpted line of her jaw. Life was so very fragile. Eden might easily have succumbed to a poisonous plant, or for that matter, to the capricious whims of human nature. Was the elderly widow Crazy Mary as insane as Bear claimed, or was she the harmless old lady Eden defended? Until he knew for certain, he would warn Eden to keep her distance.

Eden's health rebounded the following day, but during the long hours she spent alone with little to do, a new fear emerged. Could vows to honor and cherish be annulled with the stroke of a pen? If their union wasn't consummated, could Justin claim they weren't truly wed and cast her aside? She'd no longer be his wife, but once again an indentured servant with few rights and even less dignity. He could send her away. She'd never see him again, and life would seem desolate without him. Her determination of the previous day returned, harder and brighter than before. She had to make an effort.

Her head tipped to one side, Eden twisted a thick curl into a glossy spiral over a bare shoulder. That evening she had dressed with care. The gown of bright rose-colored challis was particulary fetching, its bodice low cut and long waisted, the elbow-length sleeves flaring into a wide ruffle. She bit her lower lip in indecision, debating whether or not to wear a modesty piece tucked into the front of the décolletage. Inserting the bit of ruffled lace, she stared into the mirror nailed above the chest, then jerked the lace out. Although she didn't want to flaunt her assets, she didn't want to conceal them either.

She nervously surveyed the cabin. The table was set with pewter plates and mugs. She lit the candles. Beeswax instead of tallow, they were another example of Justin's extravagance, like the fine-milled soap he preferred. He may be a man of limited means, but he had a gentleman's taste.

"Good evening, sweet."

Hearing the melodious drawl, she whirled to face him. Happiness spread through her, and she felt suddenly shy. "Good evening, Justin."

"You look especially lovely tonight." He came closer, his engaging grin sending ripples of anticipation dancing along her spine, and motioned toward the shallow bowl filled with dogwood blossoms. "Is this a special occasion? Your birthday perhaps?"

"My birthday's months away." Eden glanced toward the portal, half expecting Bear to burst through. "Will Bear be joining us tonight?" His absence was almost too much to hope for. The man's blatant hostility brought a constraint reminiscent of the meals she'd sat through at Sommerset.

"I told Bear you weren't feeling up to guests tonight. But should you be in the mood for his charming company, I'll use force if necessary to bring him back."

"No, no." Eden's eyes widened in alarm before she saw the teasing glint in Justin's.

"I thought as much." Dipping his head, he let his mouth move over hers in a gentle, unhurried kiss.

"You're a rogue, Justin Tremayne," Eden told him as her lips reluctantly left his.

"A fact I can't deny, madam. And a hungry one in the bargain." He gestured at the iron kettle he had set on the floor near the door. "Rabbit stew awaits."

While Justin washed outdoors at the well, Eden heated the stew and pulled spoon bread from the oven. She gazed suspiciously at the pan and wondered what possible disaster would befall their tastebuds next. The bread appeared harmless enough. Its crust was golden brown, not too dark, not too light. The surface was all one height, not slanting right, sloping left, or slumping in the center. Eden grew optimistic.

Justin returned, wearing a grin and brandishing a bottle of fine red wine. He produced two stemmed glasses from the corner cupboard and filled them to the brim. Once they were seated across the table from each other, Eden watched covertly as Justin sampled her latest attempt at spoon bread. "Good," he complimented around a mouthful of food.

Relieved, Eden began to eat the stew. Sookie was an excellent cook. Their meals were well seasoned and tasty. Yet Eden was eager for the time when she could prepare their food herself. Now that she had achieved some proficiency in baking . . .

Her first bite of spoon bread disintegrated into gritty crumbs. Eden stared aghast at her plate. Another failure! Tears welled in her eyes and she blinked them back, appalled that her emotions were so close to the surface. This would never do! Focusing her attention on a flickering candle, she forced her mind to empty. Slowly she raised her glass. A swallow of wine rinsed the bread past the lump of disappointment lodged in her throat.

Justin's upward glance captured the fleeting look of dejection that passed over her face like a shadow. It tore at his heart. She tried so hard. If he knew how to cook, he would gladly teach her himself. Didn't she realize how happy she made him? "Think I'll have another piece." He popped another wedge of corn bread into his mouth.

Eden was amazed. How could Justin act as though nothing was remiss? Perhaps he possessed the taste buds of a peasant. Or perhaps he was unable to distinguish caviar from crow. Eden hung her head, ashamed of her thoughts. She was being unkind. Justin wasn't eating the horrible fare because he didn't know the difference. He was eating it because she had made it for him. Justin Tremayne was the kindest, most generous man she had ever met. She loved him for it.

Loved him. The phrase rang through her mind like a church bell. Impossible. She must be growing fanciful. She *liked* Justin. Admired him. He made her happy, encouraged her to laugh. He made her come alive. But love? Eden shook her head in confusion. She wasn't even sure such an emotion truly existed.

"Eden?" Justin queried in a low voice.

She pasted on a smile. "Tell me all you know about Crazy Mary," she said, grabbing the first topic that came to mind.

Justin told her what little he knew of the widow who lived in a small cabin on his property, then added another warning to keep her distance.

"Surely, you don't believe she's dangerous?" Eden asked.

Justin shrugged. "One never knows if stories are true or greatly exaggerated. I prefer not to take any chances where your well-being is concerned."

"What kind of stories have you heard?"

Justin avoided her gaze.

"What kind of stories, Justin?"

"Bear heard once that she's a witch."

"Is that what you think?"

Justin twirled the stem of his wineglass. "I've never actually talked to the woman. I see her from a distance, but she always rushes in the opposite direction when I try to approach."

"Why do you allow her to remain on your land?"

"Where else would she go?"

"Where, indeed?" she asked, her violet eyes aglow. "Mary has found a home and a soft heart as well." Eden bestowed a radiant smile on her husband. "You're a very special man, Justin Tremayne."

Justin basked in the sheer beauty of her smile. If he lived to be a hundred, he would never tire of it.

Her expression gradually turned serious under the intensity of his stare. The atmosphere inside the cabin seemed to change. The air became heavier, thicker, harder to breathe. Tension crackled between them. Justin stood, holding out his hand. Slowly Eden rose to her feet. She reached out to him; their fingers touched and twined together. They stood gazing at each other. Neither spoke. This was the moment they'd long waited for.

Justin led Eden toward the bed. Pausing, he framed her face with his hands. "So beautiful," he breathed, placing whisper-soft kisses on her eyelids.

His lips grazed her cheek near the corner of her mouth, creating sweet torture. Eden shifted her head, trying to capture his tantalizing mouth, but Justin ignored her overture, instead raining light kisses along her jaw. She shivered as he nibbled a path down her throat, stopping to torment the wildly throbbing pulse at the base of her neck.

Her head fell back. "Justin," Eden whispered, not knowing if it was a protest to cease or a plea to continue.

"Say that you want me," he prompted, his voice low and compelling. His wet tongue rasped tantalizing forays across the flesh exposed by her low-cut bodice.

"I want you," she said with a shudder, instinctively pressing her body to his. "Only you."

Elated with her response, Justin lowered his mouth to cover hers and plundered its nectar. When her tongue hesitantly touched his, they began an age-old love play—circling, stroking, teasing, learning and savoring.

A delightful tingling began in her breasts, spreading a liquid warmth to a core deep within. Eden wanted to melt, wanted to become one with this man who stirred her so deeply. Reacting to a need to be closer still, she pressed against him with a sensual abandon that would have shocked her had she been fully aware of it.

With slow deliberation, Justin began to undress her. His hands lingered on fastenings, pausing to caress places where he encountered satiny flesh. Never had she known her skin to be so sensitive. Each caress sent her senses rioting. Newly awakened passion overruled her mind. In that brief instant, Eden forgot what was expected from a proper wife.

Her gown dropped from her shoulders to form a rose-colored pool at her feet. Justin released the ribbon at her waist, and the hoops drifted to the floor like a dainty white parasol.

"Turn around love." His breath tickled the shell of her ear.

Eden closed her eyes, waiting for Justin to unfasten the strings of her stays. He took his time, and Eden felt her impatience build. She drew in a sharp breath when his hands cupped her full breasts, capturing the rosy nubs between forefinger and thumb, and gently squeezing.

"So much fire, so much passion," he said, nipping the flesh at the juncture of her shoulder and neck. His own impatience growing, he quickly removed her underclothes. "Now it's your turn, sweet. Undress me."

With hands that trembled, Eden raised the hem of the cotton shirt and slid it upward over his rib cage. Justin hastened the task by tugging the shirt over his head and tossing it aside. Eden swallowed, her gaze level with his chest. Curiosity spurred her to touch the muscled expanse. The chestnut curls matting the broad surface were springy and crisp. When her exploring fingertips encountered twin brown pebbles, the nubs hardened under her light touch. Startled, she jerked her hand away, but Justin caught and held it firmly to his breast.

"Feel the beat of my heart," he said, his voice hoarse. "Know what your touch does to me."

The heavy pounding reverberated through the palm of her hand, up her arm, to her own breasts, until she couldn't distinguish the thudding of his heart from her own.

She moved his hand to her. "And this is what yours does to me."

Justin drew a ragged breath. Eden didn't dare let her gaze stray further than his chest while he hastily shed the remainder of his clothes. She was frightened yet at the same time filled with giddy anticipation. Soon, soon, an inner voice sang joyously. Soon she would be his.

He plucked pins from her hair and smiled when the lustrous mass tumbled over her shoulders. Burrowing his long fingers in its silk, Justin pulled Eden closer, forcing her head back. Naked, eager, their bodies fused in an unbroken line from breast to hip. Justin's mouth descended, no longer gentle but demanding.

He eased her downward to the bearskin rug. Her dazed eyes questioned. "Humor me, love," he murmured. "This is how I've dreamed of you."

Fleetingly Eden tried to marshall her willpower to lie compliant. But the bearskin added an erotic element. The coarse fur felt primitive and uncivilized against her sensitive skin. Its rough caress on her naked flesh excited her with each movement. She licked her dry lips, her attention concentrated on Justin.

Firelight washed his powerful bronzed frame. Such a beautiful man, she thought, and he was hers.

"Come with me, love," he cajoled, placing fiery kisses from the pulse point behind her left ear, down the column of her throat, to the firm mounds of her breasts. "Fly with me to a place high in the heavens—a special place reserved for lovers. Soar with me, Eden. Let yourself feel."

Justin's mouth and hands took delightful control of her body. A sensation swelled within her that was like none she had ever experienced. She twisted, writhed, and strained in her quest to discover what lay beyond. Clutching his shoulders, she arched her neck and raised her hips to accommodate his possession. She gasped as pain seared the juncture of her thighs, then subsided.

Justin's movements stilled then resumed, the rhythm smooth and forceful. "Come, love," he coaxed. "Don't be afraid."

The sensation—the need—swelled to greater proportions, carrying her to a realm of blissful wonder. "Yes, Justin." She shuddered. "Take me with you."

No longer tethered to earth, they soared as proud and

free as eagles. Higher and higher, they were swept toward the heavens. For a brief but glorious interlude, they experienced love's ultimate ecstasy—the perfect union of heart, soul, and body. At journey's end, they began a slow descent to earth, secure in each other's embrace.

Chapter 12

As April slid toward May, contentment settled over Eden. The days followed a familiar routine, but the nights were pure bliss. Each evening Eden's pulse would quicken at the thought of Justin walking through the door. Her tension would mount after dinner as the minutes ticked slowly away. At last one of them would yawn broadly; the other would solicitously suggest retiring early. Eden smiled, remembering the previous night. The moon had barely risen above the treetops when both had yawned simultaneously. Justin had made an exaggerated scramble for the bed, while Eden had burst into laughter.

He was a man of his word. He had brought smiles and even laughter into her life. In doing so, he had enriched it immeasurably.

Eden touched the velvety petals of the small bunch of violets she'd arranged in a shallow bowl on the table. The flowers had been on her pillow when she awoke this morning. No sonnet could have been as eloquent. The gesture was thoughtful, romantic, and characteristically Justin. He was a very special man.

She turned with a smile as the cabin door swung open, but her joy in Justin's arrival was marred by Bear's churlish presence. If possible, the man grew more gruff and surly with each encounter.

"Good evening, sweet," Justin greeted her.

"Good evening to both of you," Eden returned.

Bear grunted an unintelligible response.

"I didn't think you'd mind company," Justin said. "Bear will be leaving for Williamsburg in a few days. I thought perhaps there might be something you need that he can bring back."

"No," Eden replied with a shake of her head. "I can't think of a thing."

Bear's brow furrowed. "Don't know a woman alive who didn't think she needed somethin'. I'll wager by the end of dinner, y'll have a list as long as my arm."

"Perhaps," Eden murmured. She crossed to the hearth where a hen was roasting on the spit, potatoes baking on the coals. She had given up on spoon bread—temporarily.

Justin sniffed appreciatively. "Mmm. Smells good."

The comment was also typical of him. Every night he ate her burnt offerings, then asked for seconds. His consideration for her feelings endeared him to her all the more.

By the time the men washed up, she had the meal on the table. The chicken wasn't half-bad, Eden realized with a sigh of relief. She picked at charred potatoes with her fork. Thanks to the loaf of white bread Justin had brought, at least no one would leave the table hungry.

Calling on skills she'd learned at her stepfather's table in England, she tried to engage their taciturn guest in conversation. "Will you be in Williamsburg long?"

"No." Bear tore off a chunk of bread.

Justin looked up from his plate. "With decent roads, he ought to be back within a week, and Thunderbolt with him."

"Thunderbolt's a magnificent horse. Is he the reason for your trip to Williamsburg?"

Bear held the drumstick in two massive hands, his elbows resting on the table, and leveled a stare at Eden that seemed to say his actions weren't accountable to her. "Partly." His look defied her to probe deeper.

"It's Publick Times," Justin explained. "Bear wants to check the taverns to see if there are any messages."

"People leave messages in taverns?"

"Taverns supply many services besides serving drink,"

he told her. "They also provide weary travelers with a bed for the night."

"If ya don't mind sleepin' with a stranger or two," Bear mumbled.

Justin chuckled. "Williamsburg's taverns may not be ideal for a good night's sleep, but they're a fine place for merrymaking and debate. Tavernkeepers post broadsides to catch the eye, and many act as postmasters."

Eden looked askance at Bear, but he didn't volunteer any further information. She hesitated to antagonize the man further, but she was curious. What message did he hope to receive that would precipitate the long journey to the colony's capital? Did he have family or loved ones from whom he awaited word? The notion made him seem more human.

When they finished supper, Justin slapped Bear on the back. "I'll walk you partway." He turned to Eden. "I won't be long."

Moonlight speared through the newly leafed trees, providing a glow sufficient for them to follow the well-worn path. For a space, the two men walked in a silence born of years of close association.

"There's something I'd like you to bring back," Justin said at last.

"Sure," Bear grunted. "Name it."

"See if you can find a cookbook for Eden. If John Greenhow's Store doesn't stock such an item, try the Printing Office."

A low rumble sounded deep in Bear's thick chest. "If such a book exists, it'll be my gift to yer bride. Weren't for Sookie, ya'd be a bag of bones by now."

"Eden's cooking is improving."

Bear chuckled. "Heard a sayin' once: 'Heaven sends good meat, but the devil sends cooks.' " He reached into a pocket, brought out a plug of tobacco, and bit it off. "You oughta get yer wife's recipe for corn bread and use it to mortar bricks."

Justin ignored the barb. "I hope you won't be too disappointed if you don't find a message from your sister."

"Shoulda heard from 'er long ago, Justin."

"You know how unreliable the mails are."

"Somethin's wrong." Bear spat, and an arc of tobacco juice landed in the brush. "I sent passage money over a year ago. She shoulda been here by now."

"She was probably delayed. If there's no word by harvest, I'll send word to my solicitor to make inquiries."

They reached the point where the path diverged to Bear's cottage. Bear stuck out his hand. " 'Preciate that. Yer a true friend, Justin."

After the men parted company, Justin hesitated before continuing along the path. Fifteen minutes later he emerged into a clearing. The darkened Georgian-style manor stood in the center, assuming a melancholy aura in the moon's watery light. Greenbriar, the house he had been building for the last three years. Barring unforeseen problems, it would be completed by fall.

Since their first meeting, Justin had envisioned Eden moving through Greenbriar's many rooms, lending them grace and beauty. The image of her exquisite face inspired his choice of colors and selections of furnishings. But he was no longer driven by a compelling urgency to complete the house. Strangely, he was content. Everything important to him was in his small cabin.

A rustle of sound drew his attention. On the opposite edge of the clearing, a doe stood poised with its head upraised, ready to flee at the first sign of danger. Two spotted fawns flanked her side. Not wanting to frighten them, Justin remained motionless until they turned and bounded into the wood.

Ever cautious and slow to trust, Eden was much like that doe, Justin thought as he started for home. Beautiful yet chary, and ready to flee at the first hint of danger. He turned his back on the house.

In spite of their newfound intimacy, he admitted he was not a whit closer to solving the riddle of her past. What secret did she harbor? What did he have to do to gain her confidence? Without trust to bond them, what did their future hold? It wasn't enough to make love to her each evening. He wanted not just her body, delightful as it was, but all of her. Until then he wouldn't be truly satisfied.

Justin's reservations vanished under the radiance of Eden's welcome. As he closed the door behind him, he realized with surprise that he would miss this cabin when the time came to leave. Eden's presence had transformed the chinked walls and bark roof into more than a crude shelter. She had made it a home.

Setting her sewing aside, she rose to greet him. "You were gone so long I was beginning to worry."

Justin drank in the sight of her. "Have I told you yet this eve how truly beautiful you are—inside and out?"

Eden's steps faltered. Ever since she was a child, a great deal of fuss had been made over her appearance. At times, she had felt like a porcelain doll taken off the shelf, admired, then set aside and forgotten. What had Mary said? *Pretty is as pretty does.* The old woman wasn't crazy; indeed, she had more sense than most. A person's inner beauty mattered a great deal more than outward appearances.

"I trust Bear's journey will be a success."

Justin came forward and, unable to resist, placed a tender kiss on her lips. "You have already rendered the man one staggering disappointment."

"And how did I manage that?" It was a struggle to keep her wits from scattering when his fingers burrowed beneath her hair and traced concentric circles along her nape. Shivers shimmied down her spine.

"He was expecting a lengthy shopping list. He left with nary a scrap of paper." His lips lightly traced the delicate line of her jaw, leaving a trail of tiny kisses. "Are you certain there isn't anything you need in Williamsburg?"

"Quite certain, milord." Her eyes took on the dusky shade of wood violets. "Everything I desire is here within these walls."

He pulled her tight against the beat of his heart and the throbbing in his loins. "And everything I value, love, is here within the circle of my arms."

Later, still in his protective embrace, replete and drowsy, Eden lay on her side. Justin's lovemaking was a constant revelation. He played upon her senses with the consummate skill of a virtuoso, drawing out each nuance of passion, finding each chord of desire, striking until the ecstatic notes reverberated from her core to the tips of her toes. He encouraged—no, demanded—a response, making her realize he wouldn't tolerate any measure less than her all. Was this really the former Eden St. James, not a submissive but an eager participant?

Justin pressed a kiss to her forehead and ran his fingers along the gold chain circling her neck. He stopped to examine the locket that rested in the hollow of her throat. "I've meant to ask you about this. It must mean a great deal to you. I've never seen you take it off."

Eden's languorous mood fled. The locket was a subject she didn't want to discuss—not even with Justin. The memories it evoked were too painful.

"Are you aware," Justin continued, "that at certain times a faraway expression steals over your face and you touch that locket as if it were a good luck charm? Has it been in your family long?"

"It was a gift," Eden answered tersely.

Justin studied her face. "From an admirer?" He knew he sounded like a jealous husband, but couldn't help it.

Eden sighed and drew back. "No."

"Don't pull away," he coaxed, his hand idly stroking her arm. "I know so little about you. Tell me about yourself. Do you have a father, mother, a brother or sister perhaps? You can trust me, Eden. What made you flee London?"

Before he could stop her, Eden sprang from the bed, reaching for her nightgown as her feet touched the floor. "It's none of your concern." She slipped into the garment. A toss of her head sent her hair cascading down the white muslin like a bolt of black silk. Stalking over to the hearth, she was unaware that the firelight made the worn fabric transparent.

Rodney had given her the locket in a rare moment of generosity, and she had been wearing it the evening they argued. She couldn't stop remembering how he had looked with blood pouring down his face. She fondled the golden disk nervously, then realizing what she was doing, let it slip from her fingers. How would Justin react if he knew about that night? He thought her beautiful and loving. If he discovered the truth, he would surely despise her.

"I can see something's troubling you." Impatience laced his tone. Damn! What was her secret? "Please don't be afraid to talk about it."

Cold seemed to penetrate into the very marrow of her bones. Shivering, she hugged her arms around herself. "Why do you persist?" she hurled over her shoulder. "The past is over, done with. I refuse to talk about it!"

Helpless anger washed over him. He threw back the covers and came to stand beside her. "You, madam, have the devil's own pride."

"And you, sir," Eden nearly spat, turning to confront him, "have the disposition of a mule."

They stood, toe to toe, glaring at each other.

"Ah, Eden. There is fire under all that ice. When you allow the coldness to melt, the heat is powerful enough to make my blood boil." He tilted her chin up, forcing her to meet his gaze. "Other times, however, you could try the patience of a saint."

Her anger ebbed, replaced by a throbbing awareness of his naked body standing scant inches away. "And which are you, Justin Tremayne?" she taunted. "Sinner or saint?"

His mouth crushed hers, greedily seeking to drink its fill. Eden's hunger matched his, her passion an antidote for remorse and sorrow. Her hands dove through his brown locks; her slender form arched into his powerful one; her hips sought and moved against his manhood until he groaned his need aloud and swung her into his arms, carrying her back to bed.

Much later, the crackling logs in the hearth reduced to a bed of glowing coals, Justin and Eden lay wrapped in each other's arms, waiting for their heartbeats to slow, for their ragged breathing to even.

I do trust you, Justin, my love, Eden told her husband silently. With my present. My future. But please, don't ask more than I can give. The past is buried.

Early the next afternoon, Eden picked her way along the bank of the creek, determined to find Mary's home. She discovered the bush of persimmonlike fruit and reasoned Mary must live close by. Pausing to watch a hare vanish into a hole at the base of an oak, she noticed the underbrush was slightly trampled, revealing a narrow trail.

Eden followed it with quickened steps. The trail ended at a cabin even smaller than the one she shared with Justin. She marched up and knocked on the door. There was no answer. She hesitated, uncertain what to do next, her teeth worrying her lower lip in indecision. It was impolite to intrude on the old woman's privacy uninvited. She thought she saw a curtain flutter. Maybe Mary was home and didn't want visitors. Deciding to come back another day, she left a basket on the doorstep and turned back the way she had come. But she hadn't gone more than three steps before the door opened a crack.

"Wait. Don't go," Mary called. "Stay. Have a cup of tea."

Eden faced the old woman. "If you're busy, I can come another time."

"Busy?" Mary waved her inside. "Come, have some tea."

Eden felt awkward. Did rules of etiquette apply to social calls in the backwoods with an old woman reputed to be a witch? she wondered with wry humor. Taking the basket from the sill, Eden ducked to pass through the low doorway.

The interior of the cabin seemed even smaller than it appeared from the outside because of its clutter. Reed baskets and bundles of herbs hung from exposed beams. More herbs sprouted from pots on the windowsill and floor, filling the cabin with pungent scents. A small, cherry spinning wheel occupied one untidy corner, along with a quantity of bright red wool. The small room rioted with gay colors, from the patchwork quilt on the bed to the rag rugs on the floor. It was bright, cheerful, homey. Eden loved it.

"Come, sit," Mary ordered, shooing a tabby the shade of marmalade off a chair.

"I brought spoon bread." Eden said, accepting the seat the cat had vacated.

Her movements quick and birdlike, Mary shuffled back and forth, pouring water into a kettle and setting out a china teapot decorated with a garishly painted dragon. She selected a tin box, grunting as she tried unsuccessfully to pry off the lid.

"Here," Eden offered. "Let me help."

Mary gave it one last try, then shook her head in disgust. "Don't get old," she warned, relinquishing the box.

Eden's heart twisted in sympathy when she noticed the old woman's gnarled hands. No wonder Mary had struggled with the simple task.

"Rheumatism," Mary confirmed. "Damn curse."

Eden sliced spoon bread while Mary measured tea. When the beverage was ready, Mary poured the brew into cups also adorned with dragons and sat across from Eden at the table.

Eden was intrigued with the woman and eager to draw her out. She was also lonely. It had been a long time since she had had the companionship of another woman. "Your china is quite unusual."

"Unusual, eh?" Mary's rusty cackle sounded. "I like pretty things. Bought these from the peddler."

"Does he come often?"

"Every spring. Name's Jack." Mary helped herself to a slice of bread. "Like to barter, do you?"

"I wouldn't know," Eden answered, sipping her tea. "I've never done so."

Mary regarded her thoughtfully. "Don't suppose fine ladies have much need to barter."

"No, I suppose not."

Mary's teeth sank into the bread. She grimaced. "Is this what you feed that handsome lad of yours? He'll be skinny as a toothpick!"

Eden's face clouded. "I'm a terrible cook. No matter how I try, it always tastes worse than the time before."

"There, there." Mary clumsily patted Eden's hand. "Don't take it to heart. Most fine ladies never see the inside of a kitchen."

"I'm not a fine lady." Eden's chin lifted a notch, her hauteur stating otherwise.

"Nonsense! I know a lady when I see one." Mary got up from the table, went to a cupboard, and brought out still another tin box, which she handed to Eden. "Here, open this. We'll have molasses cookies with our tea. Cat can have your spoon bread after I soften it up with cream. Don't fret about learning to cook. That's what servants are for."

The old woman wasn't making sense. Had she forgotten they lived in a simple cottage? Bear might be right—perhaps Mary was a bit senile. "But I don't have servants," Eden explained gently.

"Well, of course you don't. But you will."

"Before that day arrives," Eden said ruefully, "Justin will be whittled down to the toothpick you predicted."

"Cooking's not all that hard."

"It is for me."

"If you like," Mary said diffidently, "I could teach you."

"Oh, Mary, would you?" Eden's excitement broke

through her reserve. "I'd be forever grateful. I do so want to be a good wife."

"Nothing to it once you get the knack." Mary's wide grin told Eden how pleased she was by the prospect. "We'll start tomorrow."

Eden was thrilled. During the ensuing weeks, the cooking lessons progressed better than she had dared hope. Mary was an excellent teacher, patient to a fault, content to sit back and instruct while Eden learned by doing. This afternoon they had made pound cake, and lo and behold, it smelled good enough to eat. Under Mary's tutelage, she was ready to advance to heartier fare, such as soups and stews. Eden started on her way home, the golden yellow cake tucked into a basket, along with a bottle of Mary's homemade dandelion wine.

She paused on the path. Mary had told her of a place nearby where she might find a patch of wild strawberries. If Eden's judgment was accurate, the path led in a southerly direction. *Don't venture south,* Justin had told her. So far she hadn't disobeyed his order, but the thought of plump red strawberries to top her cake overrode her reluctance.

Eden found the spot easily and sampled nearly as many as she picked. Perfect on pound cake, she mused, adding the fruit to her basket. Tonight she and Justin would toast her culinary success with a glass of Mary's wine. A strawberry poised midway to her mouth, Eden cocked her head and listened. There, she heard it again, the tap of a hammer. How strange. Why would anyone be hammering in the middle of a forest? Deciding to find out, she moved toward the sound.

The trees thinned and Eden shaded her eyes from the glare of the late-afternoon sun. She gaped at the sight of the house that loomed in front of her. She was certain it was the one she had first seen as they rounded the bend of the James River the day she arrived. How odd. She had no idea the house was so close. The distance by land versus the distance by water must be deceptive.

The house was truly beautiful, grace and elegance in its every line. It had an unlived-in look, as though in repose, waiting for its new owners to breathe life into the rooms. What kind of people were going to live here? She would probably never find out. Too much distance separated them socially. Gentry didn't mix with commoners.

Eden looked around, wanting just a peek. There didn't seem to be anyone there except for the unseen carpenter. What harm would there be in taking a single look if she didn't disturb anything?

She approached the house slowly from the back and rapped on the door, but the continued pounding of a hammer drowned out her timid knock. Suddenly the door swung open of its own accord. "Hello," she called out. There was no answer, no one in sight. Eden stepped into the entranceway and gazed around. The staccato sound of the hammer ceased and was followed by the occasional rasp of a saw. She ventured forward. Sunlight streamed through the windows, capturing dust motes. A winding staircase with a carved banister ascended to the upper floor. Her leather slippers soundless on the hardwood floors, Eden skirted piles of lumber and buckets of paint and began to explore the lower level, admiring the craftsmanship of the carved moldings, and trying to envision the transformation that furniture would make. She forgot she wasn't alone.

"What are you doing here?" The voice startled her.

Eden whirled, her grip tightening on the handle of the basket. "Justin! You scared me half to death!"

He stood with his feet slightly braced, his hands clasped behind his back in the entrance to what Eden assumed was the dining room. "I asked what you were doing here."

Eden stared uncomprehendingly. What was wrong? Why was Justin scowling? He didn't seem the least bit happy to see her. "I-I was picking strawberries when I heard hammering. I was curious."

"I specifically told you not to wander in this direction. Haven't I warned you it's dangerous to roam the woods alone? What if you had found someone else instead of me? A beautiful woman and a deserted house is a foolhardy combination. Anything could happen." He advanced further into the room, towering over her, tall and accusing.

Her mouth went dry. "Justin, you're frightening me."

"I mean to."

"But I'm alone all day at our cabin. You never seem concerned about my safety there."

"There's a lock on the door to bar strangers. If that fails, there's a gun within arm's reach."

"I don't know how to use a gun. How could I possibly protect myself?"

Justin couldn't fault her logic. It was he who was being irrational. Finding her here had caught him off guard. He was suffering a pang of conscience for keeping Greenbriar a secret. He was a fine one to tout honesty. If it wasn't for Bear . . .

Besides, this wasn't how he had envisioned Eden's introduction to Greenbriar. He wanted it to be a wonderful surprise, a home complete with furniture, paintings, carpeting, and draperies, not a house with echoing, vacant rooms. It could still be a surprise, an inner voice prompted. Eden didn't have to know just yet that Greenbriar was his.

He closed the gap between them, his expression softening. "I've been remiss in not teaching you how to protect yourself. But it's a problem that can be easily remedied. I'll teach you."

She stared at him in surprise. "You're serious, aren't you?"

"Perfectly, madam."

"All right," Eden agreed with alacrity. "Firing a gun can't be any more difficult than learning to cook."

A reluctant grin spread slowly across his face. "As long as you're here, would you like a grand tour of the house?"

Eden accepted his proffered arm, relieved that Justin no longer seemed angry. "I'd be delighted."

"Justin, this house is beautiful!" Eden exclaimed as she circled a large bedroom on the second level. It was part of a master suite, two separate bedrooms connected by an adjoining dressing room. "Who does it belong to? Will they mind our trespassing?"

Justin watched from the open doorway. "The owner is a close acquaintance. Knowing how much you like his new home will please him immensely."

Eden pressed her palms against the windowsill and leaned forward, admiring the wide lawn sloping down to meet the James River, which wound before her like a wide silver ribbon glinting in the sunshine. "It's peaceful here," she mused. "So tranquil."

His footsteps sounding hollow in the empty room, Justin crossed to stand behind her, his hands resting lightly on her shoulders. For a long moment he, too, absorbed the verdant beauty of the Virginia countryside. "The view never fails to have the same effect on me."

"Do you come here often?" she asked softly, turning toward him.

"Occasionally." He studied her upraised face, debating how much to reveal. "I oversee some of the details for my . . . acquaintance."

"Oh." Her voice fell. Eden was painfully conscious of his nearness. She wanted to brush the errant curl from his brow and had to fight an urge to lay her hand against his rock hard chest where she could feel the muscles ripple beneath her touch. Wanton, she chastised herself. Aloud she said, "Is that what you're doing this afternoon? Overseeing details for your friend?"

"You might say that." Would he ever tire of looking at her? Justin wondered, losing himself in the violet depths of her eyes. Or wanting to touch her? Or making love to her? It was doubtful. He pressed a kiss, slow and deliberate, on rosy lips that parted in anticipation. "Come."

He put his arm around her shoulders. "I want to show you the rest of the house." *Our house,* he amended silently.

Room by room, they toured the upper floor before descending the stairs. "I saved this room for last." Justin twisted the doorknob at the far end of the hall. "The music room."

Eden stepped inside. Late afternoon sunlight spilled through the mullioned windows like pale champagne. Unlike the other chambers, this one was already painted; the walls were pale blue, the moldings creamy white. A thick Oriental carpet woven in delicate shades of blue and ivory covered the floor. There was a white marble fireplace along an outer wall. Overhead, intricate prisms dangled from a crystal chandelier.

"Justin," she gasped. "It's lovely." Standing in the center of the room, Eden rotated in a full circle, eager to see everything at once. Her long hair swirled around her, then settled over her shoulders in a thick black cloud.

His hands in his pockets, Justin sauntered forward, touched by her enthusiasm. "The pianoforte will go there." He indicated a corner. "I—"he caught himself, then added, "it's been ordered from Italy."

"Are the owners musically inclined?"

"My friend has a deep appreciation of music, though no talent, but I believe his wife is an accomplished pianist. The piano is to be a gift to her."

"Your friend sounds like a very considerate husband. I'm sure his wife will love it."

"I'm sure she will," Justin replied noncommittally. "Did you say you were berry picking? Strawberries? Is that what's in the basket?"

"I've been to visit Mary," Eden confessed. "Besides telling me where to find berries, she gave us a bottle of homemade dandelion wine." She tucked her hand in the crook of his arm and smiled winsomely. "Can I tempt you with a sample?"

"You, my sweet"—he tapped the tip of her nose—"are a constant source of temptation."

"Seeing as the house is deserted, we could have a picnic."

"You needn't say more. I'll be back in a moment."

Justin was as good as his word. He returned carrying a pewter mug, a canvas tarpaulin under one arm, and the basket. Eden watched him spread the tarpaulin in front of the fireplace with a flourish and set the basket in the center. A devilish grin animated his handsome face when he turned to Eden and made a knee. "Our picnic awaits, my lady."

She joined in the festive spirit and dipped into a deep curtsy, then laughed gaily as she gracefully lowered herself to the tarpaulin. The skirt of her lilac cotton dress spread around her like the petals of a flower. Justin sank down next to her, half reclining on one side, his elbow bent, his head propped on a fist.

"Fresh strawberries." Eden reached into the basket and brought out a bowl heaped with succulent red berries. "Dandelion wine." She produced a green-stoppered bottle and set it in front of Justin. "And," she pronounced smugly, "cake that Mary vouched would be absolutely perfect." She proudly drew out the small cake which was light as a feather and done to a turn.

"Looks good enough to eat," Justin teased, though it wasn't the cake that garnered the compliment.

"You always say that," she chided. "But this time it's true." Her cheeks flushed with victory, her eyes alight with pleasure, Eden beamed at the man lounging beside her. "I used to think you had a cast-iron stomach."

"Do you still?"

She watched his long, tapered fingers work the cork from the bottle. "Not any longer." She accepted the pewter tankard he handed her.

"What do you believe now?"

The wine tasted cool and refreshingly delicious. Eden drank first, then handed it to Justin. "I've discovered you're every bit as kind and thoughtful as I hoped you'd be."

Justin turned the rim of the cup to the place her lips had touched. Keeping his gaze locked on hers, he drank deeply of the wine.

Eden drew a shallow breath. The silver eyes that studied her so intently mirrored his passion, a desire so consuming that it frightened her. Nervously, she dipped a hand into the bowl of fruit and brought a strawberry to her mouth, biting into the luscious berry. "Umm," she murmured. "Try one."

His eyes never leaving hers, he took a strawberry and dipped it into the wine. "Open," he ordered.

Her teeth sank into the morsel, fruit and wine mingling in a delicate blend. Justin repeated the ritual, this time sampling the fruit himself. Eden watched as he chewed slowly, savoring the sun-ripened berry. Her mouth felt parched. Reaching for the tankard, she finished the wine in three gulps.

It happened so quickly, Eden hadn't time to protest. Justin's hand reached behind her head, and he pulled her down on top of him. His lips slanted hungrily across hers. His tongue sought access to the sweet, moist cavern of her mouth. She granted it willingly, sensing the urgency that drove him, feeling the same need burgeon within herself.

"Love me, Eden." His voice was ragged with longing.

She wanted to tell him what he yearned to hear, but the words stuck in her throat. She knew so little of love. What she felt was a tangled confusion of gratitude, respect, affection, and passion that raged out of control at his merest touch. Was that love? Eden wondered. If only she knew.

"I need you." The admission seemed to come from the depths of his soul.

She answered the only way she knew how, responding to Justin's lovemaking with a wisdom that her mind refused to accept.

Chapter 13

Startled, Eden glanced up from her needlework, listening intently. The sound grew louder. It hadn't been her imagination. Placing her embroidery in the sewing basket, she crossed the cabin to peer out the window. Something, or someone, was tramping through the brush. Her breath caught. It was the middle of the afternoon, hours before she expected Justin to come home. What could it be? Justin's warnings flashed through her mind. A bear? Indians? She pressed her back to the wall and, reaching out, turned the key in the lock.

Her thoughts ran rampant, conjuring up vivid images of red-skinned savages hunting for scalps. Her gaze flew to the flintlock rifle hanging above the door. She had no idea how to load and fire a weapon. Perhaps she could use it to bluff her way out of trouble. Rising on tiptoe, she sighed in frustration as her outstretched hands fell short of the weapon by inches. Her gaze darted about the cabin. Perhaps, with a bench to stand on . . .

"Anybody home?" a gruff voice called.

Eden leaped backward, her heart racing.

The banging on the door continued with enough force to rattle the plates in the corner cupboard.

"Who is it?" Eden hoped her voice didn't quaver.

"It's Jack, mum. Jack the peddler."

Relief turned her knees to water. Feeling foolish, Eden turned the key stealthily, hoping the man wouldn't hear the metallic click and think her a complete ninny. The

184

elflike man on her doorstep brought a smile to her lips. "How do you do?"

"Mary sent me, mum." His bright blue eyes twinkled merrily. He doffed a wool cap to reveal a bald pate wreathed with snowy white hair. "Said you might be needin' some things. A beauty she said you were, and she was right, if you don't mind my sayin' so."

"That was kind of Mary. Please, come in." She stood aside and motioned for him to enter.

"Give me a minute, mum."

Eden watched in fascination as Jack unloaded his wares from the back of a packhorse. Pots and pans, herbs and spices, bolts of cloth, ribbons and lace. One person's trinkets, another's treasure.

The little peddler spread the goods on the pine table, and Eden listened raptly as he extolled the merits of each bit of merchandise, not pressing the issue when she showed no interest in an item, but cheerfully moving on to the next. When they concluded their business, Eden was the proud owner of a multicolored rag rug, a three-legged frying pan called a spider, and a heart-shaped trivet.

"A cup of tea to seal our bargain?" Eden suggested. "Can I persuade you to stay for supper?"

"A cup of tea, mum, but I promised Mary I'd dine with her."

In no time, Eden had water simmering in the kettle and had set out the teapot and cups. Jack kept up an endless stream of chatter, telling Eden about many of the Tidewater neighbors she had yet to meet. There was no way she'd be able to remember all those names, she thought with amusement, should circumstances warrant a meeting.

Jack's visit provided a pleasant interlude, and Eden was sorry when it came to an end. "How soon will you be back this way?" she asked.

"Come every year at plantin' time." Jack rose from the table with a spryness that belied his age. "Mary said your Christian name was Eden. Unusual name, Eden." He slapped on his cap and was about to leave. "Met a gent not long ago in Norfolk askin' about a woman named Eden. Seemed awful anxious to meet up with her.''

All the color drained from Eden's face. ''This gentleman,'' she said, her lips barely able to form the question, ''what did he look like?''

''Let me think. . . . '' Jack rubbed his smooth shaven jaw. ''Meet a fair number of people, I do.''

''Was he English?''

He snapped his fingers. ''Now it comes back! English he was. Wore a black patch over one eye and had a nasty lookin' scar peekin' out from underneath. Musta been some fight he was in. Hate to see what the other fella musta looked like,'' he added, chuckling.

Eden sagged against the door frame, scarcely aware of the peddler's leave-taking. Her worst fears were being realized. Rodney was here! In Virginia! It was only a matter of time before he found and killed her!

She pressed her hands over her ears. She could still hear his screams. *Bitch! I'll kill you for this! I'll kill you if it's the last thing I do!*

The memory filled her with terror, a fear as great now as it had been the night she had fled London with only the clothes on her back and not a farthing in her pocket. Panic engulfed her in great waves, drowning logic, swamping reason.

She was no longer safe.

Galvanized into action, she frenetically stuffed clothes and food into a cloth bag. As an afterthought, she added money Justin kept in a tin box in the cupboard. She paused at the cabin door. Moisture clouded her vision. Determinedly she blinked back the tears. For a brief time she had been happy here, happier than she had ever been in her life. But she had to flee.

Justin! Eden bit down on her lower lip. She couldn't leave without saying good-bye. A note. She'd leave him a note. Dashing to the chest, she took out quill and ink and hastily scribbled a message, then left without looking back.

Knowing she could travel faster on horseback, Eden

went directly to the weathered shed that served as a stable for two horses Justin owned. The bay and saddle were missing, leaving only a gentle-eyed mare.

"C'mon, sweetheart." Eden grabbed a bridle and coaxed the bit into the horse's mouth. "Good girl." She nervously patted the animal's neck. Tugging a block of wood alongside the mare, Eden heaved herself onto the bare back. She dug her heels into the flanks and gave the mare its head. Distance. She needed to put distance between herself and Rodney.

I can't stay.

"What the hell is that supposed to mean?" Justin reread the note for the twentieth time.

"It means exactly that." Bear gripped Justin's shoulders and gave them a rough shake. "She's left ya, friend. Yer beautiful lady wife has left ya."

"I don't believe it," Justin persisted doggedly. "I *can't* believe it!"

Bear gave him another shake. "She left a note, took clothes, food, money, and yer horse. What more does it take to convince ya?"

Justin twisted free, his hand raking his hair as he paced the length of the cabin. "Why? I don't understand why."

"The woman wasn't cut out fer life in a backwoods cabin. She pegged ya for bigger 'n better things. When it didn't work out, she took off."

"I'm going after her."

Disgusted, Bear wagged his shaggy head. Men could act such fools over a pretty face. They had been arguing about Eden's disappearance since both men had returned to the cabin shortly after nightfall and discovered her missing. They had even gone to see Crazy Mary, but the old crone could give no clues to Eden's whereabouts. It was all Bear could do to keep from saying "I told you so." He had never seen his friend so distraught. All things considered, it was probably best to keep his opinions to himself.

"Leave it be, Justin. Yer better off without the durn woman."

"Why would a woman who was planning to leave buy cooking utensils from a peddler?"

Bear threw up his hands. "How do I know what goes through a woman's mind? Maybe once she bought 'em she didn't want to use 'em."

"I'm going after her," Justin repeated stubbornly. "I have to know what caused her to run. Will you help me find her or not?"

Bear cursed under his breath. "Yeah," he mumbled. "I'll help."

"Good. We leave at first light. You head toward Williamsburg. I'll follow the road to Richmond." Justin continued to pace. "Not knowing where she is, or if she's safe, is driving me crazy. If anything should happen . . ." He squeezed his eyes shut to block out the image.

"Stop worryin' and get some rest," Bear advised. "She'll be fine. Cats always land on their feet."

Eden woke the next morning, her muscles sore and aching from a night spent curled in a tight ball. Rising, she brushed some twigs and dried leaves from Justin's cloak. At least she had had the good sense to bring something warm. The nights were still cool. She went to the creek and splashed cold water on her face, then, cupping some in her hands, drank deeply. The cloak was the only sensible clothing she had taken, she thought grimly, thinking of the three pairs of stockings and nightgown she had brought along.

After breakfasting on bread and cheese, she climbed onto a tree stump and once more mounted the dependable little mare. Her past experience riding bareback at Sommerset had finally stood her in good stead.

The skill had cost her dearly, Eden recalled. She had learned it secretly as a young girl of twelve living on her stepfather's vast estate in the English countryside. Riding bareback had been a challenge at first, a game to wile away the lonely hours. Proud of her accomplishment, she had bragged to Rodney after swearing him to secrecy. Rodney had immediately betrayed her trust by reporting her daring to his father.

Her stepfather had been livid. Though he never raised his voice, never struck her, he had more effective methods of quelling what he termed her rebelliousness. He instructed the housekeeper to strip Eden's room of all personal belongings, including her books. She was locked in her room for weeks, a virtual prisoner. Even the maid who brought her meals of gruel and bread twice a day was forbidden to speak to her. At the end of her incarceration, Eden was ready to beg her stepfather's forgiveness. She had never again attempted anything that might offend him.

Afterward, Rodney had apologized profusely and gifted her with a box of her favorite chocolates. Following weeks of eating nothing but bread and gruel, the rich candy had made her deathly ill. She had never since cared much for chocolate.

Eden urged the horse into a canter. Cruel, unpredictable Rodney. He was capable of anything—even murder.

The sound of carriage wheels alerted Eden that someone was approaching from the opposite direction. She nudged the mare to the side of the road and waited until the vehicle had passed, repeating this precaution again and again as traffic on the road increased toward midday. Spotting a lesser-used road angling from the main thoroughfare, Eden altered her course.

Fatigue eroded the panic that had driven her for over twenty-four hours. Justin slipped into her thoughts with increasing frequency. She mourned his loss as though he had died. For, indeed, leaving him was to her a death of sorts. She refused to think of how things might have been had she stayed. If Rodney had found and killed her, Justin would have been in jeopardy as well. Rodney would leave no witness to his foul deed. Eden glanced around in dismay. The lesser-used road had turned into a trail, then disappeared completely. She was hopelessly lost.

At day's end, too tired to eat, she slipped from the horse, pulled Justin's cloak around her, and once more curled into a ball at the base of a tree. She fell asleep remembering the feel of Justin's arms.

"Lookie here. See what I found."

A pair of long shadows fell across Eden, blocking out the sun's rays. Feeling disoriented, she blinked sleep from her eyes. Two men, bearded and unkempt, stood over her. The older one was large and burly, his fat stomach oozing over the waist of his pants. A crooked nose and a jagged scar along one cheekbone proclaimed him a fighter. In comparison, the younger man, not more than a year or so older than herself, was small and slight with greasy shoulder-length hair and a scraggly beard.

"Purty little thing, ain't she?" the larger one said.

"Sure is, Pa."

A shiver of unease slithered down Eden's spine. Clutching the edges of the cloak together, she inched away.

"I've always hankered for a purty little girl all my own. Can I keep 'er, Pa?"

"Who are you? What do you want?" Eden started to rise to a sitting position only to land flat on her back, a rifle butt pressed solidly to her breastbone.

"Name's Zebulon Hale." A wide grin split the man's bearded face, revealing gaping spaces where his teeth had been. "This here's my boy, Junior."

"Howdy." The younger one leered. He knelt on one knee and picked up a lock of her hair. "Ever see hair this black, Pa? Betcha it even smells good."

Eden tried to wriggle away, but the increased pressure of the gun butt prompted her to lie quietly.

"Please, Pa, can I keep 'er?" Junior wheedled. "Been a long time since we had us a woman up on the mountain."

Zebulon pulled a plug of tobacco from a back pocket and bit off a chunk. "Yup, not since Mabel up and died birthin' her brat."

"Nice tits." Junior placed a grimy hand over Eden's breast and squeezed none too gently. "Nicer 'n Mabel's."

Fury spawned by fear lent Eden courage. In one lithe movement, she pushed the stock of the gun aside and rolled to her feet. She faced them glaring, her hands curled into claws, her hair a stormy cloud around her pale visage.

The men seemed more amused than concerned.

"Ain't she somethin', Pa? I jest gotta have 'er."

"She's somethin' all right. You gotta good eye for the ladies, boy. You can keep 'er on one condition."

"Sure, Pa, anythin' you say." Junior's eyes were fixed on the rapid rise and fall of Eden's breasts, visible where the cloak had separated.

Zebulon licked his lips. "You gotta share 'er with yer old man."

"Animals!" Eden spat. "Both of you."

"She's got you there, Pa." Junior slapped the side of his leg in glee. "Mabel use ta say you was nothin' but a ruttin' boar."

The older man laughed until the gut hanging over the top of his pants jiggled.

Eden's gaze darted from one to the other. She swallowed. Her only hope was making a mad dash to the horse and outriding the pair. Cautiously she backed away. The smiles gradually faded from the men's faces. As if they had all the time in the world, they drew apart until they flanked her, one on either side. For each step she retreated, they advanced. Her breathing quickened. They were the hunters; she was the quarry.

Spinning on the ball of her foot, Eden turned and ran. She was the first to reach the place where the mare was tethered. Frantically she looked for something to stand on. from behind, someone grabbed a fistful of hair and yanked her head back.

"You ain't goin' nowhere 'less I says." A thick forearm wedged against her throat, pinning her to the man's burly form.

Eden squirmed, tugging with both hands at the arm

around her neck, but to no avail. "Save yer strength fer later, missy," Zebulon advised, his fetid breath making her stomach churn. His next remark was directed at Junior. "Get a rope, boy."

Junior obediently trotted over to the pack mule and brought back a length of hemp.

"Tie 'er hands together. No, dummy," his father growled, "in front of 'er. How you expect 'er to stay on a horse if she cain't hold on?" As soon as the last knot was secured, he released her.

Eden shakily sucked in a great draft of air. Her eyes widened in terror as she watched Zebulon unsheath a wicked-looking knife strapped to his waist. He grinned and ran his thumb along the curved tip with its razor sharp edge, savoring her terror. Eden's eyes dilated until only a thin violet circle rimmed the black pupil. With a flash of steel, he sliced the rope in two, then looped a piece around Eden's neck and tied it.

"Here, boy." He handed the free end to his son. "Keep 'er on a short leash 'til you get 'er trained."

"Whatever you say, Pa. You know best."

Squinting, Zebulon studied his captive. Eden forced herself to stand motionless when his ham-sized palm went for her throat. For a moment she feared he was going to pull the cord around her neck even tighter, strangling her. Instead the glint of gold beneath the fastener of her cloak caught his attention.

"What've we here?" He gave the chain a vicious jerk.

A gasp of pain escaped her as the metal gouged Eden's slender neck, leaving a long, bloody scratch. She swallowed hard. Her delicate locket in the man's dirty hands seemed an obscenity.

Zebulon put the locket in his mouth and bit down. "Real gold," he announced. "Oughta bring in a pound or two."

"She's wearin' a ring, too." Junior grabbed Eden's bound wrists and held her hands up for his father's inspection. "Want it?"

Zebulon aimed a stream of tobacco juice at a clump of ferns. "Durn right. Gold's gold."

"No! Please!" Eden struggled in earnest, twisting and turning, making it difficult to remove the ring. In spite of her efforts, Zebulon yanked the wedding band from her finger. Helpless to stop them, she felt tears well in her eyes and roll down her cheeks.

The older man's eyes narrowed to slits. Holding up the ring, he rolled it between thumb and forefinger. "Looks like a weddin' ring. You runnin' away from yer mean old husband, purty lady?"

Eden stared at him through a haze of tears.

Junior yanked the rope around her neck, causing her to stumble forward. "Pa ast you a question."

"Already got my answer. Better get a move on, boy." Zebulon hefted the rifle across his shoulder. "If my woman run off on me, I'd be hot on 'er trail. Her husband probably called out the goddamn militia."

Eden prayed it was so. Dear Lord! What had she done? she wondered as she rode pillion behind Junior. Zebulon Hale followed, leading her mare and a pack mule. At least by Rodney's hand in all likelihood death would have been mercifully quick. With this unsavory pair, life would be hell.

Sunlight pierced the lacy green canopy, dappling the woodland floor with patches of amber. Cardinals and jays flitted among the branches in bright flashes of red and blue. Rabbits, squirrels, and an occasional raccoon rustled through the brush. But Eden was impervious to such beauty.

Her shoulders slumped with fatigue. Perhaps tonight, after her captors fell asleep, she could attempt an escape. If she could find a sharp stone, she'd try to saw through her bonds and be gone before they woke. At the feel of something creeping up her leg, she straightened so abruptly that she almost toppled off the horse.

Junior groped his hand along Eden's leg where her skirt

had hitched above her knees from riding astride. "Wait till tonight, you purty li'l thing."

"Take your hand off me, you vermin!"

"Hey, Pa," Junior called out. "Ever heard tell of vermin?"

"Nope." Zebulon winked and gave Eden a lewd grin. "But I betcha it ain't purty ta look at, is it li'l gal?"

Junior continued stroking her leg. "When we make camp, I'll show you what a real man is like."

Tears of anger and frustration stung her lids. Eden gritted her teeth and forced herself to endure his touch, refusing to dwell on what would happen later.

The day grew warm. Beneath the woolen cloak, her cotton dress was damp with perspiration. Eden tolerated the discomfort rather than remove the cloak. Wrapped in misery, she lost track of time and all sense of direction.

It was nearly dark before Zebulon motioned it was time to stop for the night. Junior lifted Eden down and led her to a clearing. Disheartened, she closed her eyes and sat with her back against a tree stump. The men built a camp fire, despite Junior's objections. Zebulon argued that by now Eden's husband was most likely combing Richmond for his missing wife and wouldn't think to venture west toward the mountains.

Confident, the men wolfed down greasy salt pork, stale biscuits, and boiled chickory root coffee. Junior untied Eden's hands just long enough for her to eat a piece of meat and swallow a mouthful of the bitter brew. The minute she finished, he replaced the bonds. He wasn't taking any chances on her getting away.

From the screen of her lashes, she saw his lascivious gaze fasten on her. Now and then he smacked his lips as though already tasting the ultimate victory. Her flesh crawled. How could she bear to have this scum defile her? Justin! her heart cried silently. Where are you? Forgive me.

"Well, boy, it's time." Zebulon emptied the last of the thick coffee into a tin mug. "Don't forget 'bout sharin'."

Junior's Adam's apple bobbed. "Yeah, sure Pa."

Eden bit her lip. Fear raced through her veins. Hysteria threatened her composure. She was at the mercy of men who didn't know the meaning of the word.

Junior got up and swaggered over to where she sat propped against the stump. She scooted as far from his reach as possible. Her action brought chuckles from the pair.

"You ain't goin' nowhere, gal." Junior gave her a shove that sent her sprawling on her back. "It's bedtime."

Her head struck a rotting log, and pain exploded inside her skull. Before it cleared, Junior fell on her.

He clawed at the neck of her cloak. The fasteners ripped, and along with them, the last of her control. Eden fought like a tigress. Desperation spurring her on, she swung at his jaw with her bound wrists. Her punch connected with a satisfying thud.

"Bitch!" Junior yowled, drawing back.

"No son of mine takes that from a woman!" Zebulon roared. "Show 'er who's boss."

Embarrassed that his father had witnessed his humiliation, Junior viciously backhanded Eden. Her head rocked. Her lip stung; she tasted her own blood.

Junior was quick to seize the advantage. Grinding his mouth against hers, he forced Eden's lips apart, his fusty breath making her gag. Bile rose in her throat, and she swallowed it back. She twisted her head from side to side, trying to rid herself of the suffocating pressure.

Junior's hurtful hands seemed to be everywhere—pulling, pawing, pinching. The bodice of her dress separated with a loud rip and a rush of night air cooled her overheated skin.

"Atta boy! Go to it, son," Zebulon shouted.

Eden tried to kick out, but her full skirts impeded the effort. In the process, her knee connected with Junior's groin. He drew back with a yelp.

"Lady's got spunk," Zebulon observed grudgingly.

"Hold 'er legs, boy. I'll show you how a man beds a hellcat."

In spite of her struggles, they caught Eden's ankles and dragged her legs apart; her skirts tossed up. Her battle became even more frantic when she saw Zebulon Hale unbuckle his wide leather belt with its wickedly sheathed knife and let it drop to the ground. Lust brought a snake-like brilliance to his dark eyes. His pants dropped to his ankles.

"Justin!" Eden screamed as Zebulon straddled her thighs.

An explosion resounded. Zebulon Hale slumped across Eden's body. His heavy weight knocked the air from her lungs. Blood pumped from a large hole in the man's back.

"Move an inch and you forfeit your life." Justin's voice was deadly calm.

Eden craned her neck in time to see her husband step from the shadows, long-barreled pistols held steadily in each hand. Acrid smoke spiraled from one gun, the other was leveled at Junior's chest. Hunkered at Eden's ankles, Junior froze.

His gaze fixed on the ferret-faced man, Justin motioned with the gunbarrel. "Over there. Now!"

Junior scrambled to obey.

Tucking the smoking gun in his waistband, Justin reached down and hauled the dead man off Eden. "Are you all right?" he asked, his eyes still trained on Junior.

"Y-yes." Eden drew in a shaky breath. "I-I'll be all right . . . now that you're here." She tugged at her skirts with her bound hands and pulled herself into a sitting position.

"Don't kill me, mister. I didn't do nothing', I swear."

Justin's gaze swung to Eden, raking slowly over her, trying to assess the damage. He needed to assure himself she was truly safe. At the sight of her torn clothing and bruised cheek, his eyes darkened to the color of tarnished silver, and his mouth tightened ominously.

Taking advantage of Justin's distraction, Junior edged

closer to where his father's belt lay on the ground. Cunning lit his close-set eyes. Arm outstretched, he made a flying dive for the hunting knife. Justin spun and fired. There was no time for careful aim. The lead ball tore through the air, but missed its target by a hairsbreadth.

"Yer luck's run out," Junior smirked. Light glinted off the jagged-edged blade in his right hand, turning it into livid molten steel. "My turn."

A deft flick of Junior's wrist sent the knife flying. Tempered steel whined through the darkness. With deadly accuracy, it was embedded midway to the hilt in a tree trunk, chest level behind the place where Justin had stood a split second earlier.

Junior looked crestfallen when he realized he had missed his target. After mentally pitting his chances against Justin in a fair fight, Junior turned tail and ran. Justin picked himself off the ground and sprinted after him. He caught up with Junior as he reached his horse and whipped him around. Justin's fist crashed into the younger man's face. Blood spurted from a broken nose.

A snarl escaped as Junior dropped to a half-crouched position. Like unarmed gladiators, the men circled each other. Eden scuttled out of their way, fear for Justin making her heart thud painfully against her ribs.

"You yellow-bellied coward. Come on, fight like a man," Justin goaded.

Junior lunged, his fists swinging. Justin anticipated his move and neatly sidestepped, the momentum sending Junior sprawling. Justin threw himself on top of the man. Junior reached into his boot. Firelight gleamed hellishly on cold metal.

"A knife, Justin," Eden cried. "He has a knife."

The warning came too late. The razor-sharp blade sliced into Justin's arm. Both men grappled for the weapon rolling over and over, locked in a life or death contest.

Eden watched horrified, her hands pressed to her mouth.

When the end came, it wasn't with a shout but a gurgle. Neither man moved while blood seeped into the earth around them. Eden held her breath—and prayed. After what seemed like eons, Justin stirred, then shoved away from Junior's still form and got to his feet. Eden's breath escaped in a quivering sigh. Silhouetted by low-burning embers, Justin stood as tall and dark as an avenging angel, staring down at the prostrate form of Junior Hale.

Spinning on his heel, he strode across the clearing to the tree where the blade was embedded and pulled out the hunting knife. He went to Eden and, bending over, sliced the ropes binding her wrists, then carefully sawed through the one circling her throat.

Scrambling up on limbs that were cramped and stiff, she hurled herself against Justin's chest and buried her face in his shoulder, clinging to him. Tremor after tremor rippled through her as memories of the day's events washed over her in torrents of remembered terror. Because of her, both of them had narrowly escaped death. If anything had happened to Justin, the fault would have been hers. She was guilty, she realized, accepting full blame for her actions.

Justin made no move to console her. Instead he remained impassive, his hands at his side, absorbing but seemingly unaffected by the aftershocks that raced through her. Gradually, Eden became aware that no comforting arms offered her shelter, no tender words calmed her fears. She drew back and searched Justin's face. His expression was shuttered, remote.

"What's wrong?" she asked anxiously. "Are you all right?" When there was no response, her eyes quickly skimmed over his muscular frame. She gasped at the bloody rent in the sleeve of his shirt. "You're hurt!"

"It's nothing." Justin brusquely dismissed her concern, then turned away. "I have scum to bury." He found a small spade among the Hales' belongings and started to drag the bodies into the woods.

"Wait!" Eden ran to Zebulon's recumbent form. Careful to keep her face averted from that of the dead man, she knelt beside the body and fished through the contents of his coat pocket. With grim triumph, she found the items she searched for. Sitting back on her heels, she replaced the gold band on the third finger of her left hand and stared at the locket nestled in her palm. "The clasp is broken," she said softly. Getting to her feet, she slipped the golden oval into her pocket. Her spine ramrod straight, her head high, she walked slowly to the camp fire. She was still standing there when Justin returned to the small clearing much later.

"It's done?"

"Yes. It's done."

The cold, harsh tone was unlike Justin's normally pleasant drawl. Eden turned toward him, but he made no move to close the gap separating them. He was different somehow, a stranger, and just as unapproachable. Nervously she laced her fingers together and cleared her throat. "I owe you my life. Thank you."

"Thank you?" He flung the spade aside. "That's all you have to say? *Thank you?* Pray tell, madam, for what reason have I earned your undying gratitude? Because I killed two men? Because I risked my life?"

Eden flinched. Justin crossed the space between them with long strides. Involuntarily she took a step backward.

"Didn't you stop to think of the danger you were putting yourself in?" He grabbed her shoulders and shook her until she feared her neck would snap. "Do you have any idea what those men were really like? What they would have done to you? Was leaving me worth taking on a living hell?"

He released her abruptly, and she collapsed at his feet. "I'm s-so s-sorry," she whispered, trying to control her trembling.

"Sorry isn't good enough." His voice sounded ragged. "Why did you leave me, Eden? Why?"

Eden wrapped her arms around her knees and stared into the dying flames. She felt numb, first by the day's events, but worse still by Justin's defection. He had deserted her when she needed him most. It was too much to deal with. "I couldn't stay," she answered dully.

Justin's broad shoulders slumped. What had he expected, a testimonial of undying love and devotion? Eden had been honest with him from the beginning, but he had been too stubborn, too proud to admit the truth. It was time to face reality. Their love had been one-sided. Eden didn't love him now, never had, and probably never would.

He picked up a log and tossed it into the flames, sending sparks dancing like fireflies into the dark night. He watched as fire licked the dry wood. His arm throbbed and felt too heavy to raise. A leaden sensation oozed through him, spreading thick despair. He had gambled on love and lost.

Finally his practical nature asserted itself. With a sigh, he went to the pack mule and rummaged through the Hales' possessions. His search yielded a jug of corn liquor. Twisting out the cork, he took a long swallow. The liquor singed his throat and burned the pit of his stomach. He took another swig, hoping oblivion would come quickly.

His actions roused Eden out of her stupor. She walked over to him. "At least let me see to your wound." Carefully she peeled back the edges of his shirt to inspect the injury. The bleeding had started afresh, but to her vast relief the blade hadn't bit deep, leaving a clean, shallow cut. "Sit over there." She indicated a fallen tree.

While Eden tended his wound, Justin appraised her with cool detachment. The ordeal had left its mark. Her hair hung in tangles, her gown was soiled, the thin chemise visible beneath the torn bodice. But the purple discolorations on her fair skin bothered him the most.

"That should do it," she said, tying the bandage in place. Their faces were at eye level. Justin caught her chin firmly between his fingers and turned her head first one way, then the other. Eden stared into Justin's gray eyes, hoping to find a glimmer of warmth or tenderness there. She found neither. His gaze was wintery, light without heat.

Justin noticed the abrasions that banded her throat, the

angry gouge from when the locket had been torn from her neck, the bruise grazing a delicate cheekbone. A muscle bunched in his jaw from the effort to stem his rage.

Eden placed a gentle hand on his cheek. "It's over, Justin. Let go of your anger."

Justin gripped her wrist and jerked her hand away. At her grimace of pain, his hold eased. His gaze dropped to her wrists, and his fury mounted when he saw where the rope had chafed the skin raw.

"You little fool. They could have killed you." His voice was hoarse with emotion.

He shifted suddenly, pulling her into his lap. His mouth captured hers, hot and demanding. Mistaking passion for tenderness, Eden responded, exulting that they had been reunited. His need fueled hers, and together they burned hotter, brighter than ever before.

It wasn't until long afterward that Eden realized her error. The flame of passion had turned to ash.

They lay sated, their backs to each other. "Never again, Eden," Justin said, each word clipped and distinct. "If you run from me again, I'll not come searching."

A horse whickered. An owl hooted. Justin's words echoed in her mind. Eden stared dry-eyed into the darkness.

Chapter 14

"You left ill prepared," Justin commented the following morning as he sorted through Eden's meager bundle of supplies. "How did you plan to survive?"

She felt her defenses rise in response to his sarcasm. "I would have found a way." After all, she had once managed with much less.

Justin set out the last of the foodstuffs. "I didn't know riding bareback was one of your accomplishments." He handed her a chunk of bread topped with a slice of cheese and made another sandwich for himself.

Eden bit off a corner and chewed thoughtfully. "Does my ability to ride bareback distress you?" she asked, remembering her stepfather.

Justin regarded her with a strange expression. "Should it?"

Eden shrugged. "Not everyone has such an open mind."

"As soon as we finish breakfast, we'll be on our way. We have a long ride ahead of us."

Justin's uncompromising attitude made their conversation strained. "How did you find me?" she asked when the silence became unbearable.

"A beautiful woman alone and riding without benefit of saddle is apt to draw a certain amount of speculation." He didn't meet her eyes, preferring instead to watch the horses graze on grass and sweet clover. "I asked everyone I chanced to meet if they had encountered such a female.

Several said they had seen one hiding at the edge of the road. When I got as far as Richmond and no one recalled seeing the woman I described, I backtracked until I discovered a trail leading westward. I followed it, and when it ended, I noticed the tracks of four animals. One set was particularly deep, leading me to suspect the animal carried a double burden.''

Eden dropped her gaze and pleated the folds of her skirt. "How much did you see last night? Were you there long?"

"No." Justin rose and saddled the horses, using a saddle belonging to the Hales on Eden's mare. He could still hear Eden shrieking his name. Thank God he had arrived in time.

They exchanged few words during the long journey home. Justin pushed hard to cover the distance in record time. Aside from stopping to purchase food from a farmer on his way into Richmond, they paused only briefly to eat and sleep.

The silent treatment was not unfamiliar to Eden. Her stepfather was master of the technique and had resorted to it often to express his disapproval. If she could tolerate her stepfather's lengthy bouts of silence, why did Justin's indifference cut her to the quick? The Justin she knew, with his charming ways and teasing banter, had been replaced by a silent man with a closed expression. An aching sense of loss began to build within her heart.

They arrived at the cabin long after nightfall of the second day. Eden was exhausted, Justin withdrawn and uncommunicative. Bear was waiting for them. He heaved his cumbersome bulk from the bench and regarded Eden with loathing. "Found 'er, I see."

"Yes, I found her."

"Where was she?"

"Heading west toward the mountains."

"What the hell made 'er head off in that direction?"

Eden was tired of the conversation flying back and forth over her head. "If you gentlemen don't mind, could you please continue this discussion later?" She heard the petulance in her voice, but couldn't help it. After days of riding, she felt tired, irritable, and dangerously close to tears. All she wanted was to bathe away the grime of travel, then crawl between cool cotton sheets and sleep.

For the first time since the night he'd found her, Justin studied Eden closely. She looked like a bedraggled waif. Her face was pale and drawn, with dark circles beneath her eyes, the high cheekbones and delicate hollows more pronounced. Wisps of hair had escaped her braid to curl along her temples and cheeks. His gut wrenched. She seemed fragile enough to shatter into a million pieces. He wanted to take her in his arms and delude himself into believing things could be the same as before. But they couldn't, he reminded himself sternly. Squaring his jaw, he resisted the notion.

He slapped Bear on the back. "Help me unsaddle and feed the horses. I want to hear how you've managed in my absence."

Bear grunted his agreement, then shot Eden a final resentful glance before following Justin.

Eden looked around her. The cabin's quiet welcome brought a peacefulness that soothed her troubled spirit. It was as though that fateful afternoon of the peddler's visit had never occurred. With trembling fingers, she removed Justin's cloak and laid it over the back of a chair. After bathing quickly in water she didn't bother to heat, she slipped a nightgown over her head, climbed into bed, and was sound asleep before she pulled the covers up.

"Woulda been better off if ya hadn't found 'er. Woman's no good. She's rippin' ya apart."

"Dammit, Bear!" Justin slammed his fist against the weathered door of the stable. "You were right. I've behaved like a lovestruck schoolboy since I first saw her. I was so sure, so positive, that given a chance Eden would come to care for me. Well, it doesn't work that way. It's time I accept defeat."

Bear tried not to gloat. "Did she say why she left?"

Justin released a mirthless laugh. "Only what her note said. She couldn't stay. I still don't understand what the hell that's supposed to mean."

"I've been tellin' ya all along." Bear leaned against the doorjamb, thumbs hooked in his belt. "She's tired of this kinda life. Don't see no future in it. Can't blame a beautiful woman for not wantin' to waste away in the backwoods."

Justin sucked in a deep breath, then let it out in a whoosh. "Maybe you're right. I only know I can't go on like this."

"Ya need to get away fer awhile, my friend. Give yerself a chance to put 'er out of yer system. That woman has too much power over ya. She's poisonin' yer blood."

"I don't know what to think anymore, Bear. It's hell to love someone and not have them love you in return. Perhaps getting away isn't a bad idea. Maybe it's what I should do. Go and not come back until—as you put it—I've got her out of my system."

"Now yer makin' sense. Why not go up to Philadelphia and visit that kid sister of yers? See how Emma looks now that she's no longer a scrawny kid but a married lady with a little one on the way. Give 'er my regards."

"I'm not . . ."

Bear sensed his lingering doubt. "Don't worry none about yer wife. I'll look after 'er and see she stays put." He thrust out his hand. "My word's good."

Two days later, Eden watched Justin pack. Panic flooded over her just as it had the afternoon of the peddler's visit. Only this time the panic wasn't prompted by fear for her life, but fear of another sort. She was losing Justin. She knew that as surely as she knew Rodney meant her harm.

"You're still angry, aren't you?" A tentative note had crept into her voice.

Justin placed his razor and shaving brush into a leather satchel. "I need to get away."

"I told you I was sorry for the trouble I caused."

"Forget it!"

"Is Philadelphia far?"

"Yes." Justin hoped it was distant enough to make himself forget this violet-eyed temptress. He added a pair of boots to the satchel. "You needn't worry. Bear will be here to watch over you. He'll be within the sound of your voice should you need anything."

"I'm certain Bear will make an admirable guard," Eden said bitterly. She picked up a shirt of fine lawn and folded it. "I was merely wondering when to expect you home." She really wanted to say she'd miss him, but years of keeping her own counsel stilled her tongue.

"You'll be quite safe." He closed the satchel with a snap. "Bolt the door if it makes you feel better."

Something goaded her to try to break through his shell of indifference. "Aren't you afraid I might try to run away while you're gone?" she taunted.

He grabbed her wrist tightly enough to make the fragile bones quiver from the pressure. "Your word, Eden," he gritted.

She gasped, partly in surprise, partly in pain. "Justin, you're hurting me."

His hold slackened, but while it was no longer painful, it was just as inescapable. "Promise me you won't run away."

"There is nowhere to run." *Nowhere safe.*

"Good!" He let her arm fall to her side. "See that you remember."

Eden retreated to the far side of the cabin. She touched the locket at her throat. Justin had repaired the clasp and returned it to her last night just before telling her of his plans to visit his sister. What had come over him? He had become a virtual stranger, seeming to change before her very eyes. He was cold, remote, curt—like the other men in her life. Where was the gentle, caring man she had been learning to trust? Eager to believe he was different, she had been gulled by his sweet kisses and smiling eyes.

She had to make one last attempt at understanding. Her

head held proudly, she confronted him. "Why, Justin? Why are you leaving?"

He faced her across the cabin. Whether dressed in simple homespun or clothed in satin, her beauty never failed to stir him. Though he had touched her body, he had never touched her heart. Because I need you too much, he confessed silently. Because you don't need me enough. Not enough to trust. Not enough to love.

"Why?" He kept his tone devoid of emotion. "After your sudden departure, I think you, better than anyone, should understand my overwhelming desire to get away."

His words dropped like stones, building the wall higher between them.

Bear poked his head in the doorway. "I brought the horses around. Thunderbolt's saddled and rarin' to go."

"Good." Justin slung the satchel over one shoulder. "I'm anxious to be off."

"Justin?"

He paused on the threshold, but didn't look back. "What is it?"

"How long will you be away?" She was proud her voice didn't waver.

"However long it takes!"

Then he was gone.

Eden ran to the doorway in time to see Justin mount the stallion, nod to Bear, and disappear down the path leading to the Richmond Road. Her eyes burned from unshed tears. "Go away. Don't come back. See if I care," she said aloud to the empty cabin.

But even as she said the words, she knew they were a lie.

The nightmares returned.

The first time, Eden's piercing scream brought Bear pounding on the locked cabin door. She stumbled out of bed, cracked open the door, and reassured him she was all right. Bear was no fool. The terror in her scream had been real enough to raise his hackles. He had seen the way her hand had trembled as she brushed dark strands from a face as pale as chalk and dotted with moisture. He had almost felt sorry for her.

Days slid into a week, then two. Nearly a month passed. Alternately, Eden was angry, hurt, confused, and frightened. Always she was lonely. She missed Justin so much it seemed to gnaw at her insides. During the day, countless times, she recalled his piratical smile, the teasing glint in his silver eyes. At night, she remembered his touch. Her longing intensified until she feared she would grow crazed. But thoughts of Justin were a talisman to keep at bay the terror that Rodney would find her and exact revenge.

One afternoon when she felt the pangs of Justin's departure even more keenly, Eden decided to pay Mary a visit. The old woman looked equally pleased to see Eden and invited her inside for cake and cider. Mary's fondness for bright colors was once again evident, this time in the bright red scarf tied carelessly around the neck of her drab black dress.

"You look especially pretty today, Mary."

"Pretty as a mud fence on a rainy day," she said, chuckling.

Eden laughed softly as she lifted the tabby from the chair and took a seat. The cat gave her what seemed a reproachful look before curling into a ball at her feet.

"You're a strange one." Mary took a chair and offered Eden a plate of small cakes. "I didn't expect to like you, but I do."

Eden accepted a pastry. "Why would you dislike me without knowing me?"

"Jealous, I guess. You're a beautiful woman, Eden. Beauties like you tend to be vain and selfish creatures."

"Nanny used to tell me, 'Sweetkins, you'll have to be more than pretty to survive in this world.' " Eden smiled at the fond memory. Nanny Wadkins was one of the few people who had ever shown her affection.

"Your nanny gave you good advice." Mary trained her bright eyes on Eden. "For all your looks, you don't sound as though it's made you very happy. Miss your husband, don't you, dearie?''

The cake stuck in Eden's throat as she started to protest. She washed it down with a swallow of cider, then answered truthfully. ''Yes, I miss Justin a great deal.''

''Do you love him?''

Eden's eyes widened. ''Yes . . . no . . . I-I don't know.'' Her gaze dropped to study the crumbs on her plate.

''Does he love you?''

''He said he did.'' Her voice was small and forlorn.

''You don't believe him?''

''I don't know what to think.'' Eden shoulders lifted and fell. ''I know my running away hurt him. I know he's acted strangely since then. He seems . . . different. Mary''—she leaned forward in her earnestness—''is love something you can turn on and off at will?''

''There, there.'' Mary patted Eden's hand. ''I'm sure that handsome lad of yours loves you as much as ever. A little thing like you, so pretty and sweet, how could he not? Marriage is never easy, not even when two young people love each other.''

Eden twisted her wedding band. ''I'm afraid I know very little about the emotion. How do you know when you love someone?''

Mary stared at her for a long time. Had this beautiful child been so deprived of love that she didn't know what it was? Pity! She clucked her tongue. Jumping up from the table, she went to the cupboard and brought out a jug of homemade wine. ''A chat of this nature calls for sterner stuff than cider.'' She poured two glasses to the brim.

''Men fancy themselves the strong ones. Truth is, they tend to confuse brawn with power. Manys the time I've watched a maid with a comely face and fetching ways come away the victor in a contest of wills.''

The old woman proceeded to fill Eden's head with wisdom garnered from experience and observation. Instead of answering Eden's questions, Mary's advice posed new ones, riddles she would have to try and solve later.

"Enough of my rambling," Mary pronounced at last, feeling a trifle light-headed after drinking two glasses of wine. "What you need, dearie, is to keep busy. I've been thinking, do you still want me to teach you how to spin? Tell you what. I'll give you my spinning wheel."

"Oh, Mary, I couldn't accept such a gift." In spite of herself, Eden darted a covetous glance at the small, cherry spinning wheel.

"Nonsense!" Mary waggled her misshapen fingers in front of Eden. "These old hands are almost useless. Take the spinning wheel, girl, with my blessing."

Eden came around the table and, pressing her smooth cheek to Mary's wrinkled one, gave the old woman a hug. "I'll even knit the wool into a shawl for you." She smiled impishly. "Provided you teach me how."

The remainder of the afternoon passed quickly. Eden proved to be an able pupil. She had the theory down pat; all she needed now was practice. The wooden spinning wheel was awkward to carry, but Eden was determined to bring it home with her. Spinning would help wile away the evening hours.

She was halfway to the cabin when she heard a noise. Setting her burden down, she rested, straining her ears for the elusive sound. Puzzled, she picked up the spinning wheel and lugged it further. She set it down again and wiped perspiration from her brow. Perhaps Mary was right. She should have waited for help rather than struggle with the wheel herself. But with Justin away, who was there to ask? Bear? He had no use for Crazy Mary and even less for her. No thank you. She would manage.

Eden was about to pick the spinning wheel up and try again when she noticed a movement out of the corner of her eye. About ten feet away, bushes had parted, then the branches had swung together as if released from a spring— or a man's hand. Eden's heart tripped faster. Her back stiff and straight, she stood immobile, staring at the site, afraid to breathe. Nothing moved. There was only silence. It came to her then that the stillness was unnatural in a woodland swarming with wildlife. Her flesh crawled with apprehension. Someone, or something, was watching.

"I know you're out there. Who are you?"

She waited. Her breathing came easier, and she began to relax. What a ninny. She had convinced herself that she was, indeed, alone when the bushes rustled and a figure emerged.

Blood roared in her ears. A dark haze clouded her vision. Her legs buckled beneath her and she sank to the ground. For the first time in her life, Eden fainted. . . .

Air fanned her cheeks.

"Ya all right? Please be all right."

Dazed, Eden opened her eyes to find Bear's grizzled face staring down at her.

"I'm really sorry. Never meant to scare ya so. Justin will tan my hide."

Eden moistened her lips. "Wh-what happened?"

Bear used the kerchief with which he had been fanning Eden to dab at the sweat running down his face and trickling into his beard. "Ya swooned clear away."

"I'm fine." She shook her head to clear the fuzziness.

"I know I'm ugly as sin," he said, chuckling nervously, trying to make light of the situation, "but I never gave anyone the vapors before."

"You're not to blame," Eden said, pulling herself into a sitting position, her head still whirling. "Mary gave me a sample of her homemade wine, and it must have made me dizzy."

"Don't go drinkin' none of 'er stuff," Bear cautioned. "No tellin' what the crazy old woman put in it."

His warning brought a wan smile to her lips. "Mary is a sweet old soul who wouldn't harm a flea."

Bear wasn't convinced. "Why are ya cartin' a spinnin' wheel 'round the woods?"

"Mary gave it to me. I was bringing it home."

"Coulda asked fer help 'stead of tryin' to haul somethin' almost as big as yerself."

Eden didn't say a word; one look said it all. Bear, unable to sustain her censure, studied the ground. Eden was amazed to see a telltale flush creep over his face. She had thought him indomitable, but he was human after all. Her generous nature couldn't stand to see him cowed.

"Bear?" She touched his arm tentatively. "Would you please help me carry the spinning wheel home?"

His shaggy head snapped up. After what seemed a long time, he nodded sheepishly. "Glad to."

"Thank you."

Bear helped Eden to her feet and kept his hand at her elbow when she still seemed a bit unsteady. Brushing leaves and twigs from her gown, she was about to tell him she was well enough to go on when she discovered his gaze riveted on her locket. "Is anything wrong?" she asked.

"Yer locket." His voice sounded hoarse. "My mother useta wear one just like it."

"I never heard you mention having a family. This belonged to a friend of mine." She touched the smooth metal reflectively. Painful memories of a young girl consigned to a watery grave emerged from the recesses of her mind. With an effort, she pushed them back. "By the way, Bear, you never said what you're doing out here."

He hefted the spinning wheel as effortlessly as a child would a toy. "Came by the cabin. When ya was nowhere aroun', I decided to do a little checkin'. Heard someone comin' along so I scrunched down in the bushes till I seen who it was makin' all the racket. Didn't mean to scare ya."

Relieved to learn her fears were unfounded, Eden gladly accepted his offer of help.

The following week dragged. Each evening, Eden practiced spinning. Once in bed, she thought of Justin, missing him more than she thought possible. She mulled over

Mary's advice about love. If love had a face, Eden concluded, it would resemble Justin's.

The sound of voices drew Eden to the window early one evening. Pushing aside the curtains, she peered out. In the gathering darkness, she saw Justin and Bear coming up the path toward the cabin. Emotions she didn't take time to identify tumbled through her, one superseding all the others—joy. A joy so intense it was almost painful. Justin! her heart sang. He's home. Dear lord, Justin's home!

In a flurry of motion, Eden dashed to the mirror and inspected her reflection. She wished she had time to change her gown, but the men would be here any minute. Instead she smoothed back an errant curl, pinched her cheeks, and raced to the door. She paused for a moment to compose herself, then opened it wide and stepped outside.

Justin's conversation halted midsentence. He stared at the woman limned in the soft cabin light—slender, graceful, as lovely as ever. Her face was shadowed, and he was unable to read her expression. Did Eden welcome his return or merely tolerate it? He squared his shoulders and moved toward her. It didn't matter.

Eden drank in the sight of his tall, muscular form. He seemed leaner, older somehow, and infinitely precious. She wanted to run down the path and throw herself into his arms, but her uncertainty of his response curbed the impulse. Outwardly serene, a smile of welcome curving her lips, she walked down the path to greet him.

Justin watched dispassionately. He could see her features clearly now. As always, her beauty stunned him. How unfair that her allure was more potent than ever. He steeled his heart.

Her violet eyes shining, Eden stood on tiptoe and brushed a kiss across his cheek. "Welcome home, Justin."

He didn't rebuff her, but neither did he reciprocate her warmth. "Thank you." His manner was detached and cool. "It's good to be home."

Bear shifted his weight from one foot to the other.

''Maybe I should leave. We can go over the figures to-morrow.''

''Nonsense. I have to make up for lost time.''

Eden was puzzled by Justin's aloofness. Was he still angry? she wondered. She dismissed the notion. She was just being overly sensitive. ''You must be hungry after your long journey. Let me fix you something to eat.''

''Don't bother. I already had dinner.''

''Oh.'' Eden felt vaguely disappointed. ''Did you stop at an inn?''

Bear tugged at an earlobe. ''Uh, no. Justin had supper at my place.''

Her glance went from Bear to Justin. A heavy weight seemed to settle on her chest, making breathing difficult.

''I got back this morning, but I went to see Bear,'' Justin explained, then turned his attention to his friend. ''We still have work to do.'' They continued toward the cabin.

Eden stood alone on the path and stared after them. The man who had returned from Philadelphia bore little resemblance to the Justin of her dreams.

Justin went to see Bear, her mind repeated. *He went directly to Bear . . . instead of coming to me.*

Chapter 15

Two weeks passed.

Justin had it all figured out, he thought as he traipsed through the woods. The object was to keep so busy he wouldn't have time to think, to drive himself so relentlessly he wouldn't have a chance to feel, to work so hard that fatigue would smother his need. Simple. But why did a certain look from a pair of amethyst eyes nearly crumble his resolve? Intent on this train of thought, he paid scant heed to the ground underfoot until it was too late.

A trap, concealed beneath dense brush, sprang closed, grabbing his leg with enough force to throw him forward. Pain came next—swift, hot, and excruciating. Justin clutched his leg and writhed in agony. A large steel trap held his left leg in a painful vise. Its teeth had bit through his leather boot and, like monstrous iron fangs, had sunk into the thick muscle of his calf.

Gasping for breath, Justin lay on a bed of decayed leaves. Overhead the green-and-gold umbrella of leaves and sunlight shimmered, faded, then focused. The forest surrounding him was dark and primeval and, except for the manacle on his leg, unblemished by signs of civilization. There wasn't a soul around. And there wasn't likely to be. He must free himself or bleed to death.

Levering himself on one elbow, he looked around, knowing he needed to formulate a plan. Pain made thinking difficult. A large oak stood four feet away. Inch by painful inch, Justin dragged himself along the leaf-strewn

ground to the limit of the trap's anchor chain, each movement sheer agony. Sweat beaded his forehead and upper
lip. At the tree, he closed his eyes and tried to fortify
himself for the ordeal ahead.

His face ashen, Justin opened his eyes and braced the
heel of his injured leg against the base of the oak. With
his good leg, he pushed down on the lever of the trap. It
groaned open. He wrenched his left leg free mere seconds
before the steel jaws snapped shut.

"Aagh!" he cried, nearly losing his hold on consciousness as flesh and muscle were splayed wide from midcalf
to ankle. Runnels of perspiration streamed down his face.
He blinked to clear his vision, then glanced downward.
The shredded pant leg, wet and sticky with blood, clung
to his leg. Dark red liquid pooled on withered leaves.
Justin knew he had to stop the bleeding. Shrugging out of
his shirt, he wrapped the cloth tightly around his thigh
and knotted it.

"I've got to get home," he muttered. With an effort,
he pulled himself to his feet and leaned against the tree
trunk for support. "Got to get home."

Justin spotted a stout branch lying within his reach. Balancing on his uninjured leg, he bent over and picked it
up. Using the branch as a walking stick, he hobbled forward, dragging his injured leg. "Only a little farther," he
said with each slow, awkward step. "A little farther."

Upon reaching the footpath he paused to rest. Bright
sunlight filtered through the treetops. Another hot day, he
thought with detachment. How strange the day could be
so warm, yet he feel chilled to the bone. He shivered.

"Just a little farther." The whispered words became a
litany. His head spinning, giddy, Justin forced himself to
continue. Willpower alone prodded him forward. His stick
thumped the hard-packed earth, the rhythmic sound alternately followed by the scrape of his dragging leg. The
rhythm became erratic. He stopped to wipe sweat from
his brow with his forearm. The forest seemed to close in,
then recede. He shook his head, but failed to clear the

confusion. The universe spun faster and faster. With a strangled cry, he toppled to the ground.

Bear found him sprawled face down, not more than fifteen yards from the cabin. "Justin," he shouted. "Justin!" There was no response. Bear rolled him onto his back. Squinting, he ran his gaze over his friend's form. His eyes narrowed at the makeshift tourniquet tied around Justin's left thigh, then moved down to the torn boot and blood-soaked pant leg. Hefting Justin over his shoulder, he carried him to the cabin, kicked open the door, and stepped inside.

Stunned, Eden stood broom in hand and stared at her unconscious husband slung like a sack of meal over Bear's massive shoulder.

"He's hurt. Hurt bad."

She went utterly still, her figure resembling a wax mannequin, her knuckles white on the broom handle.

"Well, don't just stand there," Bear hollered. "Do somethin'!"

Justin needed her. This one thought penetrated layers of numbing indecision. As surely as if she had turned a latch, Eden locked away the shock, horror, and fear that swirled through her. There would be time for such emotions later; every moment counted now.

Tossing the broom aside, she crossed the cabin and pulled back the bedclothes. Blood dripped across the planked floor. "What happened?" Her mouth was so dry she could barely speak.

The veritable giant of a man laid his burden down with incredible gentleness. "Told ya. He's hurt."

His defensive manner contrasted with the distress on his craggy face. Eden tempered a sharp retort. "Yes, I can see that." Aside from Justin's leg, she wondered if there were any other injuries. Bending over his still form, she placed her hand on his brow, finding his skin cool and clammy to her touch. His tanned face was ghostly pale. Her hands lightly explored each limb, hoping—praying—

she wouldn't find broken bones. "What happened?" she asked again.

Bear shifted from one foot to the other. "Looks like he caught his leg in a trap."

Eden wiped her damp palms on the sides of her apron. "Is there a doctor we can call?"

"Folks 'round here do their own doctorin'." Bear took off his hat and fidgeted with the brim.

"Oh," she murmured, looking at Justin's pale features.

"Look, if it's a doc he needs, I'll ride to Williamsburg and hunt one down."

"No." Eden shook her head impatiently. "There isn't time." Satisfied that only Justin's leg was injured, her gaze settled there. With utmost care, she loosened the cloth wrapped around his thigh. At his soft moan, Eden bit her lip in indecision, then marshaled her inner resources. He needed her. She couldn't fail him. "Help me get his boot off."

The leather felt wet and sticky in her hands. Even the slightest touch elicited a groan. Eden forced herself not to think of his pain or her control would snap. "Hold his shoulders, Bear, while I cut off the boot."

"Cut it off?" Bear's practical nature asserted itself. "Durn fool woman, those are his best boots. Ordered them special from England."

"Unless we take steps to mend his leg," Eden replied calmly, "he'll have no need for a boot."

Bear hung his head. Though he hated like hell to admit it, the woman had a good point. "Reckon the boot's beyond repair anyways," he conceded, offering his hunting knife.

As Eden sliced through the mutilated leather, Justin, hovering on the fringes of consciousness, moaned and thrashed. It took Bear's considerable strength to keep his friend's shoulders pinned to the mattress. Eden refused to dwell on the travesty of mangled flesh that was exposed once the boot thudded to the floor. Gingerly, she grasped a torn edge of his pants and peeled it back.

It was difficult to assess the extent of the damage to the blood-caked limb. At least there was one thing to be grateful for. Except for some oozing around the jagged tears, most of the bleeding had ceased.

A small sound from Bear distracted Eden's attention. A quick glance at his unhealthy pallor sent her scurrying for a chair. "Sit!" she ordered, pushing the chair behind his knees.

Bear's legs buckled, and he plopped down heavily, the chair creaking in protest. His yellow-brown eyes were glassy. Eden placed a hand on his head and shoved. "Put your head between your knees. Now!" One unconscious man at a time was all she could contend with.

As she turned back to the bed, Justin's eyelids fluttered open. Eden felt his forehead. Though his skin was still cool, it was no longer moist. A good sign—she hoped. "You're going to be all right, Justin," she said with a tremulous smile. "Don't worry. I'll take care of you."

"Thirsty . . ." His teeth chattered. "S-so cold."

She had to bend low to hear his words. Leaving only the wounded leg exposed, she drew the quilt over his form, poured water into a mug, supported his head, and held the cup to his lips.

Behind her, Bear drew in a shuddering breath and ran his hands through his shaggy hair.

Eden turned to him with a look of concern. "Are you feeling better?"

He rose unsteadily. "Don't know what came over me. Musta been somethin' I ate." Bear gazed down at his friend's face while avoiding looking directly at the injured leg. "This here's all my doin'. If I hadn't thought I spotted a panther roamin' around and set that damn trap . . ."

"It was an accident," Justin told him weakly. "Only an accident. . . ."

Bear didn't resist when Eden took him by the arm and guided him to the door. "Go fetch Mary," she instructed. "Tell her what happened and bring her here as quickly as possible."

Bear balked at the notion. "What do ya need that crazy old lady fer? Ya got me."

"This is no time to argue. Do it . . . for Justin's sake."

Grumbling under his breath, Bear went in search of Mary. In his absence, Eden tried to convince herself that Mary would know what to do. Once the old woman arrived, everything would be all right. Mary will know what to do, she repeated fiercely as she gathered clean linens and boiled water. When she glanced toward the bed, she found Justin watching her, his gray eyes clouded with pain.

"I have to remove your breeches. I'm afraid it will hurt."

He nodded weakly. "Do whatever you must."

Eden cautiously unfastened the shirt tied around his thigh. While some fresh bleeding occurred, it was less than she had anticipated. Her breath gushed out in a long sigh. Taking a firm grip on Bear's hunting knife, she eased the blade along the seam, then proceeded to remove the garment.

"Your wound needs to be cleaned. I'm sorry, but it must be done." Steeling herself against the pain she inflicted, Eden gently cleansed the gaping wound. Her stomach lurched at the sight of his torn flesh, and she hoped she wouldn't be sick.

Justin clamped his teeth together to stifle an outcry. White showed around his mouth, visible proof of his effort.

Eden tenderly smoothed a sweat-dampened curl from Justin's brow. "You're very brave, though you needn't be. Cry out if you want."

When she finished, the water in the basin was crimson and her white apron was flecked with red.

Justin caught her wrist. "You've done enough. My leg isn't a sight for a lady of delicate breeding. Let Bear, or your friend Mary, tend my wounds."

Obviously during his lapse of consciousness, he hadn't witnessed Bear's near faint. Equally apparent was his lack of faith in her abilities. "I'm not as delicate as you fear."

Eden tugged her wrist free. "I'm neither a hothouse flower, nor a shrinking violet."

"I didn't mean . . ."

She instantly regretted her bristling. She drew a chair to the bed, picked up Justin's hand, and held it to her cheek. "On several occasions, you've asked me to trust you. Now I'm asking you to trust me." Her gaze held his. "No harm will come to you while you're in my care."

It was a vow, quietly spoken but binding. This man, Justin Tremayne, had forced himself into her life, forced himself into her heart. She would never again be the frightened, hapless girl she had once been. She was a woman now, one who knew what it was to love. Her admission brought her neither shock nor surprise. It seemed as basic, as natural as the sun rising in the morning and setting each eve. It gave her courage and made her strong.

"Trust me, Justin," she pleaded softly.

He studied her silently, then nodded his consent. His pain-glazed eyes drew comfort from the sweet perfection of her face and the glowing determination in her steadfast gaze.

Bear and Mary's quarreling voices preceded their entry. Mary carried a willow basket filled with pungent herbs and glass-stoppered bottles. Setting it on the table, she went to the bedside and peered down at Justin's leg. "Tsk, tsk, it's a nasty one," she observed. "Going to need stitching, lots of it. Hope you got whiskey."

Eden sprang from the chair and went to the cupboard for the bottle Justin always kept on hand. She'd considered it another extravagance—until now.

"Put some in a cup, dearie, along with a needle and your strongest thread," Mary directed.

While Eden sought her sewing basket, Mary measured out a thimbleful of colorless liquid from one of her many bottles. "Laudanum to help ease the pain."

"I don't need any," Justin objected, though his tight-lipped countenance belied the fact.

"Of course you don't," Mary said agreeably, "but it

will make it easier on the rest of us.'' She neatly tipped the contents of the glass down Justin's throat before he could lodge further protest.

Mary turned to Bear. ''Over here, big fella,'' she ordered the man who was easily thrice her size. ''Make yourself useful. Hold him steady while we douse his leg with whiskey. It's going to hurt like the devil, but it will purify the wound.'' She wedged a piece of rawhide between Justin's jaws. ''Bite down.''

''What do you want me to do?'' Eden asked, relieved to have Mary take over.

''Hold his foot steady while I pour the whiskey.'' Mary's expression seemed to ask whether or not Eden was up to the task. When she returned the stare without flinching, Mary nodded her approval.

As the alcohol seared his ripped flesh, Justin's body convulsed in agony, his back arching off the mattress, his head tossed back until the muscles in his neck stood out like thick bands. His teeth clenched the rawhide so fiercely that Eden thought he would surely bite it in half. His lithe body quivered much like a bowstring after an arrow has been fired.

''Shh, love, it's over.'' Eden dampened a cloth and wiped the moisture from his forehead.

''Not quite, dearie. You're going to have to do the sewing.'' Mary held up hands crippled with rheumatism.

Eden swallowed hard and accepted the inevitable. ''Let me wash first.'' She poured steamy water into the basin and brought out a cake of lye soap reserved for cleaning chores. Pushing up the sleeves of her dress, she scrubbed from fingertips to elbows until her skin was pink and tingly. Her face wiped clear of expression, she sat alongside the bed and fished needle and thread from the glass of whiskey. A sidelong glance at Justin confirmed he had sunk into a laudanum-induced stupor. That would make the task easier for both of them. Drawing in a slow deep breath, she began.

The first stitches were the most difficult. His skin was

surprisingly tough, with a leatherlike consistency. Initially it was hard to gauge the depth of each stitch. Eden's mind emptied of everything but the job at hand. Time and again the sharp needle pierced his flesh. Tiny red dots marked each puncture site, the blood dabbed away with a whiskey soaked cloth. She pulled the lacerated edges carefully together, sewed, then knotted the black thread and snipped the ends with embroidery scissors. She worked quietly, concentrating on making a network of small, even stitches, seeming oblivious to the reality that she stitched flesh not cloth.

Except for the sounds of her precise movements, the cabin was hushed. Straightening at last, Eden accepted the bandages Mary handed her. With Bear supporting the heel of Justin's foot, Eden wound wide strips of muslin around the injured leg from ankle to knee.

"Miracle the bone wasn't broke," Mary said. She began to tidy up, gathering scissors, bandages, and bits of thread. "Bad as it was, it could have been worse."

Bear hovered at the foot of the bed, his face still pasty. "Are you all right?" Eden queried.

"How do ya think I am?" he growled. "Seein' my friend with more stitches than a patchwork quilt? Watched ya the whole time." He shot her an accusing glare. "Didn't bother ya one whit. Yer a cold-hearted wench, Eden Tremayne."

Her expression didn't alter. Picking up the basin of bloody water, she left the cabin.

"You big oaf!" Mary drew herself up to her full four feet and ten inches, and marched over to Bear. "You ought to be ashamed of yourself." She poked a finger in his chest. "Talking to that sweet child that way. You'll rue the day if I ever hear you do that again. Understand?"

All the stories, the many rumors, Bear had heard about Crazy Mary came rushing back. The woman was reputed to be a witch. Did she mean to cast a spell over him? Not that he was superstitious, but it was best to take precautions. "Yes, ma'am," he said with a gulp, retreating a step.

Mary advanced. "Good. See that you don't." She waggled a crooked index finger under his nose. "Now find her and apologize."

"I won't—"

"Listen here," Mary cut him off. "Go tell her you're sorry. Now off with you, shoo." She waved him toward the door.

"No sense arguin' with a crazy person," Bear grumbled as soon as he was out of earshot.

There was no sign of Eden. Bear began to circle the cabin. He didn't want to find her, didn't want to apologize. He didn't even like the woman. Never had, never would. To think she had seen him almost keel over. Downright humilatin'. Wasn't his fault he couldn't stand the sight of blood. Just thinkin' about it had him queasy. Not everyone was like that cold-hearted bitch. Stitchin' up her own husband like she was at a sewin' bee. He had seen more expression on the face of a statue. Rounding a corner of the house, he stopped abruptly.

Eden was kneeling in the tall grass, her back to him, retching repeatedly. When the spasms subsided, she made no move to rise, but slumped back on her heels. Bear watched, uncertain what to do. Eden wrapped her arms about her waist and rocked back and forth. He approached cautiously and tapped her shoulder. When she turned and raised her face, he was surprised to find it wet with tears.

"Justin . . . ?" Her eyes rounded in fear. "Is he worse?"

Bear shook his head. "Uh-uh, he's asleep. I was lookin' fer ya."

"For me?" Sniffing, Eden blotted the tears from her cheeks with the corner of her apron.

Bear reached down and helped her to her feet. "I'm sorry fer what I said back there. I had no call to tie into ya."

"Apology accepted." She gave him a watery smile. "I know how close you and Justin are."

Bear felt lower than a rattlesnake. He deserved to be chewed out or set in his place, not smiled at. He kicked a clump of weeds. "Ya done a good job of sewin'."

"Do you really think so?"

"A doc couldn't a done better."

"I was so scared. When I first saw you carrying Justin, I thought for a moment he was dead." Her lower lip quivered at the memory.

"Don't go worryin'." Bear clumsily patted her shoulder. "Justin's strong as an ox. He's gonna be fine."

Justin spent the next two days in a laudanum-induced fog. When he wasn't racked with pain, fever beleaguered his body. Eden worried over the angry-looking gashes on his leg and prayed gangrene wouldn't set in.

Mary adopted a more pragmatic approach. "Nothing more you can do for him, dearie," she had said after applying a paste of Peruvian bark and beeswax that was believed to contain healing properties.

When Bear came by with a chicken, Mary taught Eden how to prepare a nourishing broth. Eden patiently spooned the liquid between Justin's parched lips when he was conscious and sponged his body with cool water when he was caught in the grips of fever. Time passed in a blur.

On the eve of the second day, the candle had burned to a nub when Eden woke from the chair with a start to discover Justin watching her. Untangling herself from the blanket, she painfully uncurled her cramped legs. Perching on the edge of the bed, she rested her hand against Justin's cheek. The skin beneath the bearded stubble was cool and dry, no longer feverish. The silver eyes were clear and lucid.

"Your fever has broken." She sighed happily. "How does your leg feel?"

The corners of his mouth curved in a wry smile. "Like I stepped into a steel trap."

"Would you like something for the pain?"

"It's bearable, but I would like a drink of water."

Eden's bare feet skimmed the floorboards. She didn't know whether to laugh or cry. Her prayers had been answered. Dear Lord, Justin would recover.

He propped himself on an elbow. Under the near-transparent folds of her nightgown, Eden's graceful form was tantalizingly evident. Her dark hair fell in a single plait over one shoulder. She was his own beautiful angel of mercy, and he was content just to watch her. Accepting the glass he handed him, he thirstily drained the contents.

"One more request."

"Anything."

"Come to bed." He threw back the bedclothes and patted the empty space beside him.

To hide her emotion, Eden turned her back for a moment and placed the glass on the nearby chest. How she yearned to be close to him again in every way possible. Did Justin want that, too? Perhaps they could begin to rebuild what they had lost.

Snuffing out the candle, she slipped between the sheets. She curled on her side and, keeping in mind not to jar Justin's injured leg, rested her head lightly against his shoulder.

"That's better," he murmured drowsily. "After everything you've done for me, I couldn't very well let you sleep in a chair."

Eden died a little inside. *Gratitude.* Now she understood how Justin must have felt on their wedding night. If gratitude was the sole reason he had invited her to share his bed, it wasn't the place she belonged. She eased away to face the wall. Tears rolled silently down her cheeks and dampened the pillow.

Beginning the next morning, Justin's convalescence progressed at a steady and predictable rate.

"I'm famished," he announced. "Though I can't fault your chicken broth, I want something I can chew."

Eden was delighted with the request. She prepared a soft-cooked egg, a piece of lightly toasted bread, and a mug of tea. When Justin finished his breakfast, he rubbed a hand over his raspy growth of beard and grimaced. "I'm sorely in need of a shave and a bath. Soon I'll look as disreputable as Bear."

Eden gave him an arch look. "I think you look distinguished in a beard." She picked up the breakfast dishes. "Much older, of course . . ."

"Well then, before I'm mistaken for your grandfather, fetch me my razor."

Eden brought his shaving things along with a basin of hot water and a hand mirror. With her help, Justin propped himself against the head of the bed, pillows cushioning his back. Sitting on the edge of the bed and angling the mirror so he could best see his reflection, she watched him lather the brush with soap and spread a thick layer over both sides of his face and neck.

The faint essence of wildflowers teased his senses. The lush fullness of her breasts brushed his bare chest each time she adjusted the angle of the mirror. "Damn," he cursed when the blade knicked his skin for the fourth time. Annoyed, he tossed the razor aside.

"The fever has left you weak as a kitten." Eden picked up the razor. "May I?"

Justin eyed her warily. Until his leg mended, there would be no escaping her. Resigned, he laid his head back while Eden plied the well-honed blade. He watched through slitted eyes. She tilted her head first one way, then the other, her lips pursed as she regarded the results. She looked soft, sweet, and utterly feminine. Tomorrow, he decided, he would shave himself—or grow a beard.

He dozed on and off for most of the day. The following afternoon he was determined to get out of bed over Eden's objections.

She looked dubiously at his bare sun-bronzed chest. "Mary said she would be by for a visit later." She rummaged through the bottom drawer of the chest and pulled out the nightshirt she had been keeping as a surprise. "Here," she said shyly, presenting the shirt. "This is for you."

Puzzled, Justin took the folded garment from her hand. "What is it?"

"A present."

He held it up by the shoulders. "A nightshirt?" he said in amazement. "You made me a nightshirt?"

"I remembered that on our wedding night you said you didn't own one." She flushed. "I couldn't think of anything else you needed and thought you might like one."

Touched by the unexpected gift, Justin smoothed his hand over the precisely stitched garment monogrammed with his initials. "I remember buying the fabric so you could make yourself a petticoat."

"I already have one petticoat. How many do I need?" She gave a small laugh.

"Thank you," he told her solemnly, then slipped the knee-length garment over his head. "It must be lonely for you isolated here in the backwoods. Yet you never complain. Why not?"

"I'm accustomed to keeping my own company. Besides," she said with a shrug, "why should I be lonely when I have you, Mary, and Bear for companionship?"

Justin felt a twinge of guilt. He had selfishly discouraged visitors, telling them his bride would prefer not to receive callers until she was established as mistress of Greenbriar. Most women would have chafed under such a restriction, but not Eden. Instead she seemed content with the friendship of an eccentric old woman, a surly overseer, and a temperamental husband. He absently rubbed his smooth-shaven jaw, feeling he didn't understand her any better now than before they had wed. What Eden needed was a friend. If he couldn't be that person, at least he could provide one. It was something to think about.

"If you're still determined to get up, let me help you to a chair."

With Eden's support, Justin hobbled across the cabin

and was sitting, his leg propped on a chair, when Bear arrived a short while later.

" 'Bout time." Bear grinned his approval from the open doorway. "Thought ya'd tire of lazyin' around. I brung ya somethin'." Reaching to the side, he produced an improvised crutch made from a young sapling. The bark had been peeled away, leaving the wood smooth and shiny. Two smaller branches protruded. The padded one at the top tucked neatly under Justin's arm, the other for his hand was located midway down and was intended to bear his weight.

"This seems the day for gifts, and it's not even my birthday," Justin quipped as he struggled awkwardly to his feet. "Thanks, friend. Let's see how well this apparatus works."

Eden watched from the table where she was slicing carrots to add to the rabbit stew cooking over an open fire outside, the weather being far too warm to use the fireplace. "It was kind of you to provide the meat. You will join us for supper, won't you, Bear?"

"Hoped ya'd ask. Could smell it cookin' halfway down the path."

"Good. Mary will be joining us, too." Eden wiped her hands on her apron. "If you gentlemen will excuse me . . ."

She went outdoors and added the vegetables to the simmering kettle. After stirring the savory contents with a large wooden spoon, she sampled the broth to see if it was properly seasoned. Perfect, she decided, except it needed a dash of salt. Remembering she had left the salt cellar on the table, she started for the cabin. She just outside the door when she heard the men discussing her cooking skills. Pausing, she listened.

"I never thought I'd see the day you were eager to accept a dinner invitation," Justin said, chuckling.

"Me neither," Bear replied. "Yer wife's turned into a decent cook. Surprised me, she did. Pity she won't get a chance to practice once ya move to Greenbriar."

Eden frowned. The conversation had ceased to make sense. "Move to Greenbriar?" she repeated, stepping into the room. "What are you talking about?"

The men exchanged uneasy glances.

Justin eased himself into a chair and leaned the crutch against the edge of the table, needing time to frame a suitable response.

His plan to show her Greenbriar when it was finished was impossible now. Oh, why had he ever listened to Bear? The situation was going to take a lot of explaining. He tried a direct approach. "Eden, I'm sorry you had to find out this way, but I'm the owner of Greenbriar."

"But I thought . . ." Her confused glance encompassed everything within the cabin's four walls.

"I know what you thought, but I deliberately misled you. The house overlooking the river is Greenbriar, not this cabin," Justin confessed.

Stunned, Eden stared at him, unable to comprehend what he was telling her. Hurt quickly followed, the sensation so intense it made her gasp. Justin had tricked her, deceived her, all the while spouting platitudes of trust. "That house is Greenbriar," she repeated numbly. "It doesn't belong to a friend, it belongs to you."

"I was going to—"

She didn't wait for an explanation. "What else do you own?" she demanded, her voice strained.

Justin cleared his throat. "There's land, and of course field slaves."

"How much land, Justin?" She advanced into the cabin until she stood in front of him, her gaze never leaving his face.

"Nine hundred and twenty acres to be precise," he admitted slowly.

"Nearly a thousand acres!" After months of believing she had wed a poor farmer, Eden found it difficult to imagine such vast holdings. But gradually the truth penetrated layers of shocked disbelief. Outrage swept over her, numbing the initial pain of his deception. "You never breathed a word, not even the afternoon you took me on a tour of the house. Just when were you planning to tell me?"

"It was already dark the day you first arrived here. I thought I'd wait until morning to show you the unfinished house. . . . "

"Don't go blamin' Justin," Bear said, tugging on his beard. "Ya see, it turned inta kind of a test."

"A test?" Eden's eyes blazed like blue-violet flames; rage stained her cheeks dusky rose.

"Yeah." Bear squirmed, uncomfortable on the wooden bench. "I told Justin I didn't think ya'd stick around if ya thought he was poor as a church mouse. So we kinda came to an agreement to see what would happen if ya didn't know nothin' about his money."

"Arrogant fool! You believed I married you for your money!" She unleashed the full fury of her anger on Justin. "When were you planning to tell me the truth? The day we moved in?"

"How do you think I felt, bringing you to a crude shelter?" Justin retorted, sounding defensive. He grimly propped his injured limb on a three-legged stool. "Later, when I saw how content you were, I thought there was no harm in waiting until Greenbriar was completed. I planned to take you to your new home as a bridegroom should, to proudly drive up to the front door, then carry you over the threshold. I wanted you to see Greenbriar in its full glory—not as an unfinished house in need of paint and plaster. I was keeping it as a surprise."

"Congratulations," she said scathingly, placing her arms akimbo. "You succeeded!"

"I never meant to hurt you. Trust me, Eden—"

"Hypocrite! How dare you speak of trust! You don't know the meaning of the word!"

"Eden!" Justin reached blindly for his crutch, only to curse when it clattered to the floor. "I understand you're upset, but—"

"Did I pass your test?"

"You're twisting things."

"Did I pass?" she demanded through gritted teeth.

Justin levered himself to his feet and hobbled toward her. "Of course you did."

She flung her hair over her shoulder. "What, pray tell, is the prize? You? Or Greenbriar?"

He reached for her, but she stepped back so quickly that he nearly lost his balance. Her eyes brimmed with tears she refused to shed. "Well, I don't want either. Not either. . . . " She turned and ran.

Chapter 16

"Want me ta go after 'er?" Bear asked.

"No." Justin sighed. "She needs time alone." He turned and, limping to the chair, slumped heavily into the leather seat.

"Guess I was wrong 'bout yer lady." Bear studied his battered felt hat as though seeing it for the first time. "I'm sorry, friend. This mess is my fault. If it'll help, I'll go find 'er and explain how it was all my idea."

Justin rested his head against the back of the chair. His eyes closed wearily. "I make my own decisions. No one forced me. I accept full blame for my actions."

"Well, I better be on my way." Bear shuffled toward the door. "Got work ta do."

Justin's leg throbbed unmercifully, but the pain was no worse than he deserved. His suffering was insignificant compared to the distress he had read in Eden's eyes when she learned of his duplicity. He laughed aloud at the bitter irony of the situation, the sound harsh in the cabin's stillness. All these months he had failed to be open and honest with her, hoarding the secret of his wealth and holdings for purely misguided and selfish motives. How often had he upbraided her for the same lack of openness he himself was guilty of? Eden was right—he was a hypocrite.

She returned to the cabin through the lowering darkness. Her mindless flight had ultimately led her to Greenbriar. Since it was Sunday the house was deserted, and she had wandered through its rooms, absorbing its tranquil beauty. She felt calmer now, her anger spent. Her foot-steps plodded along the twisting path. Would Justin be relieved to see her, or would he be angry? She paled, recalling the spate of childish name-calling she had in-dulged in. She knew full well how her stepfather would have reacted to such insolence.

Upon reaching the cabin, she paused. The fire in the outdoor pit had long since died. The iron cooking pot, crusty with charred remnants of rabbit stew, lay to one side. There was no light coming from within the cabin.

With trepidation she pushed open the door and stepped inside. Squinting while her eyes adjusted to the gloom, Eden glanced half-fearfully at the empty bed.

''Eden.'' Justin rasped her name.

She started at the sound of his voice. Turning, she found him slouched in his chair.

''Are you all right?'' he asked. ''I was worried about you.''

Eden swallowed the lump that rose in her throat. She hadn't prepared herself for his concern. ''I'm fine, thank you.'' She crossed the room and lit a candle. When she faced Justin, she was appalled by his appearance. His skin was the color of tallow; his lips formed a taut line. A frown wrinkled her brows when she observed his band-aged leg. ''The swelling is worse. You ought to be in bed. Let me help you,'' she said, starting toward him.

''I'm not a cripple.'' Grabbing his crutch, Justin awk-wardly hauled himself to his feet and hobbled toward the bed. ''I can manage.''

Fighting the urge to protest, Eden went instead to the cupboard and poured a small measure of painkiller. She held out the glass to him. ''Here, take this.''

''No.'' He shook his head stubbornly. ''We need to talk.''

''Drink it down or I'll send for Mary and her leeches.'' Recognizing the obstinate set of his jaw, Eden relented. ''Please take your medicine. Then we'll talk.''

Justin accepted the glass and drank its contents without

further argument. He caught her wrist as she was about to step away, his grip surprisingly strong considering his weakened condition. "I never meant to hurt you—you do believe that, don't you?" His hold tightened when she tried to jerk free.

"I don't know what to think after today."

"At first I only wanted to prove Bear wrong about you." He ran his tongue over dry lips. "Later, vanity got in the way of common decency. I'm truly sorry." His words slurred and his grip slackened. The strain of the past afternoon took its toll, and Justin slid into unconsciousness.

For long hours, Eden huddled in the wing-backed chair and watched her sleeping husband. She recalled with clarity the night he had brought her to the cabin; there had been moments of brooding silence between them, and others fraught with embarrassment. She also remembered Bear's antipathy. Gradually she began to comprehend what had prompted Justin's deception, and with understanding came the dawn of acceptance.

Justin's strength rebounded in the days that followed. Each day the swelling and redness in his injured leg decreased. Except for the zigzag lines of neat black stitches, his leg looked almost normal.

However, tensions between the pair escalated. They behaved like overly polite strangers, each wary of offending the other. Justin reverted to the aloof manner he had adopted upon his return from Philadelphia. Eden was miserable, but too proud to let it show. The nights were by far the worst. Their backs to each other, they hugged opposite sides of the mattress and pretended to sleep. Not once did Justin attempt to make love to her. Indeed, he hadn't so much as held her in his arms since the horrible night he had rescued her from the Hales.

A scant two weeks after Justin's accident, they traveled to Williamsburg. Eden had initially balked at the plan, arguing that Justin's leg needed more time to heal, but Justin had insisted he was fit to travel and that the trip would be less taxing than resuming his activities at Green-briar. Weighing the options, Eden had conceded that Williamsburg was the logical choice.

The city was every bit as charming as Eden remembered. The same could be said of Nora Cunningham, although during the past three days, she had subjected her houseguests to numerous small, informal gatherings that left Eden little time to brood over Justin's persistent coolness. Thus far, the carriage ride Nora suggested had provided their only opportunity to be alone. Justin avoided personal topics by acting as a tour guide. He ordered Hiram to stop the carriage in front of the Powder Magazine to watch a militia muster.

"King George's finest." Justin inclined his head toward the red-coated soldiers parading in front of the magazine. "Lobsterbacks." He pointed to a second group practicing on the green, these men garbed in homespun, some carrying muskets, others sticks. "With few exceptions, every British subject who is a free, white, able-bodied man between the age of sixteen and sixty is a member of the colonial militia. We're responsible for our own protection against pirate raids, Indian attacks, and slave revolts."

Eden couldn't help but marvel at the disparity between the two military groups. "I hope the day never comes when such a motley corps is pitted against England's might."

Justin motioned for Hiram to drive on. "Don't be fooled by flashy red uniforms and shiny brass buttons. If it comes to a showdown, courage and determination will be the deciding factors."

The well-sprung carriage continued down Duke of Gloucester Street. Heads turned to admire the handsome young couple seated inside. While women cast envious glances at Eden's exceptional beauty, men viewed her with blatant interest.

The carriage rolled past a thin man of medium height standing on the cobbled walk near a row of shops. His face was averted while he removed a pinch of snuff from a small enamel box. Eden admired his finery. In his bottle green coat lavishly rimmed with gold braid, he was the epitome of a fashionably dressed man. Delicate lace cascaded below a stock of fine Holland linen. A black taffeta bow was attached to the queue of his peruke. As she was about to glance away, he raised his head, and she saw the jagged scar that extended beneath a patch covering his left eye.

The skin at the nape of Eden's neck pricked; apprehension slithered down her spine. She swung her head for a second look and glimpsed the disturbingly familiar figure as he vanished between two buildings.

"Stop!" she cried. "Stop the carriage!"

Surprised at the outburst, Justin turned to Eden, alarmed by her sudden pallor. Gripping the side of the carriage, she stared at the space between a grocer's shop and a tavern.

"What's wrong?" Justin demanded.

"A man," she gasped. "A man with an eye patch. Find him, Justin. I have to know for sure."

Her voice was so faint, he had to lean forward to catch her words. Baffled by the strange request, he looked at the spot again, but saw no man of that description. Who did she think she'd seen? A friend? A former beau? "There's no one there."

"But he was there." She clutched his sleeve and spoke with urgency. "I saw him."

Deciding to humor her, he pried her fingers from his coat and climbed from the carriage as quickly as his injured leg would allow. "Wait here. I'll be right back."

Her heart in her throat, Eden watched Justin hobble down the narrow passageway, then disappear from sight. Anxiously, she touched the locket at her throat.

As Justin had expected, he found no mysterious stranger wearing an eye patch lurking about. He made a cursory inspection of the grocer's shop as well as the dependencies of the tavern before slipping inside the rear door into the common room. The occupants quaffed tankards of ale and rum punch. One grandfatherly man wore wire-rimmed spectacles. None wore an eye patch. Justin nodded to the serving girl and exited by the front entrance, his brows drawn together. Who was this man? He hurried toward the carriage, determined to find out.

Eden's eyes were full of questions as she watched Justin climb inside. "Home, Hiram," Justin ordered. Hiram clucked to the matched team, and the carriage lurched forward. "I searched, but there was no sign of your one-eyed man," Justin said. "Now will you kindly explain, madam, who you think you saw?"

Eden rested her head against the velvet cushions, her heart resuming its normal pace. "I must have been mistaken. He reminded me of someone I used to know. My imagination must have been playing tricks."

The incident had happened so quickly. Now that she could think clearly, she decided she may have been premature in assuming the man was Rodney. Surely, she rationalized, there were other men in Virginia who wore eye patches. She must learn to control the hysteria that bubbled in her veins each time a one-eyed man was mentioned. *But what of the one-eyed man the peddler had spoken of?* an inner voice persisted. *The one asking about a woman named Eden. . . .*

Justin's fingers drummed on the back of the seat. Eden was being evasive again, and it infuriated him. Damn! Why did she have to be so secretive? He'd once believed he could break through the shell she had erected around herself. He'd naively thought love and patience could conquer all. Fool! Love had gained him nothing—except gratitude. And as for patience, his had just run out.

When the carriage pulled to a stop in front of the house on Francis Street, Justin alighted first, then assisted Eden down. She started up the walk, but turned when she realized he had made no move to follow. "Aren't you coming?"

"I have workmen to interview and hire if Greenbriar is

to be completed by September. Tell Aunt Nora I'll be back for tea.''

Eden didn't have a chance to ponder Justin's action. An excited Nora Cunningham brushed past Prudence with a hasty greeting. "Eden, child, I could barely wait for your return. You'll never guess what came shortly after you left for your ride with Justin."

Eden smiled fondly at the woman. "Whatever it was, I can see it pleased you."

" 'Pleased' is too mild a word.'' With a dramatic flourish, Nora snatched up from the hall table a vellum envelope bearing an official seal. "This, dear girl, is a coveted invitation for the most important social event of the summer.'' She waved it triumphantly. "A ball tonight at the Governor's Palace!''

"How wonderful!'' Eden tried to imitate Nora's enthusiasm.

"Yes, isn't it? I hesitated to mention the ball sooner. I wanted to wait until I was assured you and Justin would also be issued an invitation. What more auspicious way to mark your official acceptance into Tidewater society.'' Nora patted Eden's arm. "Mrs. Peabody, the mantuamaker, will be here within the hour to make final alterations.''

"Alterations?'' Eden echoed.

"Why, yes, dear.'' Nora beamed. "Justin ordered more than a dozen or so gowns made to your measurements. The items he purchased last time were only meant to be temporary. Justin is a very wealthy young man—and a generous one as well. Most of the gowns have been delivered.'' She prodded Eden toward the stairs. "Go look at your pretty new things. I'll send Prudence up with refreshments.''

Pushing open the bedroom door, Eden drew in her breath. The room was ablaze with colors ranging from icy pastels to vivid jewel tones. Rich velvets, lustrous satins, crisp silks, both flowered and plain, along with others of cotton and linen crowded the available space. Matching accessories lay scattered in gay confusion amidst the open boxes. A young woman with an armload of garments turned from the clothespress with a wide smile. "Bess?" Eden cried in disbelief.

"Oh, Eden, I hoped we'd meet again." Bess dropped the gowns on the bed and gave Eden a fierce hug. "I'm so happy to be in your service. Life was miserable at the Wainwright's after you left."

Eden held the girl at arm's length. If anything, Bess's face was thinner than ever, giving her angular features a pinched look. But at least the anxiety was gone from her green eyes, replaced by genuine happiness. "It's wonderful seeing you again, but what brings you here?"

"Oh, Eden—I mean Mistress Tremayne," the girl hastily corrected in embarrassment, "I owe it all to your husband. He sent his friend, Bear, to buy my articles of indenture from the Wainwrights. Said he wanted someone to be your companion and to help you run the household. Wanted me to be a surprise."

Eden's vision misted, and she blinked back tears. This had to be the nicest surprise she had ever received. Justin was so dear, so thoughtful. "My husband is inordinately fond of surprising me," she replied in a voice husky with emotion, glancing from Bess to the bed piled high with new clothes.

Regardless of the changes in Justin's recent behavior, one trait had remained constant—his innate kindness. Bringing Bess to her was typical of the qualities that had attracted Eden to him from the very beginning. Somewhere along the way, however, her gratitude had been transformed into love.

Prudence interrupted with a tray of tea and cakes, followed almost immediately by Aunt Nora leading Mrs. Peabody, a small, energetic dark-haired woman, and her assistant, a young bond servant of sixteen. Eden spent the rest of the afternoon modeling gown after gown while trying to avoid being jabbed with pins or ripping out basting stitches. Most of the dresses fit beautifully with only a few needing minor alterations.

The fitting finally over, Nora escorted the dressmaker downstairs, giving Bess strict instructions to let Eden rest before preparing for the Governor's Ball.

"Oh, my lady." Bess sighed in admiration. "You look like an angel straight from heaven."

"Thank you, Bess." Eden dabbed scent at the base of her throat and behind each ear, inspecting her mirrored reflection with a critical eye. The white satin gown she had selected was strikingly similar to the one she had worn the first time she had met Justin. Had he ordered it because it reminded him of their initial meeting? Eden sincerely hoped so.

"Wish I could see Mister Tremayne's face when he gets a look at you." Bess tucked a spray of tiny silk flowers into Eden's dark curls. "Do you want me to wait up, Mistress?"

"That won't be necessary, Bess." Eden turned to face the girl. "We know each other far too well to resort to formalities. Mistress Tremayne sounds terribly stuffy. Please, call me Eden, just as you always have."

Bess traced a cabbage rose on the carpet with the toe of her shoe. "Is that proper, considerin' you're a fine lady and I'm only a bond servant? I wouldn't want Mister Tremayne to be sorry he sent his friend to fetch me."

Eden caught Bess's chin and forced the girl to meet her gaze. "Would you rather anger me?"

"No, no, of course not," Bess denied vigorously. "But I don't think I ever seen you get mad, not even with Polly or Mistress Wainwright bein' mean to you."

"I've been known to lose my temper on occasion." Eden grew pensive, recalling how she had stormed out of the cabin after learning the truth about Greenbriar. But Justin had seemed to understand her anger. His attitude—his acceptance of her—afforded her a freedom she had never known.

Picking up a hand-painted silk fan, Eden opened it with a snap. "Beware, Bess, my feathers ruffle easier these days."

Justin stood waiting in the hall just outside the drawing room. He rested both hands on the silver head of his ebony walking stick and watched Eden descend the stairs. Except for her hair, which she had left unpowdered, she appeared much as she had the evening of Lady Butterick's soirée. And just as it had that night, her exquisite beauty stole his breath away.

Drawn by the intensity of his stare, Eden's eyes met his and, for a fraction of time, steel gray melted to liquid silver.

"You look lovely."

"Violet," Eden retorted, then laughed at his bewilderment. "That was the very first word you ever spoke to me. It must be the gown," she confessed. "It reminds me of the evening we first met. Though I failed to recall your name, I remember you tried to guess the color of my eyes."

"They reminded me of wildflowers," he admitted, his tone cool, guarded. "Would you care for a glass of sherry before we leave?"

"Yes, thank you." Eden's optimism faded but perhaps a taste of wine would bolster her morale. She followed Justin into the drawing room, silently admiring his handsome figure. He was resplendent in a black coat and breeches with an embroidered silver waistcoat, clocked stockings, and silver buckles on his shoes. A froth of lace appeared at his shirtfront and spilled over his sun-bronzed wrists. Although he used a walking stick, his limp was barely noticeable.

He poured sherry from a cut-glass decanter and handed it to Eden, noting the slight tremor of her hands as she reached for the wineglass. He returned to the sideboard and poured another glass for himself. "Surely you aren't nervous about tonight."

"I must admit I'm a little apprehensive." She took a sip

of sherry. "I'm not certain how I'll be received in such an illustrious gathering. After all, people know nothing of my background. Gossip must have been rampant when Justin Tremayne wed a bond servant. People are often cruel. We might both be social misfits."

Nora Cunningham came into the room with a swish of lavender taffeta. "Of course, people will be curious. However, you'll be judged on your own merits. Given time, your beauty and charm will win them over."

"Virginians are good judges of quality," Justin agreed. "Life moves quickly here. You'll discover we're less rigid than our English counterparts."

"Don't worry, dear. Cream always rises to the top." Nora declined the offer of wine with a flick of her silk-mittened hand. "Shall we go?"

As Hiram urged the team down tree-lined Palace Street, Nora Cunningham kept up a lively commentary. "The large brick house on your left belongs to George Wythe and his wife Elizabeth. George is a fine lawyer and a member of the House of Burgesses. He's becoming fast friends with Governor Fauquier and is sure to be at the ball." Nora pointed to a clapboard house on the corner. "That's the home of Thomas Everard, the county clerk. Thomas is very active in civic affairs and will also be present tonight."

Eden murmured appropriate responses, dreading the task of connecting not only names and faces but occupations as well.

"The Governor's Palace is probably the most imposing building in all of the Colonies, don't you think, Justin?" Nora asked.

He nodded. "It serves as a constant reminder of the power of the Crown."

They waited to disembark behind a half-dozen carriages. Finally, they stood inside the entrance hall clustered among a small group of people waiting to be announced by a liveried footman. Eden was awed.

A giant sunburst formed by scores of long-barrelled

muskets, their bayoneted tips meeting in the center, was
suspended from the ceiling by unseen fastenings. Still more
muskets, along with numerous pistols and flags, hung on
paneled walls. Swords criss-crossed like palm leaves
flanked arched doorways. The royal coat of arms was
prominently displayed above the marble fireplace, an im-
pressive and intimidating reminder that the military might
of England stood behind the governor of Virginia.

From the entrance hall, guests passed through a set of
double doors leading into the ballroom. Nora Cunningham
was announced first, then it was Justin and Eden's turn.
At a signal from the footman, Justin held out his arm to
Eden.

Poised on the threshold of the grand ballroom, the footman's loud, imperious voice rang out. "Mister Justin Tremayne . . ." He paused. "And his wife, Mistress Eden
Tremayne." He stepped aside.

Eden's hand tightened involuntarily on Justin's sleeve,
then relaxed. Dozens of expectant faces turned in their
direction. Conversation ceased. A ripple of appreciation
came from the crowd as Justin and Eden smiled and entered the ballroom.

Eden's practiced serenity masked her contradictory feelings. Since leaving England, she had imagined her triumphant return to society. Now that her hopes were about to
become a reality, she discovered the prospect fell short of
her expectations. While relieved of an existence marked
by poverty and toil, she knew that worldly possessions
were no guarantee of happiness. The most wonderful period of her life had been spent in a simple log cabin tucked
deep in the Virginia woods.

She nodded to an elderly friend of Nora's who had been
present at their wedding ceremony. Justin smiled at a
florid-faced woman in magenta silk. Together they took
their place in a receiving line to be introduced to Francis
Fauquier, lieutenant governor of Virginia.

The ballroom was lavishly decorated. Crystal chandeliers hung from a vaulted ceiling, their glass prisms spar-

kling like giant diamonds. Gleaming gilt outlined the dentiled woodwork, wainscoting, and elaborate doorframes. On the opposite wall, massive portraits of British monarchs hung in gilt frames on either side of yet another set of double doors, which led into a supper room. A string quartet played in the far corner. The only discordant note to mar the room's elegance was an iron dutch stove, ugly but necessary during the cold winter months.

Eden's gaze swept the luxurious ballroom before resting on the man at her side. "All this time I thought you were a poor farmer, a man of simple means. Suddenly I find myself amidst wealth and splendor. I'm not sure how to act, or," she added with a wistful smile, "even who you are."

Justin's expression was somber. "Then we're equals, for your secrets have kept us strangers."

His words dropped like pebbles into a still pond, sending ripples of shock, disbelief, and sorrow spreading through Eden's mind in ever-widening circles. All he had asked of her was trust, and she had failed him, keeping her secrets, testing his devotion, vainly trying to bury her past. How could she make him understand? She had never learned to trust. Was it too late now?

"Governor Fauquier, may I present my wife, Mistress Eden Tremayne."

"Governor Fauquier." Eden swept into a deep curtsy.

Intelligent brown eyes peered at her kindly from beneath a full-bottomed periwig dressed away from a prominent forehead with soft rolls of curls at either side. "The pleasure is mine, Mistress Tremayne. Your rare beauty transcends this humble setting."

His countenance reminded Eden of a basset hound, a thought which made him seem less formidable. "You're much too kind, Governor," she murmured.

"Kindness musn't be confused with honesty, my dear." He smiled, then said to Justin, "You, Mister Tremayne, have earned the reputation of being a knowledgeable and able planter. Botany is a special interest of mine. I hope we can find an opportunity later to discuss the possibility of cross-breeding certain species of plants that are native to your region.''

''I shall look forward to our talk,'' Justin replied.

The reception line moved on, and Justin and Eden were absorbed into the gaily chattering crowd. The musicians began a minuet, and the floor rapidly filled with couples.

''Unfortunately my leg prevents me from dancing, but I doubt you will lack partners.'' No sooner did Justin utter the words than a young man approached and was subsequently granted Justin's permission to escort Eden onto the ballroom floor.

Another minuet followed, claimed by a bewigged gentleman whose multiple chins were drowned in starched ruffles. A series of reels followed, each one of which Eden danced with a different partner. She wasn't quite sure what had prompted her popularity—curiosity or admiration, or perhaps both.

Out of the corner of her eye, she observed that Justin's injury didn't hamper his own popularity. He always seemed to have the company of one or two sympathetic ladies to keep him amused. While he had been a guest of the Wainwrights, she had observed how easily women were smitten with his pirate's grin and dashing good looks. Still, she felt the sting of jealousy. She wished he'd pay half as much attention to her as he was to the simpering blonde hanging on his every word.

Justin didn't reappear at Eden's side until it was time to escort her into the supper room for a midnight feast. ''Are you enjoying yourself? You don't seem to be at a loss for partners.''

''And you, my lord, don't seem to lack female companionship. Indeed, you seem to have an affinity for blondes.'' Eden favored him with a sugary smile.

Justin paused, plate in hand. ''Do I detect a note of jealousy?''

''Of course not!'' But a fiery blush betrayed her and, she added a crab cake she didn't want to her plate of food.

"Truth is," Justin admitted, "I find dark-haired women much more attractive."

Now it was Eden's turn to pause. Was he referring to her? He was concentrating on the array of delicacies before him and didn't return her look. Again she admired his handsome profile with its straight nose and firm jaw harboring a hint of obstinacy. In his well-tailored black breeches and coat, he cut a striking figure. No wonder he set female hearts fluttering, hers among them.

"There's someone I'm anxious for you to meet," Nora said as she came toward them. "I've saved a place for you at our table. I've been telling George and Elizabeth Wythe all about Greenbriar."

The midnight supper passed quickly and ended with the Wythes extending an invitation to Justin and Eden to come for tea in the near future. The Wythes were proud of their stately brick home designed by Elizabeth's father, Colonel Richard Taliaferro, which was touted as an example of colonial architecture at its finest. Elizabeth, George's second wife, was happy to impart to Eden some of her knowledge on how to manage a large home and staff of servants.

The music started once again, summoning guests back to the ballroom. Eden's head was beginning to pound. Justin was conversing with another planter on the merits of open-fire curing of tobacco versus dry curing. Faced with the choice of returning to a noisy ballroom or taking a quiet stroll in the garden, Eden opted for the latter.

The night was black without benefit of moon or stars; the air enveloped her like a wet woolen blanket—heavy, damp, suffocating. Thunder rumbled ominously in the distance. An almost-overpowering scent of flowers assailed Eden's nostrils, the smell not unlike that of a fine French perfume applied with an indiscriminate hand. She knew the formal garden, with its manicured parterres, must be quite lovely in the daylight, but in the dark only the shell pathway was clearly discernible. The impending storm had discouraged all but a few guests from a late-night stroll.

The shell pathway crunched beneath her slippers as Eden

wandered down the central avenue until it intersected right and left. Not quite ready to return to the ballroom, she turned left. Where the ballroom garden ended, a fruit garden with rows of carefully tended trees began. Just a little further and she would retrace her steps, she decided. The path separated once again. To her right, high walls formed a murky outline. She strained her eyes for a better look.

A holly maze! She had discovered a holly maze. Fascination lured her toward it; curiosity pulled her inside.

If possible; it was even darker in the maze, black against black. The air was cooler, stagnant. She would go only as far as the first bend, she promised herself. It would be too easy to become hopelessly lost in the intricate winding pattern.

She was about to return the way she had come when the now-familiar prickling sensation began at the nape of her neck. Eden froze. She knew beyond a doubt that she was being watched. Fear wrapped icy fingers around her heart—and squeezed. Summoning more courage than she thought she possessed, she forced herself to turn around.

A dark figure stood silhouetted inside the entrance of the maze.

"Who are you?" Her voice quavered.

Silence.

"What do you want?"

The figure took a single step forward.

Eden retreated a pace. "Who are you?" Her voice grew shrill.

A gleeful chuckle struck a chord in her memory. "Rodney!"

The following peal of laughter drove Eden deeper into the maze. The sound rang after her until she was clutching her skirts and racing down the path. Spines of holly snagged her gown and snatched at her hair. She could no longer distinguish the pursuing footfalls from the heavy pounding inside her chest.

Her head snapped back, and she was brought up short. Fearfully, she glanced over her shoulder. A spiny protrusion of holly had entangled a long curl. Her relief was so immense that she clamped a hand over her mouth to stifle a hysterical giggle. Tugging at the snarled strand, she finally succeeded in freeing herself.

Deeper and deeper she ran along twisting, turning paths. A needle-sharp spine scratched her arm, but she was oblivious to the discomfort. The walls of holly were higher than she was tall; she could barely tell where they ceased and the heavens began. A cramp in her side almost made her double over, but she persisted. Instinct failed her, leading her into a blind end. Three towering walls blocked her exit.

As frantic as a wild thing caught in a trap, her gaze darted around, looking for an escape. There was none. Eden tried to quiet her raspy breathing, tried to instill logic into panic. A strong sense of self-perservation came to her rescue. If she stayed where she was, Rodney would find her, a helpless victim awaiting the coup de grace.

Footsteps sounded close by, perhaps even on the opposite side of the hedge where she now stood, quaking. Gathering her wits and her courage, she bolted. A trio of steps sent her hurtling into a pair of open arms.

"Eden?" A familiar voice soothed her.

"Justin!" She grabbed the lapels of his coat and clung to him, half sobbing in relief. "I-I was so frightened. I went for a walk . . . found the maze. I was only going to peek inside. There was a man . . . he laughed . . . started to follow me. I ran and ran . . . b-but got lost." Eden knew she was babbling, but she couldn't check the words that gushed out, almost incoherent.

"Hush, it's all right," he murmured. "There isn't anyone here but the two of us."

"B-but there was. I saw him." Drawing back slightly, she licked dry lips and peered around his shoulder. Justin was right. There was no one. Was her mind playing malicious tricks on her? Could she have only imagined the incident? It had seemed so real.

"What did this man look like? Did you see his face?"

"N-no." She shook her head. "It was too dark."

"Did he say anything to offend you?"

"Nothing. When I asked who he was, he just laughed."
Eden shuddered at the memory.

"It's over. You're safe now." Silencing his better judgment, Justin pulled Eden against him and wrapped his
arms around her. "It was probably a guest out for a breath
of fresh air. Undoubtedly you frightened him as much as
he did you. Poor man probably had apoplexy."

Eden allowed Justin's mellow voice to dissolve her fear.
She closed her eyes and willed her body to relax, feeling
protected in the warm shelter of his embrace. The scent
of sandalwood and tobacco, mingled with musk, awakened her dormant longings.

Justin must have sensed her yearning for his arms tightened around her, and his lips brushed her temple. "Eden,
Eden," he murmured raggedly. "What am I to do with
you?"

"Kiss me, Justin. Please, it's been so long."

He gazed into her upturned face. In the biblical Garden
of Eden, Eve had offered Adam forbidden fruit. In a secluded maze of holly, Eden tempted him with forbidden
fire, a temptation as old as mankind and just as irresist-
ible. Justin issued a groan of surrender, and the pressure
of his embrace increased. His mouth covered hers, vora-
ciously plundering, stealing, robbing the honeyed cavern.
Eden surrendered joyously to the invasion. The kiss
gentled, teased and coaxed, then ended with slow reluctance.

"If we don't return soon, people will begin to wonder."
Justin strove to put distance between them.

Eden murmured her assent, then silently followed his
broad back as he threaded his way through the tall maze.
Her unease returned each time the path divided. How very
simple it would be for a man to lurk unseen in one of the
shadowed nooks and crannies. When they finally emerged,
she released an unsteady breath.

Together they made their way back to the Governor's

Palace. Lightning flickered, turning the landscape a ghostly gray. Eden's nerves were frayed, and a deep weariness seeped into her bones. Once more her thoughts darkened. Had there really been a man in the maze? And if so, had it been Rodney? Or was her conscience so riddled with guilt that she envisioned his disfigured face at every turn?

Justin reached for her hand and, finding it icy, tucked it into the crook of his elbow. "Better now?"

She nodded. "I must look a fright." With dismay, she thought of her pell-mell flight through the maze and smoothed a wisp of hair from her face.

"I have yet to see you when you are less than beautiful." His hand covered her cold one and squeezed it reassuringly. "Even with soot on your face," he added with a small smile. "Governor Fauquier has already retired, and the guests are starting to leave. If you'd rather, we don't have to go through the palace."

"What about your aunt?"

"Aunt Nora wishes to stay a while longer and plans to come home with neighbors."

Justin escorted her around the side of the building toward the coach house, where he singled Hiram from a group of other drivers and instructed him to bring the carriage.

They endured the short ride to Francis Street without exchanging a word. Equally disturbed by the evening's events, each would have been astonished to learn how closely their thoughts mirrored the other's.

Was the man in the maze flesh and blood? Or was he a figment of Eden's imagination?

Chapter 17

A single candle burned in a brass holder on the hall table. The house was quiet. Eden paused, one slippered foot on the bottom step, and looked over her shoulder. "Justin?" she ventured.

"Yes?" The remote tone she had begun to hate was back in his voice.

"I, uh, I never thanked you for purchasing Bess's articles of indenture."

"Your gratitude isn't necessary. Greenbriar is in need of good servants."

"Well, thank you just the same. I'm sure Bess won't disappoint you." She moved to the next step, then waited, watching him shove his hands deep into his pockets. He made no effort to follow her. "Aren't you coming up?"

"Later. I'm going to have a brandy first." His limp was more pronounced as he turned and walked toward the small drawing room. "Sleep well."

"Good night, Justin." She had hoped . . . .

Chastened, Eden climbed the stairs. She was a dreamer, wishing things would be as they once had been. It would be less painful if she were a realist and accepted the fact that Justin no longer cared.

In the drawing room, Justin lit a taper, then splashed brandy into a snifter. Damn! What the hell was the matter with him tonight? He raised his head and tossed back the brandy. All evening he had been like a man possessed. The entire night he could think of nothing but making love to Eden. Beautiful, bewitching Eden. He took a thin cigar from a case, clamped it between his teeth, and bent toward the candle's flame until the tip glowed red. Eden remained as much a mystery now as the day they had wed. She still baffled him, foiling his attempts to understand her. He had sought to lessen his frustration by retreating from her both physically and emotionally. Then, in the maze, when he had taken her in his arms, his resolutions had been put to the test—and he had failed miserably.

Justin poured more brandy and sank down on the settee. His left leg propped on a low stool, he stared morosely into the shadows. The incident in the holly maze troubled him. Eden's fright had been genuine. If there *had* been a man, he had been nowhere in sight when Justin had found her.

As he sipped the brandy, another thought intruded. What about the episode near the Powder Magazine in Williamsburg? There, too, Eden's fear had seemed real. He frowned. Didn't women sometimes get overly emotional at certain times each month? His sister, Emma, certainly did, spending one or two days confined to her room. Or perhaps someone had been watching Eden this morning. What man in possession of all his faculties *wouldn't* watch?

Justin straightened when he heard the front door rattle and Aunt Nora call farewell to her friends. Predictably, she came down the hall to join him. "You're still up!" Her taffeta gown rustled as she entered the room. "I thought you'd be in bed by now."

"I raided your excellent French brandy." He raised his glass. "Would you care to join me?"

Nora refused with a quick shake of her head. "Did Eden enjoy the rout? Governor Fauquier was quite taken with her. She made a marvelous impression tonight, Justin. You can be quite proud."

"I wasn't worried. With her breeding, I was certain she'd be accepted."

"Well, you know how people love gossip. News of your marrying a bond woman spread quicker than swamp fever.

Many a young lady had designs on you, Nephew, and they weren't happy to have an eligible bachelor snatched from under their noses.''

Justin drew on his cigar. ''By now they surely have their sights set elsewhere.''

''I suppose they do seem a fickle lot. Did you accomplish everything you wanted to here in Williamsburg?'' Nora asked, fussily rearranging procelain figurines on a drop-leaf table.

''Yes, as a matter of fact, I did, and I'm quite pleased with the results.'' Justin swallowed the rest of his brandy. ''I was able to hire an additional crew of workmen. Provided they work sunup to sunset, Greenbriar should be finished ahead of schedule.''

''Eden must be anxious to move into her new home.'' Nora clucked sympathetically. ''A one room cabin must be a hardship.''

Torture would be a better word, Justin thought. And the problem was definitely one-sided. Lying next to Eden each night, determined not to touch her, was sheer agony for him. ''The sooner Greenbriar is finished, the better.''

Nora smothered a yawn behind her hand. ''Before I go to bed, I'm going to check that the windows are shuttered. The wind is starting to pick up. There's a nasty storm brewing. Good night, Justin.'' She gave him a peck on the cheek and bustled out.

Justin knew he should retire, too, but he postponed the inevitable. He got up and, adding more brandy to his glass, went to the fireplace and leaned against the mantel. Was he condemned by his own stubborn pride to a lifetime of celibacy? He was a man, not a eunuch.

He stared broodingly into the amber liquid. Hadn't he proved his immunity? Eden was his wife. If she could give her body but not her soul each time they made love, why couldn't he? Determined, Justin set the glass down and threw his cigar into the hearth. Leaning heavily on his walking stick, he awkwardly made his way up the stairs.

Once inside the guest room, he stripped off his clothes

and slid into bed. Wind gusted through an open window. The blind billowed outward, its wooden slats clacking. Beyond, thunder cracked, and a jagged streak of lightning rent the night sky. Eden stirred restlessly, kicking the sheet toward the foot of the bed. She turned toward Justin, her thin batiste night rail twisted about her hips.

Unable to resist her proximity any longer, Justin reached out and stroked an ivory thigh. Her skin felt as soft as down, as velvety smooth as a rose petal. Her sleep-heavy eyelids fluttered. "You're a sorceress, Eden Tremayne," he whispered. "Come, witch, weave your spell." He showered tiny kisses across her cheek and down the delicate line of her jaw.

Eden wondered if she was awake or only dreaming. If it was a dream, she wished it would go on forever. "It's been so long, Justin. . . . " she murmured.

"Much too long." His mouth descended on hers for a deep, drugging kiss.

Eden's hands tunneled into his springy curls and held fast. She joyously welcomed her husband's ardor and returned it in equal measure. A gurgle of pleasure escaped her lips when she felt his hand possessively sweep down her spine, then slowly travel upward and cup her breast.

"I can't stop wanting you," he said thickly. He tugged the night rail over her head, tossed it aside, and pulled her against him. "Ah, Eden, I need you so." His lips covered hers; this time their touch was almost savage in intensity.

Eden held nothing back. She was spinning away, her mind emptying of everything except the fact that Justin wanted her, needed her. Sensations took over: she felt the rasp of bearded stubble across her overheated skin as Justin explored soft curves and musky hollows; she heard his unintelligible endearments; she tasted a mutual longing so acute that she cried out.

Pellets of rain stung the windowpanes. Water slanted through the opened window and formed a puddle on the floor. But the desire raging within the four walls made the storm outside pall into insignificance. Justin and Eden were oblivious to the warring elements.

At length the fury of their passion was spent. The quiet inside contrasted sharply with the clamorous assault beyond the window of wind and rain, thunder and lightning. Eden was glowingly content to lie with her head nuzzled on Justin's shoulder while her heart slowed to a normal rhythm and her breathing became steady and even. Justin, on the other hand, was not. Disengaging himself, he crossed to the window and closed it. His arm braced against the sill, he watched branches whip back and forth like spindly flags.

Eden's contentment dissipated into unease. She raised herself on one elbow and gazed at him. In the ghostly half-light, his superb body resembled a sculpture, a study of smooth muscle and sinew. The comparison seemed appropriate for he now appeared as cold and unfeeling as marble. Outside, the rain had changed to hail. It pounded on the cedar shingles and beat against the clapboard siding.

"The storm is wreaking havoc with the crops." His voice flat, Justin kept his back to her. As wonderful as their lovemaking had been, it had left him oddly dissatisfied. Nothing had changed; Eden was still an intimate stranger.

"Are you worried about Greenbriar?"

"We'll return tomorrow."

Eden closed her eyes. It seemed as though Justin was already miles away.

They left the following morning. While en route, Justin announced his decision to live in the cabin until Greenbriar was completed. He refused to place himself in a position where he had to duck under painters' scaffolds and dodge workmen's tools every time he turned around. Besides, he added, most of the furnishings wouldn't arrive until the end of August, six weeks hence.

Another problem presented itself. Where would Bess sleep in the meantime? Eden offered to approach Mary and ask if the woman was amenable to sharing her quarters with the girl.

Now that his leg was sufficiently healed and Greenbriar no longer a secret, Justin was eager to show Eden his holdings. Two days after their return, he offered to take her on a tour of his plantation. Attired in her new riding habit of deep purple cotton twill and a broad-brimmed hat sporting a black plume, Eden paced the front porch of Greenbriar where they had agreed to meet. The groom arrived holding the reins of two black horses, Thunderbolt and a dainty mare with white fetlocks.

Justin strode around the corner of the house. "The mare is yours," he said without preamble. "Name her whatever you wish."

"Ebony," Eden answered so promptly that Justin laughed. She ran to the mare and stroked its velvet-soft muzzle. "Justin, she's beautiful. You're much too good to me."

"Am I?" he asked cryptically. "Sometimes I wonder."

Her hand stilled. He was staring at her in a way that made her heart hammer against her ribs. It seemed a long time since he had looked at her like that. Too long. Nervously, she ran her tongue over her lower lip. "Thank you," she whispered.

At Justin's signal, the groom led the mare to the mounting block. Justin lifted Eden onto the horse's back, his hands tarrying at her waist. She wanted to loop her arms around his neck and slide down his hard-muscled length. She wanted to be crushed in his embrace, to feel loved and cherished. But apparently she wanted more than Justin was willing to give. She would gladly have forgone horses, servants, even the mansion, for a simpler life in which Justin cared for her. The distance between them had widened into an abyss.

"Since you haven't ridden much recently, we'll go slow until you get accustomed to your new saddle," Justin suggested. He swung up on the stallion, and they started down the graveled drive at a sedate pace.

It was a glorious summer day; the bright blue sky was dabbed with fleecy clouds. Eden urged Ebony into a canter, enjoying the mare's rhythmic gait and the rush of wind against her face. Resolutely, she locked her troubles away, feeling for the moment almost carefree.

Justin turned off the drive, and Eden followed. They topped a rise and reined to a halt. Spread out before them as far as the eye could see lay fields of tobacco ripening on heavy stalks. The reins held loosely, his hands crossed on his saddle horn, Justin proudly surveyed the domain he had carved out of the wilderness. "My tobacco crop," he said simply.

Eden's eyes swept the panorama. Dozens of men and women moved slowly among orderly rows of plants. The men were naked to the waist, their backs glistening like oiled mahogany in the sunlight. Eden was appalled. "All these people . . . you actually own them?"

Justin turned in his saddle and when he spoke, steel laced each word. "They may be slaves, but they're treated well."

"But to actually control the lives of so many." Her brows drew together. "It's barbaric!"

"Why the concern? You knew I owned slaves."

"Just as you own me?"

"You're not a slave," he ground out. "You're my wife!"

"You bought me as surely as you bought every man and woman in that field."

"I told you once that if you weren't happy I'd pay for your return to England."

"Yes, you did—but only when my indenture ended." Eden stared out at the field. In truth, the slaves didn't look underfed or ill-treated. Some even sang as they worked. But her own experiences had heightened her sensitivity to the tribulations of others, and her heart ached knowing these people were condemned by the color of their skin to a lifetime of bondage. Realizing there was little she could do about it made the situation even more untenable.

"Are you telling me you wish to go back to England?" Justin asked in a tight voice.

Eden released a long sigh and answered truthfully, "There's no reason for me to return. I left nothing behind."

Tension drained from him. He had been afraid to ask the question, had feared her answer even more. What if she had demanded return passage? Could he have kept his promise? And at what price?

He nudged the stallion closer and caught her chin in his lean fingers. "Eden, hear me out. I know you're upset. Believe me when I tell you I don't condone the practice of slavery any more than you do. But it's a way of life in the Tidewater. There comes a point when a man must learn to accept what he cannot change. Perhaps someday," he added, shrugging, "things will be different."

Eden felt ashamed for making him the object of her frustration. A fairer, more generous master than Justin would be hard to come by. She managed a feeble smile. "I'm sorry, Justin. I had no call to lash out at you."

His expression softened. "Come. Let me show you the rest of Greenbriar."

They rode past acres of corn. Workers, mostly women and children, moved between the rows selecting ripe ears while elderly slaves, shaded under muslin sheets, sat on the sidelines and removed the corn from the husks. If their cheery greetings were any indication, Justin was well liked.

"Most of the corn will be ground into meal," he explained. "Part will be kept as feed."

They continued past the fields and down a wooded path which followed a bend of the river. Through the trees Eden heard the steady chop of an axe and the grating of saws.

"I sent a crew to clear land. Any lumber we can't use at Greenbriar we'll sell in Richmond or Williamsburg."

"More land?"

"With tobacco, it's important to rotate the crops to help

control disease. Next year we'll plant soybeans and corn wherever tobacco grows today.''

After Justin spoke a few words with Fritz Kieffer, the stout, round-faced German in charge of the operation, he began circling back to the house. They stopped at a babbling brook to water the horses. ''Until today I had no concept of how extensive your holdings are,'' Eden commented.

Justin shrugged. ''By some standards they're considered modest.''

''Modest?''

''One man, Robert 'King' Carter, is reputed to have owned three hundred thousand acres and one thousand slaves at the time of his death.''

Eden was trying to assimilate everything she had seen and heard as they rode through the slave quarters a scant mile from the main house. Small whitewashed buildings hugged both sides of a dirt road. Behind them lay carefully tended kitchen gardens. An old woman with a clay pipe clamped between her toothless gums sat on a porch rocking a squawling baby. Dogs yapped as Eden and Justin passed.

''Do you feel it, Eden?'' Justin asked. ''A oneness, a certain harmony with the land, a feeling of belonging? I love Greenbriar. Its life force flows in my veins. You're important to these people. They'll come to you for help in settling their disputes and curing their ills. I want you to feel as much a part of the land as I do.''

Eden bowed her head. ''Give me time, Justin. For some of us, love grows slowly before it flowers.''

''And for some it never flowers at all.''

At his words her stomach twisted into a knot. Surely, he didn't think she was incapable of love. Or did he? Eden worried her lower lip. She wanted to ask him what he had meant by his cryptic remark, but a glance at his implacable profile stilled her tongue.

They spoke no more until they reached Greenbriar.

* * *

One week lengthened into two, and July melded into August. Eden was grateful that preparations for the move to Greenbriar filled each day, leaving her little opportunity to brood over Justin's continuing coolness. He hadn't made love to her since the night of the Governor's ball. She often wondered if he regretted his lapse on that memorable occasion.

Seated behind a makeshift desk in Justin's study at Greenbriar, Eden glanced at the girl who was helping her check off newly arrived household goods. At least Bess's presence was comforting. Under Eden's patient tutelage, the girl was proving herself to be a quick and able helpmate. In the process, they were becoming friends.

"If I look at one more inventory list, I'll be permanently cross-eyed," Eden complained, throwing down the quill pen.

Bess was stooped over a barrel sorting through china dishes and glassware. "Two broken dishes ain't bad considerin' this stuff was sent from England by ship."

"These things probably received better treatment than we did."

Bess straightened and wiped her hands on her apron, her gaze fixed on Eden. "Funny. I keep fergettin' you come over indentured. Was the trip a bad one?"

Eden touched the locket. Just like her precipitate flight from England, the voyage to the Colonies was something Eden preferred not to dwell on. Six women cramped into quarters the size of a pantry, weevil-infested food, rats, filth, and the stench of human excrement—no, those weren't memories she wanted to hold. And there had been worse.

Amy had died in her arms. Eden had watched dry-eyed while burly seamen had wrapped the girl's frail body in canvas and unceremoniously pitched it into the roiling, gray Atlantic.

"Yes," Eden whispered at last. "It was a bad one."

Bess awkwardly patted her shoulder. "Sorry, Eden, I shouldn't've said nothin'. But things are better now." She brightened. ''You got Mister Tremayne . . . and me . . . and soon you'll be livin' in this big, beautiful house.''

Eden summoned a smile. ''You're right, Bess. Don't think I'm ungrateful.''

''What's this talk about being ungrateful?'' The old woman entered the room on silent feet.

''Mary!'' Eden exclaimed with pleasure. The woman wore the purple silk apron Eden had bought her in Williamsburg. ''I'm so glad you came to see Greenbriar at last.''

''I don't belong in a fancy house. Only reason I came was to bring you fresh-baked gingerbread.'' Mary's eyes busily took in all the details, noting the generously proportioned drawing room, then coming to rest on Eden's makeshift desk of pine boards supported by sawhorses.

''Mary, would you think me a terrible hostess if Bess gave you the grand tour instead of me? Justin will be by to meet me shortly,'' Eden finished in a rush.

''He's gonna teach her how to fire a pistol. Imagine learnin' how to shoot one of them noisy things!'' Bess shook her head in bewilderment.

''You firing a pistol? Whatever for?'' Clearly Mary didn't comprehend Eden's desire to learn to shoot any more than Bess did.

''Don't you start, too!'' Eden warned, making a neat stack of the parchment sheets in front of her. ''I'm certain I won't be the only Tidewater woman who knows how to fire a gun. After all, this is practically wilderness. Why, right now, there's a war going on. Should the trouble spread to the coast, at least I'll be able to defend what's mine. Besides,'' she rationalized, ''wild animals prowl the forests. There are panthers, bears, and God only knows what else.''

Bess and Mary exchanged glances but held their tongues. Mary set the gingerbread on the desk. ''Justin's not here yet. Go ahead,'' she urged. ''Try some while it's still warm.''

The scent of ginger and molasses pervaded the room.

Bess broke off a piece and popped it into her mouth. "Speakin' of Justin, either of you know if Bear's with him?" she asked with studied casualness.

"Interested, are you, girl?" Mary's dry cackle sent color flooding Bess's cheeks.

"Mary's only teasing," Eden assured her. "Bear is a fine man. He's been a steadfast and loyal friend to Justin for years. You could do much worse, Bess."

"My sentiments exactly." Long strides carried Justin into the room.

Bear appeared moments later. "Mmm. That gingerbread I smell?" The big man stopped short at finding himself the center of attention. "Somethin' wrong?"

"Come in, Bear." Eden motioned toward him. "Help yourself to the gingerbread."

Bear didn't hesitate to accept the invitation. He had just bit off a large hunk when Mary smiled up at him from her perch on an upended barrel. "Eat up! Made it myself."

Bear's jaws stopped in midchew. He looked as though he were debating whether to swallow the cake or spit it out.

"It's not poison," Mary assured him, chortling. "Bess sampled it, and she's still breathing."

Justin chuckled at his friend's chagrin, then turned to Eden. "Are you ready for your lesson, or have you changed your mind?"

Eden stood, smoothed her skirt, and came out from behind the desk. "Not only ready, but eager to learn."

"Then we'll see you all later." Justin waved at the others and left with Eden at his side.

Bess quickly rose. "Mary, I promised Eden I'd show you the house."

"Sit, sit." Mary brushed her offer aside with a gnarled hand. "I can manage. My feet aren't too feeble to carry me upstairs for a look around. You're a scrawny little thing, Bess. Have another piece of gingerbread." Her look slid from Bess to Bear before she shook her head and left to explore on her own.

Bess sat down again, her eyes lowered. An awkward silence fell.

Bear cleared his throat and helped himself to another piece of cake. "Mary's right, ya know. Yer much too thin."

"Nothin' wrong with thin," Bess fired back. "I'm healthy enough."

"I didn't mean no insult. There's nothin' wrong with yer looks." An even lengthier silence fell. Bear cleared his throat a second time. "Ya seem to be gettin' along real well with Eden. I been wonderin'—what was she like when ya first knowed her? Was she uppity?"

"Eden isn't uppity," Bess defended hotly. "That's just her way, is all. Most folks can't see past her highbred manners."

Bear glanced away guiltily.

"Eden always did exactly as she was told," Bess continued. "Worked harder than some I knowed. I used to think bein' beautiful was wonderful, but I don't think that no more. I saw what problems Eden went through, and I'm glad I'm plain."

"What sorta problems?"

"Take Mistress Wainwright. She was always pickin' on Eden. Even hit her a time or two." Bess brushed crumbs from her hands. "And engaged or not, Master Charles wouldn't a been able to keep his hands off Eden much longer. Then there was Cook and Polly, both of 'em mean and spiteful as can be. But Eden didn't complain, just went about her business." Bess glared at Bear as though daring him to dispute her. "Anyone could see how unhappy she was. Thank goodness Mister Tremayne come to her rescue."

Bear mulled over Bess's words. Her description didn't fit the picture he had in his head of Justin's bride. Maybe he was one of the fools Bess mentioned, the kind who couldn't see beyond highbred manners. And if he was, he had done the lady a disservice, one he wasn't sure he could remedy.

He rose heavily to his feet. " 'Preciate ya tellin' me all this." On the threshold, he turned. "Bess . . ." He hesitated, his gaze darting around the room before coming to rest on hers. "I don't think yer plain."

Bess was still smiling long after he was gone.

Upon leaving the others, Justin and Eden mounted their horses and followed a winding trail through the virgin forest. Trees towered above them like cathedral spires, spicing the air with the scent of pine. Birds chattered noisily, and small animals scurried through the brush. Branches formed a living canopy over their heads, shading them from the sun's scorching rays.

The rythmic chop of an axe rang in the distance. "We're clearing a field for planting," Justin explained as they rode along. At last they came to a clearing. "This is as good a spot as any." Justin dismounted and lifted Eden from the mare's back.

Her hands rested lightly on his shoulders, feeling the play of muscles through the thin shirt. She could see the weave of the cotton fibers, and she knew the dark chest hairs that curled over the open neckline would feel springy beneath her fingertips. She slid slowly to the ground, her body grazing his, and heard his breath catch. Her eyes lifted to find his gaze fastened on her mouth. Her heart slammed against her ribs. Desire pulsed between them.

"Come on." He set her away from him. "Let's get on with your lesson."

Eden blinked, confused by the abrupt change—confused and disheartened. She was certain that Justin, too, had felt the heady onslaught of passion. She recognized it in eyes which had darkened to the color of slate. Desire had shone there, and just as quickly had vanished. Biting down her disappointment, she waited for Justin to tether the horses and take a leather case from the saddlebags. At his nod, she trailed after him to a hollowed log at one edge of the clearing. He motioned for her to sit.

Settling next to her, Justin opened the catch and raised

the lid of the box. Eden stared at twin flintlock pistols nestled in a bed of red velvet. She studied the guns with interest. They were the same pistols Justin had used with deadly precision the night he had rescued her from the Hales. Their butts were of smooth English oak, inlaid with silver and oiled until they gleamed with a rich luster. The steel barrels winked at her.

"Sure you want to go through with this?" Justin asked.

Eden nodded vigorously.

"Why?" He studied her with piercing eyes. "Do you intend to shoot someone? I hardly think you're capable of killing a man."

Her gaze skittered away from his. He thought her a sweet, guileless innocent. Little did he suspect the darkness of her soul, the potential for violence closeted there. She had nearly killed Rodney. He could easily have died from injuries inflicted by her hand. That would have made her a murderess.

"I don't know if I could cold-bloodedly end a man's life," she answered at length, "but knowing how to fire a gun will make me feel less defenseless."

"Pray tell, madam, what do you need to defend yourself against?"

Eden picked up one of the pistols, finding it heavy and cumbersome, designed for a man's hand. "You've often cited the dangers of living in a wilderness." She shrugged diffidently. "There was talk at the Governor's Palace of the French and Indian War."

"So this interest has nothing to do with your fright in Williamsburg?"

His astute question caught Eden off guard. She dropped her gaze lest he read her thoughts for, of course, it had everything to do with her fear. If there had truly been a one-eyed man in Williamsburg, and that man was Rodney, it was only a matter of time before he traced her whereabouts—and exacted revenge. While Eden was certain she could never shoot her stepbrother, she might be able to stave him off until help arrived.

She traced the scrolled-silver inlay. What if she unburdened herself by telling Justin the entire story? Would he believe her? Would he still care? At one point, she had almost overcome her hesitancy and confided in him. But things had changed since the afternoon of the peddler's visit. A chasm had sprung between them—and kept widening.

She raised her eyes to meet Justin's stare. "Will you teach me or not?"

"Yes," he said with a sigh. "I'll teach you."

Eden looked on while he carefully poured a small amount of gunpowder into the muzzle of the remaining pistol. "How can you judge how much to use?" she asked.

"Some use a charge equivalent to one-third of the ball weight. Others lay the ball in the palm of their hand and slowly pour powder over it until it forms a neat cone shape just covering the ball."

"But you didn't measure."

"I've learned to judge the amount through years of practice. But," he added, "I want you to measure before you load."

Eden scooted closer, her thigh resting against his. Stuffing a small piece of paper into the barrel, Justin rammed it down with a rod. He produced a small scrap of cloth cut in a circle, spit on it, and placed it over the muzzle. "Always keep the grain of the cloth in the same direction." He set a lead ball on top of the patch and pushed it down the muzzle. "Never fire unless the shot is down against the powder charge, or it can burst the barrel. Understand?"

Her eyes like round moons, she nodded.

"Good." Justin indicated the gun in her lap. "Now it's your turn."

Eden imitated his actions, then waited further direction.

"You're an apt pupil. You learn quickly."

His praise elicited her happy smile. Justin was sorely tempted to plant a kiss on the tip of her nose. Eden's nearness tested his resolve to remain aloof. Knowing that she would willingly melt in his arms only made matters worse. If he succumbed to impulse, he would once more be enslaved by infatuation. His expression hardened.

He sprang from the log and crossed the clearing. "Next we will see if you can hit a target." He tacked a handkerchief to the trunk of a tree.

Eden joined him and took her place in front of the target, her legs braced. Her arm wavered as she raised the muzzle loader.

The sight of Eden trying to master the heavy weapon seemed at variance with Justin's image of her. He acknowledged silently that he had always considered her a dainty, fragile creature, one in need of protection not one capable of defending herself. But that simply wasn't true. Many times in the course of their marriage, Eden had risen to the occasion and proved herself competent. "Here, let me show you." He positioned himself behind her. "First of all, pull back the lock to cock it. Then hold your arm steady. . . ."

His warm breath tickled her cheek. Eden's eyelids drifted shut for a moment as she savored the feel of his large, muscular frame against her back. "Take careful aim." His honeyed voice purred in her ear. "Now gently squeeze the trigger."

She opened her eyes a slit and fired. The explosion rocked her backward, and her arm vibrated clear to her shoulder from the force of the blast. The pistol belched thick black smoke. Absently, she wiped a sweat-dampened tendril of hair from her face, unaware of the black smudge she left behind. A hole gaped in the upper right-hand corner of the target.

"Not bad for a beginner. Let's see how you do without my help." Justin handed Eden the other primed pistol and stepped back.

She took careful aim. This time the shot went wide, the ball rebounding off the trees beyond the clearing. Justin mistakenly assumed she would be content to quit, but then he remembered her tenacity. Plunking himself down on the fallen log, he watched her reload both pistols.

The first shot joined the other, the ball embedding itself into a sturdy maple. Eden wiped her sweaty hands on the side of her dress and impatiently brushed aside the same unruly lock of hair. From the corner of her eye, she saw Justin propped against the trunk of a tree, his arms folded across his chest. Picking up the other gun, she looked down the length of the pistol.

The muscles in her arm ached from the strain. The barrel wobbled. She shifted her stance, biting her lower lip in determination. It was suddenly important that she vindicate herself. Using her left arm to steady her right one, she drew a bead on the target and fired. When the cloud of smoke cleared, there was a hole just off center of the handkerchief.

"I did it!" She squealed in delight and hurled herself into Justin's arms. "I did it!"

He held her stiffly, waging war against his personal demon. One part of him remained unaffected, while another wanted to share her exuberance. Resolutely, he set her at arm's length, a reluctant smile curving the corners of his mouth as he gazed down at her. "You look like a chimney sweep." He held her powder-blackened hands in front of her.

Eden stared at them in disgust.

"Your face is dirty, too." Justin traced dusky smudges from cheek to ear. "And your gown . . ."

Appalled, Eden glanced down at the soiled skirt of her yellow muslin dress. Gunpowder striped each side where she had wiped her sweaty palms.

Justin chuckled. "Bear always says that anyone who's afraid to get his hands dirty had better stick with lace doilies. You definitely aren't afraid to get your hands dirty."

His attention wandered to a bead of perspiration slowly trickling from the hollow of her throat. He watched, fascinated, while it disappeared into the cleft between her breasts. His expression turned serious. "You could use a bath."

His husky drawl emboldened Eden. Placing grimy hands on the front of his spotless white shirt, she raised on tiptoe and brushed her lips across his. Her touch ignited the dry and brittle tinder of Justin's repressed emotions. The kiss deepened. Flames of longing burned, devouring his injured pride, consuming his caution.

Eden's arms twined around his neck. Shamelessly she arched against him, her hips pressing against his aroused manhood. Her full breasts flattened against his chest. "Justin," she half sighed, half sobbed. "I need you so. Love me, please love me," she begged, racing fevered kisses down his throat to the open vee of his shirt.

With a groan, Justin lowered her to the ground. Their hastily discarded clothing soon formed a blanket beneath them. Flesh touched flesh; need fueled passion. They were lost, victims of a raging conflagration that neither could contain.

Long after the flames had turned to smoldering embers, they lay in each others embrace, two bodies melded into one. Eden dozed for a while, then awoke to find Justin watching her. For the first time in months, his expression was unguarded, allowing a trace of his former tenderness to shine through. Charcoal smudges lay across his naked form like shadows, visible evidence of where her hands had touched. "I'm not the only one in need of bathing," she said with a smile.

His lips quirked. "I know how to remedy the problem." Getting up, he reached for her hand and hauled her to her feet. Bending, he scooped the clothing up in his arms and her along with it.

"Justin," she protested, laughing, "what are you doing? Where are you taking me?"

"Hush." He silenced her with a kiss. Her mouth opened invitingly; their tongues met and sparred in a playful duel. "Ah, Eden, what a temptress you are." Justin sighed as their lips reluctantly parted.

He carried her beyond the clearing to a place where a creek twisted through the forest, then widened to form a basin before shifting course. Eden felt as though they were the only two people in existence, the pine-scented forest their exclusive paradise. Nestling in the haven of Justin's arms was heaven on earth.

"Your bath awaits, milady." Flinging their garments to the bank, Justin waded into the pool with Eden in his arms.

"But I don't know how to swim." Her luminous violet eyes regarded him trustingly.

"There's no need, love, the water isn't deep." He released her, letting her body skim the length of his as her feet sought the sandy bottom. "Now make yourself presentable. You look like an urchin."

"An urchin!" Eden feigned outrage, then kicked up a spray of water at him.

His face streaming, Justin shook the moisture from his eyes. "Why, you little minx, you deserve a good dunking."

Her eyes widened at the threat, and she edged closer to shore. "Remember, Justin, I can't swim." He grinned, then ducked below the surface and disappeared.

Eden felt something nibble her calf and quickly stepped aside. Now her other leg was under attack. She splashed toward the bank, but lost her balance and toppled back into the pool. Sputtering and coughing, she regained her footing. Water sprayed in all directions as she shook herself like a frisky pup. Her braid had come unfastened during their romp, and her hair whipped from side to side. Justin caught a handful and pulled her close.

"Why, you, you . . ." She searched for a suitable word.

"Honest, love, until this minute I never laid a hand on you. You can't blame me because you swallowed half the creek. Besides," he added, grinning, "I brought you a present." He held out a palmful of sand. "Your soap, madam."

He sifted the fine grains into her cupped hands, then

looked on as she used it to scrub away the grime. She splashed water on her face and rubbed vigorously. Justin's gray gaze never wavered, its intensity rekindling a warmth that started in the pit of her stomach and spread like wildfire.

The water came barely to her shoulders. Beneath its clear surface, Eden's breasts gleamed opalescent, their peaks a dark, dusky rose. Unable to resist the tantalizing sight, Justin reached out and weighed their plump fullness, one in each hand. His thumbs drew lazy circles around the nipples until they puckered into hard pebbles.

Eden glided closer. With her hair slicked back, her delicate features were etched in stark relief. Beneath the fringe of thick lashes, the color of her eyes deepened, enticing him like exotic purple orchids. Her flawless beauty weakened him, sapped his will, annihilated his resolve. Make her yours once more, his body urged.

"I never seem to get enough of you," he confessed in a ragged whisper.

The admission was the only encouragement they needed. Justin dropped his hands to her waist and pulled her tight. His mouth sought hers, hot and wet, cajoling and demanding. Eden sucked in a breath when his hands moved to her buttocks and lifted her with gentle pressure. "Don't be afraid, sweet. Wrap your legs around me."

Her sheath lubricated by desire, Justin entered her effortlessly. He guided her buttocks down, positioned himself, then began to move. Eden tipped her head back, her neck arched. Loosened from its braid, her hair floated about them like a giant fan, the water was an erotic caress against her bare flesh. Justin kissed her throat, the crest of her breast, and suckled a rosy areola. Eden's thighs clutched his flanks. He surged, striking a rhythm as ageless as the pounding surf. Together they strained, Eden's legs locked around him. She cried out her release as he erupted inside her.

She was floating. How simple it was, she marveled. The water suspended her as easily as a mattress. Beside her,

Justin lazily stroked toward shore. Eden felt the slope of the sand bottom. She stood and waited until he was even with her.

"Justin?" She caught his hand. "Why did things change between us? Why can't it always be like this?"

"Everything changes, Eden." He disengaged his hand. "Nothing stays the same."

Was there regret in his eloquent eyes? Had a note of wistfulness crept into his melodic voice? How her heart ached. The afternoon had been an enchanted interlude, a time to treasure. But a few hours of happiness did not vouchsafe them a future.

With escalating regret, she left the pool.

Chapter 18

By the beginning of September, every rug and every piece of furniture was in place. Greenbriar was finished.

Eden wandered from room to room, the sound of her slippered footsteps absorbed into the stillness. It was a lovely house, but would it ever become a home? With the passage of time, would it become a place of love and happiness? Or would it forever remain simply brick and mortar, wood and shingle?

As on the afternoon when she had first discovered the magnificent house, the music room was the last room she entered. An item had been added since her last inspection—a gleaming mahogany pianoforte stood in front of the windows. She moved forward as if in a trance, her fingertips tingling with anticipation. It had been so long since she had even practiced a simple scale that she wondered if she still remembered how.

A swift glance at the door assured her she was alone. She sat on the piano bench and spread her skirts. Her hands poised above the keyboard, then tentatively pressed the keys. At first her fingers felt clumsy, but as they moved across the keyboard they grew limber. A melody she'd learned long ago filled the room, the notes swelling as her confidence rebounded.

Bess slipped unnoticed into the room. When the music ended, she burst into applause. "Oh, Eden, that was beautiful. I couldn't help myself. I hope you don't mind my listenin'."

"Of course not." Each time Eden looked at her friend, she was struck anew by the remarkable changes in the girl. Bess had blossomed since coming to Greenbriar. Her face had lost its sallow, pinched look, but the most startling change of all was the girl's demeanor. She no longer seemed ready to jump at her own shadow.

"Do you like Mr. Justin's surprise?" Bess asked, her eyes sparkling. "He made sure the piano was delivered while you were off visitin' Mary. Kept it hidden behind the painters' scaffold where you couldn't see."

Eden swallowed. "It's a wonderful surprise." Justin was the kindest, most thoughtful husband in the world . . . at times. "You'll never know how much I missed being able to play."

"I'm glad you like your gift," Justin said, strolling into the room, casually elegant in buff breeches, high black boots, and a ruffled cambric shirt.

"Justin!" Eden hurried to greet him. She wanted to thank him with a kiss but felt self-conscious in Bess's presence. Why blame Bess? The question brought her up short. Her reluctance had nothing to do with the girl. It stemmed from her inability to predict Justin's reaction; she was afraid of being rebuffed. "Thank you," she said simply, her eyes full of the emotion in her heart.

Justin cupped her chin in his hand and feasted on her incomparable beauty. "My pleasure, pretty lady."

"Here ya are." Bear blundered into the music room, looking every inch his namesake and just as out of place in such refined surroundings.

Justin let his hand drop and turned to his friend. "I thought we settled everything. Did I forget something?"

Bear nodded to the women, his eyes lingering on Bess. "Ya said ya wanted to go over the figurin'. Thought you might be needin' this." He thrust a ledger at Justin.

"Supper is about to be served," Eden spoke up. "Bear, you and Bess must join us. You'll be our very first guests."

Bess's hand flew to her chest in horror. "Oh, I couldn't.

That wouldn't be fittin'. People will talk 'bout havin' a bond servant eat dinner with you.''

Bear twirled the brim of his hat. ''Bess is right. I'm just the overseer. It's not my place to be sittin' at no fine table.''

Justin stared at his friend, amazed at his sudden concern for propriety.

''Overseer! Bond servant! What utter nonsense!'' Eden marched over to the giant of a man and, placing her hands on her hips, glared up at him. ''We were good enough to share meals with before. Did you do it only to gloat over my burned rabbit and scorched bread?''

''Course not.'' Bear glared back.

''Then why did you?''

He shifted his weight. ''Cause me and Justin's friends, that's why!''

''Exactly.'' Eden nodded so emphatically that her curls bounced. ''And friends share meals. Or do you no longer consider us friends because we've moved to a different house?''

A dull red suffused Bear's bearded countenance. ''That's a dumb question. Me and Justin's friends, same as before.''

''Good. Then you'll stay for supper.'' Eden threw him a sunny smile as she turned to Bess, who had watched the scene slack jawed.

Bess took half a step backward and was brought up short against the piano. ''B-but, Eden, bein' an overseer is one thing . . . but a bond servant?''

''I haven't forgotten, Bess, what it's like to be indentured. However, in the last weeks, you've become more than a servant. I don't know how I would have managed without you. Justin and I will invite whomever we choose to our table and will tolerate no snide gossip from others.''

''Well said.'' Justin stepped to Eden's side and draped an arm over her shoulders. ''Now will the two of you cease your objections and join us?''

Bess bobbed her head, looking pleased beyond words, while Bear muttered an almost-incoherent acceptance.

Justin squeezed Eden's shoulders, feeling inordinately proud of her. "I couldn't have stated our case more eloquently."

A soft knock prevented further talk. A slender negro woman wearing a starched white apron and neckerchief over a blue homespun dress stood on the threshold. "Supper's ready, ma'am."

"Thank you, Liza," Eden returned. "We'll be having guests. Please add two more place settings." Liza, her dark face impassive, nodded, then left. Hooking her arm through Bear's, Eden urged him toward the dining room.

"Madam." Justin offered his arm to Bess and favored the flustered girl with a heart-stopping smile. "Supper awaits."

An oval cherry table and Queen Anne chairs graced the the room. Pale gold wallpaper covered the wainscoted walls, and matching fabric covered the cornices above the tall windows and decorated chair seats. A gilt framed mirror hung above a sideboard along one wall. Underfoot lay a fashionable floor cloth of black and gold hexagons.

Justin gallantly held out a chair for Bess. Blushing to the roots of her hair, she mumbled a thank-you and slid into the chair. Bear, aping his friend's action, did likewise for Eden. Before sitting down, Bear dubiously studied his own frail-looking chair, gauging its sturdiness against his substantial bulk. Gingerly, he took a seat.

"A toast." Justin held up his wineglass. "What benefit is good fortune without friends to share it? To friendship."

They raised their glasses. While the ladies sipped daintily, Bear quaffed the fine wine as though it were ale, then looked around. From the expressions on the others' faces, he belatedly realized his mistake and set the stemmed glass down with exaggerated care.

"The tobacco crop looks the best we've had thus far." Justin indicated to a servant to refill Bear's glass.

"Yeah, sure does." Bear lapsed into silence.

Eden quietly instructed Liza to serve the first course.

Liza and Didi, a girl in her late teens, circled the table and ladled savory split-pea soup into individual bowls. Bear stuffed the linen square into the front of his shirt, picked up his spoon as though it were a shovel, and began to eat. His noisy slurps brought titters from the young servant. A frown of disapproval from Liza brought Didi under control, but too late. Bear dropped the spoon and pushed the dish aside.

"Soup's delicious," Bess ventured timidly.

"Yes, it is," Eden agreed.

"Sookie was an excellent choice for a cook," Justin commended. "I'm glad you didn't heed my advice when it came to selecting house servants."

Eden smiled across the table. "I'm grateful you decided to indulge me. I don't think you'll regret it."

Justin turned to Bear. "I had planned to purchase house servants at a slave auction in Williamsburg, but Eden persuaded me to consider some of my field hands."

Eden nodded encouragement to Didi as the girl whisked away the soup bowls. "Unlike some planters, Justin has a policy of never separating families, so actually there were a number of women to choose from."

"Eden handpicked each servant." Justin speared slices of cold roast beef and ham from a platter that Liza offered. "She chose some because of their prior experience in other households. The others had nothing to recommend them except their eagerness to better their lot."

Bear gulped when he glanced at the array of silverware, dismay written across his face in bold letters. Seeing his dilemma, Eden gently cleared her throat to draw his attention, then indicated which fork to use for the meat course.

"Me and Eden gave classes. Just like real schoolin'," Bess volunteered. "First Eden tol' me what she expects of her servants, then we gave lessons in cleanin' and carin' for the house, how to set the table, how to serve a meal. We taught 'em everythin'."

"Never stopped to think about all it takes to run a house," Bear conceded. "But I do know how much work it was teachin' Justin about farmin'." He gave Bess a broad wink that made her blush again.

Eden joined in. "Together, Bess and I decided who was best suited for laundress, cook, and other jobs in the kitchen, dairy, and the house itself. If anyone was truly unhappy with his or her position, I promised work elsewhere."

Bear's eyebrows came together as he studied Eden with new respect.

As tasty as the food was, Eden unexpectedly lost her appetite and reverted to her old habit of cutting her meat into small pieces and scattering them on her plate. "Cook was the easiest job to fill. Sookie, as you probably know," she explained to Bess, "did the cooking for us while we lived in the cabin. Without her, Justin would be skin and bones."

"Not with your determination," Justin was quick to add. "You became a fine cook once you got the knack."

"For that I have Mary to thank," Eden acknowledged. "Although she's too crippled with rheumatism to do much herself, she was a wonderful teacher. She even shared her herbs and spices. Because of her, I finally learned the trick to controlling the heat of an oven."

"I've been doing a great deal of thinking," Justin said, accepting a generous slice of vegetable pie. "I've become remiss in my social obligations during the construction of Greenbriar. My friends have been quite tolerant, but now it's time to pay my debts."

Eden waited, her fork poised in midair, already anticipating his next words.

"As soon as the harvest is in, I'd like to have a housewarming. Do you think you can manage one in a month's time, Eden? If not, I'm sure Aunt Nora would be happy to assist you."

"With Bess's help, I'm certain we can arrange it."

"Good. Keep me informed of your progress. I want no expense spared."

By the time peach cobbler was served, Bear seemed more at ease in the new surroundings. He coughed and nervously leaned back in his chair. "It's still early, Bess. How 'bout a walk? We could go down by the river."

Bess dropped her gaze and carefully refolded her napkin before returning it to the table. "A walk by the river sounds . . . lovely," she said, using a word she had often heard Eden use.

Bear ambled to his feet and extended his arm to Bess. The pair said their good-nights and left the dining room.

Justin stared after them in amusement. "If I didn't know better, I'd swear Bear was courting the girl."

"Bess seems quite taken with him as well." Eden smiled behind her teacup. "You don't object, do you?"

"Why? Because she's a bond servant?"

Eden nodded. Bond servant. She had come to hate that term.

Justin downed the remainder of his wine. "Bear was once a bond servant himself. When we first met, he was just finishing his indenture. He planned to buy a small plot of land with his freedom dues and farm tobacco, but I convinced him it would be more profitable to work for me instead."

"If Bear was once a bond servant, why did he resent me so much?" Eden asked.

"It was because of your indenture that he distrusted you. He believed you married me for my wealth, as a way to avoid your obligation."

"I see," Eden answered quietly. Having observed the way Bear's mind worked, she could easily understand his reasoning. What she couldn't accept was that Justin must have believed it also, otherwise he would never have allowed her to continue thinking that the cabin was Greenbriar. Trust between them had been a meaningless platitude, a missing ingredient since the very beginning, on both their parts.

"If you'll excuse me." Justin got to his feet. "I have a ledger to review."

Eden rose, too. "It's been a long day. I think I'll retire."

The weariness she felt as she trudged up the curving staircase had little to do with physical exhaustion. She paused on the landing and looking over her shoulder. The wide entranceway was empty. As empty as she felt inside.

As the housewarming approached, gifts arrived with increasing frequency from friends and well-wishers, tokens of esteem celebrating both their marriage and their new home. Eden received several callers, women from neighboring plantations who were eager to meet Justin Tremayne's mysterious new bride.

This particular afternoon Eden was entertaining Clara Howell, whose husband, James, was a former Harvard classmate of Justin's. Clara was several years older than Eden, tall, buxom, with thick auburn curls and pale green eyes. The couple, along with their young son, had stopped to visit on their way to Richmond. The men were at the stable inspecting Justin's new bay.

"You're not at all what I expected," Clara said, helping herself to a second pecan tart. "Millicent Wainwright led me to believe you came from a common background."

Eden raised a brow. "Are you and Millicent good friends?"

"Mercy, no." Clara laughed. "If the truth be known, I can't abide the woman. Millicent always has to have the last word. And it's sickening the way she dotes on her children. . . . " She clapped a hand to her mouth. "I shouldn't have said that. James is always warning me I talk too much."

"Talk all you want. It's wonderful to have company. I'm so happy you and your husband will be spending the night."

"Mommy, mommy, come see the horsey." Three-year-old James Junior burst into the room followed by his father and Justin.

"Later, sweetheart." Clara chucked the child's dimpled chin.

"Justin has an eye for good horseflesh," James said, slapping his friend on the shoulder. "As well as for beautiful women. You are to be commended, Justin, on your choice of a wife. After Millicent's remarks, I feared you had taken leave of your senses."

Justin went to the inlaid mahogany sideboard, poured two glasses of bourbon, and handed one to his friend. "Millicent was undoubtedly disappointed when she learned I wished to marry Eden instead of Caroline."

"From what Caroline hinted, she's found a new beau. An English lord, no less! Won't Millicent brag." Clara's eyes danced.

"I wish Caroline the best." Eden offered James the plate of tarts. "I hope she'll be very happy."

"I nearly forgot. I have something for you." James polished off the sweet in two bites. "We stopped at a merchant's in Williamsburg. When we happened to mention we'd be traveling to Richmond, he asked if by any chance we were planning to visit Greenbriar. Wait here a moment." He left the sitting room and returned minutes later with a box wrapped in silver foil.

Eden and Justin exchanged curious glances while Clara sat forward on the settee. "I think it's a wedding gift. The merchant asked if we'd bring it and save his boy a trip."

James presented the package to Eden. "Actually I think he was more interested in pocketing the coin he got for delivery."

"Go ahead, Eden," Justin urged, stepping closer. "Open it."

Eden quickly unfastened the wrappings and lifted the lid. From a mound of cotton stuffing, she pulled out a beautifully crafted hand-blown glass kitten.

"Pretty!" the little boy cried in delight. "Pretty kitty."

Eden held up the object. Light caught the crystal and

was refracted. It was superbly fashioned. In a three-inch piece of glass, the artist had captured the animal's playful mood in the slight tilt of the kitten's head and the lift of one front paw.

"Oh," Clara sighed enviously. "What a clever piece! Just look at the detail. It's almost lifelike."

"Who sent it? Is there a card?" Justin asked.

The tiny glass figure in the palm of her hand struck a vaguely familiar chord in Eden's memory. Still trying to identify it, she frowned slightly and handed the object to Clara. She searched through the wrappings to no avail. "The card must have been lost."

"Too bad." James shrugged. "Perhaps the merchant forgot to include it. You'll have to wait until someone accuses you of not acknowledging their gift."

Throughout supper Eden's thoughts returned to the glass kitten with disturbing regularity. An almost-forgotten incident struggled to resurface, but she couldn't quite grasp it.

"Would you excuse us while we go up and say good night to our son?" Clara asked, laying down her napkin.

"Clara is an overly indulgent mother." James gazed at his wife affectionately. "She spoils the boy terribly."

"And my husband is even worse," Clara replied.

"By all means, bid good night to your son," Justin said, standing. "Join us in the music room. I believe Eden can be persuaded to play a piece for us, then perhaps we'll play a game of whist?"

"Add a glass of your French brandy, and you have yourself a deal," James joked, looping an arm around his wife's waist. The couple left to check on James Junior.

As Eden rose to leave the dining room, Justin caught her arm. He couldn't help but notice her distraction during the meal. Bending his head to hers, he spoke softly. "Is anything wrong?"

Concern turned his eyes smoky gray. He was so precious, so dear, and she loved him so much. Had she lost his love before she ever learned the true meaning of the word? She couldn't, wouldn't, let it slip away without a fight. She affected a casual air. "Nothing's wrong. I'm fine, thank you."

He searched her face. "You don't look fine. You seem a bit pale." Eden was a master at hiding her feelings, he knew, but he could have sworn her mask had slipped. Worry shadowed her violet gaze. Perhaps he had become more attuned to the subtle nuances of her expression. Hope sparked. Perhaps she was less guarded—and more trusting. Caution kept this fledgling notion a low, burning flame. It was better to be careful than to expect too much and risk disappointment.

Eden smiled a shade too brightly. "There's been much to do of late what with moving, making preparations for the coming winter, and arranging the housewarming party only a fortnight away. I'm a little tired, that's all."

"I've yet to hear you complain." He tucked her hand into the crook of his arm, and they slowly walked down the hall to the music room. "I've been so busy with the harvest, I didn't stop to consider the extra burden a houseful of guests would entail."

"Shh." She stopped and laid a finger to his lips. "Stop treating me like a china doll. I'm quite capable of handling the house party. You'll see. You'll be proud of me."

Justin nipped at her finger with his teeth. "I already am, sweet."

Before Eden could frame a reply, Justin's mouth touched hers with a soft, exploring pressure, triggering an intense pleasure she felt clear to the soles of her slippers.

"I guess this is what one must expect when one visits newlyweds," James Howell declared from the entranceway. "Too bad little James fell asleep so quickly."

"James!" Clara gave her husband a good-natured nudge in the ribs.

Justin and Eden broke apart.

"Ladies," Justin said, making a sweeping motion of his hand and stepping aside so the women could enter the music room.

Eden's cheeks were still pink when Clara pleaded with her to play a selection on the piano. Eden was happy to comply.

As the haunting melody flowed around Justin, Eden's accusation intermingled with the notes. *Stop treating me like a china doll,* she had protested. He was guilty as charged. Blinded by her beauty, he often failed to recognize the capable woman beneath the pretty surface.

The music wove a spell over him. Justin propped his chin on a fist and closed his eyes. Even if she were as plain as pudding, Eden deserved his admiration. She had long ago proven her mettle. No, she wasn't china, more like finely tempered steel. And that made him love her all the more. His eyes snapped open, and he sat up straighter in his chair.

He loved her.

All his efforts to resist her had been for naught. He had discovered a simple truth: love wasn't something you could control. God help him, he loved her more than ever. What he had felt earlier had been a schoolboy infatuation compared with the way he felt now.

Chapter 19

The terrifying memory pursued Eden in her dreams. Restlessly she thrashed about. Blood gushed from an eyeless socket. Rodney's agonized face danced before her closed eyelids. A scream slid along her throat, but died before it was born. She shot bolt upright in bed, her breath coming in short, uneven gasps; sweat glued her nightgown to her skin. Alone in the darkened bedroom, she shivered violently.

She lowered herself to the mattress, her body as rigid as a corpse, and stared at the ceiling. It had been months since she'd had the nightmare. What had brought it back? The glass kitten? The gift without a giver? Suddenly it became imperative that she examine the figurine more closely, to discover why it was so disturbing to her.

Tossing aside the tangled bedclothes, Eden shrugged into a silk wrapper and padded downstairs. The glowing bed of coals in the hearth cast a hellish light. She went to the fireplace and, with trembling fingers, took the crystal kitten from the mantel. Little James was right. It was a pretty piece, executed in minute detail. Once, when she was eight, Nanny had given her a real kitten. Eden traced the glass image with a fingertip. It had been gray with four white paws. She had called it Boots. Fear swept across the plains of her heart, then took root, swiftly, cruelly.

"No," she whispered, "it can't be." But she could no longer deny the truth. A painful memory resurfaced. In a burst of rage, Rodney had taken her pet and tossed it into a bonfire. Screeching in pain, the kitten had leaped from the fire, a furry ball of flame. Hysterical, tears streaming down her cheeks, Eden had chased her pet until a gardener took pity and ended the animal's anguish. "No," she whispered again.

With hands that shook as though palsied, she held the crystal toward the meager light. Fine lines were plainly etched around each small foot, giving the appearance of four stockings . . . or boots!

"Eden."

She whirled. The glass kitten slipped from her hands and crashed to the hearth, where it splintered into tiny shards. Blinded by remembered terror, she stared at Justin blankly.

"Eden!" His hands bit into her shoulders, and he shook her—once, twice, three times. Her head snapped back, her eyes unfocused. "Eden! It's all right. It was only a piece of glass."

"G-Glass?"

He wrapped her in his arms and pinned her against his bare chest. Why couldn't she let go of the demons that terrorized her? She felt small and frail in his embrace, infinitely in need of protection. She shuddered convulsively, then held on with a nameless desperation. "Hush, darlin', don't be frightened," he murmured, stroking her tangled curls. "Talk to me. Tell me what's wrong."

She squeezed her eyes shut. No doubt, after the episode in the holly maze, Justin already feared for her sanity. He wasn't even aware of Rodney's existence. Would he believe her if she told him her stepbrother had vowed to kill her—and with good reason? Probably not. Her charges would sound like the ravings of a mad woman.

"I had a nightmare." Her voice sounded as though it were coming from a great distance. "I came downstairs because I couldn't sleep. You startled me."

Justin didn't doubt for a moment that he had startled her, but he was equally certain she was holding something back. He checked the urge to shake her again. Why wouldn't she confide in him? He was deeply concerned about her. Patience, he counseled, she'll tell you when she's ready. Until then, real or imagined, the devils would remain hers. "It's late." He sighed. "Let's go back to bed."

Holding her close to his side, Justin guided Eden up the stairs. They paused outside her bedroom. Her enormous eyes in her colorless face beseeched him. "Sleep with me," she pleaded.

Justin groaned silently. He had waited a lifetime for this request. To refuse would be the ultimate self-deception. He loved her; she needed him. With a nod, he followed her into the room.

Once in bed, he wrapped his arms around her. Gradually the tension drained from her body, and she relaxed against him. He made love to her with slow, exquisite tenderness. Finally, she slept, cradled in his embrace. Would he ever understand her? he wondered as he watched shadows chase across the ceiling. What phantoms haunted her dreams? Who was the one-eyed man she thought she had recognized in Williamsburg?

The Howell's visit had provided a pleasant interlude. Justin persuaded them to attend the housewarming a fortnight later before returning to Baltimore. With rumors that French-instigated Indian attacks against the British were increasing, it might be some time before they returned to Virginia. Eden was happy they agreed. It would be good to see Clara Howell's warm and familiar face amongst a houseful of strangers.

In the days to come, the odor of curing tobacco hung over Greenbriar. When ready, the tobacco was packed in hogsheads and rolled to the river landing to be shipped to Williamsburg, and from there to England. While Justin was thus occupied, Eden prepared for the housewarming. They saw each other only at mealtimes.

Mary popped in for a visit one afternoon and viewed

the commotion. "Too many people, too much noise," she said, and went away grumbling.

Eden was relieved her nightmare hadn't recurred. Fatigue seemed to dog her footsteps during the day, and each night she tumbled into bed too exhausted to dream. Resignation blanketed her initial terror. Rodney knew where to find her. It was only a matter of time before he tired of this cat-and-mouse game and made his move.

By the third week of September, all was in readiness.

A hush shrouded the great house; anticipation charged the atmosphere. Eden felt like an actress waiting in the wings for her cue. No one seeing her serene countenance would guess her palms were moist, her heart racing. By midday, guests began arriving and Greenbriar was jolted out of its lethargy.

The first people to arrive were Emmett and Bernice Dodd, an elderly couple with grown children. "So nice of you to invite us, dear." Bernice eyed Eden with frank interest. "Emmett and I have known Justin since he was a boy. To be honest, we've been curious ever since Millicent Wainwright told us of his marriage."

"You picked yourself a beauty, boy." Emmett slapped Justin's back. "Bernice and I were friends of Justin's parents," he explained to Eden, then turned to Justin. "Only wished they had lived to see you settled. Bernice used to fuss you'd never marry and raise a family. But I told her all in good time. Never saw the likes of it before. Every step you took was well planned and thought out. Even as a lad, you weren't one to settle for second best."

Justin's eyes strayed to Eden, a tender expression on his face. "I'm still not."

She hugged his words to her heart. They sustained her as Greenbriar's rooms filled with houseguests.

A young woman whom Eden guessed to be in her early twenties was assisted from a carriage by a man easily thrice her age. An apricot-silk gown accentuated the woman's dark, petite beauty. "Georgina and Frederick Benton," Justin informed Eden in an undertone as the pair mounted the low porch steps. "They own Fairlawn, along the James River between here and Williamsburg. Georgina's from South Carolina."

Eden stood proudly beside Justin while he made the introductions. "I'm pleased you and your father were able to accept our invitation," she said.

The young woman tittered while the man's face grew florid. "Humph!" he sputtered. "Georgina is my wife."

Eden would have gladly sunk through the floodboards. Justin came to her rescue. "Take it as a compliment, Frederick. Your charm defeated many rivals, most much younger than yourself, to win your lady's heart."

Frederick Benton appeared mollified. "A natural mistake, as you pointed out." His frigid expression thawed. "Forgive me if I sounded churlish, Mistress Tremayne."

"You had every right to, Mr. Benton," Eden apologized. "The fault was mine."

When he had recovered from his pique, Frederick stared boldly at Eden's uncommon beauty, and the irritation on his face changed to admiration. "Please, my dear, call me Frederick."

"I'm thrilled we're practically neighbors." Georgina's honeyed drawl was more pronounced than Justin's, each word low and provocative, meant to deliberately entwine and ensnare the senses. "We jus' love company. Until now, Justin only accepted a handful of our invitations. Perhaps now that he's married, you can coax him into comin' more often. Women get so bored out here away from everythin'." Flirtation brightened her dark eyes as she beamed at Justin.

The Howells, with their ebullient young son in tow, were next to arrive, followed by Nora Cunningham. Eden embraced the older woman with genuine affection.

"Well, Nephew." Nora gave Justin a peck on the cheek. "Greenbriar is all that you promised—and more. You are to be commended. I demand a guided tour of your lovely new home," she said, linking her arm through Eden's.

Justin and Eden were happy to grant her request. Since

they were familiar with the house from their previous visit, Clara and James Howell elected to remain behind and tend their rambunctious three-year-old. The other guests followed, eager to view Justin's gracious home. The house met with unanimous approval.

"Oh, Justin," Georgina cooed, "what excellent taste you have. Don't tell me you picked out all the furnishin's yourself."

"Much of them belonged to my late uncle. I arranged to have it shipped from England when I was there last year."

"You have a good eye for color, Nephew," Nora commented. "If I didn't know better, I would swear your selections have a woman's touch."

"In a way that's true," Justin admitted. "At the time, I had just met the woman who was to become my future wife. She served as my inspiration."

Eden cast a glance at Justin. Did he mean that? Had their first meeting had such a profound affect on him? Pain, swift and saber sharp, pierced her heart. How foolish she had been, how terribly naive. She had held his love in the palm of her hand and, not recognizing its value, let it trickle slowly through her fingers.

"What a romantic you are, Justin." Georgina sighed enviously. "Perhaps you could give Frederick lessons."

"And my Emmett," Bernice added so emphatically that she drew laughter.

After touring the upper level, they returned downstairs. As Justin anticipated, the music room brought the greatest praise.

"A pianoforte!" Georgina exclaimed. "I've been beggin' Frederick to buy one for me."

"You confessed, my dear, that you hated piano lessons and never learned more than a simple scale," Frederick reminded his wife pointedly.

Georgina pouted. "Well, then, you can hire someone to play while I sing."

Emmett Dodd whispered to his wife. "Place like this

must have cost a fortune. Could of built a house half this
size and bought more land for tobacco.''

"Oh, Emmett," Bernice scolded. "Is tobacco all you
ever think about?''

"I have a surprise in store for tonight," Eden announced. "But now it's time for tea. There will be libation
for the gentlemen, if they prefer." She rang a tiny silver
bell, and Liza entered promptly with a tea service, Didi
with a tray of pastries.

After refreshments, the guests went to their designated
rooms to rest and repair themselves for supper. Recon-
vened later in the sitting room, they were engaged in conversation when Liza stood hesitantly in the open doorway
and beckoned to Eden.

"The Wainwrights have arrived."

"Show them in, Liza."

Justin came up behind Eden and, placing his hand on
the small of her back, bent his head to question softly, "Is
anything amiss?''

She shook her head. "The Wainwrights have just arrived."

Millicent Wainwright sailed into the room, her huge
breasts jutting before her like the prow of one of His Majesty's ships. "We're late, but it couldn't be helped. Something or other on the carriage broke.''

"An axle, Millicent. An axle," Jasper supplied, entering. He pumped Justin's hand.

"Whatever the cause for the delay, we're happy you're
here now," Eden responded graciously.

Millicent brushed Eden's welcome aside. "We brought
along our houseguest. I hope you'll be able to accommodate another person. I, of course, always make arrangements for an extra guest or two, but perhaps you aren't
familiar with such niceties.''

At her side Eden felt Justin tense.

"What did I tell you before, woman?" Jasper growled.
"Mind your manners!''

"Why, Jasper!" With wide eyes, Millicent splayed a

hand across her ample bosom. "I was merely being truthful. I wanted Eden to know that we're all aware she's rather new at acting as hostess and are prepared to make allowances for her inexperience."

The woman's attempt to portray herself as a paragon of thoughtfulness made Eden's lips twitch in amusement. "I appreciate your concern, Millicent." She tucked her hand through the crook of Justin's arm. "However, the doors of Greenbriar are open to both friend and stranger. Your guest is more than welcome."

Justin squeezed her hand. "My wife is quite remarkable. I've yet to see her fail to meet a challenge."

"Humph!" Millicent sniffed and looked askance. Spotting a sympathetic friend, she excused herself and made her way toward Bernice Dodd to air her grievances. Jasper followed, relishing a discussion of tobacco prices with Emmett.

Charles and his pregnant bride, Rosemarie, were the next to appear. He looked dapper, wearing a peruke to cover his close-cropped blond hair, and a sapphire blue coat. Rosemarie hung on his arm, looking weary and bedraggled. Eden felt a quick stab of pity for the girl.

Charles made a knee. His pale glance fixed avidly on Eden. "My, my, from serving wench to royal princess. A far cry since you were last seen riding off in a shabby dress and borrowed cloak."

Eden inclined her head. Her firm grip on her husband's arm cautioned restraint. "Because of Justin, I have much to be grateful for." Her gaze softened as it played over her husband's features before returning to the couple. "Rosemarie," she said, addressing the young woman, "I see congratulations are in order. In your condition, you must have found the journey trying. Let Didi show you to your room so you can freshen up."

"Thank you." Rosemarie managed a tired smile. "That would be lovely." Eden summoned a servant, and the girl gratefully followed her up the winding staircase.

Charles swept an assessing look over the guests, then

singled out Georgina Benton. "Excuse me," he murmured. "I must say hello to an old friend."

"Oh, Eden." Caroline's excited voice preceded her into the drawing room. "Your house is truly beautiful."

Eden's gaze skimmed past Caroline. The man accompanying the girl arrested all her attention. A loud droning blotted out the chatter of the guests; the room dimmed. Frantically, Eden clutched Justin's sleeve. "Rodney!" The name escaped her bloodless lips.

Feigned disbelief spread across the saturnine features of the foppishly-clad gentleman wearing a magenta velvet coat and tight satin breeches. A jagged scar peeped beneath the patch covering his left eye.

"Eden!" Imbued with joy, his voice carried to the far reaches of the room. "Eden! I can't believe it's really you!" He enfolded the dumbstruck woman in a fond embrace.

Eden's knees turned to jelly, and she caught Rodney's shoulders to keep from falling. To everyone observing, it appeared to be a fond reunion.

Justin scowled at the man gripping his wife in a bone-crushing hold. Who was this popinjay with the clipped British accent? Friend? Former beau? Was he the mysterious one-eyed man Eden believed she had seen in Williamsburg? And what right did he have to treat her with such familiarity? Justin felt an overpowering urge to rip her from the interloper's arms. His hands balled into fists.

"Let me feast my eyes on the beauty I never thought to see again." Rodney stepped back and pinched Eden's chin between thumb and forefinger. His words were gentle, the contact cruel.

Justin noisily cleared his throat. Without looking at him, Eden sensed her husband's burgeoning wrath. Recovering somewhat, she jerked free of Rodney's touch. "Justin, permit me to introduce—"

"My lord, you know this woman?" Millicent Wainwright elbowed her way to the front of the guests now crowding around the trio.

Rodney gazed at the circle of expectant faces, clearly gratified by the stir he was creating. His thin lips curled in a gleeful smile. "Know her, madam? Indeed, I know this lady quite well. Eden is my dear baby sister."

Murmurs of surprise rippled among the onlookers. None was more shocked than Justin. "Sister?" he rasped. Until now, he had believed Eden without benefit of family. He felt like a fool, learning of the existence of a brother in front of a houseful of guests. What else had she kept from him? he wondered with growing fury.

"Your brother, Eden?" Nora Cunningham peered from one to the other. "I fail to see a family resemblance."

Color slowly seeped into Eden's chalk-white face. "Rodney is my stepbrother," she clarified.

"Eden was little more than an infant when my father married her mother. Unfortunately, the lovely lady died in childbirth the following year. Father raised Eden as though she were his own."

Millicent Wainwright was incensed. Eden Tremayne, the chit, a former bond servant, was long-lost kin of the Earl of Rutherford? The coincidence was too great to bear in silence. "If she's truly your sister, as you claim, why did she arrive in the Colonies as an indentured servant?"

Her audacity drew gasps. Jasper reached for his wife's arm, but she obtrusively pulled free of his touch.

"Ah, dear lady, my fault entirely," Rodney acknowledged with a sorrowful shake of his bewigged head. "I was trying to provide for her welfare the only way I knew how—by arranging a suitable marriage. Alas"—he sighed—"if only I had known how unhappy that would make her. You should have confided in me, Eden my dear. I'm not the monster you fear."

Eden held her tongue and regarded her stepbrother warily. This wasn't at all how she had imagined her reunion with Rodney would be. Granted, he spoke in half-truths, but he could hardly reveal the unvarnished facts without doing irreparable damage to his character.

"Why did she flee England?" Millicent demanded.

Eden sensed that Justin, too, awaited the answer.

"Ah, Millicent." Rodney smiled unctuously. "My sister was a proud, headstrong young girl. I hoped a match with an older gentleman such as Lord Ashcroft would curb her impulsiveness. Eden, however, refused to accept my decision. Instead she ran away. I turned London upside down searching for her, but"—he spread his hands in a helpless gesture—"to no avail."

Everything Rodney said was true, Eden admitted bitterly, but there was more, much more that he left unsaid. He made no mention of the fact that Lord Ashcroft was not only old but also impotent. He also failed to remark on his plan to bestow her virginity, albeit unwillingly, on his friend Geoffrey Killington to repay a gambling debt. When Rodney had tried to use force, a struggle had ensued. Eden had struck him with a crystal vase, a blow that had cost him his left eye. His screamed threats to kill her had driven her into the night with only the clothes on her back. Fear and guilt had plagued her since then.

A motion in the doorway caught Eden's attention, and she looked up. Liza mouthed that supper was ready to be served. Eden drew a breath to steady herself. "Supper is ready," she announced quietly, hiding her turmoil behind a bland expression. "We can continue this conversation later, if you wish."

"About time," Emmett Dodd muttered. "A man can't survive on fancy pastries. He needs meat and potatoes."

Conscious of his role as host, Justin took Caroline's arm and escorted her into the dining room. Rodney presented his arm to Eden with a flourish. Wanting to avoid a scene, she accepted it and followed her husband's broad back. With the exception of Rosemarie, who pleaded fatigue and asked that a tray be sent upstairs, it was a noisy, chattering bunch who gathered around the supper table.

Eden's new status as stepsister to the fifth Earl of Rutherford gained her instant respectability from those who had come to scoff. Even Millicent Wainwright's irascible tongue was leashed. Once supper was over, the men adjourned to Justin's study for brandy and cigars, while the ladies were treated to persicot in the music room.

Didi poured thimble-sized glasses of the golden liquid from a cut-glass cruet and passed them among the ladies. "Please try some," Eden encouraged. "You'll find Sookie's persicot quite good."

Nora sniffed appreciatively and took a sip. "Mmm." She closed her eyes. "Delicious."

Georgina, Bernice, and Clara followed suit. Millicent stared into her glass as though expecting to find a worm crawling at the bottom. "What's in it?" she asked suspiciously.

"Sookie's recipe is a closely guarded secret," Eden replied smoothly, "but I believe it's made of peach, apricot, and cherry pits steeped in French brandy and seasoned with cloves and cinnamon."

"Humph! Spirits!" Millicent shook a warning finger at Caroline just as the girl was about to sample her drink. "None for you, missy. I don't want you becoming a tippler."

"But, Mother . . ." Caroline whined.

Millicent leveled her finger at her daughter. "No arguments, missy." As soon as conversation resumed, and with no one watching, Millicent raised her own glass and took a large swallow.

When the men rejoined the ladies, a magician and a mime supplied the evening's entertainment. With Publick Times about to commence, it had been a simple matter to obtain talent from the skilled bands of performers who passed through on their way to Williamsburg.

During the magician's sleight-of-hand performance, Eden felt herself the object of Rodney's one-eyed stare. When she looked in his direction, he bestowed a benign smile that gave no clue to his real thoughts. Eden glanced away, more confused than ever. What did he want of her? Nothing in his calm, sophisticated veneer indicated he intended to harm her, but with Rodney she could never be sure.

One thing she was certain of—Justin's displeasure. He stood on the far side of the room, feet slightly braced, arms folded across his chest. Tight-lipped and unsmiling, he watched the mime's clever, wordless act. Not once did he glance in her direction. Luckily, most guests were too enthralled with the performances to notice their host's grim preoccupation.

Mime and magician accepted the enthusiastic applause and bowed their way out of the music room.

Imperiously, Rodney stood and snapped his fingers. A male servant carried in a large package tied with a satin ribbon. "With the splendid entertainment, I nearly forgot the wedding gift I brought. I purchased it in the fond hope that my hostess and my long-lost sister would be one and the same. Eden is an uncommon name, after all," he added by way of explanation.

Not to be outdone, Nora Cunningham rose to her feet. "Since you two married in such haste, I, too, brought along a belated wedding gift." Others echoed similar sentiments and hurried off to return with gaily wrapped packages.

Eden sat in a wing-backed chair, Justin at her side, and one by one opened the gifts. The goodwill of the guests clustered around them acted as a tonic to her flagging spirits. For a time, she relaxed and enjoyed being a bride. A handsome mahogany dressing box, a Chelsea figure of a shepherdess, a polished-brass spice caster, and a pair of silver candlesticks passed from hand to hand.

"I see you've saved mine for last. Go ahead," Rodney urged guilelessly. "Open it."

'Yes, please do, Eden," Caroline urged. "Let's see what your brother brought."

Rodney negligently crossed one leg over the other. "Please do, little sister. I spared no trouble selecting the appropriate gift." His long, bony fingers adjusted the velvet patch covering his left eye.

Eden followed the movement. Her momentary feeling of well-being vanished, replaced by alarm. Justin's hand, warm and reassuring, pressed into the curve of her shoulder. "Go ahead, love, open it." The low command vibrated like honed steel.

Her gaze fell to the box in her lap. Her movements slow and awkward, she tugged at the bow, slid aside the paper, and lifted the lid. Sifting through the padding, her probing fingers closed around a solid object and pulled out a lead-glass vase etched with roses. Candlelight caught and refracted a rainbow of colors.

"Oh, how lovely." Georgina sighed. "Frederick, you'll have to buy me one just like it."

Eden's heart hammered in her ears. She was scarcely aware that Justin had taken the vase from her numb fingers and was examining it.

"It's a replica of one we had at Sommerset," Rodney explained. "My sister, it appears, is quite overwhelmed."

A replica? Did Rodney think she was a fool? It was the mate of the one she had struck him with on that unforgettable night. The vase had broken, a spiked edge gouging Rodney's face. A jagged shard had impaled his left eye. There had been blood, so much blood. A shudder rippled through her, and bile burned her throat. Eden feared she was going to be ill.

"Perhaps your gift will comfort my wife should she find herself lonely for England," Justin commented before placing the vase in Georgina Benton's greedy hands.

"That's my cherished hope," Rodney said with mock sincerity. "Does it bring back memories, my dear?"

"Yes." Eden's answer was barely audible.

"You look a bit peaked, sister." Rodney picked an invisible speck of lint from his coat.

"The poor thing," Nora commiserated. "With all the preparations Eden's had to contend with, she's probably dead on her feet but too polite to say so."

Justin studied Eden closely. Her skin was so pale it seemed translucent. Her violet eyes were as dark as purple ink, and just as impenetrable. She looked more fragile than the Chelsea shepherdess. Damn her insufferable hide!

Fragile or not, he was angry enough to throttle her. Yet at the same time, he wanted to protect her. How could he ever have thought life was simple? Eden added a complexity he had never imagined.

"I don't know about the rest of you, but I have a son who gets up with the roosters," Clara intervened.

A loud snore came from Emmett Dodd.

"Emmett's an early riser," his wife explained. "When it's past his bedtime, he falls asleep. Doesn't matter where he is, could be the Governor's Palace, it wouldn't matter to Emmett."

Eden roused herself and stood. "I hadn't realized the hour. May we bid you all good-night?"

The guests drifted toward the stairs in groups of twos and threes. Rodney lagged behind. Nervously, Eden laid her hand on his sleeve. "Rodney, we have to talk." She spoke softly, quickly, taking care her words wouldn't carry to Justin, who stood in the entranceway speaking with Charles.

Rodney patted her hand. "After all these months, surely what we have to say can wait." He placed a dry kiss on her forehead, something he had never done before, and left her staring after him in bewilderment.

Justin took Eden's elbow and led her up the stairs toward the bedroom they were sharing because of the number of guests. Eden risked a glance at her husband. His congenial manner was deceiving, for the painful grip on her arm was far from friendly. The latch on the bedroom door had scarcely clicked shut when his anger erupted. "Your brother!"

"Shh!" Eden cast a worried glance at the closed door. "Justin, please, everyone will hear you."

"Brother?" His voice lowered to a loud whisper. "You never mentioned a brother. You deliberately deceived me into thinking you had no family. Why?"

"Rodney is my stepbrother. We've never been close." Eden crossed to the dressing table and removed amethyst studs from her earlobes. "If you had asked me whether or not I had a stepbrother, I wouldn't have lied to you."

"So this is all my fault for not asking the right questions?" Justin shrugged out of his coat and flung it across the foot of the bed.

"I didn't say that."

His waistcoat followed in a crumpled heap. "What else are you keeping from me? Perhaps you also left behind a fat husband and two snively-nosed brats."

"Stop it. You're being ridiculous."

"Since when is it ridiculous to want to know about the woman you're married to?" he countered, jerking his stock loose. "Just once, can't you be open and honest? Do you always have to be so damn secretive?"

It had been a long day, and Eden had endured as much as she could stand. Turning, she marched over to him, hands on hips. "How do you expect me to tell you anything when you're acting like a bully?"

He bent and brought his face close to hers until they stood nose to nose. "Bully, is it?"

"You heard me." She folded her arms across her chest and glared mutinously at him. "You're a fine one to speak of honesty, Justin Tremayne. You very conveniently forget your own duplicity. For months you allowed me to think you were a poor farmer, that Greenbriar was a simple cabin."

"I explained why I did those things and told you I was sorry." His voice lowered, the angry edge turning mellow. "I am, Eden, and I'll always regret my actions."

Staring into those fathomless gray eyes, Eden found it impossible to sustain her outrage, especially knowing Justin had every right to be furious. Her shoulders drooped with defeat. She should have told him the truth about Rodney long ago, but she couldn't bear the thought of his love turning to loathing. "You have every reason to be angry," she conceded in a small voice.

"Damn right I do!" He straightened, her admission deflating the last of his rage. "Why didn't you tell me you left England because your brother was forcing you into a marriage you didn't want?''

''And why can't the past stay buried?'' She spread her hands in supplication. ''You seem to think that being open and trusting should be as easy as breathing, but it's not like that for everyone.'' She went to the mirror and began plucking pins from her hair with quick, agitated movements. Glossy ebony tresses spiraled down her back and around her shoulders.

Justin approached and gravely regarded her reflection. ''Then tell me what it's like for you. Don't keep us strangers.''

Her hands paused in midair. Strangers? Is that what they were? Her eyes met his in the mirror, and she nearly faltered. Slowly, she turned to face him.

''My childhood was much different from yours. You've never known what it's like to be unloved and unwanted. I did. I never had anyone to confide in, anyone I could trust.'' She walked to the bed and sat down on the edge, lacing her fingers together nervously. ''My father died before I was born. When I was hardly more than a baby, my mother remarried a man much older than herself, an English lord with a young son. She died a year later. I don't even remember her. To my stepfather I was an unwanted burden. To Rodney I was a threat.''

She stared down at her hands. ''My stepfather was unfeeling and often cruel. He was extremely critical of both of us and could be quite merciless when we did anything to displease him.''

Justin listened in shock and outrage while she revealed details of her unhappy life at Sommerset. He couldn't help but contrast Eden's childhood with his own. Secure in his parent's affection, he had always felt free to express himself. He sat beside her and took her hands in his, amazed to find them icy cold. ''Eden, I'm sorry. Until now I never knew what it was like for you.''

She raised her eyes to his. ''I learned at an early age to keep my thoughts and feelings to myself. I've been this way for so long it's become a habit . . . a pattern. It's not something I can discard like last year's ballgown just because someone says 'Trust me'. I am trying, Justin, believe me, but it's very difficult to change.''

Justin was moved by her impassioned entreaty. He smoothed her hair and cupped her face in his hands. ''I promise I'll try to be more patient and understanding. I love you, Eden Tremayne, and I always will.''

''And I you,'' she echoed against his broad chest.

Chapter 20

It was happening again. Rodney grabbed the back of a chair and swayed slightly. A fuzzy gray cloud descended over his good eye. His vision blurred. Cold sweat beaded his upper lip and trickled from his armpits.

"The bitch!" he cursed. "The little bitch!" He was going blind, and it was all her fault.

Groping his way around the chair, he fell into the cushion and buried his face in his hands. As anxiety mounted, his breathing came in short, rapid gasps. His vision would return. It always did. Another minute. Another minute, and it would came back. Dear God, why was it taking so long?

Hadn't the most recent doctor he had consulted warned him that this would happen? According to him, the attacks would become more frequent, last longer . . . until the day when his eyesight would not return.

The first time the blurring had occurred was aboard ship. The aberration was so fleeting he had deluded himself into thinking he had only imagined it. But after docking in Baltimore, it had occurred again. All the physicians agreed on three issues: there was no treatment, no cure, and in all probability, his pending disability was not related to the injured left eye. After eliciting the information that his grandfather had gone blind while still in his prime, the doctors had shaken their heads and said there was nothing anyone could do. Soon he would be blind, totally helpless, dependent on others for the rest of his days.

"Oh, God," he wailed to the empty room. "What did I ever do to deserve this?"

Close to despair, Rodney dropped his head against the back of the chair. A mantle clock ticked ceaseless minutes. Gradually, the cloudy veil lifted. Objects in the room became foggy outlines, then their edges sharpened, and the image cleared. Rodney's breathing slowed to normal. His immaculate linen shirt clung to him, damp and chill against his skin. He inhaled deeply and smelled the fetid odor of his own terror.

Shaken, Rodney got up and crossed to the washbasin. After scrubbing his flesh with perfumed soap until the skin tingled, he donned a fresh set of clothes. He fixed a gummed patch of black velvet cut in the shape of a mandolin to his cheek, then adjusted the eyepatch. He scowled into the mirror. Beneath the close-fitting, heavily powdered bagwig, his complexion appeared sallow. His scowl deepened. His days were numbered. Soon, quite soon, he wouldn't be able to see his mirrored reflection ever again.

Impotent rage coursed through him. Damn! He swept the pitcher from the washstand and hurled it across the room. What good were doctors? What did they know? They'd never convince him Eden wasn't responsible for his infirmity. If it was the last thing he did, he would make her pay. Stepping over the broken glass, he left the room.

A leisurely afternoon ride through the countryside had brought the house party to a picturesque spot along a bend of the James River. Autumn had begun to brush the woodland in shades of crimson and gold. Feathery clouds scudded lazily across a bright blue sky. Summer's humidity had vanished, leaving the air fresh and clear. Earlier that day, servants had dug barbecue pits and lined them with hickory chips. The mouth-watering aroma of roasting meat filled the air.

"A perfect day for a picnic," Nora pronounced.

The others agreed. They spilled from open carriages and swarmed into the grove. The level, grassy spot was ideally suited for lawn bowling. Nearby iron stakes driven into the ground invited quoits, a game in which players tossed metal rings at a peg. Guests issued good-natured challenges, then chose teams.

Rodney appeared at Eden's elbow. "Well done, little sister. Thanks to father's tutelage, you've turned into an excellent hostess."

"Rodney, you've been avoiding me."

"Nonsense. You're imagining things." He smiled and walked away. "There'll be time for talk later."

Eden watched him saunter off, puzzled by his manner.

Justin had observed the brief exchange. "What was that all about?" Granted, Rodney was Eden's only kin, but there was something about the man he didn't trust.

"Oh, nothing." She shrugged. "It's just that with the party, we haven't had a chance to talk privately."

Justin studied his wife through narrowed eyes. "Forgive my saying so, but you don't seem overjoyed to have your brother at Greenbriar."

"If you'll recall, we didn't part on the best of terms."

"Do you want me to tell him he isn't welcome here?"

Eden slanted him a startled glance. "You'd do that?"

"You should know I'd do anything for you."

Sounds from the grove filtered to them. Without making the slightest physical contact, Eden felt as if Justin were holding her in his arms. For a short moment, Rodney's presence ceased to be a menace. Justin cared. He would protect her.

Her lips curved upward. "Throwing your wife's only relative out on his ear would never do. It would be an insult to Virginia hospitality."

Not caring who looked on, his mouth plucked the smile from hers. "You, madam, are worth the price."

"There you are, Justin. I've been lookin' all over for you," Georgina Benton drawled, slipping her arm through his. "Surely you can spare your husband for just a tiny little bit." She smiled sweetly at Eden, then turned limpid brown eyes on Justin. "All Frederick wants to do is watch

Emmett and Jasper toss quoits. How tiresome. He's no fun at all. Come on, Justin." She tugged on his arm. "Be my partner for lawn bowlin'."

"Go ahead, I don't mind." Eden spoke up before Justin could tactfully decline. "I only hope you enjoy Justin's company half as much as I do, Georgina. He's never tiresome." She tossed the last over her shoulder in a perfect imitation of the girl's Carolina accent.

Justin flashed Eden a roguish grin before a remark from Georgina demanded his attention. "You had all your friends worried to death at your runnin' off and marryin' a bond servant . . . of all people. Shame on you, Justin!"

"As you can see, your worry was unnecessary."

"When you sent word you weren't receivin' callers until you were settled at Greenbriar, why"—she peered up at him through a thick screen of eyelashes—"we all thought you were havin' second thoughts about your weddin'."

"Quite the contrary. I've never been happier."

Her dark eyes boldly swept his length. "You certainly look fit."

"Now that you've met her, what do you think of my wife?"

"Actually she's quite attractive," Georgina admitted grudgingly. "And knowin' she's related to an earl makes her socially acceptable."

Justin's expression turned frosty. "Even without her stepbrother's presence, Eden would have gained approval on her own merit."

"Oh, dear me." Georgina fluttered her eyelashes. "I didn't mean to be insultin'. It's all very romantic—you elopin' with a servin' girl, then hidin' her away for months on end. I only wish Frederick was more like you." She sighed, moving against him in such a way that her breast brushed his arm. "You have no idea what it's like bein' married to a man so much older than oneself."

"Frederick's a good man."

"A good man, but a borin' one." She pouted. "Sometimes I get so bored I think I'll go crazy."

Justin glanced uneasily at the throng of people. "This is hardly the time or place to discuss your marriage."

"Why, Justin, you read my mind," Georgina cooed. "With all these people to see to, your wife is bound to be busy. If *you* get bored, perhaps we can find ourselves a diversion." The invitation in her doelike eyes was unmistakable. Her tone dropped to a conspiratorial level. "I bet you know all the ways of pleasin' a woman."

Justin removed her hand from his sleeve. "I think not."

Georgina took the rejection with good humor. "If you should change your mind. . . . " She strolled toward the green where the Howells, along with Charles and Caroline Wainwright, waited to begin the game.

Eden moved around the grove, stopping frequently to speak with her guests and oversee the servants. Amidst shouts of laughter and encouragement came the clang of quoits striking their target and the clank of wooden lawn bowls. Everyone seemed to be having a marvelous time. Eden wandered to the spot in the shade where the older women were gathered.

"Join us." Nora indicated a chair next to hers.

Bernice looked up from her needlepoint. "Please do, Eden."

"I was just saying what a pity that Rosemarie didn't feel up to coming along. The poor dear has such a delicate constitution." Millicent spoke fondly of her daughter-in-law. "Being in the family way is proving to be a trial for her. I told her that soon the queasiness will subside, and she won't feel tired all the time."

Bernice clucked sympathetically. "First one's always difficult. When I carried my Harry, I was sick the entire nine months."

"You must be thrilled to be expecting your first grandchild, Millicent," Nora commented.

"Absolutely." Millicent beamed. "Rosemarie proved so fertile, we're looking forward to half a dozen or more babies." She turned to survey Eden's slim form. "How disappointed Justin must be that you aren't expecting yet. You know how men are about siring an heir. Pity. You've been married nearly six months."

"Really, Millicent!" Nora was aghast.

"It's all right, Aunt Nora," Eden soothed. "I'm certain Millicent didn't mean to be offensive. Did you Millicent?"

"I was merely making an observation." The woman affected an injured air.

"What a wonderful surprise it must have been to find your brother after so long," Bernice commented with a bright smile.

"Yes." Afraid her voice lacked conviction, Eden tried to infuse it with enthusiasm. "Yes, indeed. A surprise that left me quite speechless."

"Lord Rutherford is a most charming and sophisticated man. Jasper was introduced to him in Williamsburg and invited him for an extended visit. Caroline is quite taken with him. It would be a wonderful match. Lady Caroline Rutherford has rather a nice ring to it, don't you agree?" Millicent looked at the group expectantly.

"You poor dear." Bernice clucked her tongue and patted Eden's hand. "How difficult life must have been when you arrived in the Colonies."

"Humph," Millicent snorted. "Not many fine ladies can claim the dubious honor of being former bond servants, can they? Fortunately for you, Eden, your indenture was brief." She turned to Bernice and Nora. "In all my days, I've never seen anyone so clumsy or inept. Eden was a disaster. The only suitable place for her was the scullery."

Eden sucked in her breath at the affront. Her cheeks burned.

"That was totally uncalled for, Millicent," Nora upbraided the woman. "Considering Eden's background, I'm certain she performed admirably."

Millicent shot Eden a spiteful look. You stupid chit, it seemed to say, if it wasn't for you, Caroline might have married Justin and become mistress of Greenbriar. From the corner of her eye, Millicent saw her husband and Lord Rutherford approach and prudently refrained from further comment.

Rodney stood at Eden's shoulder and rubbed his hands together. "Well, ladies, are you prepared for the day's entertainment?"

Dread crept over Eden. "What entertainment?" she asked quietly.

"Why, the cockfight," Jasper supplied heartily.

"It's all the rage in England."

"Your stepbrother suggested we liven up the party, and I agreed." Jasper slapped Rodney on the back. "We selected two of the meanest roosters we could find and brought them along. Soon as a couple of our slaves are done digging the pit, we can start."

"Anyone care to place a wager?" Rodney inquired of the group. He beckoned to a young negro toting two wood-slatted cages, one in each hand, each containing a brightly colored gamecock. "Step up, folks, and take a closer look. Pick your champion."

"Place your bets, ladies and gentlemen," Jasper urged. "Emmett here will hold the purse."

Eden searched out Justin. Judging from his frown, he didn't seem any more pleased at the prospect of a cockfight than she did, but any objections they might have voiced were drowned by the enthusiastic response of the guests. The gentry's inordinate fondness for gambling was once again evident.

At Rodney's instructions, everyone congregated around a shallow pit enclosed by rough-sawn boards. Rodney opened one cage, Jasper Wainwright the other. Each man held a rooster in a firm grip, allowing it to peck away at the other until the birds worked themselves into an angry frenzy.

"Ready, set, go," Rodney shouted.

He released the birds. Immediately they began a battle to the death. With a noisy whirr of wings and raucous cries, they clawed at each other with the long spurs on their legs. When the larger of the two was the first to draw blood, half the group let out a loud cheer.

The sight of the gamecocks ripping each other to shreds sickened Eden. As she backed from the arena, she glanced over her shoulder. She found Rodney observing her, his thin mouth curled in a malevolent smile. His expression removed any doubt from her mind that he'd staged this revolting display solely for her benefit. She left the excited voices behind and walked toward the riverbank.

She felt ill. Out of sight, she eased herself to the ground and leaned against a tree. Closing her eyes, she tried to forget the bloodied feathers and the noisy squawks. She had nearly succeeded when footsteps sounded behind her. Opening her eyes, she craned her neck and saw Rodney coming toward her.

He wore the same parody of a smile. "Anything wrong, sister? Didn't you enjoy the entertainment?"

Her eyes flashed. "Cockfighting is barbaric! It ought to be banned!"

"It certainly didn't agree with you. Your face is positively green. Not your best color, dear sister." He pulled a lace-edged handkerchief from a pocket and fastidiously spread it on the grass before lowering himself beside her. "Lovely weather, I daresay."

Eden glanced sharply at him. "Surely you didn't follow me to discuss the weather. What are you doing here, Rodney?"

"In the Tidewater?" He raised a brow. "Well, actually, I heard there was money to be made in the Colonies. I've been thinking about investing some capital in a shipyard. Rumor has it there are vast tracts of virgin forests just waiting for the axe."

"I was referring to your reason for being at Greenbriar."

"The Wainwright's were gracious enough to include me in their invitation."

He was being deliberately evasive, Eden realized with

exasperation. "Now that you've found me, what do you intend to do?"

"You've grown skeptical. It's not a very attractive trait." He flicked a speck of dust from his sleeve.

"Why did you lie about the vase?"

"Whatever do you mean?"

"Stop playing games! We both know the vase wasn't a duplicate of one at Sommerset."

"Oh, that," he said dismissively. "What did you expect me to do, tell people the sordid details? Imagine the sensation that would have created." He reached into an inner pocket, pulled out a jeweled box, and took a pinch of snuff.

Eden anxiously stroked the gold locket. "The last time we saw each other," she said haltingly, "you threatened to kill me."

"And would have, with my bare hands had I been able."

At last he had said something Eden could believe. His final look of hatred that night was scored into her brain forever. She swallowed. "And how do you feel now?"

"I've always been hot tempered. You know that. My rage cooled, although I admit it took a while. Even a volcano loses much of its energy given time. I didn't come to Greenbriar with murder on my mind—if that's what you're afraid of."

"Then why did you come?"

"Back to that again, are we?" He chuckled. "I wanted to find out once and for all if Eden Tremayne, former bond servant of Jasper and Millicent Wainwright, and the Eden St. James from Sommerset were one and the same."

"Now that you know, what are your plans?"

He shrugged his narrow shoulders. "I'm eager to return home. From all accounts, the Atlantic is treacherous in winter."

Eden quietly let out a sigh of relief. He would be gone soon. She would be safe.

"From the astonishment on your husband's face last

night, I surmised you kept my existence a secret. I expected to hear quite a row and perhaps be tossed out bag and baggage. Since I wasn't, I can only assume you didn't tell your stalwart young buck the terrible truth about your wicked stepbrother. I see you still wear the locket I gave you.''

Eden's hand flew to the gold disk at her throat. She nodded dumbly.

''A reminder of better times, dear sister? Or your guilt?'' With care, Rodney adjusted his eye patch.

His astute question caused her stomach to churn. Though she had tried to convince herself she wore the locket simply because it was her only connection with her past, she now wondered if that was the real reason. She *was* responsible for Rodney's disfigurement. Could it be that she wore the locket, a constant reminder of him, as a penance of sorts? As unconscious atonement for a vicious deed? The notion was unsettling, and she attempted to dismiss its implications.

She stared at the smooth sweep of river as if hoping to share its tranquility. ''I try to forget that horrible night ever happened. I don't like to think about it.''

She failed to see Rodney's face twist into a malignant mask. Bitch! How dare she try to forget the night she left him blind and disfigured. As God was his witness, he'd make sure she remembered it every day of her miserable life.

''I'm truly sorry, Rodney.'' Eden's voice throbbed with contrition; her eyes pleaded for absolution. ''All I wanted was to get away. I never meant to harm you.''

Guilt had become her intolerable burden. It was true she tried to forget—but she found it impossible. Not a day passed in which she didn't recall how Rodney had looked clutching his eye, blood dripping down his cheek, seeping between his fingers. In her sleep, she heard his screamed obscenities. Time and time again she wondered if the final outcome might have been different if she hadn't resisted.

The answer was always the same. Rodney's demands

had been preposterous. It was unthinkable to believe she'd surrender her virginity to repay a gambling debt, then marry another who fondled her with clammy hands and slobbered kisses. Rodney had literally backed her into a corner. Like any cornered animal she had fought to escape.

The struggle had cost Rodney an eye and sent Eden racing through London's dark streets. She had stopped near St. Paul's Cathedral to ease the stitch in her side. Tacked to a post had been a broadside advertising passage to the Colonies in exchange for services. Rising from his lounging position on the church steps, a recruiter—or spirit, as they were called—had sidled up to her. He'd shrewdly assessed the situation, offering comfort and making extravagant promises—food, clothing, lodging, a position as governess to a wealthy family of planters. And eventually, waiting like the proverbial pot of gold at the end of the rainbow, freedom dues—money and the means to begin life anew.

There had been no one to counsel her, no relatives to offer shelter. Nor could she depend on the few friends she had made during her brief stay in London to shield her from Rodney's wrath. She had only herself to rely on. In a foreign land with an ocean separating them, she would be safe. Rodney would never find her.

"Come," the spirit had cajoled. "Let me take care of you." And the man had been true to his word. He had taken Eden to a roach-infested room in St. Katherine's near the Thames where he had kept her supplied with meat pies and cheap wine until it was time to board the ship. The door had been locked from the outside. "For your own protection, miss," the man had told her. Later Eden had wondered if this was true, or if it was a precaution to keep her from escaping.

Rodney's hand on her arm startled her from her reverie. "I'm not blameless either," he said. "I must have been crazy to agree to let Geoffrey take your virtue. I've always been one to act first, regret it later. My conscience is somewhat sluggish," he added with a dry laugh.

"Then you've forgiven me?"

"Let's just say I'm prepared to let things be."

Eden searched his saturnine features, looking for clues to his sincerity. Her gaze rested on the black patch covering his left eye and the wicked-looking scar extending along his cheek. She had done this to him. If he was willing to put the past behind him, he merited her eternal devotion.

Reaching out, she gently touched his scarred cheek. "Thank you, Rodney."

"So this is where you two went off to." Justin's tall figure broke from the trees.

Eden accepted her husband's outstretched hand and rose from the ground. "I hope people won't think me rude, but the cockfight was making me queasy," she explained.

Rodney got to his feet as well and brushed a blade of grass from his pant leg. "My sister's always had a squeamish stomach."

Justin placed his arm around Eden's shoulders and drew her closer. The silvery gaze he directed at Rodney was accusing. "Knowing this, why did you go to so much trouble to bring gamecocks?"

"It's just a sport." Rodney picked his handkerchief from the ground, shook it, and carefully tucked it into his waistcoat. "Aren't you placing too much emphasis on a simple event? Or are you one of those doting husbands who caters to his wife's every whim?"

"I've been fortunate to be blessed with a very considerate husband," Eden said quickly. She flashed a look at Justin, silently entreating him to curb his temper.

Rodney smiled thinly. "Well, I for one am always happy to see people get what they deserve." He turned to Justin. "No offense intended. The birds were just there for sport."

"Then no offense taken." Justin's voice had lost its edge.

"Good." Rodney pulled out his snuff box and offered it to Justin. When he declined, he took a pinch for himself before returning the box to his pocket. "My stepsister and I had a long-overdue talk. I think we reached an understanding."

"Yes." Eden squeezed Justin's hand. "Everything's going to be all right now."

"Good." Justin returned the pressure and tucked her hand in the crook of his elbow. "I'm happy to hear that."

They started back to join the others. Eden felt optimistic that Rodney meant her no harm. He'd soon be gone—not only from Greenbriar, but from the Colonies. Best of all, he bore her no grudge. The glowing smile she bestowed on her husband conveyed her full happiness, and the lambent flame in her violet eyes declared her love.

A speculative gleam brightened Rodney's remaining eye.

Chapter 21

"Oh, Eden." Bess sighed. "You look like a princess."

Eden pivoted in front of the mirror, twisting first one way, then the other. The scarlet brocade was a perfect foil for her dark hair and creamy skin. It was patterned in the fashionable French style known as the sacque, or Watteau gown. The front and sides hugged her slender figure then flared over side hoops, leaving the pleated back hanging in a continuous length from neck to hem, displaying the lush fabric. Her hair was dressed high with two long curls falling over a bare shoulder.

Bess, her head cocked to one side, regarded Eden critically. "Sure you don't want your hair powdered? You'll be the only lady at the ball without white hair."

"All the more reason not to. That alone will single me out from the others."

"You're mistaken, madam." Justin, elegant in a black velvet coat and breeches and a richly embroidered black satin waistcoat, sauntered in from the adjoining dressing room. Pristine flounces of white linen cascaded over his wrists and beneath his stock. "You could braid your hair like an Indian squaw and you'd still be conspicuous. Next to your radiant beauty, others pale."

Eden smiled at his lavish praise. "And you, sir, with your pretty words, could turn the head of any poor lass."

Justin's eyes met Eden's and held. Taking her hand, he raised it to his lips.

317

Bess tittered in embarrassment. "You're both beautiful. I've yet to see a more handsome couple."

Justin turned to regard the girl. "What's this I hear from my wife about you refusing to join the festivities?"

"I got things to tend to. Besides"—Bess shrugged—"it wouldn't be fittin' an' all for a servant to mingle with gentry."

"That sounds like something I would expect to hear from Bear," Justin commented dryly. "Too bad he's in Richmond purchasing livestock. Do you miss him by any chance?"

Hectic color flooded the girl's face. "He's only been gone a week, but it seems like two."

Justin eyed the blushing girl. "It sounds as though things are getting serious between you two."

Flushed cheeks and sparkling green eyes elevated Bess from plain to almost pretty. " 'Neath all that growl and bluster, he's kind and gentle as can be. He's wonderful, Mr. Tremayne."

"That he is, Bess," Justin agreed solemnly.

"If you change your mind about joining the party, Bess, feel free to borrow one of my gowns." Eden hurried to the clothespress. "The pale green silk would look especially nice. Take it as a gift." She thrust the gown into Bess's hands.

"Oh, but I couldn't!" Bess gazed longingly at the dress. "I—"

"Nonsense." Eden cut off further protest. "The color will suit you much better than me. Green always makes me look sickly," she said, unwittingly echoing Rodney's earlier comment.

Bess gulped, blinking back tears. "I've never owned anythin' this fine."

Justin put his arm around Eden's shoulders. "I've learned from experience never to argue with my wife once her mind's made up."

"Why not wear your new dress when Bear returns. Per-

haps he'll take you walking by the river," Eden suggested
as she and Justin left the room.

"Playing matchmaker, are you?" Justin teased.

Eden's face was upturned to her husband's when a door
opened at the far end of the hall. Concealed in shadows,
Rodney watched the pair descend the broad staircase. His
stepsister was much too happy with her lot. It was a pity
that the stupid colonial had offered matrimony.

When Rodney had accidentally discovered that a woman
named Eden was indentured to the Wainwright family, he
had been overjoyed. The idea of Eden as a bond servant
had almost made him believe there was a God. For a time
he had envisioned buying her articles of indenture. Having
his beautiful stepsister at his beck and call held great appeal. Rodney fussily adjusted his lace-edged sleeve. News
of Eden's marriage had thwarted his plan, but he wouldn't
be cheated out of his revenge.

As Justin and Eden stood in the entrance of the ballroom and greeted their guests, more than one person
shared Bess's opinion that they did, indeed, make a handsome couple. In addition to the group already assembled,
owners of neighboring plantations had joined the guests,
filling the gracious home with exuberant chatter. Dozens
of beeswax candles in crystal chandeliers and wall sconces
shed their glow on a rainbow of colorful garb. In one
corner, a trio of musicians tuned their instruments. At a
nod from Justin, they began to play a minuet.

With a flourish, Justin led Eden onto the dance floor.
More couples followed suit until everyone in the room
moved to a synchronized rhythm.

Justin and Eden, their faces set in the prescribed
expressions of polite boredom, bowed and postured to
the slow tempo. The hem of Eden's gown swished the
polished floorboards as they flawlessly executed the complicated pattern of steps, glides, rises and dips, bows and
curtsies.

"You're an excellent dancer, my lord," Eden complimented, gracefully pointing one satin slipper. "I'm happy to see your injured leg no longer hampers you."

"I must remember to thank my nurse . . . later." His low voice was ripe with promise.

When the first set ended, James Howell claimed Eden while Justin danced with Clara. The music changed; partners shifted. Minuets, reels, and marches followed one after the other.

Eden stood next to Charles Wainwright at one side of the ballroom, sipping punch. She caught an occasional glimpse of Justin as he performed intricate steps with a series of ladies who were clearly captivated by his easy charm. Age seemed to make no difference to the women's susceptibility. Eden felt a twinge of jealousy. She wanted to be her husband's partner, the only one he smiled at.

"Am I boring you?" Charles asked.

"Of course not, Charles." Eden forced a smile. "With so many guests to attend to, my attention strayed for a moment."

He took a swallow of punch. "This whole affair has been quite disappointing to Mother."

"I'm sorry to hear that." Eden kept her tone carefully bland. "In what way?"

"Mother was certain the party would be such a disaster that it would fuel gossip for the entire winter." Charles chuckled. "She planned to comfort Justin on his miserable choice of a wife, along with making subtle reminders of how Caroline would have been more ably suited as mistress of Greenbriar. In short, Mother came to gloat."

"Poor Millicent," Eden said. Her gaze swept over the ballroom which resounded with music and laughter. "How terribly distressing this gathering must be for her. Everyone seems to be having a splendid time."

"Splendid, indeed." Charles's light blue gaze fastened on Eden's face. "And so are you. Justin is a lucky man."

Startled, Eden stared at him. How could she have ever thought Charles handsome? Or had desperation only made him seem so? With the passage of years he would undoubtedly become a masculine version of Millicent. Already a fine network of veins spread across his nose and cheeks. In time his complexion would change from ruddy to florid, his solid girth turn portly, his arrogance become pomposity. Eden felt sorry for Rosemarie. "I haven't yet congratulated you on your impending fatherhood," she said to divert her thoughts.

Charles grinned broadly. "Naturally we're all pleased."

"I wasn't aware you were fond of children."

"I'm not."

Her eyes widened at the blunt admission.

"You needn't look so shocked, Eden. After all, you're no longer a maid. Getting your wife with child, and especially as quickly as I did, is proof of one's manhood." He set his empty glass on a servant's tray and accepted a full one.

If Eden had felt sorry for Charles's bride before, her pity now grew twofold. "Though we haven't had much opportunity to become acquainted, Rosemarie seems a lovely girl," she commented.

"My wife has a delicate constitution. If she's not throwing up, she's nodding off. I must keep reminding her of her wifely duties." Charles's words held little warmth for the woman he had so recently chosen to wed. "Must we spend our time talking of Rosemarie?" he asked querulously. "I find you much more interesting. Who would have guessed that under the guise of serving wench was a lady of quality?"

How strange, Eden thought. Her privileged position, followed by her subsequent lack of station, had never mattered to Justin. Whether she was clothed in homespun or satin, he had always accorded her the utmost respect and consideration. Her eyes instinctively searched for his tall figure among the dancers. Justin was dancing a second round with Georgina Benton. He chanced to look in Eden's direction and found her watching from the sidelines. She sensed rather than saw concern darken his eyes when he noted Charles Wainwright beside her. She sent him a re-assuring smile.

"You could have knocked me over with a feather," Charles continued, "when Lord Rutherford embraced you as his long-lost baby sister."

"Stepsister," Eden amended. "Forgive me, Charles, can we continue this conversation another time? There are preparations I must see to."

"By all means." Charles caught Eden's hand and bent over it. "I anticipate our next meeting with great pleasure."

Eden realized it was rude to leave the man standing there, but it would be even worse to remain and allow her growing dislike to show. Good heavens! Did most men view siring a child as a tribute to their masculinity? Would Justin feel the same way? Her hand smoothed the brocade over her flat stomach. She sincerely hoped not.

Eden decided to slip away. Perhaps she'd seek out Bess and ask her about the sleeping arrangements for their additional guests. Upon leaving the ballroom, Eden passed Justin's study, which had been converted into a card room. Men sat around tables, placing bets and discussing tobacco prices, their voices slurred from having liberally imbibed Justin's brandy. The air was blue with cigar smoke; the pungent odor polluted the hallway.

Eden noticed Rodney standing just inside the open door, a brandy snifter in one hand, a cigar dangling indolently from the fingers of the other. It was impossible to pass unnoticed. At the rustle of her skirts, he looked up and stepped into the hall.

Eden paused. "Are you enjoying the party?" she inquired politely.

His lips curled. "As much as possible—under the circumstances." He adjusted his eye patch.

Unease slithered through her. Rodney was a complex man. Often he'd lulled her into false complaisance, only to remind her later that she'd gravely misjudged his intent.

"What circumstances are you referring to?" she asked now.

He motioned toward the study with his snifter. "A singularly uninteresting bunch, these provincials. As a group, a rather dull lot."

"Perhaps the dancing would be more to your liking." Eden started past him.

"Don't rush off." He tossed down the brandy, set the snifter on a marble-topped table, and trailed after her. "A breath of fresh air is exactly what I need."

Eden felt concerned. There was no way to avoid Rodney's company without appearing shrewish. After all, she consoled herself, he would soon be returning to England. She stepped outside with him and began to circle the garden slowly.

"What about you, Eden? Aren't you sick to death of this dreary backwoods? Don't you ever long for the opera, the ballet, or a conversation that doesn't revolve around tobacco?"

"I admit I found Colonial ways strange at first, but I've grown accustomed to them."

"You mean you have no wish to return home?"

"For me, this is home."

"Surely you're not serious! There's nothing you miss? Absolutely nothing?"

Her lips twitched in amusement. "Perhaps if I think really hard, I'll remember something." She pretended to ponder the matter as they rounded a turn in the path. "Springtime in England is superb. And I used to love curling into your father's leather chair in the library on a rainy day and sipping Swiss chocolate while nibbling Cook's butter scones."

"Remember the afternoon we rode through Hyde Park in my new curricle?" His tone grew reminiscent. "I don't know which turned more heads, you or the curricle. Do you recall how one young man was so busy gaping that he walked into a tree?"

Eden laughed softly. "That was when I first arrived in London."

"And I experienced a sudden rash of invitations from eager young swains anxious to be introduced to my beauteous stepsister. I had quite a gay time. Ah, yes"—Rodney sighed wistfully—"I'm eager for home."

"When will you be leaving?"

"As soon as I can book passage. Is there any chance you might return for a visit someday?"

"It's unlikely." Eden experienced no regret at the thought. "Justin has much work to do establishing Greenbriar."

Completing their tour of the garden, they returned to the front entrance. "This is just a rhetorical question, you understand"—Rodney paused on the wide porch—"but what would Justin do if you decided to return to England? Would he let you go? Or would your dashing young husband follow you to the ends of the earth?"

Eden stared at the lovely house. Every window was brightly lit. Laughter and music wafted on the night breeze. Greenbriar was solid proof of Justin's pride. Months ago, her mindless flight had struck that pride a crippling blow, one that had damaged their relationship almost beyond repair.

"No," she answered quietly, melancholy stealing over her. "I ran from him once. He vowed never to follow me again."

Without further comment, Rodney watched her go up the front steps and through the main door. An idea formed in the cunning recesses of his brain. Chortling at the simplicity of his plan, he made another circle of the garden.

Eden and Justin held another ball the next evening, a lavish repetition of the first. On this particular evening Eden, not Justin, was attired in black. The satin gown featured a deep square-cut neckline, the waist coming to a sharp point in front, the wide hoops extending sideways.

The bodice and long, fitted sleeves were bordered with lace frills. Eden had allowed Bess to powder her elaborate coiffure, and in a moment of daring, had applied a heart-shaped patch near the corner of her mouth. Worry darted across her features. Did the bodice feel tighter than it had at an earlier fitting? Was her bosom more provocatively displayed?

"Wish I could be a fly on the wall," Bess said, giggling and stepping back to admire Eden's appearance. "I'd give another year's indenture to see Mistress Wainwright's face when she sets eyes on you."

"The only person I wish to impress is Justin." Eden's eyes gleamed with determination. "With Georgina Benton batting her big brown eyes at every man in sight, I want to make sure I'm the woman my husband notices."

"Mr. Benton's too busy with his card game to pay any mind." Bess began straightening the clutter on Eden's dressing table. "Why would a woman marry a man old enough to be her father?"

Remembering Rodney's plan to marry her off to a man even older than Frederick Benton, a man wealthy enough not to require a dowry, Eden frowned. "There are many reasons, Bess. Among the nobility, marriages are arranged. Few couples marry for love. Before I met Justin, I doubted an emotion such as love even existed."

Bess made a face. "Can't see me marryin' anyone 'less I loved 'em."

"Perhaps I shouldn't pry," Eden said softly, placing her hand on Bess's arm, "but by any chance are you falling in love with Bear?"

The silver hairbrush in her hand forgotten, Bess turned toward Eden, her eyes downcast. "I think about 'im all the time. My heart starts flutterin' whenever we're together." She timidly met Eden's gentle look. "I know I'm not pretty like you. Even all dressed up, I'll never be much to look at. But . . ." Her face grew rosy. "Oh, Eden, he makes me feel pretty inside."

Eden caught her in a swift hug. "You *are* pretty, Bess, in the only way that matters."

Bess sniffed back tears, then pushed away. "Here." She held out an ivory-handled fan. "I'm gonna make you late for your own party."

With a snap of her wrist, Eden spread the fan wide and peered coquettishly over its edge. "Georgina Benton had better behave—or else," she declared in a mock drawl. Bess was still giggling as Eden left the bedroom.

Standing on an upper landing, Eden viewed the scene below, marveling at the Virginian's unquenchable thirst for merriment. Even with very little sleep, they showed no signs of tiring. She descended the stairs slowly, regally. Conversation dribbled off as one by one the guests paid silent tribute to their hostess's stunning beauty. Gradually talk resumed, flowing as freely as before.

Justin greeted Eden at the foot of the staircase. His gaze swept her in sober perusal, lingering on the heart-shaped patch that dared a man to ignore her soft pink mouth, then lowering to the tantalizing swell of her breasts. "Your appearance, madam, leaves me racked with indecision. I'm torn between having your portrait painted and locking you away for your own good."

"I prefer the latter." A beguiling smile curved her lips. "Provided you're locked in with me."

"I'll instruct the jailer to throw away the key." Justin fervently wished there wasn't a houseful of people. He'd like nothing more than to sweep Eden into his arms and carry her back upstairs to the bedroom. He stole a brief kiss before resuming his duties as host.

The sweetness of his kiss lingered on Eden's lips during countless sets of dances with bewigged and smiling gentlemen. She was grateful when it was time for the midnight supper, and Justin rescued her from Emmett Dodd's rambling discourse on the merits of soybeans.

Justin lowered his voice. "You may think me inhospitable, but I'll be happy when everyone departs and I can have more than five uninterrupted minutes of your time."

"I must confess I'm equally guilty." Eden accepted his arm and accompanied him into the dining room. "What with the harvest, and now the housewarming, we've had little chance to be alone."

"Soon, sweet," he promised with a look that set her pulse speeding.

Long tables supported heavy platters of food. Smoked ham, roast turkey, and sliced beef with assorted trays of crabs, oysters, and clams were displayed in an appetizing manner. Another table held nothing but desserts—pies, cakes, and puddings, no two of which were alike.

"Sookie deserves a reward for her efforts," Eden said. "She's a credit to Greenbriar." She spotted Liza in the doorway. When the servant beckoned, she reluctantly excused herself.

"Justin," Georgina pouted, tugging on his arm, "I've been lookin' high and low for you. Eat supper with me, pretty please. All Frederick's interested in are those silly old cards."

"Of course, I'll eat supper with you." Justin and Georgina fell into the line forming at the buffet. "Eden was called away, but I'll save a place for her."

"What a shame," Georgina drawled. "At least we have each other for company."

The first problem was no sooner resolved when a second claimed Eden's attention. By the time she finally made it back to the dining room, only a few stragglers still dawdled over the meal. Music coming from the ballroom signaled that the dancing had resumed. Eden felt her head swim and blamed it on not having eaten. She fixed a small plate of food before the servants carried away the almost-empty platters. Didi brought her a cup of tea. Finishing the meal, she took the tea and slipped out the door into the garden. A few stolen moments of solitude would fortify her for the remainder of the evening.

At first she thought she had the garden to herself. Everyone else, it seemed, was occupied with dancing, playing cards, or imbibing. but she had just settled herself on a wrought-iron bench in a niche in the privet hedge when she heard someone approach.

"You've been ignoring me ever since we arrived. I won't stand for it!" The woman sounded close to tears.

"Ignoring you! Ha! That's a laugh," Charles retorted angrily. "It's you who have been ignoring me, since the day we returned from our honeymoon."

"I can't help it. I've been sick," Rosemarie whined.

"Well, what do you expect from me? Do you want me to hold your hand for nine months? A man has needs, Rosemarie. I'm not a gelding."

"Charles!"

"Come on, honey, let's not fight."

During the brief silence, Eden debated whether she could leave her secluded nook undetected. But before she could react, the argument continued, pinning her to her seat.

"Charles!" Rosemarie's tone was outraged. "How dare you fondle me like some common slut—and out here where anyone could find us." She rushed past Eden in a swish of silk.

"You never want me touching you," Charles yelled. "Before the night's over, I'll find a woman who does."

His agitated footsteps paced the brick walkway not far from where Eden sat. She leaned back, hoping to blend into the shrubbery. She might have succeeded if her powdered hair hadn't formed a stark contrast against a dark background.

The pacing ceased. "Eden? Is that you?" Charles demanded.

"I'm sorry, Charles." She carefully set the teacup on the bench and rose to her feet. "I didn't mean to eavesdrop."

Charles rubbed the nape of his neck. "My wife doesn't understand me. Perhaps she could take lessons from you on pleasing a man. Justin always looks like the cat who swallowed the cream."

"Speaking of Justin, he must be wondering what has

happened to me." Eden tried to edge by Charles, but the wide hoops of her skirt made passing difficult.

"It isn't polite to ignore a guest. Stay a while." Charles grabbed her arm and hauled her close. "No need to worry about your husband. Georgina Benton's taking good care of him."

"Please take your hand off me," she ordered, her voice low.

"Come on, Eden," Charles wheedled. "What's a little kiss between old friends? You never used to mind." He jerked her against his chest, his hot mouth choking off her protests.

Eden's hands were caught between their straining bodies. Using the only recourse left to her, she caught his lower lip between her teeth and bit down. With a muffled oath, Charles released her, wiping at his bloodied mouth.

Her breasts heaved in anger as she confronted him. "If this is an example of your lovemaking, I pity Rosemarie." Eden spun on her heel and sped down the path Rosemarie had taken minutes earlier.

She hesitated on the threshold. Was her hair mussed, her cheeks flushed? She needed to bathe her face in cool water and calm herself. A final glance assured her that the guests were engaged in having a good time. Unobtrusively, she slipped upstairs.

From his vantage point inside the ballroom, Rodney observed Eden's flustered manner. As soon as she disappeared from sight, he sidled up to Justin. "You must have your hands full fending off my stepsister's admirers. In London, she had so many ardent suitors, I practically had to beat them off with a stick."

Justin frowned. "Is there something you wish to tell me, Lord Rutherford? Or are you trying to strike up an idle conversation?"

"Let's not stand on formalities, Justin. After all, we are related—in a manner of speaking."

It wasn't like him to dislike a man for no apparent reason, but Justin felt an instinctive mistrust of his wife's only kin. Perhaps the eye patch lent a sinister appearance. Perhaps the man embodied a certain effeteness. Whatever the reason, Justin would be glad when Rodney sailed for England.

"Poor thing," Rodney murmured sympathetically. "Eden and I had a long chat. I fear my sister is dreadfully homesick. She couldn't ask enough questions about her friends and the happenings in London. She even misses Cook's hot chocolate."

Justin clasped his hands behind his back and stared at the couples bobbing on the dance floor. "Eden has said nothing to make me think she misses her old way of life."

"Of course she hasn't, my dear fellow. She's too much a lady to appear ungrateful. She's beholden to you." He idly took a pinch of snuff. "After all, without your intervention, she'd still face years of Millicent's drudgery."

"I thought that issue was resolved," Justin said in a weary tone. "How many times need I remind her I don't want her gratitude?"

Rodney smiled inwardly. These colonials, how naive, he mused. He could play them like a fiddle. "My sister is quite fond of you. She wouldn't hurt your feelings for the world. But take my word"—Rodney placed a consoling hand on Justin's shoulder—"given a choice, Eden would board the swiftest ship and leave this wretched country at a moment's notice."

Justin clenched his teeth so tightly that a muscle ticked in his jaw. "Eden doesn't seem unhappy or discontent."

"You're not very observant, are you? Haven't you learned?" Rodney shook his head sadly. "My sister is adept at hiding her true feelings. Always has been."

"Why would she tell you how she feels?"

"I told you, Eden and I talked. You're forgetting I'm her only living relative. If not to me, to whom can she unburden herself? It was pitiful really, the way she poured her heart out." His hands in his pockets, Rodney moved off to mingle with the other guests.

Justin stared after him. The future suddenly loomed as colorless as a barren landscape. Did Rodney speak the truth? Eden *was* adroit at concealing her thoughts and feelings. Was she as eager to return to England as Rodney intimated?

Justin wondered if he could selfishly bind her to him if she were truly unhappy. But was he strong enough, courageous enough, to sacrifice his happiness for hers?

Chapter 22

On the sixth day, the last of the guests departed. The inhabitants of Greenbriar heaved a collective sigh of relief. They had achieved their goal: Greenbriar's reputation for gracious entertaining had been firmly established.

One of the first things Eden did was to make certain her servants knew how much she appreciated their efforts. With this thought uppermost in her mind, she visited the kitchen.

"Sookie, you're a gem." She smiled at the jolly, moon-faced cook. "I wanted to thank you again for the splendid job you did during the housewarming. Justin and I couldn't have been more pleased."

Sookie chuckled at the compliment, an infectious sound that made Eden's smile widen. "Glad you happy with ol' Sookie's fixin's."

"Our guests raved about your cooking. Some even wanted to take you home with them."

Apprehension wiped the merriment from the woman's broad face, and Eden wished she were able to call back the careless remark. She should have remembered that the lot of a slave was precarious. "You have no reason to fear, Sookie." She placed her hand on the cook's arm. "Greenbriar will always be your home."

"Sure do like it here, Miss Eden. Don't want no other place ever. You sure is good to all of us."

On a pine table Eden spied an apple pie cooling and

inhaled its mouth-watering aroma. "Mmm, this smells delicious."

Sookie chuckled again and waddled over to stir the contents of a copper kettle. "Miss Eden, no matter how much cookin' ol' Sookie does, you still skinny as a broomstick. But you watch." She waved a spoon in Eden's direction. "I'll fatten you up. Wait till you taste my plum puddin." She smacked her lips and rolled her eyes heavenward.

Eden laughed though she had no doubt the woman was serious. As she turned to leave, she remembered another reason for her visit. "My friend Mary will be coming by later. Her rheumatism is bothering her, and it's hard for her to prepare meals. Would you please fix a basket of food for her?"

"Yes'm, I'll see she don't go hungry. Shore 'preciate her givin' me cuttin's from her herb garden. Make some mighty tasty dishes with those herbs, just you see."

Eden strolled down the bricked path, past the dairy and the laundry. Smoke spiraled lazily from the smokehouse, spicing the crisp autumn air with hickory. From the fattening coop came the cackle of geese and hens.

The gate at the far end of the garden opened a crack, and a familiar, stooped figure slipped through. Mary wore her customary black muslin dress, a vivid turquoise apron tied about her waist, and she carried a willow basket slung over one arm. She saw Eden and hurried toward her with small, quick steps.

"Brung you makin's for dye," Mary announced.

Eden smiled fondly at the lined face and took the basket from her. "You needn't think you have to find an excuse to visit. You're always welcome here."

"I know, I know, but I like bringing you things."

"Why don't we find a quiet spot, then you can teach me the fundamentals of dyeing wool." Eden linked her arm through her friend's, and they continued down the walk.

Near the rear corner of the laundry, they encountered two young slaves tending a great pot of boiling grease and lye suspended over a low-burning fire. After questioning the pair as to the portions of ash and grease being used, Mary seemed satisfied. "Whole secret of soap making is the strength of the lye," she counseled Eden as they moved off. "If a potato will float in the lye so you can see a piece of its surface as big as a ninepence, the lye is just strong enough."

Eden signaled a passing servant and directed the girl to bring refreshments to the rose arbor, her favorite retreat. There they sat on a bench shaded by vines. Summer's last blooms perfumed the air. "Justin said he had the rose arbor built as a permanent reminder of the place where he proposed to me," she mused, a dreamy smile on her face.

"Have you told him yet?"

"Told him?" The question startled her out of her absorption.

"About the babe you're expecting," Mary explained patiently.

Instinctively Eden's hand came to rest on her stomach.

"What are you waiting for, dearie? Tell the lad he's going to be a father."

"I wanted to be certain, and then everything's been so hectic. I was waiting for just the right moment. How did you know?"

"A woman has ways. There's a certain glow about you these days, like a rosebud unfolding. You looked a little peaked for awhile, but that's behind you. I remember being sickly the first three months or so myself."

"Mary!" Eden exclaimed. "I didn't know you had a child."

"A boy." Mary stared unseeingly into the distance. "He died before his second birthday," she said after a lengthy pause.

"I'm sorry." Eden placed her hand over Mary's. The blue-veined skin felt tissue thin beneath hers. "So terribly sorry."

Mary's seamed face looked even more crumpled. "If

the boy hadn't died, my husband might have stayed. As it was, I lost them both.''

''What happened?''

''Run off with a pretty young thing, my Willard did. Love of my life, he was. Never saw him again.''

''Is that when you came here to live?''

Mary nodded. ''Couldn't stand people feeling sorry for me. Didn't want pity then, don't want it now.'' She gave Eden a meaningful look.

''You're a strong woman, Mary. I don't pity you, I admire you.'' Eden gently squeezed the fragile hand.

''Enough time spent on what's past.'' Mary cleared her throat. ''Let's get down to the reason for my visit.'' She reached into the basket and began pulling out cloth pouches tied with bits of bright yarn and cloth. She lifted a packet secured with a narrow strip of black fabric. ''Scrub oak mixed with red maple bark. Good for dying cloth black. . . . ''

Eden listened intently, trying to absorb the information while Mary proceeded to describe the contents of each small package.

''This here's dyer's moss. Grows on rocks and is used for red wool. Barberry root makes a pretty yellow,'' Mary instructed, pulling out another packet. ''Wild indigo makes any shade of blue you could want. To make green, dye the wool with indigo then boil it with hickory bark and laurel. And last of all''—she fished the remaining item from the basket—''walnut hulls if you want brown.''

Eden was truly impressed with Mary's knowledge. ''Whatever would I do without you?''

Mary waved away Eden's praise. ''You'll soon have a houseful of little ones to look after. You won't need an old woman like me hanging around.''

''I'll need you more than ever,'' Eden corrected. ''Who else but you could act as grandmother to a houseful of children?''

''Grandmother, eh?'' Mary's dark eyes were suspiciously bright. ''I like the sound of that.''

While the two women shared a companionable silence, Bess joined them with a tray of lemonade and ginger cakes.

"Sit and rest for a moment, Bess," Eden told her, pouring three glasses of the drink. "You haven't stopped all day."

Bess accepted the invitation and plopped down with a grateful sigh. "What with winter on the way, there's much to be done."

"I know," Eden agreed. "I've come to depend on you a great deal. Justin must be thanked for his foresight in sending for you."

"Your husband is also to be commended for finding Sookie," Mary said, sampling a ginger cake. "Don't think he'd find a better cook if he sent to London."

"Bear says she's the best in the Tidewater," Bess chimed in.

"Sookie certainly has a sunnier disposition than other cooks I've met, including that of the Wainwrights."

Bess munched on the treat. "Bear thinks Millicent Wainwright could keep two cooks busy with the amount of food she eats."

Bear's name seemed to come out every time Bess opened her mouth. Mary and Eden exchanged glances, but refrained from commenting until after Bess had returned to her tasks.

"What the girl sees in that big oaf, I'll never know." Mary brushed crumbs from her apron.

"She's obviously in love with him."

"Think he loves her?"

"I don't know, but I'd hate to see Bess hurt."

"Well, there's only one sure way to find out." Mary jerked her thumb toward the garden gate. "We'll ask him." Eden followed the direction Mary was pointing. The object of their speculation was ambling down the walk.

Bear was nearly upon them when he noticed the two women seated in the arbor. He nodded a greeting and would have continued on his way but Mary called out to him. "Over here, you big lout."

"Who, me?"

"Yes, you," Mary snapped. "Who do you think I'm talking to?"

Deliberately ignoring the old woman, he addressed Eden. "Justin and me got business to discuss."

"Was your trip to Richmond a success?" Eden inquired pleasantly, knowing he had returned that very afternoon.

"Yeah. Justin will be real pleased with the deal I made."

"Enough shilly-shallying," Mary declared. "Eden and I have been talking. We're concerned about Bess. Seems the girl fancies herself in love with you. Though for the likes of me"—Mary shook her head—"I can't imagine why."

"What Mary is trying to say," Eden continued, "is that we want to know if your intentions are honorable."

Astounded at their boldness, Bear roared, "My intentions? Ya want to know my *intentions?*"

The women looked at each other. As if at a given signal, they rose simultaneously to their feet and stared at the blustering man with unnerving calmness.

"You heard us," Mary said. "We're fond of Bess and want to protect her. We don't want her to be a light-o'-love."

Eden folded her arms across her chest and raised a brow. "For all we know, you could be a lothario taking unfair advantage of an innocent girl. Are you in love with Bess?"

"Or are you out to steal her virtue?" Mary poked a crooked finger in his ribs.

"Course not, ya durn fool women." Indignation brought a ruddy glow to Bear's bearded face. "What do ya take me for? I like Bess. Matter of fact, I like 'er a lot."

"But do you love her?" Eden persisted.

Bear shifted his weight from one foot to the other. He stared at the vines, the bench, the ground, the flowers—anywhere except at the women.

"Are you going to marry her?" Mary prodded, jabbing her finger for emphasis.

Bear's face grew redder. He took off his battered felt hat, ran a hand through his shaggy mane, and jammed the hat back on his head. "Don't know if she'll have me."

"Then you do love her!" Eden confirmed with a smile.

"Yeah." Bear's voice was a gruff rumble.

Mary and Eden traded grins. "Then Bess will have you." Eden went up on tiptoe and placed a light kiss on the startled man's cheek. "Congratulations!"

"Yeah, well, gotta be goin'." He doffed his hat and backed away from the rose arbor, feeling bested by two small women.

He was at the gate when Mary called out again. "Break that girl's heart, and you'll have me to answer to."

With a final glance over his shoulder, Bear vanished from the garden. Crazy old woman, his look seemed to say.

A wide expanse of polished mahogany separated two place settings on the dining room table. Didi looked up from laying polished silver in a precise row and noted her mistress's frown. "Anythin' wrong, Miss Eden?"

"Yes, there is." Hands on hips, Eden mentally measured the distance from one end of the table to the other and came to a decision. "From now on when my husband and I dine alone, please see that we're seated next to each other."

A knowing gleam flared in the servant's black eyes. "Yes'm. I'll do jus' that." Smothering a chuckle, Didi left.

Restless, Eden roamed from room to room. Tonight she would tell Justin that she was expecting his child. How would he react? she wondered. Would he be pleased? Like Charles, would Justin regard pregnancy merely as proof of his virility?

She hoped her husband would welcome their child. She prayed he would love it. A child deserved better than she had known. Eden couldn't recall a single day during her childhood when she hadn't felt she was a burden. Her stepfather had been a cold, heartless man with no love to give his own flesh and blood, and even less to bestow on the daughter of another man.

Eden entered the music room. Poor Rodney, she thought with a sigh. He had tried even harder than she to win their father's affection. Neither had succeeded, and the failure had left invisible scars. Eden suspected it had warped Rodney's character. She sat on the piano bench and idly ran her hands over the keyboard. Soon the strains of a hauntingly sad melody filled the house.

When the last note was absorbed by silence, Justin pushed away from the door frame. "You play beautifully."

"Justin!" Eden turned with a start. "I didn't know anyone was listening."

"Evidently not." He strolled toward her, his hands behind his back, his face somber.

Eden waited, trying to assess his mood. He didn't look angry, but neither did he look approachable. The shuttered expression was back, the one she had grown to hate during the long days of their estrangement.

"You must have taken your lessons seriously as a young girl."

"I suppose I did," she said, gauging him cautiously.

He leaned casually against the pianoforte, his arms folded across his chest, one ankle crossed over the other. "Do you ever think of England?"

"Well, yes, as a matter of fact I do."

"Do you ever wish to return?" There, he had done it. He had voiced the concern uppermost in his mind. The conversation with Rodney had spawned nagging doubts which had since multiplied.

Eden rose to her feet and placed a hand on his sleeve. "Greenbriar is my home now. I wish for no other."

His eyes, as turbulent as a summer storm, studied her face as though trying to read her soul.

An unnamed fear ruffled her newfound contentment, and Eden's grip tightened on the sleeve of his coat. "Justin . . . ?" She spoke his name tentatively. "You're frightening me. Have I done something to displease you?"

He pried her hand from his arm and raised it to his lips. "Your happiness matters more to me than my own." His mouth brushed the back of her hand, then turning it over, he pressed a kiss into her palm.

As Eden thought of the child growing within her, a radiant smile bloomed on her face. "You've made me happier than I ever dreamed."

It was impossible for Justin to be unaffected by her singular beauty. For the moment, his fears melted under her sunny smile. He gathered her in a fierce embrace and held her as though he would never let go.

Didi chose this inopportune moment to announce supper. With a rueful grin, Justin released Eden, offered his arm, and led her into the dining room. Only after they were seated did his private devils return to taunt him, and he lapsed into brooding silence.

He picked up his wineglass and stared at Eden over the rim. Rodney had been right when he had reminded him of Eden's talent for concealing her feelings. The music she had been playing when she thought herself alone had conveyed an aching melancholy. Was she being honest, or did she secretly long for England and Sommerset?

Eden spread butter on a muffin and wondered if she should wait until later to share her news. How did one go about telling one's husband he was going to become a father? It didn't seem the sort of thing to blurt out between the soup and the fish.

"The housewarming was a tremendous success. You're to be congratulated." Justin saluted her with a raised glass.

"My stepfather always insisted on having lavish parties," Eden returned absently. "I was trained to act as his hostess since I was a young girl."

"The Colonies must seem rustic in comparison."

Preoccupied, Eden didn't hear him. Perhaps it would be

better to wait until they were in the privacy of their chambers, she thought, rearranging bite-sized pieces of roast duckling on her plate.

"Do they, Eden?"

She glanced up blankly. "I'm sorry, I was woolgathering."

With a shake of his head, Justin leaned back in the chair. "Never mind, it's of little import."

Throughout the remainder of the meal, Eden stole frequent glances at Justin. She wanted this evening to be special, but nothing was going as planned. Something was troubling Justin, though she had no idea what. She tried to engage him in conversation, but he answered in monosyllables. Eventually she, too, lapsed into silence. When supper ended, Justin retired to his office to review papers, and Eden retreated to her room. Though she tried to stay awake, she eventually gave in to her body's insatiable need for sleep.

As he paced the confines of his cramped quarters at Raleigh Tavern, Rodney, the fifth Earl of Rutherford, cursed his fate. The physician in Williamsburg had been his last resort. Soon, the doctor had warned him, he would be totally blind. The situation was hopeless.

Her fault! It was all her fault. The bitch! He kicked a leather valise and sent it flying across the room to land with a thud against the far wall. "Was there any blindness in your family?" Rodney mimicked the physician's voice. He didn't give a damn what the stupid doctor said. Swiping a pewter candlestick from the desktop, he hurled it against the door.

"Quiet down!" a patron yelled from an adjoining room. "A man needs his rest."

"Quiet down yourself," Rodney yelled back. He gleaned a measure of satisfaction from causing someone else discomfort, however slight. It was trivial compared to what he was facing. His hands locked behind his back, he prowled the small room.

Who did the bumbling quack of a doctor think he was? What did he know? Rodney snorted in disgust. How significant was it that Rodney's grandfather had been blind? In his youth, Rodney always considered it strange that a blind man owned an extensive art collection. Upon questioning this when he grew older, he had been informed that his grandfather hadn't lost his sight until he was in his late thirties. By then, he'd already acquired the prized canvases.

The bed ropes creaked beneath his weight as Rodney sank down on the edge of the bed. Soon, he, too, would be a blind man with a stick, an object of cruel childish pranks, just as his grandfather had been the object of his. A tremor of despair ripped through him, and burying his face in his hands, Rodney sobbed.

When he'd shed the last of his tears, he brushed his wet face with a coat sleeve, heedless of staining the dark red velvet. Snuffling, he got up from the bed and went to the desk, dropped down on the straight-backed chair, and found writing materials. His rage and frustration needed a target, an object upon which to vent his anger at life's injustices. Eden. It was eminently more satisfying to blame her than a grandfather molding in his grave. Rodney dipped a quill pen into the inkwell. Just as his fate was sealed, so would be hers.

His message reached Greenbriar the following afternoon. Eden instantly recognized her stepbrother's spidery scrawl. Directing his courier to the kitchen for refreshment, she retreated with the missive to the privacy of her bedroom. Sick with dread, she tore open the envelope. "Meet me at the deserted cabin," the note read. "Come alone. It's a matter of utmost urgency."

The deserted cabin? During his recent visit, Rodney must have stumbled upon the home she and Justin had once shared. What did Rodney want? Why had he returned to Greenbriar? Did he seek to make good his threat to kill her? Eden's blood chilled. Obeying an impulse, she took the heavy flintlock pistol from a chest drawer and slid it into the pocket of her gown.

Running down the stairs and out of the house, she followed the winding drive and disappeared down a path that angled into the woods. In her haste, she failed to notice Bear coming around the corner of the house.

A combination of apprehension and haste left her breathless. She paused for a moment at the cabin door to compose herself. Patting the gun in her pocket for reassurance, she pushed the door open. Rodney was waiting.

"I see you got my message," he said conversationally as he rose from the bench near the table.

Eden stood poised on the threshold. "What are you doing here? What do you want?"

"You've grown cynical, dear sister." Rodney's thin mouth twisted in a humorless smile. "And very suspicious." He advanced toward her, his sallow face with its black eye patch appearing sinister in the cabin's shadowy interior.

The heavy weight in her pocket gave Eden the courage to stand firm. If need be, she could defend herself. "I thought you were planning to return to England. What urgent matters brings you here?"

"Come in." Rodney gestured toward the bench. "I have a favor to beg, and if it pleases you, I'll ask on bended knee."

Eden eyed him with suspicion, making no move to enter. What sort of trick was this? she wondered.

"I swear I didn't come to harm you. Please, Eden," he coaxed. "I need your help."

"If this is a trick . . ." She ventured a step inside.

"If only it were," Rodney said with a bitter laugh. "I beg you. Hear me out."

Warily, she took a seat and glanced around. The cabin appeared small and forlorn. All their personal effects, including the calico curtains and bearskin rug, had been removed weeks ago. Only the pine furniture remained, coated by a thick layer of dust.

"I thought we said our farewells days ago. But"—he cleared his throat—"I find myself in need of a friend. There was no one else I could turn to. You've always been kind to me, Eden, even when I didn't deserve it."

She studied her stepbrother thoughtfully. Rodney seemed less arrogant, more warm. This was a side of him she had rarely seen. "Are you in some sort of trouble?"

"There were many things left unsaid between us, bad feelings left unresolved. I came today to seek forgiveness and to plead for your understanding."

It was the last thing she had expected to hear. "I hate the animosity between us even more than you do," Eden admitted. "I always hoped we might someday be friends."

Good, Rodney crowed silently. This was easier than he had hoped. He roamed about the small cabin, taking care not to touch anything that might soil his richly embellished coat. "Truth is, Eden, I've been jealous of you since the day Father brought you and your mother to Sommerset. I never was fond of sharing anything that belonged to me. Especially Father's attention."

"I'm sorry you felt that way, Rodney. I never wanted to interfere."

"Your presence alone was an interference. You were always so damn pretty. Father loved dressing you up and showing you off. I, on the other hand"—he laughed mirthlessly—"proved an embarrassment. I was homely, skinny, and short. No matter how I tried, I could never please him. After awhile it became easier to point out your shortcomings in order to prevent Father from looking too closely at my own." He paused in front of her.

The memory of her stepfather's haughty, unsmiling mien flashed through Eden's mind. Rodney had been as starved for affection as she and just as victimized by the man's callousness. Sympathy rose within her, replacing her earlier fear of reprisal. "We can't change the past." She reached out to touch his hand. "But we can start afresh."

He sat beside her and took her hand in his. "I was crazy to even think of exchanging your virtue for a gambling debt. My actions were despicable, reprehensible. You know I often do things I later regret.'' A wistful smile curved his mouth, giving him a boyish appeal. "Forgive me?''

She nodded slowly. Granted, Rodney's sense of right and wrong was slow to function, but no matter how vile his behavior, he had always been repentant. "I'll forgive you, if you'll forgive me.'' Her voice became strained. "I meant it when I told you I never intended you harm. I'm so sorry about your eye.''

He touched the eye patch. "Ah, yes, my eye.'' Releasing her hand, he stood abruptly and walked to the fireplace, where he turned to face her.

Eden shifted uncomfortably under the intensity of his one-eyed stare. He adjusted the ribbon of his eye patch with a calculated movement, and she realized it was guilt that made her uncomfortable.

"I stopped in Williamsburg long enough to consult a physician,'' he began. "As a result of our . . . disagreement . . . that fateful night, I'll soon be blind.''

"No!'' Eden sprang to her feet. "No, Rodney, it can't be! Tell me it isn't true!''

"I'm afraid it is. Already my vision has dimmed. Very shortly I won't be able to see at all.''

Eden's hand flew to her mouth to stifle a cry. Tears stung her eyelids; guilt assailed her. Never had she willfully hurt another human being, yet because of a single rash act a man would be blinded for life. Swallowing the lump in her throat, she approached him hesitantly. "What can I do to make this up to you? How can I be of help?'' She regarded him beseechingly, her violet eyes pooling with moisture. "I'm so sorry. I'll do anything, anything at all.''

Rodney masked his triumph. "I need a place to stay until my agent can book passage on a ship for England. Thanks to Publick Times, Williamsburg is teeming with people. The tavernkeepers are sleeping three or four in a single bed. I must have privacy while I come to terms with my affliction, yet I hate to impose further on the Wainwright's.''

"Say no more, Rodney. You're welcome at Greenbriar for as long as you like.''

Resting his hands on her shoulders, he favored her with a smile. ''The last thing I want is to be a burden. Lord knows''—he grimaced—''that time will come soon enough.''

"Of course, you won't be a burden. Don't even talk like that.''

"Are you sure your husband won't mind? I wouldn't want to cause problems between you.''

"Once he knows the story, Justin will be more than happy to have you as our guest indefinitely.''

"Eden.'' Rodney's grip tightened. ''Be kind in relating the facts. The entire truth could prejudice your husband against my cause. Promise?'' he demanded, giving her a slight shake when she hesitated.

"Promise,'' she agreed, reluctant to deceive Justin, yet feeling obligated to Rodney. ''I'll admit only that we argued. That your pending blindness''—she almost choked on the word—''is entirely my fault.''

"Good.'' He released her and stepped back. ''All this traveling has left me exhausted. I'll wait here until I receive word of my welcome.''

After Eden had left, Rodney stretched out on the bare ticking, his hands behind his head, one leg propped over the other. Silly, gullible Eden. A concoction of honesty, gross exaggeration, and a handful of lies had proven an inspired formula. Congratulating himself over the easy victory, he relaxed and awaited the official summons to take up residency at Greenbriar.

The furtive glance Eden had cast over her shoulder before disappearing into the woods had alerted Bear's curiosity. He had decided to follow her. Peeking inside the cabin window, he had been shocked to find a man, a stranger, already there. After weighing his loyalties, he had hastened to Justin with the news that his wife was having an assignation.

"I hate like hell to be the one to tell ya, but . . ."

Justin strode the length of the library. "You're mistaken. You've never liked Eden."

Bear held up a hand in protest. "Tellin' yer best friend that his wife's seein' a lover ain't my idea of fun. Figured ya had a right to know." He twirled the brim of his hat and kept his eyes fixed on the carpet. "Just when I was gettin' to like the lady, too."

"I don't believe you." Justin went to the sideboard, poured a generous glass of brandy, downed the contents, then poured another.

"An Englishman he was by his dress. A real dandy."

The brandy burned the pit of Justin's stomach, the pain trivial compared to the grief in his heart. "Eden wouldn't cuckold me."

"I wouldn't a believed it neither if I hadn't seen it. But there they was. Couldn't hear what they were sayin', but he was holdin' her real tight and smilin'."

How many times had he himself done the same? Justin thought. A man could drown in those violet eyes. By the time Eden returned, he had worked himself into a righteous fury.

Chapter 23

"Well, madam." Justin glowered. "What do you have to say in your defense?"

Thick carpeting muffled Eden's footsteps as she crossed the study and scanned Justin's angry face. Her mouth went dry. Did he know the truth about what she had done to Rodney? Did he know the violence of which she was capable?

Out of the corner of her eye, she saw Bear standing, hat in hand, at one side of the room, renewed hostility glittering in his yellow-brown eyes.

"What lies have you conspired?" Justin's voice was as hard as ice. It made her shiver.

"I've never lied to you, Justin." Eden spoke with quiet dignity, though she was quaking inside. "I won't start now."

"So . . ." Justin drew out the word. "You admit you were with another man."

"Don't bother denyin' it," Bear warned. "I followed ya. I seen the way he was lookin' at ya."

Comprehension flowed through Eden. Outrage followed. How dare Justin question her loyalty? Where was the trust that should exist between them? Did Justin pay the word only lip service? Why must she trust him when he had so little faith in her? She wanted to strike out and hurt him just as his assumption wounded her. Raising her chin defiantly, she answered in crisp tones, "Yes, I met a man this afternoon."

Justin lowered himself into the desk chair, his eyes taking on the brooding, shadowy hue of encroaching dusk. "At least your honesty, if not your fidelity, is to be commended."

Bear crossed his arms over his barrel chest. "Don't know what she sees in a scrawny weasel wearin' an eye patch." He shook his head, unable to comprehend such a notion.

"Eye patch?" Justin's head swiveled in Bear's direction. "What's this about an eye patch?"

"Bear saw me with Rodney," Eden said quietly. Then she explained to Bear, "Rodney is my stepbrother."

Bear gaped. "Stepbrother?"

Cursing his stupidity, Justin leaped to his feet, came around the desk, and stood in front of Eden. "What a jealous fool I've become." He reached out to touch her cheek, but she flinched. "I'm sorry, sweet," he said with quiet sincerity.

"Stepbrother!" Bear scratched his head, his forehead puckered in a frown. "Didn't know she had family."

"You were away when Rodney arrived with the Wainwrights." Though Justin's words were addressed to Bear, his gaze never wavered from Eden. "Rodney left with them and was planning to return to England."

Shamefaced, Bear advanced a step and stumbled to a halt. "Sorry. I, uh, didn't know."

The couple standing in the center of the room trying to gauge the other's innermost feelings seemed unaware of his presence.

"Stepbrother!" Bear muttered, clapping his hat on his head. "If that don't beat all." Neither Eden nor Justin noticed his departure.

"Can you find it in your heart to forgive me?" The velvet was back in Justin's voice.

Her vocal cords seemed paralyzed. She could only stare at him with eyes that reminded him of rain-drenched violets.

"I used to consider myself a sensible, practical man.

Life seemed simple. Then I met you." Justin outlined her lips with his index finger. "You showed me life's greater complexity, taught me to look below the surface for its subtle textures, made me respect the many variations. But, above all, you forced me to realize that things are seldom as they appear." He tipped her chin back so he could see her expression more clearly. "I'm sorry if I momentarily forgot that this afternoon. All I could think of was you in the arms of another man."

The last vestiges of Eden's anger dissipated. She loved him so much she could forgive him anything. "Justin, don't . . ." she whispered.

"Don't what?" He reached for her, but she retreated beyond his grasp.

His tenderly spoken words only made her feel worse. "Please don't put me on a pedestal. I'm not the fine person you think. If only you knew . . ."

He reached out again, and this time pulled her against his chest. "Eden, love, what is it?" He rubbed his jaw along the top of her head, then pressed a kiss into her fragrant curls. "Come, tell me what's bothering you."

She felt deluged by remorse. Squaring her shoulders, she placed her hands on his chest and pushed away. "It's time you knew the truth about the kind of person I am." She dropped her gaze.

"I already know."

"Wait," she cried. Lacing her fingers tightly, she retreated as far as the room allowed, then faced him, her skin the color of parchment. "Justin, there's something I must tell you before I lose my courage."

Seeing her determination, he relented. "Out with it then, but remember one thing. It won't alter my feelings for you." He perched on the desk, one leg dangling over the edge, and waited.

Eden drew a deep breath, then let it out in a rush. "Rodney has asked for sanctuary. He'll soon be blind, and it's all because of me."

The stricken look on Eden's face seemed to slash his heart. "How is it your fault?"

"Back in England we argued, and I struck him. I never meant to hurt him." She began to pace in short, agitated steps, twisting her hands in distress. "I—I hit him with a vase . . . the mate of the one he brought as a wedding gift. It broke in j-jagged pieces and g-gouged out his eye. There was b-b-blood all over." She shuddered convulsively.

The library at Greenbriar receded, and Eden was once again at her stepfather's London town house. In her mind, she relived the horror of that night. "I—I wanted to help him, to stop the b-bleeding, but he kept screaming at me to stay away. He kept threatening to kill me. When he lunged forward, I-I ran." She wrapped her arms around herself to still the trembling she couldn't seem to control.

Justin was at her side, holding her, stroking her hair. "Don't torture yourself this way. It was an accident."

"He's going blind, Justin." She clutched the lapels of his coat and buried her face against his chest. "Rodney's going blind, and I'm to blame. It's . . . all . . . my . . . fault." Her fist weakly beat against his chest to emphasize each word.

"Shh, sweet," he crooned. "You'd never hurt anyone deliberately. It was an accident, an unfortunate accident."

"You don't understand," Eden sobbed. "Rodney is going blind, and I'm responsible. I have to take care of him. Please let him stay here. At least for a little while."

"Rodney can stay at Greenbriar for as long as he likes." Justin would have agreed to house the devil himself to insure Eden's peace of mind. He led her to a leather sofa and pulled her into his lap, shifting so that her head nestled against his shoulder.

As the October twilight thickened, deepening shadows spun a thick cocoon around them. Except for the muted tick of the tall case clock and the crackle of the fire in the grate, all was quiet.

Gradually, Justin sensed Eden was calmer. "You have

nothing to be ashamed of, sweet.'' His knuckles grazed her cheek. ''It took courage to defy your brother's wishes and flee to the Colonies.''

''Don't judge me brave when I'm not,'' Eden cautioned shakily. ''The truth is I'm a coward. When the memories are particularly painful, like the night Rodney lost his eye, I lock them inside and try to pretend they're not there.'' She swallowed and held back her tears. ''I might have killed him, Justin. Because of what I did, he'll soon lose his sight.''

''Come,'' he urged. ''This has been a long day. Let me send a servant to fetch Rodney and have Didi bring a supper tray to your room.''

Eden didn't protest when Justin gently set her on her feet and, with his arm firmly around her waist, propelled her out of the study and up the stairs to her bedroom. A few quiet words sent servants scattering to do his bidding.

Candles were lit and a spark ignited kindling in the hearth. Eden faced Justin. ''I was afraid that once you knew the truth, you'd turn from me in disgust.''

''Never. We've all done things we're not proud of. I once promised myself I'd learn to be patient,'' Justin confessed wryly. ''I've failed more times than I care to count, including this afternoon when I judged you without waiting for an explanation.''

A smile teased the corners of her mouth. ''You may not always have been patient, but you've always been kind.''

''I love you, Eden,'' he said quietly.

Harmony flowed between them that had been lacking of late. Eden decided to take advantage of this newly restored closeness. ''Justin?'' Smiling tremulously, she rested a hand on his cheek. ''I'm going to have a baby.''

As he gazed down into eyes that glowed like amethysts, his breath caught in his throat. Never had she looked more beautiful. ''A baby?''

She nodded happily.

Justin's wonder gave way to pure, undiluted joy. He scooped her up and swung her around. ''A baby!'' He threw back his head and laughed, a rich masculine sound that filled the chamber with exuberance.

Eden was giddy when he placed her on the feather bed. He would have straightened, but her hands dove into his luxurious brown curls and pulled his mouth down to hers. He didn't need further encouragement.

They made love slowly, exquisitely, their bodies and minds perfectly attuned. A clash of symbols, a blare of trumpets, could not have proclaimed their shattering union more triumphantly.

Perhaps another cup of tea would clear the cobwebs from her brain, Eden thought, pouring herself a third cup.

"Eden?" Bess spoke timidly from the doorway.

"Bess! Please join me." Eden gave the girl a weary smile. "I'm afraid I overslept this morning. Justin ate hours ago. It's lonely here by myself."

Bess hesitated, then shyly ducked her head. "All right." As she took the chair next to Eden, her gaze swung around to admire the elegant surroundings. "I still feel out of place in such a fancy room."

"It is a lovely room, but much too large for only two people. I'm always happy when you and Bear dine with us." Eden poured another cup of tea, added cream and sugar, and handed it to Bess.

"Most gentry would have fits if they knowed you had servants dinin' with you." Bess cast a quick glance toward the doorway to make certain no one was listening. "Liza's always givin' me funny looks. Like she thinks I don't know my place."

Eden made a mental note to speak with the woman. "Why were you looking for me this morning?"

"I wanted to tell you that the wool dyein' is nearly done. Next we'll be ready to do the cardin'." Bess studied Eden over the rim of her cup. "You look tired. Your stepbrother again?"

Sighing, Eden set down her cup. "Rodney was out of sorts last night. Memories of England seem to soothe him, so we talked about London and Sommerset until the small hours.''

Bess wrinkled her nose. ''Seems he's always out of sorts.''

''I realize he's temperamental, but we mustn't forget he's going through a very difficult period. He can only make out shadows now, and soon''—sadness seeped into her voice—''even those will disappear.''

''I've got news oughta cheer you up.'' Bess hunched forward, her thin face flushed, an eager sparkle in her green eyes.

Eden forced her worry about Rodney aside and focused her attention on Bess.

''Bear asked me to marry 'im.''

''Bess! That's wonderful!'' Eden got up and gave the girl an enthusiastic hug. ''I'm so happy for you both. Have you set a date?''

''We thought Christmas would be nice.''

''A Christmas wedding!'' Eden returned to her chair, plans beginning to form inside her head. ''You can be married here at Greenbriar. The music room would be ideal. It will look lovely decorated with greens and holly.''

''Oh, Eden, you don't have to go through all the bother—''

''Nonsense! What are friends for?'' Already Eden had the perfect wedding gift in mind—Bess's articles of indenture. Naturally, she would first have to persuade Justin, but she felt certain he wouldn't object. Caught up in her own thoughts, she paid scant heed to what Bess was saying until a certain word snagged her attention. ''What did you say?''

''I said, Bear finally told me his Christian name,'' Bess repeated patiently. ''It's Cecil.''

''Cecil?''

''Surprised me, too.'' Bess giggled. ''He looks more like a Bear than a Cecil, don't he?''

''Yes, he does.''

''Guess he wasn't always the size he is now,'' Bess said,

chuckling. "Best news of all, though, is that Bear just got word his sister ought to be here in time for the weddin'. He was so worried about 'er. That'll be the best present of all."

The sound of breaking glass and Rodney's screamed invectives halted further conversation. Eden pushed back her chair and, picking up her skirts, headed toward the stairs. "We'll talk more about your wedding later," she said over her shoulder.

Upon entering the guest room, Eden assessed the situation in a glance. Rodney, a mound of fluffy pillows at his back, was propped high against the headboard of the bed. His arms folded belligerently, he scowled into space. Didi stooped to pick up randomly scattered biscuits. The girl's usually cheerful face appeared on the verge of tears.

"What seems to be the problem?" Eden asked.

"The problem," Rodney sneered, "seems to be your cook. I distinctly asked for scones. Instead the stupid cow sent bricks. Your servants ought to be dealt with for taking advantage of a blind man. My eyesight is gone, not my tastebuds."

"I tried to explain, Miss Eden." Didi's lower lip quivered. "Sookie don't have no scones this mornin'."

"Who's mistress here?" Rodney demanded querulously. "Eden, are you going to put up with such impertinence? Give her a taste of the whip. Show her who's boss."

Didi eyes rounded and welled with moisture. Eden indicated with an almost imperceptible shake of her head that the girl wasn't to worry. Didi quickly picked up the last biscuit and fled, narrowly missing a collision with Justin on her way out.

"Well, well," Justin drawled, entering the room. "What's all the commotion about?"

"A dispute regarding the differences between biscuits and scones." Eden tried to verbally smooth the frown from Justin's brow. She realized Rodney's presence was a tribulation. He was exacting, rude, and petulant. From the moment he had been ensconced in the guest room nearly a month ago, the atmosphere at Greenbriar had become emotionally charged. Yet Justin remained unfailingly cordial.

"Eden lets people take advantage of her. Always has." Rodney smothered a yawn behind pale fingers, then placed one hand over the other on the embroidered counterpane. "I'm so bored," he complained. "Eden, read to me."

"Of course, I'd be happy to." She was halfway across the room and reaching for the leather-bound book on a bedside table when Justin's voice stopped her.

"What Eden needs most is fresh air and sunshine." He quelled her unspoken protest with a stern look. "I took the liberty of having Ebony saddled. I thought a ride might be just the thing." He snatched the book from her reach. "I'll keep Rodney amused while you're away."

Eden's uncertainty vanished. It was as though the doors of a gilt cage had swung open. A heady sense of freedom beckoned. "Thank you," she mouthed.

"I love you," he mimed.

"What's going on?" Rodney shifted irritably. "Why are you both so quiet?"

Justin pulled a chair to the bedside, settled his long length comfortably, and opened the book to the marked page. "I believe this is where my wife left off. . . . "

From the hallway, Eden blew him a kiss, then hurried to change into her riding habit.

Every minute of that glorious autumn morning was golden. The air had a certain crispness, a subtle reminder that fall ultimately surrenders to winter. The sky was azure, with clouds as frothy as Sookie's meringue. As Eden enjoyed a sedate ride across fields barren of tobacco and corn, she felt the warm sun beam down on her. In others, field hands plucked vine-ripened pumpkins and squash, which they would store for winter use. Thanks to Mary's counsel, Eden was able to relax and enjoy the outing without fear that moderate exercise would harm her unborn child. All too soon, however, she recalled her duties and nudged the mare toward Greenbriar.

Throughout the remainder of the day, Rodney continued to be in a foul mood. He swore at the servants and criticized everything Eden tried to do for him. Secretly, she acknowledged she would be relieved when he left Greenbriar. But even as she entertained these thoughts, guilt pricked her conscience. How would he manage without her? Who would care for him?

Eden was so absorbed by gloomy thoughts that she failed to notice Justin's troubled glances throughout supper. "You look worn out," he commented.

"It's been a trying day." She gave up all pretense of eating and gave him a wan smile. Shortly afterward, she pleaded fatigue and went upstairs to bed while he retired to his office.

But the neat entries he made in the ledger could have been hieroglyphics for all the sense they made. Disgusted with his lack of attention, Justin got up, poured himself a brandy, and leaned back in his chair, his feet propped on a corner of the desk. Eden's association with the Colonies had been unhappy from the outset. He recalled his conversation earlier that day with her stepbrother. Rodney had said the two of them had talked about England for hours the previous night.

Justin raised the glass to his lips and drank. Should Eden choose to return to her world, how would he react? Should he stop her? And what about the baby? Didn't his unborn child have a right to his or her heritage? As he had told Eden, life no longer seemed simple.

Chapter 24

The gray November sky threatened rain. Not even a cheery fire in the hearth could dispell the afternoon's gloom. Feeling uneasy, yet not knowing why, Eden set aside the small shirt she was stitching and paced the bedroom floor. The great house seemed unusually quiet. Justin had left at daybreak to visit the Dodd's and wasn't expected to return until the following afternoon. Rodney was napping.

For the first time in weeks, her stepbrother seemed in good humor. That very morning he had received word that his passage had been booked on a ship leaving from Norfolk, Virginia. He had ordered his trunk packed immediately. In all likelihood, he would be gone before Justin returned.

A slight sound drew her attention. Eden stopped pacing and whirled around. Rodney stood just inside the bedroom, leaning nonchalantly against the closed door.

"Rodney!" she gasped. "You startled me."

A thin smile curled his lips. "Good."

It struck her as peculiar that he had come to her room unassisted. Now that he had completely lost his eyesight, he rarely left the guest room. "How good to see you up and dressed." Eden noted his meticulous grooming, from the powdered bagwig down to the polished leather shoes and silver buckles.

"I'm going on a sea voyage, my dear Eden, and you're going with me." From the skirt of his peacock blue coat,

Rodney withdrew a pistol and leveled it at her. "I'll give you ten minutes to throw your clothing into a valise."

Eden's gaze darted from the gun in his hand to the smirk on his face. "You're mad, Rodney." She managed to keep her voice from quavering. "I have no intention of leaving Justin—ever."

"You don't understand; I'm not giving you a choice. First, though, I want you to pen a note to your beloved husband." He inclined his head toward the Queen Anne-style writing desk. "Now!" he ordered when she hesitated.

Eden glanced again at the pistol aimed at her chest and moved toward the desk. A deep-seated dread enveloped her. It was not so much fear that Rodney would shoot her, for that type of death would come quickly, but rather a fear that she would never see Justin again, for that would be the worst agony of all—a torturous death by slow degrees. "Rodney, please." Eden ran her tongue over dry lips. "I beg you. Don't do this!"

His laugh was chilling. "I've waited a long time for this moment. Revenge isn't merely sweet, it's ambrosia."

Eden sank down on the dainty chair in front of the desk. "I thought you were completely blind."

"Always a gullible little goose," he said with a sneer. "That's precisely what I wanted you and everyone else to believe. Alas, it will be true soon enough. And you, my dear, devoted sister, will be a slave to my every whim. You owe me." He came toward her. "Enough stalling. Now write!"

She wouldn't let Rodney get away with this, couldn't allow his plan to work. Eden slid the desk drawer open and reached inside. Her fingers touched the smooth butt of Justin's flintlock pistol. Catching her bottom lip between her teeth, she angled her shoulder so that Rodney couldn't see into the drawer, then gripped the handle more securely, and quickly pivoted to confront him.

As his initial surprise gave way to amusement, Rodney

laughed with genuine mirth. "What do you propose to do with that thing? Challenge me to a duel at twenty paces?"

"I know how to fire a gun. At this range, my marksmanship is excellent." Proud that her grip didn't waver, Eden rose. "Put your gun down, and we'll forget this ever happened."

Rodney stepped closer. The seat of the chair pressing against the back of her knees kept Eden from retreating. "You're the one who should put the gun away. It's not in you to shoot a man. You couldn't harm a flea, and we both know it." He advanced another step.

"Don't come any closer," she cautioned. The pistol seemed heavier than she remembered, or perhaps it was tension that made it seem so.

"Give me the gun, Eden." Rodney held out his hand.

A fine sheen of perspiration beaded Eden's forehead. The pistol was primed and ready to use. A slight pressure on the trigger and she could blast a hole in his chest the size of her fist. If she could pull the trigger . . . She swallowed, hard. She couldn't.

Flinging the pistol at his head, she dashed toward the door. Rodney dodged the missile and grabbed her arm as she tried to skirt around him. With a vicious jerk, he twisted her arm behind her back until the pain was so intense that she cried out. He released her, shoving her forcefully against the desk. Once again he aimed the gun at her breast. "You're wasting time," he snapped. "Write."

Eden dipped the quill pen in the inkwell and wrote what he dictated. When she finished, she looked at Rodney. "Justin will never believe this. He'll know it's a lie and come after me."

"I think not, sister," Rodney contradicted easily. "I laid the groundwork well. And remember, you're the one who told me that if you left again, your husband wouldn't come after you."

Indeed, those words were etched in her memory. *Never*

again, Justin had said that dark June night. *If you run from me again, I'll not come searching.*

Eden had believed it then. She believed it now.

"Pack!" Rodney waved the gun barrel toward the clothespress.

Resignedly, Eden tossed belongings into a valise. Her mind replayed her last flight, when all she had taken were three pairs of stockings and a nightgown. Justin had chided her ill preparedness. *Justin.* Eden closed her eyes against a fresh onslaught of pain.

"Let's go." Concealing the hand with the pistol beneath his coat, Rodney clutched her arm with his free hand and steered her toward the door.

The steel barrel jabbed her side. Eden thought of the child growing within her and went docilely. The house was quiet. The servants efficiently going about their chores were nowhere in evidence. Rodney had planned well. It was a simple matter to slip unnoticed out the entrance fronting the James River.

A breeze teased Eden's cloak around her legs. A sharp poke in her rib cage nudged her away from the stables and down a sloping path to the river landing where the tall mast of a sloop formed a spire against a dull, pewter sky.

"Quickly now!" Rodney gave her a push. "While my luck still holds."

Eden dropped her valise into the craft, carefully climbed aboard, and sat down near its center. Impatient to be off, Rodney followed. His sudden weight set the small boat swaying from side to side, and he cursed soundly.

"Are you certain you know what you're doing, Rodney?" Eden asked, anxiously clutching the side of the craft. "If you aren't used to sailing, Justin has horses—"

"You'd like that, wouldn't you? Not only would our departure be slower, but it would be easier for Justin to follow should he suffer a change of heart."

Eden knew it was useless to hope Rodney would relent. If she thought it might do any good, she would beg and plead, but she knew him too well. He would love to watch her grovel, then laugh in her face. He was determined to go through with his scheme. So far the odds seemed in his favor. Eden clenched her teeth so tightly that her jaw ached. Raising her chin, she turned her back on Greenbriar and faced the opposite shore.

After hoisting the sails, Rodney sat on the windward side, arranged the voluminous folds of his coat, and untied the lines. Sails billowing, the small craft glided forward.

Tears welled in her eyes and trickled down her cheeks. Once, she had been adept at masking her emotions, but no longer. Eden wanted to scream, to gnash her teeth, to tear her hair. She felt as though her beating heart were being wrenched from her body. And she didn't care who knew.

Justin stood in the entrance, shrugged out of his coat, and handed both it and his cocked hat to a servant. "Tell Mistress Tremayne I'm home," he ordered. "And Didi, have Sookie fix me a supper tray. My stomach's been rumbling for hours."

"Uh, Master Justin . . ."

"Yes, Didi, what is it?" he inquired impatiently. He was tired, hungry, and eager to see his wife. He had ridden long and hard that day in order to arrive home early. In spite of the Dodd's urgings to spend the night, he had been anxious to return to Greenbriar.

The girl avoided his gaze. " 'Bout Miss Eden—"

"If she's asleep, don't wake her."

"Yes, suh—I mean no, suh." Didi seemed fascinated by the pattern in the marble floor. "Miss Eden ain't sleepin'. . . . " Her voice trailed off.

Apprehension replaced his impatience. "She's not sick, is she? It's not the baby?"

Didi raised her eyes to the embroidered trim of his waistcoat. She looked as though she wished she were somewhere else—anywhere else. "Well, Master Justin, Miss Eden ain't here. Ain't seen 'er since dinner. Thought she was nappin', but when I called 'er for supper, well . . .''

Justin rammed his hands into his pockets to keep from shaking the information out of the girl. "Well, what?"

"Miss Eden wasn't in 'er room." Didi's face puckered. "Nobody's seen 'er."

"What do you mean no one's seen her? Surely someone knows where she is. People don't vanish like a puff of smoke." Justin took his hand from his pocket and shoved it through his hair as he stalked the length of the entrance-way. "Did anyone think to check with Mary?" He tried to tamp down his mounting panic. Visions of Eden hurt or in danger danced fiendishly through his mind.

"Bess went to see if Miss Eden was visitin' Mary."

Justin's foot was on the bottom tread of the stairs when another thought occurred to him. "What about Lord Ruth-erford? Did anyone ask what he knows of Eden's disappearance?"

Didi gulped. "He's missin', too."

Justin didn't wait for more. He bounded up the stairs two at a time. In Eden's bedroom, he found what he most dreaded. A single sheet of parchment lay on the polished surface of her writing desk. His stomach twisted into a knot as he read her slanted script. Slowly, he crumpled the sheet into a tight ball and flung it across the room. Pivoting on his heel, he left the room.

Didi hovered anxiously at the foot of the stairs. "Send someone to find Bear," Justin ordered. "Tell him to come at once." The girl ran to do his bidding. "And fetch a bottle of brandy," he called after her.

Justin strode into his study and slammed the door behind him. Hands locked behind his back, he prowled the room. Damn Eden! How could she? Didn't he mean anything to her? His emotions swung to and fro like a pendulum, from anger to despair, rage to desolation, then back again. Did her angelic countenance hide a scheming she-devil? Would he ever know his unborn child? He couldn't bear to think of the babe he might never see. Eden had claimed she loved him. Or was it a lie? Like a besotted swain, he had swallowed every word as truth.

Following a timid knock, Didi eased open the study door and slipped inside. The light from a solitary candle threw exaggerated shadows on the wall, adding to the gloom. In the eerie glow, Justin's face appeared all planes and hollows, making it seem aristocratic and intimidating. After a hasty glance in his direction, Didi put the tray down so abruptly that the glasses clinked against the crystal decanter. "Let me start a fire. Only take a minute."

"Don't!" Justin barked. "I don't want a fire."

"Anythin' else, suh?" she asked fearfully.

"No," he snapped. He felt a twinge of conscience when the girl jumped at the harsh reply. "No," he repeated with less vehemence. "That'll be all, Didi. Thank you." She fairly ran from the study.

Justin walked to the sideboard, and after pouring himself a generous portion of brandy, took a large swallow. He had to pull himself together. What did he hope to gain by taking out his frustrations on a servant? It wasn't the girl's fault he had a runaway wife. He raked a hand through his already-disheveled hair. The entire way home he had anticipated a warm welcome: the house blazing with light, a fire crackling in the hearth, and Eden waiting. The thought of her smiling reception had spurred him through every muddy mile.

Taking a cheroot from a case, Justin clamped it between his teeth, then forgot to light it as he began to pace. Eden. He remembered her in a variety of different moods—glowing with accomplishment at her first successful loaf of bread, serenely beautiful at the Governor's Ball, radiantly replete after making love. He catalogued every nuance of her expressions, whether playful or serious. Without her presence, he'd be no more than a wooden puppet, a shell without a heart.

Bear cleared his throat from just inside the study door. "Came as fast as I could." He doffed his battered hat.

Justin pulled the cheroot from his mouth and studied the unlit tip without really seeing it. "Eden's gone."

"Gone?" Bear repeated. "Again?"

"Yes, gone. As in ran away." Justin hurled the cheroot into the fireplace. "Again."

The situation warranted a stiff drink. Not waiting for an invitation, Bear went to the sideboard, poured brandy for himself, and refilled Justin's glass. "Ya mean she up and left. Like that?" He snapped two fingers.

"She's returning to England with her stepbrother. Her note said that if I truly cared for her I would let her go." Justin stood, head bent, shoulders sagging, and stared blankly into the amber liquid. Slowly, he raised the glass to his lips. Even as he did, he realized the futility of the gesture. Getting drunk wouldn't bring Eden back. The unvarnished truth was that his feelings went beyond simple caring—he loved her enough to set her free.

"Rodney's been telling me all along how homesick she is, but I chose not to believe him. I counted on the fact that now that Eden is expecting a child, she'd reconcile herself to life here in Virginia."

Bear was at a loss for words. Finally he asked, "Goin' after 'er?"

"No." Justin set his glass down. "I did once and vowed I'd never do it again." Striding to the fireplace, he leaned forward, both palms pressed against the mantel, and nudged an andiron with the toe of his boot. "God help me!" He bit back an anguished groan. "I could have sworn she was happy here."

"She was."

Neither man had noticed Bess's return. She ignored their startled looks and advanced into the room. In the meager light, her face looked pinched and drawn. "Eden was happy here. A woman can sense these things. If she left, it was for a good reason."

"Bess, I appreciate your trying to cushion the blow," Justin said, straightening, "but I have to accept things for what they are."

Bess placed her hand on his forearm. "Don't let your pride stand in the way. Eden could be in trouble. I don't trust her stepbrother."

"Are you saying what I think you are?" Justin shook off Bess's hand and grabbed her shoulders. "Are you implying that Rodney might have taken Eden by force?" The magnitude of her words was almost too great to comprehend.

"Why, that snivelin' one-eyed weasel!" Bear exploded. "Thought ya told me he was blind as a bat."

"I did." Justin released Bess and paced the room with short, agitated steps. "He is. Or rather he claimed to be."

Bess nervously twisted her hands in her apron, her eyes as round as saucers. "And if he ain't blind?"

Her question hung in the air.

Hope flashed against despair, a brilliant light against sulfurous black, then was extinguished as suddenly as it had appeared. Justin stopped pacing and stared at the girl. "If you're right, Eden could be in grave danger. Have someone saddle a fresh horse and gather supplies. I'm going after them."

Bess's face lit in a smile before she ran out to attend to the details.

"Glad to hear it." Bear pounded Justin's back. "Hell, I've been wrong about that woman of yers more times than I care to count. Only one way to find out what's goin' on is ta go after 'er and ask 'er."

Justin's thoughts raced. "If Rodney plans to return to London, he'll head for the nearest seaport."

"Norfolk."

Bess returned with the news that Eden's mare was still in the stable. The men swapped looks over her head. "Don't suppose they took the sloop, do ya?" Bear asked.

Her eyes wide with fright, Bess anxiously looked from one man to the other. "I had Thomas check. He said the sloop was missin'."

"Eden can't swim." Justin's long strides had already carried him from the room.

Bear and Bess hurried after him. "I'm goin' with ya," Bear insisted, shoving his hat over his ears.

"The river's impossible to navigate at night. They'll have to seek shelter along the way. I'll follow the river-bank and try to find the boat. You stop at every house between here and Williamsburg. Ask every man, woman, and child if anyone's seen them."

Outside, a groom waited, holding the reins of a chestnut gelding. Justin vaulted into the saddle.

"Be careful," Bess called softly.

"Good luck," Bear added gruffly.

Turning his face to the wind, Justin dug his heels into the gelding's flanks.

In spite of a swift start, Rodney and Eden's journey lagged. The wind on that overcast November day was capricious. It had died as abruptly as it had swooped in from the north, leaving them becalmed for hours. Rodney, his hand on the tiller, alternately cursed and fidgeted.

"At this rate, it would be faster to swim to Norfolk." He glared at the sail, which hung as useless and limp as a broken wing. "But I forgot, you don't swim, do you?"

"No. I never—"

"It doesn't really matter." He shrugged. "Neither do I. Oh, I can tread water and splash my feet, but one can't really consider that swimming, can one?" He didn't wait for a reply. "I never was particularly athletic, even as a youth. That, I'm afraid, only gave father something else to fault. Never could please him. I was a total failure where he was concerned."

His bitterness punctured the numbness that had enveloped her. Eden roused herself with an effort. "You and your father are alike in many ways. Although he wasn't one to display his feelings, I always thought he was proud of you."

"You really think so?"

In spite of everything that had transpired, Eden was touched by the wistfulness in his tone. Part of her wanted to answer truthfully, no, your father was a cold, heartless man who never loved anyone but himself, not even his own son. But at the fragile glimmer of hope flickering across Rodney's scarred face, Eden knew she couldn't be that cruel, not even to him. Aloud, she said, "I think your father probably loved you very much, but was too disciplined to show his feelings."

Rodney stared off toward the shoreline. A measure of peacefulness and contentment smoothed away his usually petulant expression.

How sad, Eden mused, that the cruelty of one man should warp the lives of two young children in his charge. She thought of Justin, thought of the child growing within her, and her desperation grew. Perhaps it was hopeless, but she had to try again to make Rodney change his mind.

"Rodney," she said softly, "I'm going to have a baby."

He faced her slowly. "What do you expect from me? Congratulations?"

She leaned forward in her earnestness. "Rodney, please, don't go through with this. Please reconsider. Give my child the chance we never had. Give him the opportunity to know what it's like to be wanted, to be loved." She rushed on, her voice thick with tears. "Justin will love this baby. He's good and kind. He'll be a wonderful father. Please, Rodney, I beg of you."

He studied her, his lips pursed thoughtfully. In the waning light, his good eye appeared flat and almost colorless. "Yes," he said at last. "I'm certain Justin would prove an excellent father, but it's too late. I need you." His hand sliced the air to prevent her further protest. "Enough! I'll soon be blind. I need you to take care of me. I have no one else."

The implacable expression on his face warned Eden that further argument would only make him more obdurate. She wisely subsided into silence.

Shortly afterward, the wind tugged at the sail, propelling the craft further downriver. Dusk dropped over the countryside, obscuring the riverbank behind the pearly veil of fog. The wind blew briskly now. Eden pushed unruly strands of hair away from her face with one hand while keeping the other tightly curled around the edge of the boat. She cast a sideways glance at Rodney. In the lowering twilight, she could decipher his grim tight-lipped expression. All his concentration seemed occupied with controlling the vessel.

The craft misbehaved like a willful child. Ignoring parental control, it tacked along a haphazard course.

"Rodney?" Eden ventured. "Couldn't we stop for the night and find shelter? Justin's not expected home until tomorrow. Even then, I doubt he'll come looking for me."

"We'll stop when I decide to stop." Rodney jerked on the lines of the sail. "Enough time was wasted waiting for this cursed wind. The way my luck is running, the ship will leave the harbor without us." He wedged his cocked hat more securely on his bewigged head.

It became harder and harder to distinguish the shoreline. Rodney's hands clumsily sawed at the lines and yanked on the tiller, his abrupt movements causing the craft to dodge and swerve alarmingly. Eden bit her lip until she tasted blood to keep from crying out. The last thing she wanted to cause was a distraction. Her life, and that of her unborn child, were literally in Rodney's inept command. Scattered drops of rain began to fall on her upturned face.

Rodney swore. Taking his hand from the tiller, he tugged his coat collar up around his ears. In that instant, a gust of wind caught the sail, sending the small boat careening across the river at a drunken angle. The lines whipped from his grasp. The boom swung around. Eden ducked, but the steel pole, coming from Rodney's blind side, caught him unaware and struck his temple with a sickening thud. In horrified fascination, she watched as he was neatly flipped over the side and into the river. Eden felt herself sliding, slipping, clawing for a hold. The sloop capsized, toppling her into oily, black water.

Eden gasped and drew in a lungful of water a second

before she sank below the surface. She felt herself plummet downward. Panic more than conscious thought prompted her to kick her feet and wave her arms in an effort to surge toward the surface. Breaking free, she coughed and sputtered and struggled desperately to recall Justin's advice on how to stay afloat, but her legs kept tangling in the yards of her cumbersome petticoats. The heavy clothing threatened to suck her under the waves. Eden thrashed about, frantically trying to keep from being pulled down.

Rodney's head and shoulders emerged from the surface. He was close, almost close enough to reach out and latch onto. His hat and wig were gone, washed away by the river, as was his eye patch. The yawning cavern that had once encased his left eye seemed to smile at her vacuously, hideously. A jagged track was gouged above and below the gaping hole. Blood trickled from a gash at his hairline and dripped down to mingle with drops of water.

It was the face in her nightmare.

Only this time, she was fully awake.

Eden opened her mouth to scream just as she dipped below the surface a second time. Unexpectedly, she felt a stinging pressure at the crown of her head, and the next thing she knew she was gulping air. Rodney had seized her hair and pulled her to the surface.

With a grunt, he released her braid and pushed her toward the upturned hull of the boat. "Grab on," he shouted.

Eden didn't need to be told twice. Grasping and clawing, she fought for a hold. Her fingers slipped and slid on the water-slicked hull until her hand curved around the keel.

Peering over her shoulder, she discovered that Rodney had found a tenuous hold near the stern. He had saved her life. Gratitude and remorse rushed through her. "Rodney," she gasped. "I'm so sorry about your eye. I never meant to harm you. I'm so sorry." The flow of words was almost incoherent, but Eden felt unable to stem their release.

To her utter amazement, he tossed back his head and laughed. "Silly goose! It's not your fault I'm going blind. Blame it on an accident of birth. It's a family curse." He swiped at the mixture of blood and water streaming down his cheek. "Be a good girl and help me get a better hold on this damn thing so I can figure out what to do next."

Inch by precarious inch, Eden worked her way along the overturned sloop. "Take my hand." She cautiously extended her arm, but the bow of the sloop pivoted, and Rodney's attempt fell short. His fingers slipped further from hers. "Rodney!" A scream tore from her throat.

"Eden, Eden, where are you?" Hysteria throbbed in his voice. "Eden, I can't see!"

"Over here, Rodney." He was floating beyond her reach. Her left arm outstretched, muscles straining, Eden locked her fingers onto the keel and positioned herself so that her right side touched the boat. "Straight ahead, Rodney. I'll catch your hand."

"I can't see," he whimpered. "God, please, I don't want to be blind."

"I'll take care of you," Eden promised. At that moment, she would have given anything to erase the utter desolation in his voice.

"I don't want to be blind. . . . " His arms ceased flailing. Without another sound, he disappeared beneath the waves.

Chapter 25

Gradually, Eden became aware that the boat had stopped drifting. Turning her head wearily, she saw an uprooted tree leaning out over the river. Its spidery network of branches had ensnared the little craft and tethered the boat to shore. Eden shoved strands of wet hair from her face with a trembling hand and debated whether or not she could maneuver around the spiny tangle of limbs and reach the shore. Even if she managed to do so, she was doubtful she could secure a hold on the trunk. It looked much too high and well beyond her reach.

She would be wiser to wait until the sky lightened to gauge the risk. But could she survive until then? Tiredness crept over her, a fatigue so intense that it sapped her determination. She was so cold. Her sodden clothing felt weighted with bricks. Eden was aware that if she lost her hold, she'd plunge straight to the river bottom and remain there.

A thought occurred to her. As was the custom, she wore a pair of pockets tied around her waist under the hooped foundations. Access was provided through side slits in both the dress and petticoat. She carefully released one hand from its death grip on the keel. With fingers that felt numb and cramped, she pushed aside her cloak and fumbled through a side slit in her dress to the drawstring of her hoops and petticoats. Gritting her teeth with effort, she yanked at the cord and felt a surge of satisfaction as the knots gave way and her heavy hoops and petticoats slipped from her waist and were washed away.

Unburdened of the extra weight, she returned both hands to the sloop and rested her cheek against the cold, moist wood. "Don't c-close your eyes," she mumbled, "or you'll meet the s-same f-f-fate as Rodney." She clenched her jaws together to keep her teeth from chattering.

Justin urged his horse along the rutted road. Fitful bursts of rain had begun to fall; mud sucked at the gelding's hooves and impeded its progress. So far there had been no sign of the sloop, no sign of Eden. Would he find her? Had she left of her own free will, or was Rodney responsible? He would not rest until he learned the answers.

Moonless, starless, the night was like pitch. Oaks and maples formed skeletal sentinels along both sides of the road and silently marked his progress. The road wandered in a southeasterly direction toward Williamsburg, occasionally running parallel to the river. Justin reined the horse to a halt at the water's edge and strained to see in the darkness. A man could barely discern his own hand in front of his face on such a night, much less navigate a winding river. Surely Rodney wasn't crazy enough to try. Fear for Eden's safety ate at Justin like acid.

His face set in grim lines, he nudged the horse forward. The surefooted animal pranced sideways. Glancing down, Justin spotted a piece of cloth that had been washed ashore and was about to be trampled beneath the gelding's hooves. He quickly swung to the ground to examine the fabric. When he held up the dripping mass, his breath caught. A petticoat! Was it Eden's? He could feel the delicate embroidery stitched along the edge. Justin's eyes burned, and the muscles in his jaw bunched as he strived for control.

"Eden!" he screamed hoarsely. He stood, feet planted on the muddy bank, the sodden petticoat trailing from his hand. "Eden!"

Rage shot threw him. It wasn't fair! Her life couldn't end so senselessly, so abruptly. He couldn't lose her.

Wouldn't! Anger cemented his resolve. The petticoat dropped unheeded. Justin remounted the gelding and continued his search, retracing his steps upriver in the belief that the petticoat must have been washed downstream from wherever Eden was. He was terrified of what he might discover, yet hoped, prayed . . .

Over and over, he shouted her name.

His voice echoed through the forest.

As he rounded a bend of the road, the horse whinnied and shied away. Justin drew back on the reins. An uprooted tree blocked his path. The roots partially anchored the tree to the ground, while the trunk was tipped at an angle, its limbs jutting over the water. Justin stared in disbelief. Caught in the branches was the sloop.

"Eden!"

With her black hair and dark cloak, he almost didn't see the small figure clinging to the hull. Slowly she turned her face toward the sound of his voice. She opened her mouth to answer, but couldn't speak. She blinked, afraid to believe he was real, but the beloved figure refused to evaporate into a wisp of fog. *Justin.* Once again, he was her knight in shining armor. He had kept the faith. *Justin had come for her.*

He had already shed his boots and coat and was diving into the water. Eden felt firm hands circle her waist. "You're safe, love. I've got you."

She relaxed her hold and slid into his arms.

Shock combined with fatigue, and Eden yielded to exhaustion. For the next several hours, a thick cushion seemed to enfold her, blocking out the day's terror, protecting her from the reality of Rodney's death. The energy required to open her eyes was too great. She succumbed to a strange detachment, a feeling that was not unpleasant but rather filled with peace and contentment. Only fleeting sensations intruded: the rocking motion of a horse; the smell of wet wool; the soft, reassuring murmur of Justin's voice.

A kiss, as soft as an angel's wing, whispered across her

temple and roused her from the seductive lethargy. Eden opened her eyes, and Justin filled her vision. ''I love you,'' she whispered. The avowal came from her heart.

''I love you, too.'' The tenderness in his eyes brought a lump to her throat.

For awhile, she was content to lie quiescent. Then details began to register in her befuddled mind. She was warm, dry, and secure in Justin's embrace. A low-burning fire in the hearth threw shadows around the familiar room. Slowly it came to her that she was in her bedroom at Greenbriar. With a blissful sigh, she snuggled closer to Justin, savoring the familiar feel of his strong limbs and hard muscles, exalting in the joy of being alive, of being loved.

Recalling the events of the previous day, her happiness dimmed. ''Rodney . . . ?''

Justin raised her chin and gazed into her eyes. Not wanting to cause her more distress, he struggled to find the right words.

She correctly interpreted his hesitation. ''I already know.'' She closed her eyes briefly, then opened them. ''Rodney's dead.''

''As soon as it's daylight, Bear will notify the authorities.''

''Poor Rodney.'' Her voice choked on a sob. ''In spite of everything, he saved my life. If he hadn't helped me reach the boat . . .'' She trembled, remembering.

Justin held her tightly until her tears subsided, realizing again how close he had come to losing her.

''When the boat capsized, Rodney didn't really try to save himself. I don't think he wanted to live without his sight,'' she concluded with a sigh, her hand resting lightly on Justin's chest. ''He told me it wasn't my fault. He called his blindness an accident of birth.''

''Shh, sweet,'' Justin soothed. ''It's all over. Try not to think about it.''

''I was afraid he would kill me.'' Eden's words were so softly spoken that Justin could scarcely hear them. ''He's the reason I left England, why I insisted no one know about my background. I wanted to be safe." She swallowed hard. "Rodney's always had a terrible temper. He flew into a rage when I refused to go along with his scheme."

"What scheme?"

The pause that followed lengthened into painful silence. Justin waited, hoping that the final barriers between them would come down.

A shudder rippled through her. "Rodney always resented me. . . ." With these words the entire story of her relationship with her complex stepbrother began to unfold. She found it was a wonderful relief to be able to unburden herself.

Justin swore savagely when she told how Rodney had attempted to force her to yield her virginity to Geoffrey Killington after betrothing her to Lord Ashcroft. "The bastard." His hand balled into a fist, and he pounded the mattress. If he had known this sooner, Rodney would never have set foot on Greenbriar—impending blindness or not. The fact that Eden could forgive him and feel remorse attested to her generous, loving nature. Justin pulled her closer and brushed a kiss across her forehead.

He held her for what seemed a long time, neither of them speaking. "At first I was afraid you had left because you were unhappy here in the Colonies. Unhappy with me," he said softly against her hair. "But I had to find out for myself. I would have followed you all the way to England if need be. I couldn't let you walk out of my life, couldn't let you go."

"I'd never leave you." Eden met Justin's gaze. "Rodney forced me to go with him at gunpoint. He said it was my duty to take care of him, that he had no one else."

"I love you so, Eden, sometimes I can't think straight," Justin confessed, his voice raw with emotion. "I can't describe how deeply I regret withholding the truth about Greenbriar. What started as a simple omission became a tangled web of deception." He took her chin and looked deep into her eyes. "I want us to start anew. Together we'll share life's disappointments and celebrate its triumphs. You have my word that there will be no more secrets between us—big or small—ever again."

"No more secrets," Eden vowed, reaching up and unfastening the clasp of her locket. "Rodney gave this to me years ago. For a long while it was my only link with the past. But it's time I put the past to rest"—she dropped the locket on the bedside table—"and face the future." Twining her arms around her husband's neck, she smiled the radiant, glowing smile he adored and raised her mouth to his.

Outside, the sky lightened to a pearly gray; a thin crimson band appeared above the horizon. Dawn heralded another day, a new beginning.

ELIZABETH TURNER

ELIZABETH TURNER, a native of Michigan, describes herself as a chronic daydreamer, a hopeless procrastinator, and just plain stubborn. When the fantasies inside her head grew to book length, she tried to relieve the pressure by committing her ideas to paper. Although it took years to finish, her first attempt at writing eventually became her first sale. These days her busy schedule permits little time to procrastinate. In addition to writing, Elizabeth juggles a full-time job as a nurse/technologist with being a wife and mother of two teenagers. Reading continues to be her favorite pastime, and she never leaves home without a book. Someday she hopes to write a runaway bestseller and play a decent game of golf.